The HuGuenot

And

THE HEATHEN

II

The Prodigal Returns

The 4th Novel in the Huguenot Series

The Huguenot and The Heathen II
is a work of fiction.
Names, characters, places, and incidents either are the
product of the author's imagination or are used
fictitiously. Any resemblance to actual persons, living
or dead, events or locales is entirely coincidental.

LIBRARY OF CONGRESS CATALOGING-IN-PUBLICATION DATA

Force, D.C.
The Huguenot and The Heathen II: a novel / D.C. Force

ISBN 978-1-7339762-7-5
eISBN 978-1-7339762-8-2

Published in the United States of America

Book Cover Design by
The Book Cover Whisperer

The HuGuenot

And

THE HEATHEN

II

The Prodigal Returns

By

D.C. Force

The 4th Novel in the Huguenot Series

Books by D.C. Force

The Huguenot Series

The Huguenot*: Flight From Terror*

The Huguenot II*: Building the Dream*

*The Huguenot and **The Tower of Constance***
(an e-book novella)

*The Huguenot and **the Heathen***

*The Huguenot and **the Heathen II***

Other Books by the Author

Family: a Century of Blood and Tears
released 2007

Visit our website to leave comments, ask questions, learn about the
author, or catch previews of books to come.

www.dcforce.com

www.amazon.com/author/dcforce

This series is dedicated to all the men, women, and children throughout history who have suffered severely and cruelly because of their sincere and non-political beliefs in and love for our lord, Jesus Christ.

Contains scenes not appropriate

for those under the age of 18.

"Let grace and goodness be the principal loadstone of thy affections.
For love which hath ends, will have an end; whereas that which is
founded on true virtue, will always continue."

– Dryden

"The belief in a supernatural source of evil is not necessary;
men alone are quite capable of every wickedness."

– Joseph Conrad

"Love is to the moral nature what the sun is to the earth."

– Balzac

"Land and sea, weakness and decline are great separators,
but death is the great divorcer for ever."

– John Keats

Chapter 1

The Frontier –Late Spring 1725

For the first time in over ten years, Captain John Power wanted to visit home. He felt whole again. He felt like a part of him that had been missing for a very long time had returned and settled in with a contentment and tranquility that had eluded him for over a decade. He was thirty-three and in the prime of life. His career was established. He had a sensually beautiful wife he loved with a passion and children to bring joy to their lives. Now it was time to revisit the parents he loved and missed and renew bonds with his siblings. And deep in his pocket he had something that needed a final rest. Almost absentmindedly, he touched his coat pocket and heard the crinkly sound of parchment assuring him the packet was there.

John turned on board ship to look at his wife standing in the shade of one of the masts and enjoying the river breezes. Her hand was raised to the wide brimmed hat she wore atop her neatly dressed curls, keeping the wind from blowing them asunder. She was attired in a pale green, feminine frock patterned by Mistress Greeley, the fort commander's wife, from the fashions she had observed on her last visit east. With a tightly corseted bodice, trimmed horizontally in a series of dark green ribbon ornamentations, her bosom and slender waist were encased and displayed quite handsomely, colonial style. Puffed sleeves trimmed in lace hid her arms to well below the elbow and the full skirt was billowed by several stiff petticoats and pushed out from her green velvet cloak. Little Sunshine with her blonde curls and brown eyes found those skirts comforting in the bustle of the crowds of strangers they had had to contend with ever since leaving the relative quiet of the frontier and hitting the first sizable settlement on the Delaware River.

John was proud of his wife whose name he had shortened to *Ronnie*. He knew she preferred her more simple native dress but she was becoming accustomed to dressing for his world and with her statuesque figure, she wore her clothing very well. Mistress Greeley had taught her how to dress her dark, luxuriant hair after the fashion of white women. There was an exotic dignity about her that set her apart and John found his pulse racing at the thought of evening when they would be able to retire to the relative privacy of their tiny cabin after the children were asleep.

Gray Wolf's Son was playing at his mother's feet with a cone and ball on a string amusing Sunshine and he could hear the blonde toddler's gleeful chortling laughter drift out over the deck. Her brown skinned, black eyed older brother of four was down on one knee in his short pants, little shirt, vest, and stiff leather shoes. His little black braids had been cut off and his straight black hair shorn to the short, easy style of a white boy. He still complained each morning about having to put on the stiff, hard shoes, begging for his moccasins, but Ronnie always distracted him with some other more pleasant discovery for the day and they were confident that soon he would be used to the foreign foot gear.

Indian children went naked or in a leather tunic depending on the weather, until they understood the eliminating functions of their bodies. Once this milestone was achieved, the boys began to wear a little leather clout like their fathers. This spring as they began to ready themselves for travel, John had told Ronnie most white boys of four still wore dresses until they were seven or eight. She thought at first he was joking but he explained it was much easier to lift a skirt when necessity called than undo laces or buttons on breeches and generally the dresses were more like long nightshirts. She could not shame her son by putting him into a dress, she said, and fashioned little breeches which he easily learned to button and unbutton as necessity required for he knew better than to soil his clothing. John bowed to a mother's wisdom.

As far as John was concerned, Ronnie's children were his children. He intended on looking into formal adoption proceedings in regard to Sunshine who was his daughter in all but her conception. Her natural father had denied her because she looked white and John was the only papa she knew. Ronnie had white blood but her second husband did not know that when he whipped and beat her for being an unfaithful wife and might have killed their infant. Ronnie had never loved him but she had never been unfaithful. She had run away in the Indian version of divorce, escaping from the threat of having her nose sliced off and she had fallen in love with John. Ronnie had asked John to name the infant as was the custom of her people, and he had: Mary Elizabeth Sunshine Power. People easily assumed she was his and he never bothered to correct them. Gray Wolf's Son was another matter.

John had pledged to be a father to the boy but he had no intention of trying to replace his natural father's memory. The boy was a Mohawk warrior by birth and while he would have the education of a white boy, John was not going to deny him his heritage. Ronnie had loved Gray Wolf fiercely just as he had loved her. John had come to terms with that within his own heart. After all, had he not loved before as well? And just as he knew how very much he loved his wife without any lessening of the love he had once had for his first wife, Alana, or for lovely young Freyja whom he had lost, so too, he accepted that Ronnie could love him as passionately in return, which was no insult and had nothing to do with the love she still carried for Gray Wolf. John would not try to deprive the warrior's ghost of his rightful progeny and the most appropriate name the boy could have in the white world was Gray Wolfson.

And Ronnie had given John his own son. Napping in the basket beside her was a feisty, dark haired boy with light skin and blue eyes that had only recently begun changing to what was looking like a light shade of gray. Healthy, strong, and growing by the proverbial leaps and bounds, John couldn't ask for any better. He left the rail and walked to his wife, taking her hand and giving it a kiss. She looked at him with her large brown eyes fringed in smoky black lashes and gave him a broad smile of courage, flashing white teeth against her delicately golden skin and willing herself not to reveal her fears at meeting his people.

Ronnie's thoughts were rarely far from the subject of meeting John's family. She dressed like a white woman now and allowed herself to pass as a white woman. The farther from the frontier they came, the easier it was. People made assumptions and neither she nor John corrected them. It tugged at her conscience, however, that she so easily betrayed her own mother and father, her people. Her people. Jack's people were her people now, weren't they? Just as her mother had gone with her father and his people had become hers. She tried to tell herself that this was natural, normal, the way of things but she knew there was a difference. Her mother had never denied her first tribe. And they had never denied being Delaware before they had become Mohawk. But if she was not exactly denying she was a Mohawk, she was acting like a white and not speaking of her old life. She was pretending to be white. Even her son. She looked down at the child. He looked like the little white boys. If Gray Wolf were alive he would not recognize his own son with his hair shorn. What would he think of the way she dressed the boy? She imagined the look of hurt pride on his proud countenance and she felt a sudden stab of guilt.

Ronnie felt her heartbeat race and willed herself to calm. Gray Wolf was not alive to see his son. If he were alive she wouldn't be here. If he were alive, she would never have fallen in love with Jack. But Gray Wolf was dead. And she was married to Jack now, and she prayed his people would accept her. She must make him proud of her. She must adapt to the strange world of the whites. Just then John walked over to her and kissed her hand. She loved him completely. He was her life now and she would follow him wherever he led.

She worried but said nothing to her husband. What would his family think of her? She had become acutely aware of how the whites thought of the Indians when they had passed through the first several frontier towns. It had been a painful awakening, seeing brothers spit upon, mocked, and generally insulted for no particular reason. She had seen braves with no dignity begging coins for the white man's drink.

She remembered a storekeeper in a general store who had been very pleasant to her when she first walked into his establishment, her infant in her arms. Then he caught sight of Gray and picked up a broom coming after the child.

"Get out'a m' store, ya little beggar, I've told ya little varmints often enough not t' come in here," the older man shouted as he raised the broom threateningly.

"Stop!" Ronnie cried out in panic, stepping between Gray and the broom.

"Look, lady," the clerk frowned but paused. "I don't allow 'em in my store. They're nothing but thieves and beggars."

"He is not beggar. I want to buy him shoes," Ronnie said defiantly still not really understanding the man's anger.

The clerk thought for a moment and then, shrugging, he put down his broom. Every once in a while there was some do-gooder female who would try to *civilize* the nearest injun, he thought mildly. "Don't know why ya wanna waste your money on shoes for the likes of him. He'll have them off and be back runnin' barefoot before you can say Jack Robinson. If I was you, lady, I'd buy myself something pretty instead." He tried to smile solicitously, his humor restored with the thought of a sale.

Ronnie was confused. Did he know her husband *Jack*? But he was Jack Power not Jack Robinson. She pulled Gray around to be measured for shoes which the clerk did without ceremony.

"What's this kid to you anyway, lady? You can't shoe up every beggar red-skin brat in this town."

"I tell you he is no beggar. This is my son," she replied honestly just as John walked in the door carrying Sunshine. The clerk actually stepped back from her in revulsion as though she were diseased.

"Is there a problem?" John asked coming up behind her in the full uniform of a British army officer and scowling at the clerk.

"No," Ronnie had replied quickly, only wanting to get the shoes and be gone as soon as possible. "I find shoes for Gray, Jack. Can we have these?"

"Of course." Then he turned to the clerk. "How much?"

"Those are a shilling," the man replied through tight lips.

"A shilling! Must have gold hidden in the soles, right?" John exclaimed humorlessly and tossed the coin down on the counter before turning from the clerk. Without another word, John shepherded Ronnie and the children back out onto the street.

Yes, she had learned enough already of the whites' general attitude toward her people. Would Jack's family be able to accept her? The question kept running through her mind as they drew closer and closer to Chartes Landing on the New Jersey coastline.

Phillip Power was deeply involved with the books in the saw mill office and only vaguely aware that someone had walked in. He hadn't heard a knock on the glass windowed door which buffered the small office from the sounds of the mill. He expected it was one of the workers wanting something and took his time finishing the entry he was making before looking up from the ledger surrounded by stacks of odd sized pieces of paper.

"Yes?" he said absently as he set the inky quill carefully aside and looked up straight into a face that was so very familiar and yet eleven years different from when he'd seen it last. "My God! John?" he questioned his own eyesight. He spun around and realized his brother had entered through the door to the outside.

"The one and only," John grinned broadly down at his dark haired brother. There was a time when the two brothers had looked very much alike except John was blond with gray eyes like their father and Phillip was dark haired with brown eyes like their mother's father.

Phillip rose from behind the desk, speechless, stunned, his eyes suddenly moist with emotion. He went to his brother and embraced him. The two brothers held each other for a moment and then with masculine bravado tried to joke and laugh away the awkward tenderness of the moment.

"God, look at you!" Phillip stepped back and walked around his brother, older by less than two years and still dressed in uniform. "You look hard as rocks and meaner than a snake," he jested and threw a mock punch to the gut as they used to when they were children. John did not even flinch as if a true punch would have had no more effect than a sponge thrown against a brick wall.

"And you look just a trifle soft and over fed," John joked back, poking at Phillip's slightly thickened middle and full-cheeked appearance.

"It's all that damn good cooking, between Caroline and Mother… Mother?! Does she know you're back? Have you been to see the folks yet?" he asked quickly.

"No, thought I'd stop here first and see if there's anything I should know about before I step in something easily avoided," John admitted.

"The folks are both in good health, everyone is in good health… well, that is except… did you know Louise's husband died? You remember Rafe?"

"I knew they married but I never met him. He was off doing the trading post trek the whole time I was here last."

"Right. Well, that is what he had been doing every year for Father along with our Richie. But this past season he and Richie were set upon by some damn war party. Rafe was killed outright while Richie came home wounded. He's fine now but Louise is in mourning. She's bearing up pretty well, I think. And Isabelle is going to be married soon."

"Little Izzy? No!" John exclaimed in disbelief.

"Little Izzy is quite the lady, I'll have you know. Spoiled rotten and full of airs but you never saw such a little beauty and deep down in that self-centered little body she has a soft heart. They say she looks just like our *grand-mère* when she was young. Caught the eye of some banker and they had a time of it getting Father's approval. The banker intends to move her away to Boston… in fact, you are just what the doctor ordered to get their minds off of losing their *baby*," Phillip said, slapping John on the back and squeezing his shoulder affectionately before reaching for his own coat. "Come, I have to take you to the house myself. I can't wait to see the look on their faces. You're like Lazarus come out from the grave," he grinned.

"Wait a minute, Phillip," John stayed him. "I haven't told you everything yet."

"Of course not," he responded easily as he slipped into his fitted coat, "it's going to take a while to catch up on eleven years, I should hope, or else they've been damned boring years," he laughed.

"Phillip, I'm married."

Again Phillip was rendered momentarily speechless. It took a moment and then he broke into a broad grin. "Well, congratulations, big brother!"

"And I have a family."

Phillip was chuckling now. "Your comic sense of delivery is much improved, you ought to be on the traveling stage. What other little surprises have you to drop? No, wait," he put up his hand and went back around the desk to take his seat. "There, I'm sitting. Now, what else? Have you become Royal Governor without our even knowing it?"

John frowned slightly. "She's an Indian." The jovial smile froze on Phillip's face and then faded. He remained speechless for a few long moments and then realizing he must say something he grasped for words in embarrassment.

"That's… that's one hell of a surprise. It's going to take a little… ah… a little time to get used to." Phillip's expression had gone very serious as he rubbed his forehead nervously, wishing he were better at hiding his feelings. "The family's latest experience is that they killed Rafe and damn near killed Richie."

"All Indians are not the same anymore than all whites. You can't blame us for what the French do, can you?"

Desperately trying to cover his shock, Phillip bent to open a lower desk drawer and brought out a bottle with two small glasses. "I guess this calls for a drink," he said numbly.

"It took me ten years to find love again, little brother. Do you think I could deny it just because of that?"

"No, no, of course not," Phillip gestured to the second glass while he tossed back a shot of whiskey. After inhaling again he went on more smoothly. "John. I'm sorry. You must think I'm an ass. I still say congratulations and I mean it. It's just that things on the frontier are so different I'm sure, but back here… well, we've become very civilized now. This isn't the frontier anymore and you know how people are."

"I know how people are… but what of my family?"

"Your family is your family, you know that. We love you and want your happiness. So, to us it doesn't matter."

"Well, it's only my family that matters to me. It's only my family that I've come home to see. I'm not staying, our life is back on the frontier."

"Well, you sure as hell better make it a long visit, that's all I can say, or Mother and Father will never get over it," Phillip's merry countenance had returned. "And now, are you going to introduce me?" he asked, picking up his hat and brushing the short plume lightly.

They walked out to the waiting carriage. The instant Phillip saw Ronnie his fears were dispelled. She didn't even look like an Indian, he observed. He had expected some grunting squaw in buckskins with a papoose carrier on her back, jabbering some gibberish and smelling of bear grease. But the woman he met was lovely, quite beautiful in fact, with an air of grace and an exotic accent to her slow careful English. With familiar gallantry he bowed and kissed her hand in greeting. Her children looked like regular children, Phillip noted, even the boy who John explained was hers by a previous marriage. He looked like he could be Spanish or perhaps Italian. No, Phillip thought optimistically as they made the short journey home, no one would even have to know.

It was a short ride to the Power home from their saw mill and lumber yard. Inside the carriage John had set Sunshine on his lap to make room for Phillip. The house, a full three story imposing frame with a decidedly French flavor, looked remarkably the same as he remembered as they rode along the circular drive. John dismissed the driver after they had all alighted and the luggage was unloaded. Then, Phillip stood back with Ronnie and the children while John rapped politely at the front door. As fate would have it, Marie, his mother, having just returned home herself chanced to answer the door in person.

The woman stood for several moments, her changeable eyes widening and darkening, her smooth, firm, heart-shaped face startled, her mouth dropped open in disbelief and astonishment. Her daughters had convinced her to henna rinse the gray from her hair and for those emotionally filled moments she looked even younger than John remembered her, all five foot two of her. Then, she collapsed against him allowing the tears to flow and John was aware of a fragility in her he had never noticed before. She clung to him tightly, though he barely felt it and he tried to calm her and cajole her into smiles.

Then, she let loose with a fireball of French that even he did not completely understand and really did not want to have translated. He understood enough. Her little fists pummeled his hard arms and sides with no effect and he even felt her hands smacking across his backside over his uniform coat in a spanking which did bring him to a point of flushed embarrassment.

"Mother, please, Mother, stop. Mother, I'm sorry," his face was turning red under its swarthy tan. "I'm sorry. I know I should have written more, I'm a terrible letter writer. Please. Mother... I've missed you." That stopped her and she threw her arms up so he could bend into her embrace and she kissed him repeatedly on his sun-burnt face.

"Oh, John, *mon fils, mon fils...* welcome home, John, welcome home!" she smiled at last and her lovely face lit up again.

"I have someone I want you to meet, Mother," John stepped sideways and drew his mother out to Ronnie. "This is my wife, Ronnie, and her son, Gray, our daughter, Sunshine, and our baby, Matthew."

At first Marie gasped in surprise, then her eyes sparkled with delight as she looked at the tall young woman and the handsome children. "Your wife! Oh, *mon Dieu!* How wonderful! Welcome to the family," she said and drew the tall girl down to administer a kiss on both cheeks. "John brings me another daughter and more grandchildren. It is wonderful! Wonderful! My cup, it overflows. Come, come into the house," she began to gesture. "Oh, I do not believe it." Marie laughed with delight. "*Mon Dieu!* I do not believe! Such a beautiful family and you never wrote a word!"

Jacques-Jean Charte Power, patriarch of the Power Family, had escaped from France almost four decades earlier during the re-occurrence of the Huguenot persecutions. Once heir to title and lands he could never claim because he embraced the Protestant faith, he instead had built a life and a legacy in the New World with his own two hands. But he had not done it alone. With him in his flight, had come his best friend, Richard Bonchance, and a young peasant girl of honest ambition named Marie. They began building their wealth by fur trapping and trading. Soon the men installed Marie in a trading outpost on the frontier which with the construction of the lumber mill grew into a harbor settlement and eventually became Chartes Landing. While Marie's trading post evolved into a fully stocked general store, Jacques ran the sawmill, developed his own apple orchards and expanded further into the importing and exporting trade.

Jacques took life a trifle slower and easier since his children were grown and able to assist in his many commercial endeavors. It was now his habit to awake after sunrise, not before. On icy winter mornings, he was even known to keep Marie locked in a fervent embrace while cuddling within the warm blankets for an extra half hour. They enjoyed a leisurely breakfast together in the company of their daughters still at home, and various grandchildren. Next, Jacques spent a fierce half hour fencing with a rotating list of partners. After refreshing himself and dressing more formally, he set about business which took him out of the home and usually down to the harbor. When he returned, he almost always entered by his own private entrance and remained in his office attending to correspondence and reading undisturbed until late afternoon. At that time, he would come out and spend the remainder of the day with his family.

Marie saw Jacques approaching the house and rushed John into Jacques' office as a surprise. She quickly shut the door to the study from the hall and saw to refreshments for everyone gathered in the drawing room across the hall.

When Jacques walked in via the side door, he saw boots and legs sticking out from the old wing backed chair so he wasn't startled. He knew someone was waiting for him. It wasn't unusual. He just didn't know who. He wasn't expecting anyone this day and it was not like him to forget.

Jacques was aging well and in excellent health it seemed. An exceptionally handsome man in his youth, he was now arrestingly distinguished and still extremely attractive and debonair. His wig-less pale blond locks had darkened with age, just as John's had, but Jacques' were now silvery gray. His lightly tanned face remained firm and animated with a trim, neat silver moustache and warm gray eyes which generally appeared to dance and sparkle. At fifty-nine, the elder Power retained his trim physique by walking all over the harbor front daily, riding his horses over acres of orchards, and continuing to exercise with the foil. His fencing reputation was well-known and he took pride in staying in top condition and retaining his skill. His posture and carriage were marked with the grace, poise, and assured light-footed balance so often seen in a good swordsman.

Now, he approached his guest with a degree of curiosity and was little prepared to see his own younger likeness staring up at him with a huge smile.

John rose immediately and walked into his father's embrace.

"John! *Mon Dieu!*" Jacques exclaimed in accented speech.

"Father!"

"*Mon fils!*" Jacques' voice had become very husky with emotion as he held his first born son. And John was pleasantly surprised by the strength he felt in that embrace. The men finally pulled back from each other and looked eye to eye. John was slightly taller and Jacques held the back of his son's neck with a tight grip. Then, the father let go and stepped back. His eyes traveled his son's length, up and down, studying. When he was finished, his expression said he was pleased with what he saw and he turned to the decanter on his desk and poured them each a small glass of cognac. "Welcome home!" he saluted.

"Thank you, Father. But I don't want to mislead you. I've made the military my career and I will be returning."

Jacques nodded solemnly. "Does the military not allow you to come home more than once every ten years?" he asked dryly.

"Of course. I… well, you know why I couldn't come back sooner."

"No, John, I do not," he said graciously, only seeking to understand. "Phillip told us you fell deeply in love with Olafson's eldest daughter and of the tragedy that befell her, God rest her soul. And I understand grief, but why should grief separate you from your family?"

"It wasn't just grief. I need to tell you the whole story and I promise I will before I leave again… but I was filled with darkness. Not fit to be around."

"And now?"

"I've healed."

"Good! Better than good. Excellent! It is more than time."

"But I didn't do it alone."

"Ahh, no?" Jacques lifted a well arched brow, holding back a smile.

"No, I had help."

"And what is her name?" Jacques smiled knowledgeably, intuitively guessing his son had brought home a wife.

"She is the best thing that ever happened to me. She's beautiful and warm, loving, giving, and she's struggled through so much."

"You have just described your ma-ma when I married her," Jacques nodded. "So are you married?"

"Yes, and we have children."

"*Mon Dieu!* And you could not write? You break your mother's heart, John. The least you could do is pick up a quill once or twice a year, how difficult would that be, eh?" Jacques was serious in his gentle reproof. "It is not like when I was first come to the New World, stranded in the wilderness, no way to get back word. These days the couriers run constantly from fort to fort, do not tell me you could not send a letter regularly."

"You're right, sir. Mother has already taken me to task. She even spanked me in front of my wife," John complained with good humor and a crooked smile.

"Spanked you?! Hah! That is my Marie," he chuckled aloud. "God, I love that woman! If you have half the woman I have, you will be a very happy man for the rest of your days."

"I do. I mean she's more than half. I mean… well, Ronnie reminds me of mother in many ways."

"Ronnie?" Jacques questioned amiably.

"Yes, it's what I call her." He paused then and took a breath. "I don't pronounce her name very well."

Jacques was looking at his son in amused confusion. "And why is that? Is it foreign?"

"In a way… She's part Indian and part white." John was certain he could feel a sudden coolness radiate from his father. "Please. I don't know what your experiences were with the Indians years ago. You never seemed to have any trouble with them. But don't prejudge her. Please, for my sake. Don't… don't do to me what you did to Uncle Richard."

"What are you talking about?" Jacques asked in puzzlement.

"You know very well what I'm talking about. All those years, Uncle Richard coming to our house like a man stepping out of a void, never talking of his wife, never speaking of his children all because they were Indians and he knew you didn't approve."

"No, John. That is not right," Jacques refuted with dignity.

"I saw it, Father. I saw the way he was with us, wishing he could share his family with us but you were so prejudiced against them."

"Is that really what you saw?" Jacques asked softly.

"It is the truth, isn't it?" John challenged.

"No, not at all." Jacques was quiet for a moment and then took a deep breath and spoke. "You are a man now, John, and fully grown, there is no reason to disguise the truth from you." He poured them each another small drink and sat down into his deep chair motioning John to sit as well. "Richard has been closer to me than a brother. Even though we have always been very different in our ways, he is and has been my best and dearest friend from the time we were very small children. Aside from your ma-ma, he knows me best. He volunteered to come to the New World with me even though it was a sacrifice for him to leave France. Do you have any idea what that meant to me? He helped to make my ostracism into an adventure. We shared that adventure together, the danger, the struggle, the success, the failures, the freedom, and the unknown. But the one thing we could not truly share was your mother."

John looked up sharply into his father's eyes. Jacques was looking at him steadily, a touch of sadness in his expression.

"Yes, he has always been deeply in love with your ma-ma. But, of course, he could not have her, that is quite an impossible situation for him, you see. He did not have *a* wife and *a* family. He had women up and down the wilderness trail he traveled, and offspring everywhere he went. That was not… moral… proper. Hardly the kind of libertine behavior to which I wished my growing children exposed. I will not pretend that I ever had any attraction for the Indian women, even when I was single. But, then, I believe I was already in love with your ma-ma although I did not realize it for a while. The point is, if Richard had settled with one, married her, raised a family, they would have been more than welcome. But he could not, you see, because he never really loved any of them, not to the exclusion of all others, not enough to marry. Not at all compared to what I felt for your ma-ma, and what he confessed he felt as well. So, Richard has had only mistresses and bastards and he had the good sense not to speak of them in front of my children."

"How did you know?" John asked in shock.

"About his women?"

"No, about his being in love with Mother. Did he actually tell you this?"

"Confessed is the more correct word. He was near to tears that day and we did not see him again for two years. We have never spoken of it since, but he loved her all the same, and I am sure he still does. Raphael was the only son he ever acknowledged, born of his liaison with a French woman who committed suicide when Rafe was only three. They also were never married but this Richard did not tell to his son."

John sat quietly digesting what he had just heard.

"You must swear never to speak of any of this. It is Richard's secret, both his love for your ma-ma and Rafe's birth outside of wedlock. On your honor as an officer and a gentleman?"

"Of course. Where is Uncle Richard now? Is he all right?"

Jacques' eyes were filled with a different kind of emotion for an instant and then again were composed. "He has his room upstairs. This winter, he took ill," he cleared his throat. "but your ma-ma nursed him through. He has been declining. All those winters sleeping on the ground in some drafty wigwam or other appears to have broken his health. But the death of Raphael broke his spirit. He sits in his room a great deal. He uses difficulty with the stairs as his excuse though truly I believe he makes it seem worse than it is."

"Phillip mentioned about Raphael," John said softly, "but he never said anything about Uncle Richard."

Jacques nodded. "You never met Rafe, did you? Ah, that is right. He had already left for the season when you returned from Europe. He was your age. Very tall, like his father, strong, very handsome with a good and honest heart. It has been most difficult on your sister, Louise," Jacques gestured indulgently. "Each season when he returned, it was like another honeymoon for them," he said with a mixture of humor and sadness. "She and Raphael had a true passion for each other. And now she has five fatherless children to raise. Perhaps you might find a moment to talk with her, John? She is still in *Grand-père's* wing. You understand passion and loss… perhaps better than we."

"Of course."

"It was a difficult winter for our family."

"I'm sorry, Father," it was almost a whisper.

"I know. I know," Jacques sighed. "Rafe is sadly missed."

"No, I mean, of course I'm sorry about Uncle Richard and Raphael, but… I'm sorry… for what I thought about you."

Jacques leaned forward and squeezed his son's arm and nodded. "I think it is time I met your wife and family," he said graciously.

John introduced Jacques to his newest daughter-in-law and grandchildren. And after a while, when he saw Ronnie was comfortable, John slipped upstairs and knocked on Richard's door.

"Uncle Richard?" he opened the door quietly. It was apparent the older man had been napping before the fire.

"Jacques?"

"It's John."

"John?" He seemed startled at first, then disbelieving, and finally quite pleased. "John! Let me look at you."

John grabbed the older man's hand and arm and pulled him up to receive a hug.

"Do you remember how we all used to climb all over you and wrestle? Every time you returned from one of your treks. Jane would inspect you to make certain you brought in no dirt and we would pile onto you and roll all over the foyer floor."

Richard laughed. "Yes, yes. I remember. Jane still inspects us all, God love her. Fighting dirt as though it were a lethal enemy. It is so very good to see you. Are you home to stay?"

"No, Uncle Richard. I'm on leave for a month. Brought my wife home to meet everyone. I want you to meet her as well." The initial flush of interest was beginning to fade as Richard sank back on the small settee, so John sat as well. "I was shocked to hear about Rafe. I never got to meet him. I'm very sorry, Uncle Richard. I've suffered losses but I've never lost a child. I can't imagine."

The large man reached out and grabbed John's shoulder. "You're a good boy, John. You do your father proud. Rafe was my pride. He was the very best of me, the one really good thing I had to leave behind."

"But that's not true."

Richard looked up into John's gray eyes.

"You have been like a second father to all of us. All the winters you spent playing and talking and teaching us. We hold those memories and we'll never forget them. And you're not the man to bury yourself away. Come down, Uncle Richard, join the rest of the family. Please. Meet my wife. We won't be here for that long."

Richard nodded. "Very well, I will... but not now John. I'll come down to supper later. I promise."

Chapter 2

The prodigal son had returned, not with his inheritance squandered but with a heathen wife from the land of Canaan, which some considered far worse. The parental arms were wide open, the lambs were figuratively slaughtered, the feast was spread. And the reactions among the Power family members varied.

At one time John and Phillip had been very close. That had been almost a dozen years ago when Phillip had been very young and still willing to submit to John's natural dominance. Now, after over a decade of having a free hand in the position of the eldest, at least the eldest remaining on site, the position of second eldest felt a bit snug like shoes that one has outgrown. And tight shoes can raise blisters with lengthy wearing. Phillip and his family went over to the old home often. He told himself and his wife it was the thing to do to let John know he was missed, to make Ronnie feel welcome, to show supportive acceptance. And perhaps, he thought to himself in clear self-assessment, to stay informed.

His wife Caroline was tolerant, even gracious to Ronnie and her children who at their first meeting had watched Caroline in wonder because of her flaming copper red hair. But Caroline did remember John as being rather unsettled and carefree while her husband had been laboring seriously at the family lumber business now for years, just as she continued to labor faithfully in her mother-in-law's retail establishment. She was a little on edge wondering exactly what John's presence bode for the future and if he planned to assert any eldest son rank over her husband at this stage in life.

"You don't think he's thinking of leaving the military service, do you?" she asked her husband casually in the privacy of their bedroom as she brushed out her sleek, bright copper tresses.

"I shouldn't think so," he replied as he eased out of his boots for the day. "John never cared much for business." Phillip stretched easily then catching a glimpse of himself in Caroline's dressing mirror, he sucked in his stomach as he considered his lean and hard muscled older brother. "He seems to have carved his own niche, I'd say. Seems to agree with him. Besides, I don't get the impression she would be pleased to stay here. It's a long way from her kind of life. Didn't she say she has a mother and brother back there somewhere?"

"Um-hmm," Caroline nodded in agreement.

"She seems a fairly intelligent girl, she has to know living here would be very... difficult for her kind."

"Hmmmm," Caroline sighed in a way that said he was undoubtedly correct and wisely refrained from saying any more on the subject.

Oldest sister Helen was glad to hear John was happily married although when she was told *what* he had married, she was a bit shocked. She herself was in a very comfortable marriage. She and Thor liked and respected each other. They were best friends and loyal supporters of one another. Thor's father William Boot and his second wife, Ingrid, were decent people who held to certain boundaries of interference in someone else's life. And with that came a certain distancing or lack of demonstrative affection. And if Helen did not comprehend what could possibly have caused her handsome eldest brother to "disappear" for almost a dozen years, she was not to be faulted. She had no real frame of reference for *passion.*

Helen had grown up wondering how she could be her parents' daughter. Her mother was notably pretty and her father was very handsome. But she looked like neither of them. What cabbage leaf had they found her under, she had often asked herself? Louise looked like Mother, and Isabelle so closely resembled the miniature of *Grand-mère* which Papa kept in an honored position on the mantel in his study, it was uncanny. And while Helen was named in honor of *Grand-mère,* Mama had only made vague references to Helen resembling a "Juliette,' one of Mama's sisters back in France.

Thor had taught Helen everything she needed to know as a respectable woman to make her husband happy in the bedroom. And she was more than happy to comply. It wasn't difficult. In fact, it was rather simple and often his satisfaction came rather quickly. Unfortunately, Thor did not seem to know as much about giving her satisfaction. There was a reluctance to experiment, to vary established routines or to explore new choices. And Helen found herself totally intimidated from initiating any discussion with Thor on the subject even in the very private sanctuary of their own bed. Somehow she always had the feeling it would be viewed as indecent.

Her mother, Marie, had taught her everything she needed to know about making and keeping a well run home, supervising servants, and demonstrating love and affection with her children. But once Marie had mentioned something the French call *le petit mort* under the assumption that Helen, a married woman with (at that time) two children, knew exactly what Marie was talking about. Helen tried to gracefully cover up the fact that she did not. *Petit mort* meant little death. Helen knew her French but that French made no sense. A woman did not spew seed like a man, she was simply the receiving vessel, the fertile ground the seed took root in, wasn't that so? And so Helen left the matter be.

Helen considered that Thor was an exemplary husband in many, many ways. At close to seven feet tall he was a very powerful man, he loved her faithfully and his eyes did not wander. He appreciated the home she made for them and often gave her generous compliments. Once his father retired, Thor had assumed the responsibility of managing the mill floor for Jacques. Thor was more than generous and gave her an ample allowance for her household and personal needs. He was happy to do just about anything she would ask of him. He did not gamble. He drank with temperance. He had what one could call a cheerful disposition and was even-tempered with their four children. What more could a wife possibly want? It didn't seem to matter to Helen that she didn't know what *petit mort* was supposed to mean or that she had never experienced it. But if such passion resulted in feeling so badly one must run away from the world and family for a decade like John, then perhaps it was not such a desirable thing, she told herself. Just look at poor sister Louise.

Louise was pleased to see her long lost brother but her affection was overshadowed by the sudden, unexpected, and tragic loss of her husband and the ensuing emotional instability in which she found herself drowning. Having just turned thirty, she was suddenly feeling quite middle-aged and matronly, as well as deserted and alone. She saw herself spending the rest of her life being a fifth wheel, the widowed aunt to whom everyone had to be charitable. Men didn't look at older women, they wanted young beautiful ones, like Isabelle and like their new sister-in-law. John was thirty-three but you didn't see him marrying a thirty year old woman, did you? No, of course not. The girl was barely twenty and even though she was an Indian, she was ten times better looking than Louise and could attract a catch like John.

Louise sighed and felt herself dangerously close to tears again. It was all so unfair. She had loved Raphael so deeply; they could have had such a long, happy life together. Her friend Henrietta would welcome her husband's death. He was mean and stingy and would probably live to be a hundred. Louise lapsed into another depression and because of it all, she didn't come out of her rooms to visit with her elder brother as often as she might have.

Financially, she would not have to worry but there was more to life than just being financially secure. She and Raphael had indeed shared an explosively passionate attraction to each other that never dimmed and their annual eight, nine months apart always made their hearts grow ever fonder for each other. They had been insatiable lovers and never tired of trying new ways to please. Louise could not imagine having that with anyone else ever again. She liked to think she and Rafe were much like mother and father who, she happened to know since she lived at home, still enjoyed an intense private life. Fate had brought Raphael to her and the Fates had taken him away. There was no one in Chartes Landing to hold a candle to him and with five children, she could not see herself meeting people anywhere else.

Peeping into her looking glass the image looking back at her certainly was not "middle-aged" or "matronly" although it was often red-eyed and puffy. In fact, with a smile to lend a sparkle, Louise was her mother's daughter and still a most desirable looking woman. She was, in fact, lovely, having inherited her mother's delicate heart-shaped face, large soft golden hazel eyes and slightly turned up nose. She had a neat little figure of hourglass proportions and had been endowed with a substantial dowry thanks to her French grandfather. But she did not see any of these positives. She was still too deep in her grief and it was Indians that had killed her peerless Raphael. Indians had brought her this sorrow and loss. Indians had torn her heart in two and left it a bloody tattered scrap. Indians had pushed her into the pits of despair. And while she might forget for moments that her new sister-in-law was an Indian, her dark son literally caused Louise to shudder.

Often Louise found herself weeping in the midst of other people's happiness and trying not to make them uncomfortable made her exceedingly uncomfortable.

"I'm sorry, Mother, I'm just not fit company right now," she often begged off at Marie's invitations and stayed in her bedroom in the large ground-floor suite originally built for their grandparents' visit.

"But it is you who needs the company, Louise. The best thing is for you to be with your family," Marie offered sympathetically. "We are not strangers you must pretend with. And your children, Raphael's children, they need you." Suddenly tears were streaming down Louise's cheeks again. "It was only a suggestion, *ma petite*," Marie said gently, caressing her daughter's head.

Marie was very glad her middle daughter had never sought a home of her own. With Raphael gone more than half of every year, it was most convenient for her to have the help and company of her parents in his absence and the young couple had filled up the family nursery again. Sarah, Marie's head nursemaid, was overjoyed to have a steady stream of healthy new babies to coddle.

"You're right, Mother, you're right. Thank you," she sighed a bit dully, sniffing back her tears and forcing herself to at least go to the nursery to check on her children, ages twelve, ten, seven, four, and two.

Helen was truly pleased to see John although she had reservations about his choice of a career and a wife. She invited John and his wife to their home for dinner several times, although they chose not to invite their friends or even Thor's siblings at those times. It was a mercy, Helen told Thor. Ronnie was hardly a sparkling conversationalist and seemed to have enough difficulty just getting used to them. There was no reason to subject her to the scrutiny of more strangers. And John had become… Helen considered a moment. Stiff. That was it. And serious. Yes. He was very little like the young gallant of his youth and seemed to have lost his social *savoir-vivre*. Besides, there was really no reason to tell the world her brother had married a half-breed. Still, the Boots went to the family home to visit often enough to demonstrate their conviviality.

"Oh, you didn't bring the children with you?" Helen asked graciously as a serving girl showed John and Ronnie into the richly appointed Boot parlor. "I was looking forward to seeing the little cherubs."

"I did not know they were invited," Ronnie said quietly, intimidated by her surroundings. There was a cold formality in the luxury of the Boot home that did not exist in the home of John's parents. Surrounded by what was a stifling abundance of rich velvets and satins, delicate china and glassware, a myriad of candle flames reflected off all the highly polished wood and crystal, and into the two huge opposing gold gilt mirrors which reflected it all infinitely. It was a truly dazzling and somewhat dizzying effect.

"Well, perhaps you are right," Helen smiled lightly, "it gives the adults a bit of time to themselves. I know how exhausting looking after little ones can be, my dear. I hope John provides you with a nursemaid. Do you, John?" Helen asked her brother as she took Ronnie gently by the arm guiding her over to a blue velvet settee. "Please sit down. You more than deserve a little time for yourself."

"But I do not find…" began Ronnie a bit bewildered. She hadn't meant to get away from her children, she thought, she didn't want anyone to think she found her children tiresome. They were her treasure. She delighted in their care.

"Never mind, darling," John whispered in her ear as he bent over the back of the settee. Then he righted himself and with just the vaguest hint of mischief in his voice he asked, "Where are your children, Helen, aren't they joining us?"

"Oh, well, no. Since it is only us adults. They're having their meal in the kitchen and Hannah will see them to bed shortly," she replied dismissively, "you wouldn't begrudge me a little peace would you?"

Helen was mother to the oldest grandson, Thomas, who had just turned thirteen, and Sybelle, Joseph, and Jean matched Louise's children at ten, seven and four. For a time it seemed she, Louise, and Caroline were always *enceinte* together but Helen had expressed the desire to stop and Marie had shared her knowledge of an after-morning tea that seemed very successful in preventing conception.

Richie, at almost twenty-nine, had accompanied his namesake's son, Raphael, on ten sojourns into the Great Lakes Wilderness. Raphael had learned from his father, Richie had learned from Raphael. Young Richie knew the locations and set ups of the various trading posts, most of which were being run by long trusted acquaintances of Richard Bonchance and friends with the *Wendake* or Huron who controlled the fur trading channels in the great Northeast. Originally, in the event of Richard's death, everything was to become Jacques' although Jacques had long protested that arrangement. When Richard introduced them to Raphael, Jacques insisted Richard's half of the trading post businesses was to be Raphael's if anything happened to Richard. Then, both Raphael and Richie had been set upon by a stray Algonquin war party. Raphael was killed instantly by an unfortunately accurate arrow and by the smallest bit of luck Richie escaped with his life and only a non-lethal wound. Now Richie was the natural candidate to continue with the business and he did, with the goal of splitting the profits with his sister Louise, Raphael's widow.

Richie had grown into a quiet, rather introverted young man who had been in awe of his easy graced and charming older brothers. Young Richard favored his mother in appearance, having her thick light brown hair streaked with gold, hazel eyes, and neat small nose. Although a substantial six full inches taller than his mother, he was shorter and narrower in the shoulders than his brothers and father. There had been something equally ascetic and winsome about the growing youth that had many of the village maidens striving for his attentions, no matter that he lacked any comfort in talking with them. Young and old women alike wanted to mother him and would have instinctively drawn him to their bosoms at the first opportunity. But Richie loved the wild, its remote solitude and tranquility. By the age of twenty-four, he had chosen to build a home in a quiet, remote location some distance away in the hills. He might have never married and become a near recluse if Clarissa St. Johns had not had the boldness to act upon her own instincts. A quiet, shy girl who hid a boyish figure beneath modest garments, she shared Richie's love of the wild. They had been married for three years but had no children of their own. So, with Rafe's death she planned to dress in breeches and travel with her husband in order to spend every day with him.

Fully recuperated from his wound, Richie postponed leaving for the Great Lakes when John arrived unexpectedly. The low-keyed, serious young man appreciated Ronnie's lack of pretense and quiet demeanor. He and Clarissa spent time getting to know their new sister-in-law and their newest niece and nephews. Richie especially took to Gray who being the eldest child was the easiest to talk with and had the most to say.

"Keep your children as unaffected as they are," he said quietly to John one evening as they stole a few minutes in the garden together smoking. "They're like a breath of fresh air around here."

John smiled. "Do you not plan to have a few of your own?"

Richie shrugged. "It's not important to us. Anyway, I think maybe Clarissa might be barren."

"Sorry," John murmured awkwardly.

"It's just as well. I'd not be around much to help her raise them. And I don't think she'd take happily to being left behind anymore."

"You're going to take her with you?" John asked in amazement. "Into the wild?"

"We're going to try it," Richie nodded. "Well, don't look so surprised. You're taking your wife back into the wilderness, aren't you?"

"Yes, but… I mean… it's not quite the same, is it?"

"How's that?"

"Ronnie was born there, it's her world. Clarissa is a white woman, she's from civilization."

"John, listen to yourself. It sounds as if you still think of your own wife as a savage. Not quite civiliz…"

John cut him off growing slightly flushed in the face. "That's not what I meant at all. But the fact remains, my wife grew up sleeping on the ground and using the forest for her drawing room."

"And my wife didn't but it's what she likes none the less."

"Seriously?" John paused and looked questioningly at his younger brother. "And the danger?"

"The route we travel is pretty tame, that attack last fall was a bit of really bad luck." Richie shrugged in the same typically Gallic manner often displayed by his father. He continued to look at his brother and a grin pulled at his mouth. "Did you ever swim naked together in a cold river?"

John shook his head.

"Your roger shrivels up until you think you've lost it altogether but when you feel the heat of her you can grow into her like magic," Richie grinned.

"Your *roger*?"

"Yes, you know… your pecker. Well, what do you call yours… your little johnnie?" Richie chuckled deeply at the idea. John looked away feeling his face turning red. That was exactly what he used to call it, he thought in chagrin, but damned if he'd admit it now. "Have you ever felt the wind whistle up your arse just when you hit the mark?" John just stared. Richie went on, "It makes every inch of you sensitive as hell. God, it's great!"

John continued to stare a little dumbfounded at his younger brother. This was Richie talking, little Richie. The quiet one, the serious, withdrawn one. Then, John broke into a smile.

"As a matter of fact," he grinned but refused to elaborate. He had had an experience something like that. That first time he and Ronnie had made love on that hilltop. But he hadn't really thought about the breezes. He'd been too absorbed in how incredible she had felt.

Richie slapped John on the back. "Really, John? Maybe there's hope for you after all," he chuckled deeply. "I'm of the opinion that you have a lot of woman there and I'd not like to think you don't represent the men of this family well."

Why the audacity of the young whelp! John reached out and grabbed his brother by the back of the neck. "Quite well, I think, though I'll not be comparing notes to prove it," John growled suddenly in mock irritation, "and I'll thank you to keep a civil tongue in your head when you speak of my wife." Then, he grinned again broadly.

James, the youngest brother, was twenty-five and in the middle of courtship. He'd been turned down by his first sweetheart several years before and was torn between spending time with his returned brother and pressing his suit with his newest ladylove. He remembered a time when he had almost worshiped the ground John walked on but that was long ago and they had grown apart. He'd already decided the time was not right for him to start inviting his sweetheart home to meet the family since he wasn't certain how she might react to having a half-breed sister-in-law. Personal interest won out and John and Ronnie saw very little of James.

"And where is Jamie this evening?" Jacques asked with a frown as they gathered to the dinner table. "It is Sunday supper, Phillip and Helen have each brought their children and our youngest son cannot spare his family a few hours of his time?"

"He was invited to Sunday supper with the Throckmortons, Cynthia's family," Marie explained, very much as she had for many Sundays of late. "*C'est l' amour, mon cher,* that is love," she spoke softly with a small smile and said no more.

John had hopes the soon to be nineteen-year-old Isabelle would become close to his wife. John recalled his baby sister fondly and had thought she amongst all the siblings would have the most in common with Ronnie. They were, after all, both women and almost the same age. Isabelle had always had a rather devil-take-the-hind-most attitude toward convention. He imagined that she would see Ronnie for the person she was, not for her race. But Isabelle was not home for their arrival. She was on a chaperoned trip up to Boston, he was told, where she was spending time with her husband-to-be. Staying under the protective care of her fiancé's family, the trip was the concession she had wrung from her parents when they had postponed her wedding out of respect for her sister's loss.

A letter arrived and Marie shared the greetings and information at the dinner table.

"It is from Izzy. She has seen the house Hamilton is building for them, she writes. It is so nice when your children take the time to write," Marie added with a pointed look at John over her reading glasses. "She says she spends a part of almost everyday at the construction site and when she leaves to return home she intends on stopping in New York to do some additional shopping for home furnishings with her fiancé's letter of credit."

"Good heavens," Phillip joked, "the fellow is leaving her on her own with a line of credit? He must be totally besotted or slightly stupid."

"Phillip!" Marie chided good-naturedly. "Hamilton is not stupid. And your sister can be quite responsible when she wants to be."

"Do you approve of her being on her own in a place like New York Towne?" John looked to his father.

"She is not entirely on her own," Jacques responded. "Rachel is traveling with her as a chaperon and they will be staying with the Craigmores. Do you remember our friends who owned the General Store there?"

John nodded. "The Wingates."

"Yes. That is their eldest daughter. She was widowed and sold their homestead, moving back to town with her children. She has remarried a Monsieur Alexander Craigmore. As it turns out he owns one of the competing stores. A very respectable family and one to which we now give all our business."

Marie was frowning slightly in thought as she looked at the date on the letter. "This was written some time ago. Jacques, perhaps you could check with the packet boat captain. To discover when the *Golden Willow* is due to arrive in New York harbor from Boston. According to this, Izzy may be home in only a few days."

"Of course," Jacques smiled at her obligingly.

As the dinner proceeded, the family joked and told stories of how little Izzy had been the belle of Chartes Landing from the time she was fourteen with a string of beaus and suitors calling at the house like it was a traffic center. Marie had even had to stay at home just to insure decorum since her "baby" bedeviled the governess and took no heed of her admonishments.

"That was before we knew Rachel," Marie added, shaking her head to refuse a serving of potatoes.

"Who is this Rachel you keep mentioning?" John asked casually while serving up a generous helping of everything coming out of the kitchen. He had almost forgotten how good all the food was at his parents' table.

"Rachel is a god-send," Marie responded warmly.

"Rachel is a tenacious British bulldog," Phillip chuckled, very pleased with his unique turn of phrase.

Jacques also chuckled as he poured them all more wine. "We took her in as a house servant but she has shown her true value in her ability to keep your sister in line. If it were not for Rachel, Isabelle would not have left this town without me at her side."

"I must admit I did wonder how you were convinced to do so," John ventured and tried to imagine exactly what this formidable woman must look like. "And now you must tell me who this *Hamilton* is?"

Hamilton was a very successful Boston banker, John learned, who came to Chartes Landing looking for a unique investment opportunity for his bank. Jacques had brought him home for dinner on the first evening of his visit having no idea that the young and good-looking banker would be completely smitten with the vivacious little siren his youngest daughter had become. The young man had ended up staying in Chartes Landing until he had wooed her and won his suit with Jacques for her hand.

On the day Isabelle was expected to return, John went down to the harbor himself, in his officer's full dress uniform, to surprise her. Standing, feet slightly apart, hands behind his back and with a broad grin on his face he silently watched as the delicate little figure gathered her skirts about her and began searching the wharf for signs of her family escort, her parents perhaps, or the servants. He felt her eyes float over him and saw them focus on the family carriage several yards away. He thought he saw recognition as she continued to look and puzzlement showed on her delicate little face. Then, suddenly the large gray eyes were back on him again and, after an instant, he saw the recognition as she began to run down the gangplank.

"John!" Isabelle squealed in rapturous delight as her tiny feet flew lightly over the uneven footing and she rushed into her handsome big brother's arms. He lifted her into the air much as he used to when she was very young. "You've come home for my wedding! I knew you would! I just knew you would! I told Mother, 'John will come home for my wedding, just you wait and see if he won't.'"

John chuckled. "Let me look at you, midget," he teased setting her down and holding her at arms length. She was just as pretty and effervescent as everyone had said with soft almost silver blonde curls and huge dove gray eyes set in a face of very delicate features. Her skin was almost translucent in its fairness and the hypnotic black rims circling her gray irises were just like

John's.

"Good lord, how you've grown up. And when is this big event I keep hearing about?" John smiled warmly.

"We had to postpone it," her mouth curved into a delightful little pout.

"When was it supposed to be?" he asked amiably.

"Didn't you get my letter?" she asked quickly.

"No," he shook his head.

"I swear, you can't depend on anything that goes to the frontier!" Then, she leaned forward to whisper in confidence. "It was supposed to be at the end of summer as soon as Rafe and Richie returned. I mean, Hamilton proposed late last summer. It's been almost a full year but now Father says we must wait until Louise is officially out of mourning. It's not fair. When Phillip decided to marry they just up and married. Helen and Louise only had to be engaged a few months. It seems like by the time it came around to me, they just keep pushing the engagement longer and longer."

"You're their baby," John grinned, giving her a little squeeze. "It's hard to give you up."

"But I'm not a baby. I'm almost two years older than Phillip was when he got married and I'm a woman!"

"But then we know why Phillip got married so quickly," John winked. "I hope you're not saying you've a similar concern?"

"No. Of course, not." She swung to punch his arm with her tiny lace gloved hand. "But Helen got married at eighteen, Louise was only seventeen and here I am nineteen! Well, almost."

"Tsk-tsk-tsk," John clucked. "A veritable old maid. And as I recall, both your sisters had lengthy engagements waiting *patiently* until their birthdays."

"John," she frowned, trying to exude dignity. "it's just not fair that we have to wait until after the new year. It's so silly. Louise doesn't care. And it's not like she has to stand up for us or anything, she can still wear her widow's weeds, no one will notice. Talk to Father, John, please?"

"Hey, I didn't just arrive to start getting into your little arguments," he laughed.

"It's not a *little argument*," she stamped her tiny foot, "it's my life. And Hamilton is so disappointed. Of course, he's being an angel about it. I mean, he'll do anything for me. But why does my wedding have to be put off just because my sister married a wandering fur trader?"

"That's a trifle hard, isn't it?" he quirked a brow at her as he gathered her things into his arms and began to walk toward the carriage.

"Oh, you know what I mean," Isabelle sighed. An older woman, robustly plump and as tall as a man, came up carrying more baggage.

"And who is this?" John nodded to the older woman knowing very well who she was but reminding his young sister that an introduction was due.

"Who? Oh, this is Rachel. The Spanish maidens have their *duennas* and I have Rachel. She's my chastity belt."

John almost dropped the luggage. "Your what?! Never mind, I know damn well I heard you, though I don't believe what I heard."

"Oh, don't be silly," she grinned saucily. "I'm grown up now, John, I know about a lot of things."

He ignored her last remark and hoisted the baggage into the rear of the carriage and then turned politely to the older woman. "Rachel," he acknowledged her with a slight bow, "I'm John Power, this scamp's oldest brother."

"Pleased t' meet ya, Master John," Rachel said in a distinct Cockney accent and dropped a small curtsy which looked totally out of place. Although her shawl and dress covered her arms discreetly, John had the feeling her biceps could win most challenges at tabletop arm wrestling.

"I understand it is your job to chaperon my sister."

"You 'ave that right, sir, an' pleased I am t' be of service."

"I don't envy you the job. I imagine she runs you ragged," he smiled and helped the older woman into the carriage.

"No, sir. I mean, she h'ain't no real trouble, sir. Just a ball o' energy is all."

"Yes. To be sure." John looked down upon his sister and saw her expression darken. He could tell she was about to protest his talking about her to a mere servant or maybe it was because he had assisted the older woman to her seating ahead of his own sister. "Now, don't get your ruffles up. You're coming up front with me," he cut her off as she opened her mouth. He picked her up and placed her, billowing skirts and all, onto the carriage seat.

"Oh, John," she cried out in surprise and then fell into giggles. "No one's done that since I was a child."

He smiled as he took his seat beside her and flicked the reins. "Sorry, I'm afraid I still think of you as a child. You're hardly any bigger than you were when I left." He saw her look of protest. "But then you've filled out very nicely," he added and it mollified her.

"I wonder if anyone saw us," she mused looking all about. "You really are quite dashing and handsome in that uniform. The tale will go round that some officer abducted me off the wharf." She giggled to herself.

"I can't believe you're all grown up and about to be married."

"Yes," she sat straighter, "but good heavens, if people were to put off getting married because of non-blood relatives dying, if you had a really, really large family, there would never be any weddings." She smiled at him infectiously.

"Then the family couldn't get very large," he grinned back.

"Oh, John," she feigned exasperation.

"So, it's *Hamilton*, is it?"

"Yes," she smiled broadly again, this time with a faintly distant, dreamy expression crossing her face.

"Hamilton, what?"

"Hamilton… Chadwick… Grenville… Carter. He's so wonderful, John. You'll like him. He's tall… but not too tall… with very dark hair and bright blue eyes. He's very handsome and very smart. Well, he had the good sense to fall in love with me, didn't he?"

"I never heard where falling in love had much to do with good sense or smarts," he teased. "It's entirely other matters."

"John," she slapped playfully at his arm. "That's so naughty."

"Look whose talking."

"Anyway, he *is* very smart and, of course, he's very successful."

"Hmmmm, of course," John murmured obligingly.

"Father brought him home to dinner one night and every time he looked at me I had this melty feeling in the pit of my stomach. I couldn't eat a bite. Hamilton says he fell in love with me the very moment he saw me." Then she gave a high tinkling giggle. "You should have seen Father's face when Hamilton asked if he could call on me. And when he asked for my hand, Mother and I both had to convince Father that Boston is not on the other side of the moon."

"Far enough. The better part of a week by ship, I'd wager."

"Oh, not nearly a week," she replied sweetly, "only a few days."

"Well, I hope I get the chance to meet this paragon who has swept my baby sister off her feet."

"Why, of course you will… I mean, why shouldn't you? Oh, John, you're not going to disappear again are you?" She grabbed his arm earnestly. "If you are, then we really must have the wedding before you go."

"And what does Father say?"

"Pish-posh, you know Father, he always ends up agreeing with Mother," Isabelle pouted again daintily but her voice had the clarity of a little bell.

They continued to chat amiably on the short trip to the Power family home. John was still smiling when he drew the horses up in the drive, jumped down and helped Isabelle and Rachel from the carriage. Then, swinging his sister around to face him he exclaimed, "All right, enough about you for a moment, brat, I want you to meet someone."

"Who?" Isabelle asked breathlessly.

"My wife."

"Your wife! Oh, John, you're married?! Why didn't you say so?" She stopped and clapped her hands in childlike glee. "I don't believe it. I was just saying not too long ago that you had best marry soon before you grew so old and set in your ways no woman could stand you." She grinned broadly. "That's one of the reasons I told Mother we had to get you back here for my wedding… so you could meet some nice young ladies. I said to Mother, who could you possibly meet on that horrible frontier where there's nothing but savages and soldiers."

"It's not totally devoid of beautiful females, as my wife will prove," he replied evasively. They walked through the door and Isabelle found herself facing Ronnie in the entry hall.

"Darling, this is my little sister, Isabelle or Izzy as we've been calling her since she was in diapers," said John warmly.

"Hello," Ronnie said graciously and extended her hand as John had taught her to do.

"Hello." Isabelle barely touched Ronnie's fingers with her own as she looked the much taller woman over. She certainly had an exotic look about her. In contrast to her own porcelain white skin, the woman looked positively dark. Had John met some Spaniards on the frontier? But she was so tall and Spaniards were supposed to be little people.

"This is my wife, Ronnie," John said proudly.

"Ronnie?" Isabelle smiled mischievously. "What an odd name. Surely that's not your real name."

"No," Ronnie smiled hesitantly, "it is what your brother calls me because my name does not come easily to his lips."

"Can't remember your own wife's name, huh, John?" Isabelle teased with a sassy look at her brother, then she turned back to the taller woman and continued to appraise her. "So, what is your real name, if I may ask?"

"*Ohronkene Hahser.*"

"That's very... exotic, I don't know that I could say it like you do either," Isabelle said cautiously. "So you're foreign."

"Foreign?" Ronnie questioned the word.

"English doesn't seem to be your mother tongue," Isabelle responded.

"Ah, no, your brother teaches me English," replied Ronnie with a quick glance at John.

"What is your first language?" Isabelle asked, her eyes narrowing slightly.

"*Lenni Lanape,*" Ronnie replied. "But since I be eleven I speak *Kanyenkeha.*"

"Goodness." Isabelle stared for a moment and then looked to her brother in ill-disguised irritation. "I'm sorry, I don't recognize that, is she Portuguese?"

"The Portuguese speak Portuguese," John replied stiffly, not happy with how the conversation was going.

"Oh, I know that," Isabelle huffed, "but I don't know every country in the whole wide world, nor what every language sounds like. What for heaven's sake is *Lenny la nappie*? Where is she from? She's obviously foreign. Not that that's a bad thing," she turned to the taller woman with a small smile. "My goodness, Mother and Father are French and didn't speak any English when they first arrived. Bengt Solinson who is a neighbor has parents who came from Sweden and they didn't speak anything but Swedish when they first arrived. So where did your parents...?

"Is that all you can talk about? Trying to dig up my wife's pedigree? Where are your manners, Izzy? I expected better of you," John was frowning and Isabelle flushed. His upset was intensified because he realized he was actually trying to evade a direct answer to her questions as if he was ashamed. A quick glance at Ronnie made him feel even worse for he saw that she knew it, too.

"I'm sorry," Isabelle said contritely. "Welcome to the family, of course. I guess anything that gets John to come home and visit his family is a good thing. How long have you been married?"

"Actually, it's been a while," John replied, continuing to be evasive while his self irritation put an edge in his voice. "We have several children."

"What?" Isabelle giggled infectiously as she chattered. "I bet that put everyone into a spin. Not only are you married but you already have a growing family before anyone even hears about it. Several children... that's at least several years while we've been thinking of you as this big, lonesome bachelor. And all this time, the whole ride home you never said a thing. Oh, John, you are bad. I'm beginning to think you were on the other side of the world. Is that it? Were you in one of those far off exotic places like... like China or Japan... or Arabia? Is that where you are from, Arabia?" she turned again to Ronnie.

"Ronnie is an Indian," John said softly his eyes locked to his wife's.

"You were in India!" exclaimed Isabelle. "Oh, how romantic. Isn't that where they wear those turban things and sell exotic spices and..."

"I didn't join the navy, Izzy," John looked at her. "I'm in the British colonial army, we stay on the continent."

"But then how did you meet a girl from India?" Isabelle looked at him in puzzlement.

"Ronnie isn't from India, she's from right here," John said in exasperation.

"But you said she was... Oh, my God! You mean a savage?!" Isabelle looked at her brother in horror as realization struck home. "John, how could you? Does everyone know?"

John couldn't believe his sister's reaction. She hadn't even tried to hide it. "I'm not certain what you mean by *everyone*. I haven't been up on the rooftop lately shouting proclamations to the world. The family knows, of course. What difference does it make? What's the matter with you? Are you afraid she's going to take out her tomahawk and scalp you?"

"Oh!" Isabelle gasped indignantly. "Evidently you left your own manners back in the wilderness! What do you expect a person to say when you give them a shock like this?!" she snapped peevishly. Then, with a tight nod at Ronnie she added, "I'm sorry but I really must go to my room now. I've just returned from a very tiring trip. You'll have to excuse me," and she flounced up the staircase.

John stood for a moment in the wake of his sister's departure, staggered by his own disappointment. "I'm sorry," he said at last in the aftermath of silence.

Ronnie stood silently, without expression. She was capable of hiding her emotions but he noticed her posture was rigid. He walked over to her and put his arms around her drawing her to him. She didn't resist but she didn't soften either. "I apologize for the little brat. I'm afraid I expected better from her."

"She is very young."

"Young? She's the same age as you are," he growled, "well, almost."

"At least she is honest," she replied softly but still she did not relax.

Marie Power's nature was warm, loving, and generous. She was overjoyed to have her first born home once again and she was equally happy that he had found someone to love. It had been almost eleven years ago when Phillip had come home and told them John had suffered greatly at the Olafson daughter's death. It had been a horrible story but Marie had wondered how John could have grown that fond of the young woman in so short a time. And when John continued to stay away from home she had asked Jacques about it.

"Does it seem reasonable to you?" she had murmured one night as they had lain in bed holding each other.

"What is that, *ma belle*?" he had whispered to her.

"That John should grieve so… Jacques, he only knew her a few weeks." She had felt his shoulders move in that easy Gallic shrug of his.

"A few weeks, a few hours… when a man falls in love with a woman, the length of time he has known her matters not, only the depth of his passion." He was silent for a moment and then spoke again. "I believe something happened in Switzerland."

"What do you mean?"

"I remember his letters. They were… how might I say, unfocused? A little strange perhaps? Like a man who does not know where his future is headed. We know our John, he has a home here, he sought to be a better doctor for Chartes Landing and suddenly he becomes unfocused? What is the most likely cause for this in a young single man?"

"A girl," Marie had said softly.

"I think there was a girl and something happened. What? I do not know, it is John's secret but it left him changed, broke his heart perhaps… but he was different when he returned. You saw it too, did you not?"

"Yes… yes," she nodded quietly

"And if our John had such a hole in his heart and this Freyja filled it…" he took a deep breath. "And then she took her own life…"

Marie remembered she had moaned. "Oh, my poor child."

"To lose her in such a manner… I cannot imagine…" Suddenly his arms had tightened around Marie and she had felt him give a shudder.

"What is it?" she had whispered in concern.

"I have only to think of losing you and…" he had fallen silent for a long time and Marie had sensed he was struggling to keep his composure. Finally, he had continued in a controlled low voice. "I realize that it is the fate of all to finally leave this life, *ma cœur*, but I must admit I am selfish and hope when that time comes I go before you. I no longer have the courage to live without you by my side."

In the darkness she had turned to him, caressing him and drawing him closer. "Ohh, *mon amour, mon amour*. Dare not to leave me all alone."

"I can understand all too well how John may be feeling. Thank God he is very young. I hope he learns to survive and perhaps someday he will heal and even find another love."

"Yes…" Marie had sighed gently. "I pray for that as well."

That had been eleven years ago and now John had found someone and Marie couldn't help but be happy for him. Ronnie was a lovely girl, a very competent mother and she seemed completely devoted to John. She must be, thought Marie, to be willing to come so far from her home and put up with the inevitable shortcomings of so-called civilization. And since she was brave enough to do that, Marie decided, she would show her daughter-in-law that civilization was not all bad. There were certain advantages.

And so Marie took Ronnie down to the Chartes Landing Emporium, the retail establishment Marie had spent her adult life building. The older woman was delighted to see the expressions of wonder, amazement, curiosity, and pleasure so honestly displayed on the face of her new daughter-in-law. Rather how she, herself, must have looked when she took her first good tour through the markets of New York when she was a girl, Marie thought.

The older woman helped the younger pick out a wide assortment of sundries. Sweet smelling soaps, dusting powers, lotions, and creams. Things she, as a woman, could appreciate having at the frontier and things Marie knew John, as a man, would never think of introducing his wife to since he most assuredly had no acquaintance with most of them himself. They were feminine things, things of fine textures and scents, to allow a lady to pamper herself and feel more beautiful. Marie remembered vividly her own days at the frontier.

"It is too much," Ronnie protested modestly as Marie gathered more and more items onto the counter.

"Nonsense," Marie shook her head with a smile and continued to add things, "consider it part of my wedding gift to you. It makes me happy to give you these things. I know good and well how hard it is to be at the frontier. Are there any other women for you to keep company with?"

"The major's wife has been very kind to me. She taught me how to dress like a white woman. I would like to bring her a present," Ronnie said timidly.

"Of course. What do you think she would like?"

"She comes to the coast to visit her family some times. She and the major have no children." There was a touch of sadness in the younger woman's voice.

"I could not imagine life without my children. Even with Jack, we would be missing something."

Marie smiled. "I understand exactly how you feel. And you have beautiful children, but then you and John are both very handsome, why shouldn't you have beautiful children? Speaking of which, we must pick out some materials for clothing. But first, we'll pick out something nice for your lady friend."

They took their time and found, at last, a small bit of statuary which Ronnie thought the major's wife would like very well. After depositing that with the rest, Marie was leading her over to the bolts of cloth when Ronnie caught sight of some children's primers and stopped suddenly.

"Books!" she uttered a little breathlessly. She fingered one and opened it. "This good to learn to read?"

"Why yes, of course. Do you know how to read, Ronnie?" she asked earnestly.

"I try to learn. At fort, major's wife, she has books."

"Wonderful. Reading will help you to understand the language even better. At least it was that way for me. Well, you must take a set of these for your home so you can teach your children when they grow a little older. But then you might want to read through them yourself, yes?" Marie took a set of primers and carried them to the counter to join the growing pile, then she led the way and they set about selecting materials.

At the house that evening, Marie showed Ronnie her small library. She had started borrowing books as a young girl newly arrived in New York Towne, she explained, and from them she had learned to read and helped to teach Jacques and their friend Richard to read and write in English.

"My first job when I came to this country was as a nursemaid and the little boy who was perhaps nine years old, I remember not exactly anymore, but… he loved to play the schoolmaster. He was the one who taught me first to read."

Ronnie smiled in response but her eye had fallen on a book sitting upon a small table by Marie's favorite chair. It was bound in leather and had a bright red satin ribbon page marker. "M..M..oll F..lan..ders," she sounded out as her fingers traced along the tooled leather. "What is that?" she asked in curiosity.

"*Moll Flanders* is the name of a woman. It is one of the new books I just received in this last shipment from England. It is by Defoe… oh, but you have undoubtedly never heard of Defoe. Here, wait a minute," Marie went over the shelves and after a brief time in which she stood still with her eyes looking rapidly over the volumes. "Here it is!" she said with excitement and she plucked a volume from the shelf. It was covered in finely tooled leather. She handed it to Ronnie in exchange for the other. "This is a wonderful story… by the same man."

Ronnie stood with the dark wine red volume in her hand trying to sound out the words.

"Robinson Crusoe," Marie stated at last. "That, too, is a name. Only this time it is the name of a man. It is an adventure story. I am certain you will like it. I see not why you could not work your way through this. You must take it and after you have accomplished the primers you can begin to work your way through some more adult fare. If you become frustrated with any word or do not understand the meaning of something, John will help you, I am sure."

"But…" she began to protest. She had not understood everything. Marie was speaking too quickly.

"No, you must take it. I can replace it."

"Thank you very much," Ronnie replied looking at the handsomely bound book and holding it almost reverently.

"I would let you have them both, but I am still reading the other. It is quite… umm," she cleared her throat, "entertaining. I have already sold out of all the copies I had at the store. And when I am finished, both my older daughters will want to read it. It is not something I would allow Isabelle to read… yet. By the next time you visit, I am certain we will be able to part with it." Marie smiled broadly.

"Why would you not want Isabelle to read?"

Marie chuckled. "Well, it is a little risque." Then Marie understood by Ronnie's face that she did not understand. "Ahhh, sexually suggestive?" Marie offered.

"Sexual… means pleasures?"

"Well," Marie grew thoughtful. "Sexual can mean pleasure or it can mean pain but it does refer to sex."

Ronnie thought for a moment. She had pleasure with Jack. She had had pleasure with Gray Wolf, even with Tonoaki but the white men had given her pain. Yes, she understood.

"But why should Isabelle not read? Is important to know pleasure is there to be had." She thought of how long Gray Wolf had wanted her but she had been too afraid.

"Yes, but… well… I…" Marie thought for a few moments, then smiled. "Perhaps you are right."

Ronnie smiled back. She liked Marie. A small woman, she was, however, surprisingly animated and energetic and seemed larger. Ronnie had never had a mother-in-law before. Gray Wolf had had no family at all and Tonoaki's mother was dead long before they were joined.

The Indian woman was still trying to become accustomed to the boldness of white women. Jack had taught her to walk beside him and even to preceed him through doors and up staircases ahead of him. She was so used to following behind, as all Indian women were taught to do, that she was still somewhat uncomfortable obeying Jack's wishes in this. The major's wife had helped to explain it to her at the fort. This was the white man's custom. But now, surrounded by many white women she was both fascinated and uncomfortable with how they spoke up in front of their husbands and menfolk. The Power women even looked men outside the family in the eye which took much for Ronnie to get used to. It made her exceedingly uncomfortable, as though she herself were doing something wrong. But she quickly realized the men took no offense but her keen observations noticed that other women did not do this. They were more timid. Ronnie concluded that this must have something to do with Jack's father being a chief among his people and in the white man's world his status gave this privilege to his women. White women even disagreed with their husbands in front of others, at least she witnessed it to be so within the family home although she had not been out amidst the whites enough to know if this was also true with other women.

It was a fascinatingly different world she had to admit but still she longed for home. She was very aware that some from Jack's family did not approve of her and it made her uneasy and uncomfortable. At first she thought she was doing something wrong, that somehow she was responsible for them disliking her. Then she reminded herself how easy it had been for her to hate all whites without knowing them and she understood or at least she tried to. Louise's mate had been killed by an Indian arrow. But understanding didn't make it hurt any less.

Chapter 3

"**B**ut Mother, if Hamilton finds out we now have Indians in the family, he could call off the engagement. I can't lie to him. Why if he found out after the marriage, if it came to light that we now have Indian blood in the family… who knows, it could be grounds for divorce. I would be totally disgraced!"

"Do not be ridiculous!" Marie glared at her youngest daughter. "You do not suddenly have Indian blood. This is your brother's wife, it is his children who have the Indian blood."

"Still, Boston society is not like it is here, people have very high standards and Hamilton has a very important position to maintain. It would cause a scandal, an absolute scandal," Isabelle was fuming as she sat over her morning tea.

"So, have we not high standards?" Marie looked at her daughter sharply. "It is not standards you speak of but snobbery. There was enough of that in the Old World, we do not need to cultivate it here. And if that is the kind of shallow young man Hamilton proves himself to be, then I do not want my daughter married to him," Marie replied rather curtly. She was more upset than she appeared. Her youngest daughter's blatantly disagreeable attitude toward John's wife had Marie's nerves worn raw.

"And doesn't anyone care what I want anymore?" Isabelle retorted, twisting her napkin in her lap. Her young heart was set on marrying Hamilton, being a banker's wife, and moving to the growing metropolis of Boston where she saw herself heading up the next generation of Bostonian society. And she saw all her dreams disappearing because her brother had shown up unexpectedly with, of all things, an Indian wife.

"And what exactly is it that you want, dear sister?" John asked coldly from the doorway of the sunlit breakfast room. He stood dressed carelessly in his breeches and boots with a jerkin on over his shirt which was open at the neck. He was looking hard at his sister.

John had awakened early and brought the baby into bed for Ronnie to nurse, leaving her to doze while he shaved and dressed. He had heard the voices as soon as he'd left his old bedroom and now he closed the breakfast room door, not wanting the conversation to carry up to Ronnie.

Marie looked at her son. He looked so remarkably like his father at his age, about as close a copy as any father and son could be but still with a difference other than John's lack of a moustache. There was a little more sharpness to John's chin which she took to be her influence. It went with the sharp toughness, almost hardness she also saw in her eldest son, a hardness Jacques had never had. Jacques still retained a charming Gallic gallantry that made him seem somehow a little more easy going, a little more romantic of spirit. John had had it once, long ago, when he was very young. Before he left for France, Marie thought, before Switzerland and whatever had happened there. Before the incident at the lumber camp and whatever horrors John had seen since. It was gone now.

"Good morning, John," Marie said pleasantly, then added in a voice which was soft but without a trace of weakness. "Please allow me to continue this conversation with my daughter myself."

"Good morning, Mother," John said pleasantly as he filled a cup with hot tea from the sideboard. The cook had brought eggs, bacon, ham, sausage, breads, and muffins which were all being kept warm in the chafing dishes while the seasonal fruit, which right now was strawberries, was setting on its own. He didn't seem to notice any of it. "But I would very much like to know," he continued with feigned calm as he seated himself casually across the table from Isabelle. "What is it that you want, Izzy? Do you want me to dump my wife and children into the bay and pretend they never existed?"

"Don't be sarcastic!" Isabelle snapped impatiently.

"Or do you want us to dishonor their heritage by disavowing it, by making up lies to hide the truth?" he continued, arching a brow at her.

"You don't have to lie, you just don't have to blab it to everyone," she replied.

"I don't *blab* to anyone. But what you are asking is that my wife and children never make reference to their former home, never speak of their customs and folklore, never share memories of life with other kin, because any of these things will allow the astute to deduce that they are New World natives. And if I shamed them by asking them to do these things, despite the fact that they have more right to be here than you or I do, it still only takes one person to come right out and ask 'Are you an Indian?' for the truth to come out because I will not ask them to lie!" John brought his fist down hard on the table for emphasis and the dishes clattered in vibration.

"Oh, why did you even bother coming home?" Isabelle cried out tearfully. Her pretty face was twisted in self-pity and anger, her pale blonde locks bouncing in disarray as she brought her napkin to her eyes.

"Ahhh, now we come to the heart of it," John said with a deceptive smile. "What you'd really like is for me and my family to simply disappear back from where we came, wouldn't you?" He continued to look at her. "Well, wouldn't you?"

"Yes! Yes, yes, yes. You've been gone all this time. We barely heard a word from you. You didn't care if we went to rot. So, why show up now just to spoil things!" Isabelle cried out in equal anger, jumping up from the table and running from the room.

The room became very quiet. The soft sound of rapid footsteps ascending the stairs ceased, followed by the sharp closing of a door. The only sound now was John's teaspoon hitting the side of the china cup as he stirred the cream and sugar into his tea.

"Maybe she's right," John sighed quietly, "maybe..."

"John!" the pioneer strength of a woman who had helped carve Chartes Landing out of the New Jersey wilderness came through in the poised woman's voice. "I asked you to allow me to have my conversation with your sister. Instead, you chose to argue with her and accomplished nothing." She looked him straight in the eye and he had the decency to look discomfited. "You are my first born, John. She is my last. I love you both without measure. But I am not blind or stupid and I do recognize the differences in how you were raised. You were born in the early days, you were even birthed in an Indian hut. You played with the little Indian children, you remember when they were around. She was born fourteen years later after life had become quite... different. She is spoiled. I know this. Things have been much too easy for her and too *civilized* perhaps. The Indians had disappeared by the time she came along. She never had any little Indian playmates. More and more white people had moved here and many have had very unkind things to say of the natives. People they never even knew but it was their children with whom your sister played and, in all fairness, she has seen the face of prejudice you never did.

"She knows not what it is like to play in a dirt floor cabin, she has never had to get those lily white hands dirty." Marie sighed. "Well," she shrugged almost to herself, "why do parents work and slave and struggle if not to provide a better life for their children, eh? But sometimes the life, it becomes too good… and the children lose the lessons that can be learned from the struggle." Marie put her hand on her son's arm. He was staring into his cup and the movement brought his eyes up to her face.

"This is the first thing in her silly, shallow life that confronts her, that disturbs her, and that she cannot control. It is the very first opportunity she has had to learn something of some real importance about people different from us and about life. She needs these lessons, John. It grieves my heart that this lesson comes at the expense of you and Ronnie. But I can tell Ronnie is capable of understanding. Please, you are the older, you are the wiser. Do not make this easy for her by retreating."

John sat back and looked intently at his mother. Her eyes were bright and full of life giving them that almost golden-green appearance and her whole face was youthfully energetic and warm. He reached out and took her hand.

"You're quite a lady, Mother," he said, his voice rough with emotion. "I can fully understand why Father married you. I hope you and Ronnie really get to know each other well. You're the two most important women in my life."

"Ah, *mon cher*," Marie smiled engagingly, put her other small hand over his larger one, and patted it affectionately. "To have your adult child tell you this… it is the grandest compliment to a mother's heart… but best you not forget to include your daughter," she smiled teasingly. He nodded with a grin and after a moment became serious again.

"You know we can't stay long," John said quietly as he brought his mother's hands up to his mouth and kissed her fingers lightly.

"How long?" she asked wistfully.

"For a while yet," he replied, smiling at her.

Marie maintained her composure. "And then, next time, you must not wait so long," she encouraged optimistically.

John nodded. "The ghosts I had to deal with are buried now."

"This is good," she said serenely. "There is too much juice to be squeezed out of life to let the past paralyze you."

He nodded again in agreement.

"And Ronnie… she, too, has had *ghosts*?"

"Yes," he replied quietly.

"I thought so. She has been through much in her young life and it has made her very strong. I can see it. I can tell. She is right for you, John. You will face challenges but you will be very happy together."

"I already am," he smiled broadly.

"Yes? Then, you must make the cook happy, too, and eat some breakfast."

"Yes, ma'am," John responded obediently and rose to go to the sideboard and fill a plate with food.

John was almost finished with his breakfast when Jane, their long-time housekeeper, stepped into the room and told John when he was finished his father would like to see him in his study.

"Thank you, Jane," John smiled, wiped his mouth and refilled his tea cup to take it with him.

Jacques' door was open. "Good morning," he waved his son in when he saw him approach.

"Good morning, Father, there's still some tea left if you'd like."

"No, no, thank you. I am fine." Jacques motioned John to a chair opposite his desk and rose to shut the study door. "John, there is something I wish to share with you." Jacques returned to his seat. "Many years ago when you were in Switzerland, I wrote a rather emotional letter warning you of the news that my parents had died and so you must stay out of France, do you recall?"

"Yes, of course, sir, I still have it."

"You do?" Jacques looked touched.

"It may not seem like it. I may not have given you reason to think so, but my family does mean a lot to me."

Jacques swallowed. "As you mean so much to us, *mon fils*," he said softly.

"I've never doubted that, Father."

"Good, and now," he cleared his throat, "a loose end to tie up before you return to the frontier. Perhaps you recall how I questioned your *grand-mère's* death. I asked if you believed a person could simply will herself to die. I was very crushed at the time to think my dear ma-ma did not care enough to come to us… and live."

"I remember."

"Perhaps because you are my first born, perhaps because you are a physician, I know not… but you are the only person aside from your ma-ma to whom I expressed this. And now, I want to correct the record."

John listened closely. He remembered how he too had questioned. Just as he knew the anger he had felt when Freyja had chosen to die.

"John, your *grand-mère* did not choose to die, she…"

"They killed her?!" John gasped.

"No-no, they put her into prison. She was alive all these years, well provided for by my father's will and working to improve conditions within the prison for the other women. I received a letter, her last letter to me, sent by my father's old law firm at her request upon her actual death some nine years later. They had watched out for her all those years and apologized for the deception which had been at her insistence."

"But why? Why did she hide it? Did she not think you would want to hear from her?" John was shocked.

"She wrote that the only thing she could think of to give me peace of mind was for me to think that she was dead as well. She said she was terrified that I would somehow try to fly to her rescue and get myself imprisoned or killed."

"Was it a valid fear, sir?"

Jacques looked sadly at his son. "I have not an army to lay siege and storm the walls of a prison to demand my mother's release. But oh, how I would have loved to receive letters from her." Jacques sighed. "In fairness, she never thought I would find out but complications arose involving the distribution of my inheritance."

John looked puzzled but said nothing.

"The trusteeship that provided for *ma mère* was set up to dissolve and all assets come to me once she passed. I am afraid the lawyer was at wits end with how to explain a nine year gap from when he reported her dead and when I received this last part of my inheritance."

"So she vouched for their integrity," John nodded.

"Yes. *Ma mère*, God rest her soul, could have a will of iron and the strength of a legion. My father had planned an escape route for her. He told me my cousin was a serious threat and so, it was Pa-pa's plan to whisk her away and aboard one of Dufee's ships. But she refused to leave until my father was buried. And so, the authorities took her."

"Perhaps she felt some guilt?"

"Perhaps, she made a point to tell me that she was certain she would have died in the crossing anyway and so she, in fact, had lived nine years more than she might have if she had died on board ship. Who can argue with a letter from the grave?" Jacques shrugged sadly.

"I remember she had been very seasick when they arrived to visit," nodded John.

"Hmm, but she did have a will of iron."

John got up and went to the window, restless energy needing a release. "Why do the people we love not realize… Father, I have something I too wish to tell you about." And John proceeded to tell his father all about Alana, his first wife in Switzerland, and how hard she had fought for life against a blood disease that finally killed her. And how angry he had been at beautiful, innocent Freyja who had given up on life by hanging herself when she was kidnapped for white slavery. And then ten years later, how his heart had opened to Ronnie, in part, because she had fought so very hard to be a survivor. When he had finished, the study was still.

"*Mon fils*, I can say as a father, I am truly sorry for the losses you have suffered," Jacques said sympathetically, "but as a man, I must confess it makes you much stronger than I."

John looked over at the man he had looked up to, admired, and even resented a bit all of his adult life. Resented for being so perfect. He quirked a questioning eyebrow.

"John, you have survived losing two women you have loved passionately, *n'est-ce pas?*" He looked at his son and John nodded. "And you have not just survived you have gone on to take another chance and love a third." Jacques was slowly shaking his head. "I will not lie, I had other women before I came to this country, but there was never anyone for whom I felt such passion. Until your ma-ma… and truly I feel more and more like a weak coward when I think of being left without her. I think of my friend Richard and realize the courage he has had… to love her and yet accept without malice living so closely with us but never having her. I think the man is a saint but I would never tell him this."

It grew quiet again and John wanted to say something to comfort his father.

"If my opinion as a physician is of any value, I can say from observation that both you and Mother appear in excellent health and thoughts of departing should not weigh on your mind." He smiled. "Never allow anyone to bleed you. And thank goodness for Jane and her cleanliness campaign all of these years. I've spoken with Doctor Ajax and he appears to still be adhering to all the suggestions I gave him. I think once he had a look into my microscope, he understood. He'll keep a good eye on you and Mother and if anything serious happens, please send word. And yes, I promise to write more often."

Jacques smiled. "It is good to know. And son, can I ask once again if you might speak with Louise. She needs some of your strength."

"I will, but Father, may I also encourage you to share *Grand-mère's* true death with the rest of the family? It's important they not think of her as someone who gave up on life… no matter the reason. And you should be proud of what she did in the prison. She too had strength."

Jacques nodded as his son left the study.

After depositing his tea cup and saucer in the breakfast room, John found his way to Louise's room and knocked on the door. He heard a muffled "Come in." Opening the door he saw his sister sitting at the window seat, propped against pillows, a handkerchief in her hand.

"Hello," he said softly.

"Hello, John," she replied flatly.

"Mind if I come in?" he asked but proceeded into the room without waiting for permission. He shut the door, and brought her small dressing table stool with him to the window seat.

"John, I really don't feel like talking right now," she grimaced and turned her head to look out the window as he sat down on the small stool.

"I know," he replied. "Just let me do a little talking, all right?"

That brought her head around to look at him.

"I am truly sorry I never had the opportunity to meet Raphael. Two reasons. First, he was your husband and you obviously loved him very deeply and second, because he was Uncle Richard's son, the only one he ever brought home, so to speak, so Richard must have loved him a great deal as well."

"He was raised by nuns," she said softly. "Can you imagine Uncle Richard giving his child over to a group of nuns?" she almost smiled. "He had the most beautiful manners. Uncle Richard would say 'who could imagine a fur trader with the manners of a prince?' And Mama would whisper to me… 'just like your pa-pa.'" Louise reached out then to her brother and John put his arms around her while she cried into his chest.

"Lu-lu," he said, resurrecting a name that had been buried in the nursery, "I'm not going to tell you everything is going to be all right because, frankly, at this point that is much too far in the future for you to accept. And I'm not going to tell you to be strong for your children because you already know more about what your children need than I do and I never had to deal with that… but Lu-lu, I do know what you are going through. I know exactly how you feel."

Louise pulled away and looked into her brother's face. She was about to dismiss the loss of a sweetheart of a few weeks to whom he had not even been married as hardly an equivalent when he spoke again.

"I was married in Switzerland. She was absolutely everything, everything I could hope for or dream of or desire and our passions about everything knew no bounds… except for one. She was dying and there was nothing anyone could do about it. I am a doctor, her father was a doctor and she was a doctor and we impotently watched as she faded away. Her father had written to embassies as far away as China in the hopes that somewhere someone had discovered a cure. Or if not a cure perhaps a treatment that would give her even a few more years. There was nothing. She died in my arms." John looked into his sister's eyes and she saw all the pain. "Believe me, being there when the love of your life dies is no better than not being there. Maybe it's worse. It rips out your gut and leaves your insides hanging raw in the wind."

"Ohhh, John, then Freyja wasn't…"

"Freyja was a God-send, I thought. Innocent, young, beautiful, intelligent, and self-educated even in that lumber camp… and healthy. She was very special and she was like a balm over a raw wound, proof that I still had a heart and it could still love. She made me feel whole again and I truly thought God had set her in my path as the replacement for the woman He had taken away."

"Oh, John," Louise reached out and kissed his lean cheek. "We never knew."

"No, no one over here did. I have now told father, he can tell mother. No one else knows, except Ronnie… and now you. I prefer it not be turned into easy family gossip."

"Of course not," she looked hurt.

"I told you because I want you to know, you will never forget Raphael but you do learn to live again. Everyday the pain gets a little duller. You won't notice it at first and it takes however long it takes until one day you realize you *can* live life again. But you'll always feel just a little broken, that pinch of pain when you speak of him even decades from now. But you can live again. And no one knows the future, sis, it took me ten years but I finally found another woman I could give my heart to and I'm holding on to her with everything I've got. And someday, when you've stopped crying, you just may look up and find someone too. You know when your eyes aren't all red and swollen and your nose isn't all drippy, you aren't a half bad looking woman," he said more lightly.

"But I'm no longer young," she protested.

"Oh, fiddle, you look the most like Mother and look how good she looks even at her age." To that Louise had to nod in agreement and gave a small smile. The first small smile she had had for months. The first since late last autumn when Richie arrived home with the news.

The large dining room in the Power home was lit with a half dozen candelabras each holding a dozen candles. As the heat rose, it vented out the transom windows above the French doors that led out to the gardens, thus keeping the room tolerably pleasant without the need for anyone standing duty pulling the cord connected to the pulley system that flapped the large woven reed sheets hanging overhead. Jacques Power, with perfect posture and an elegantly aristocratic manner, sat at the head of the long highly polished table which was draped in a snow white covering of linen. He and Marie were having the entire family for dinner to say farewell to Richie and Clarissa before they left on their trek into the interior.

At Jacques' right sat his son Richie, then Clarissa, James, Helen, Thor, Isabelle, and finally thirteen year Thomas who was seated at his grandmother's left hand. On Jacques' left was Ronnie, then John, Caroline, Phillip, Louise, Richard, and fourteen year old Charity. Marie sat directly across at the far end of the table.

The rest of the grandchildren were ensconced in the breakfast room where the twins, Faith and Hope, nosed out their cousin Rebecca as eldest, and Faith had the final word having been born five whole minutes before her sister.

Jacques was very proud of his family and so very pleased to have his eldest son back home if only for a while. It was more than he had been able to do for his own father. Once Jacques had fled from France almost forty years ago, he had never been allowed to go back again. But here, this night, seeing his family all together around the table, made Jacques wish to savor the moments, like a fine wine. Richie and Clarissa would be leaving tomorrow, then John again would leave. Who knew when or if they would ever be all together like this again. His heart was so full and he was feeling very blessed.

After saying grace, Jacques signaled for the wine to be brought out. Two serving girls came forth each with a large bucket of icy cold water in which rested a very large bottle which had been chilling in the spring-house. Jacques made a small production of removing one bottle which they wrapped in a fresh towel and he proceeded to untwist a wire encasement which was around the stopper. "Now, watch out," he warned and suddenly the cork fairly exploded from the bottleneck shooting across the room and falling harmlessly into the corner.

"What on earth…?" John rose from his chair and searched for the stopper, finding it and taking it back to his seat amidst a variety of gasps and exclamations. "Looks like the wine is bad, Father," offered John studying the cylindrical piece of tan material he held. "I guess it is not surprising, there seem to be holes in the stopper."

"It is cork," Jacques grinned. "An amazing material and the wine is perfect," he poured a gushing froth of bubbles into a glass, "it needs only to breathe for a moment."

Phillip smiled. "That's the way it's suppose to be," he explained to John in reference to the cork stopper. "They harvest it from tree bark in Portugal."

"I had the wine smuggled in," Jacques explained with a conspiratorial smile. "It is from the Abbey du Champagne, northeast of the Pouvoir lands."

"I've never seen *pinot gris* that is fizzy," John murmured.

"No-no, not *pinot gris* though I am pleased to see you have not forgotten your lessons in wine while you have been at the frontier," Jacques nodded approvingly and began to pour the highly effervescent liquid into the glasses on the tray the maid was holding. "It is the inspiration of a very skilled vintner, Dom Pierre Perignon. Monsieur Perignon developed a very unique blend of grapes, some say it was a happy accident." Jacques chuckled, "but then, is that not what they always say when a vintner comes upon a truly superb blend?" He placed a glass in front of Ronnie, another in front of Richie, and one above his own plate. Then, he nodded for the girl to serve the rest of the glasses around. "It is very exciting and most original. And thanks to my contacts I was able to obtain some. Sent to Dufee's ship disguised as barrels of pickled herring." Jacques laughed deeply at the thought. "If the customs officials had known what hid in the bottom of those barrels, they would most certainly have confiscated it. Supply cannot keep up with demand. Wait until you taste it. It dances down your pallet as lightly as a feather."

"It is raining upside down," murmured Ronnie as she passed her index finger back and forth over the top of her glass feeling little sparkles of wet jumping into the air above the rim. She looked wide-eyed at John.

"How charmingly put," Jacques nodded to his newest daughter-in-law. "Here," he held the bottle toward John, "lift this."

John grasped the bottle his father extended forth, raised his eyebrows, and examined it closer. "Very heavy," he observed.

"That is English glass," responded Jacques, "I understand the Abby had to send to England for bottles. The pressure within the sealed bottle is tremendous and the thin glass of normal French wine bottles cannot contain it."

John handed the bottle back as the serving girl had reached him. He took the last remaining glass from the serving tray.

When everyone had their wine in hand Jacques raised his glass in a salute to his wife. "To my partner in life, my wife, my friend, my heart, and the mother of this fine family: my beautiful Marie!" he toasted gallantly.

"Here! Here!" "To Mother." "Mother." "Mama!" "Grandma!" came the responses. They all sipped, then drank, and giggles burst forth from the women. The sparkling wine tickled their noses and their pallets and was extremely easy to consume. Another round was poured out. Only Ronnie needed no refill as she had only briefly sipped the strange liquid.

"And now," Marie held her glass up, a brilliant smile on her countenance, "to the man without whom my life would have had little meaning and none of you would be here tonight. The man I wake up beside each morning and thank the Lord that it is so. My husband, my lover, my friend, and your sire: my dearest, darling Jacques!"

"Here! Here!" "Father." "To Father." "Grandfather!" "Papa!" Again the voices responded.

Ronnie had another sip of the wine but could feel its effect going to her head immediately and set her glass down. She turned and smiled at Jack.

"What is it?" he asked her quietly.

"Your father and mother," she bent shyly and whispered. "They are like… newly married."

"I know. When we Power men love a woman, she stays loved," he whispered in her ear and grabbed her knee playfully beneath the table.

The food was served amidst a variety of small talk starting with how delightful the new wine was and quickly going on to other things. The continuing wars in Europe were always of interest as their effects were often felt even in the colonies.

"It is no wonder people continue to come to the colonies in such numbers. They are sick and tired of war, war, and more war," observed Jacques sagely.

"It sounds like the frontier," John quipped lightly.

"I know the unrest on the frontier is constant," Jacques replied, "but believe me when I say it is nothing like Europe. There… ah, how can I explain? The devastation of the armies. It is so complete. The armies scourge the lands, fields and crops are burned for miles and miles, it creates famine and starvation which leads to diseases and plagues. We are talking very large armies after all, not small Indian bands. The people suffer for years trying to rebuild. Believe me, it is not the same. This country is so rich in its bounty."

"I read the new colony of New Orleans had to bring German immigrants in to farm for them," Phillip spoke out. "I don't know what kind of Frenchmen chose to settle there but they don't seem to have the sense to be able to feed themselves. Every year they were begging food from France."

Jacques chuckled. "Sounds like a lot of foppish dandies who strayed too far from court and do not recognize the workings of a hoe and plow."

As the conversation and the meal continued everyone grew more and more gay. The first bottle of champagne was emptied and they began on the second. Even Richard was coming out of his shell. Most of the ladies were feeling more than a little light headed. Charity and Thomas had been allowed only half glasses under Marie's watchful eye. Thomas craned around the heads of his aunts and uncles to peer down the table.

"What are you looking at?" Isabelle hissed when she saw him.

"I was just looking at my new aunt, she sure is pretty, ain't she?" he replied.

"Don't say *ain't*, say isn't," she scolded.

"Well, then, isn't she?" he persisted.

"I suppose so if you like Indians," Isabelle muttered begrudgingly.

"Really?! Is she an Indian?" Thomas asked and suddenly the voices around the table grew quiet. The young boy looked around to see everyone staring at him. His face turned beet red and he immediately looked straight down at his plate.

"I don't believe I've told you about the time I was held prisoner in an Indian village," said John smoothly. "My men and I were out on a scouting maneuver when we were ambushed. I was the only survivor but I was so messed up I walked right into the arms of this group of braves who thought I was the enemy but I wasn't armed so there was no honor in killing me. They dragged me back to their village and dumped me with the shaman… that's the medicine man… so he could heal me enough for them to stick a weapon in my hand and kill me in a hand to hand combat challenge. Ronnie was the shaman's adopted daughter so she helped him. Nobody spoke English or French and I couldn't speak their tongue but when I got well enough to shave, Ronnie recognized me as the doctor who had helped her a few years before."

"Didn't you recognize her?" Richie asked.

"No, I didn't because she had grown from child to woman. Anyway there was this one hot-headed brave who couldn't wait to fight me but Ronnie knew I was still too injured to stand a chance so she helped me escape. I could never figure why this lovely young woman had risked her own punishment to help me and save my life… until later when I was back in the village with an interpreter. The irony is these Indians were Mohawks, our allies."

"And they were going to kill you?" Helen gasped.

"Well, yes, but they didn't know that we were on the same side."

"Savages," Helen muttered.

"If we are telling Indian stories," Marie spoke. "I have some wonderful stories of my own to tell." She saw heads from the breakfast room had popped into view at the doorway. "Jacques, do you mind if I tell the children about Looking Glass? It was so long ago, surely they can see that our marriage has survived."

Jacques knew exactly what his wife was up to and simply smiled graciously to her over his lifted glass, with a small nod of his head.

Marie had everyone's attention, including the listening grandchildren, as she began to tell them about the Indian brave she had named 'Looking Glass' many years ago when she had first come to the harbor valley.

"He was very strong and very fierce looking but also very handsome in his own way. And I must say, he did not think very much of your grandfather for leaving his woman… that was me… alone so much and all by myself. In time, I came to understand that to an Indian's way of thinking, the only normal living is within a tribal relationship. A warrior may go off for a time to hunt or trade or fight but he always leaves his wife with others to watch over her and keep her company."

"Is that true, Ronnie?" James asked lightly.

"It is true," Ronnie spoke softly. "Only those who are outcasts or renegades live outside the tribe. And for a wife to be left alone would be considered a punishment or desertion."

"Ahh, you see," Marie nodded, "so this poor brave is out there, watching over me and thinking that we are crazy for not staying back with our own kind and then to make matters worse, that my husband is always punishing me by deserting me for no good reason," Marie smiled.

"How did you know he was watching you, Mother?" Louise asked.

"Oh, I'm coming to that. It was during our second year on the frontier, your father was trapped in the wilderness all winter and I was left all alone in our cabin. You remember the old cabin? My old storage building before we tore it down?" she asked, and the heads of the oldest grandchildren nodded. "That was the cabin we lived in. Where I stayed all alone. Oh, the months were so long, the winter set in and I became very, very melancholy. Your father and Uncle Richard had left in the spring and were supposed to return in the autumn. But autumn came and autumn went. I watched for him every day, then the snows came and I knew he was not coming. My mind came up with a thousand different fears and, finally, I was certain he was dead, although I refused to admit it, and I did not know how I could continue on. You see when you are alone like that all the little hob-goblins come out to torment you. And soon you are drowning in a sea of sadness and worries and fears for the worst. It became impossible for me to think of anything but the worst. One night I cried myself to sleep and I forgot my fire."

"Forgot your fire, Mama," Isabelle asked with a frown, "whatever do you mean?"

"I forgot to attend to my fire, to bank it for the night. It was a little two room cabin with only one fireplace at the time. There was no one and nothing around for miles and miles and I only had one fire. Not like here now with neighbors everywhere. So, I fell asleep and my fire went out. When I finally awoke it was only because I had to pee so badly I was ready to wet my bed."

There were scattered giggles around the table and from the breakfast room door.

"The worst thing you can do in the winter time is fall asleep out in the cold," Marie went on seriously, "you know this, of course." She saw several nods from her audience. "And I had gone to sleep, forgetting to bank my fire. When it went out the chimney became like an open window to admit the cold. The cabin was soon freezing, it was little better than being outside. I would have frozen to death in my sleep if my bladder had not made me get up.

"Well, I came to find out several hills over Looking Glass lived with his tribe. And I did not know it, but much later his sister told me that every day he would look to the harbor to see if he could see the smoke from my chimney. When he saw my chimney smoke, you see, he knew I was up and about. That day when he did not see it, he immediately took his sister and they walked all the way in the cold and deep snow to bring me fire."

"Gosh," Thomas sighed.

"Surely you had flint, Mother," Helen said practically.

"Yes, of course I had flint although starting a fire from scratch on an ice cold hearth crusted over with ice crystals is no easy task let me assure you. I thought I would never achieve it. It took me hours. My whole body was shaking and shivering so, despite the long warm cloak of fur my Jacques had given to me as a wedding gift. Anyway, where was I? Oh yes, Looking Glass… he did not come so much to bring me fire perhaps as to check that I was all right, that I was not sleeping myself to death, or that I had not an accident and was hurt. It was most caring, do you not think?"

There was a quiet murmur of agreement which Marie cut short by continuing her story. "When they arrived they found me well for I had just managed to get a small fire going. And to my surprise, I discovered I could talk to them. Looking Glass' sister had been married to a white man, a trapper I think, and had learned some English and by that time I had learned English, as well."

"What was her name, Grandma?" Thomas asked, caught up in the story.

"Her name was She-Who-Laughs-In-Her-Sleep." There was a titter of amusement. "This was the first time I had met her and she was able to speak to me and interpret for her brother, whose real name, I then discovered, was Son-of-Sky-Hawk. And with his sister to interpret he offered for me."

"He offered for you, what does that mean?" young Charity asked in puzzlement.

Marie looked at Ronnie and the young woman responded.

"It means he offer to be her mate," she explained hesitantly in her low, husky voice. Gasps were heard around the table.

"What?" Helen cried.

"An Indian wanted to marry you?" Isabelle was aghast.

"His sister told me he was kind, he never beat his wives…"

"Good gracious! He was already married?!" Isabelle felt her cheeks go hot. "How insulting!"

Marie looked at her youngest daughter. "He was a good provider, a good hunter. His family ate well and he often left fresh meat for me. He was a kind man and considerate and he was offering to take care of me and give me children. Do you think that I thought this was an insult?"

"Mother!" Helen gasped looking quickly around in embarrassment like a parent whose child has just made a rude noise in public. "Unless he was offering to give you one of the children from the tribe, I think we all know what that really meant." Her face grew flushed.

"But he was already married," Louise was incensed.

"And so were you!" Isabelle stated almost accusingly.

"Yes, but many cultures allow for multiple wives, do they not? Does not the Bible tell of Isaac having several wives? And King David? And King Solomon? It is not the Christian way, we know, but this is not just a peculiarity with the native Indians. And he thought my husband had deserted me or was dead. Again I ask, do you think I thought it was an insult?"

Marie's sons were all looking between her and Jacques who sat quietly, expressionless, only his eyes betraying his attention on his wife. Her daughters were uncomfortable and fidgeting, looking down, unable to make eye contact. Only her daughters-in-law, Richard, and the grandchildren were able to look at her calmly as they remained quiet, listening.

"Well, tell me," Marie demanded. "I was a woman completely alone on the wild frontier. Your father was gone, perhaps forever. This warrior wanted to give me a home with family and companionship. Do you think I should have thought this an insult?"

The table had grown completely quiet. One by one, her daughters raised their eyes to look at her.

"Let me assure you I was not insulted," Marie looked out at the room of faces with proud defiance. "I was, in fact, flattered. And although I turned him down, explained to him that I loved my Jacques and could only be married to one man, I thanked him for his concerns for me, gave him a gift in thanks and called him *win-ka'lit* which means *friend*. He remained certain, however, that your father was never returning. And he would not allow me to remain alone. He left his sister there to stay with me through the rest of the winter so I would not be so lonely that I might do something foolish. He may have saved my life after all."

Everyone around the table remained quiet watching the small, dignified but animated woman. "And now, my children, I ask you. If your father, God bless him and give him good health, should have died out there in the wilderness and I had decided to accept that warrior's offer, where do you think you would all be right now?" After a long pause she answered her own question. "Perhaps in an Indian village somewhere in the mountains since we have driven all the Indians from here?" She picked up her glass, draining the remaining wine from it in one long swallow. Then, she reached over and drained Isabelle's glass as well. When she put the glasses down, she continued.

"There is no reason for anyone to feel superior. We are each and all here because of circumstances, tiny twists of fate, decisions, small and large, that transpired all along in our lives and even before we were born. How can you feel superior about that? What you make of yourself here and now, this is all you can feel proud of, yes? And even that is done only with the Lord's blessing and kindness." Again there was a pregnant silence.

"Very well said, my darling," Jacques finally spoke and the smile he gave her was absolutely melting, "and now I find I have married a philosopher." Marie looked to Jacques and felt her skin warm pleasantly under his attention. She returned his smile as if for a moment no one else existed in the room and for a moment no one else did.

Supper was over and the entire gathering went outdoors for a stroll in the coolness of the garden. The children were allowed to play hide and seek in the fading light while Jacques had the brandy cart brought out with tobacco for the men. Most accepted a pipe, Thor did not smoke and John alone rolled a leaf from the humidor as had become his habit. It didn't take very long for the ladies to complain of the mosquitoes. The insects didn't seem to bother the men which they decided was a benefit of the tobacco smoke.

At Marie's invitation the ladies retired again into the safety of the indoors while the children remained at their games outside in the lingering twilight. Marie guided Ronnie to join her on a small settee in the drawing room while the others settled comfortably around. Marie liked a touch of sherry after supper and Louise was pouring for everyone.

Isabelle did not need any more wine but she took a glass, looking a bit sullen and thinking of her fiancé. She was grateful Hamilton was attending to business in Boston. All this talk of Indians tonight was embarrassing. She didn't want to have to introduce him to John's wife. Hamilton was very astute and wouldn't be as distracted as she had been. He would undoubtedly realize right off Ronnie was an Indian and if he asked, Isabelle knew she dare not lie to him.

No matter what Mother said, this wasn't the old days when everything was wild. It was the beginning of the second quarter of the eighteenth century. Boston was a very civilized community and decent people did not mix with people of color whether they were red, brown, or black. It just wasn't socially acceptable. They were staff or slaves or beggars in the street. Even if what Mother said was true, if she had married an Indian then, as she said, they'd all be Indians living in the interior somewhere. She would never have met Hamilton. They wouldn't be white and part of white society. And she was certain Hamilton would find any shirttail Indian relation a disgrace. Mother could tell all the stories she wanted, the young girl thought, it still didn't change the circumstances right now and she wished her new sister-in-law would just disappear before the whole of Chartes Landing knew and word carried back to her fiancé.

"Would you like some sherry?" Louise asked Ronnie politely.

"No, thank you," she replied softly.

"I noticed you didn't drink your wine at dinner," Isabelle looked directly at Ronnie. "Don't you like our wines?"

"It was not unpleasant but I do not drink spirits," Ronnie answered truthfully.

"What a waste. And to think Father had to have the champagne wine smuggled in. Our wines come all the way from France, that's a long, long way across the big water," she said condescendingly. "I don't suppose you have any idea where I'm talking about." Louise shifted in her chair, uncomfortable with Isabelle's tone. Clarissa was looking into her lap. Caroline was watching Marie and Helen's mouth almost gaped. Marie was staring hard at her youngest daughter. The girl remained oblivious and unconcerned. She chuckled maliciously, her head light from alcohol. "And here I thought your people liked firewater."

"Isabelle!" Helen finally erupted with the admonishment, unable to hold her tongue any longer. "For God's sake be still!"

Isabelle looked disdainfully at her sister and giggled.

"Firewater is a plague upon my people," Ronnie said coldly.

"Really?" Isabelle responded. "A plague? That's a bit dramatic I think. A true plague attacks unseen. With drink, one always has a choice."

"If you see what I see firewater do, I think you not find it amusing," Ronnie spoke calmly but a telltale vein at her temple throbbed.

"Oh, really, and what is that?" Isabelle challenged sitting abruptly on the chair opposite Ronnie.

Ronnie knew it was a challenge. Despite the kindness of her mother-in-law, she was tired of the condescension, the polite hypocrisy, the air of tolerant superiority from these other women. White people had no manners, she had decided. They spoke falsely and made pretenses with a two sided tongue. They were the invaders. They were the outsiders. They were the foreigners. And even though she shared their blood, her native pride surged within her.

"The first time I see my people drink firewater I was ten years old. It was pushed on them by deceitful white men until they knew no better. They acted stupidly, like children, not aware of treachery around them.”

“Well, most people who drink too much act stupidly but aside from a bad headache the next morning, there's really no harm done. One could hardly call that a plague,” Isabelle bantered.

“The white men give firewater to my parents until they no longer them- selves. Then one rape me while he shoot off my father's face with pistol.” She spoke very matter-of-factly, knowing she was shocking the assemblage. “Bits of my father's flesh and blood fell on me while I lay crying. Do you think that is 'no harm'?”

“Oh, my God!” “Dear Lord!” “Mercy!” “Good Lord!” came the startled voices in response. Marie forced herself to remain silent as did Isabelle who looked a little stunned despite her attempt to hide it.

“Next morning without father and uncle to protect us, mother, aunt, me raped again and again. My four year old brother was tortured, burned with a fire log. Marked with scar he live with rest of his life. He swore when he was grown he would kill every white man he see. Then, we learn we part white and there is no reason to hate people we do not even know.”

Isabelle flushed. “I don't believe you!”

“You think I lie?” Ronnie challenged back.

“Why not? That's all you're good for.”

“Isabelle! I am ashamed of you!” Marie spoke severely. “I did not raise any of my children to exhibit such a disgraceful display of bad manners. Ronnie is your brother's wife and a guest in my home. You will apologize!”

Isabelle said nothing but lowered her eyes as if deciding, weighing, what to do next. She knew she had overstepped the line. Now her mother was angry with her, ashamed of her. All Isabelle wanted was for the woman to leave and go back to wherever she came from.

“I prefer truth to lie,” Ronnie spoke. “Do not make her say words she does not mean.” Then she turned to look again at Isabelle. “I do not lie. I do not un- derstand why you think I say this if not true. Ask your brother. He see my in- juries at hands of white men. He see scar my brother bears on arm. Your brother save my life. And it from him I learn not all whites are unfeeling and cruel. I hope someday you learn not all Indians are savages.”

Isabelle began blinking rapidly. Ronnie's words that not all whites were un- feeling and cruel had been said as though a direct accusation and they twisted in her conscience. Was she being *unfeeling and cruel*? The little blonde swal- lowed hard before she spoke. “Why did they burn your little brother?”

“They wanted us to whore for them,” Ronnie retorted curtly. The young women stifled more gasps of shock. “Because I fight, they burn my brother, threaten worse. They torture children to bend us to their lusts.”

“You must really hate us,” Isabelle said staring intently, her eyes narrowing slightly, almost daring the other to contradict her.

"Yes. For many years I hate you, all of you, without knowing you," Ronnie agreed flatly. "For many more years I fear you, but I no hate anymore. To hate whites just because they are white would be to hate part of me and part of my children. And through your brother I know some white people kind. I love your brother with all my heart."

Isabelle felt her skin growing hot as the blood rushed to her cheeks. She could feel her sisters glaring at her, her own mother's intense displeasure with her. They all supported this stranger against her. How dare this…… this half-breed make herself out to be such a saint. They could believe her if they wanted, Isabelle thought, but she didn't believe a word of it. If it was true, how could this person talk about it so calmly, so detached? Didn't anyone else see that but her? Was she the only one who could see right through this savage's lies? Suddenly Isabelle stood. "I'm sorry," she said in a low tight voice. It was only a capitulation to her mother. "Excuse me everyone, I'm going to bed." And she left the room in embarrassed indignation.

"Good heavens!" Louise breathed softly. "Mother, whatever brought that on?"

Marie reached out and patted Ronnie's hand, choosing to ignore the question rather than draw out the unpleasantness any longer. But at the same time, polite conversation now seemed very trivial. After a few awkward moments, Caroline excused herself as she and Phillip prepared to gather their children and leave for the evening as did Clarissa who went out to seek Richie. Helen went to gather up her children before finding Thor. Thomas who balked at being hustled away so quickly came into the parlor to say farewell to his grandmother before leaving for home. He also made a point of bidding his "new" aunt a very fond farewell in such a very courtly manner it made Marie smile.

"You've gained another admirer," the older woman chuckled when Thomas and Helen had left. "He reminds me of his grandfather."

"Silly little boy," laughed Louise.

Ronnie frowned slightly. "Among my people, he would be considered a man and would have the right to assert his will even with his mother."

"Oh," Louise retorted lightly, "don't give him any ideas. He'd get his fanny paddled if he tried that with Helen."

"Fanny paddled?" Ronnie looked to Marie in puzzlement.

"Fanny… ah, bottom." Marie made a gesture, raising her own bottom slightly off her seat and patting it. "Paddled… well, that means he would get a spanking."

"Spanking?" Ronnie questioned. The word was not part of her new vocabulary.

"Yes… you know, a punishment," Marie gestured again in a mock spanking of her own bottom.

"You mean beating?!" Ronnie's eyes opened wide.

"No-no," Marie assured her. "Not a beating, that is too severe. Well, perhaps you could say a small beating, to teach the child to do right."

"You know," Louise added, "surely you spank your own children when they are naughty."

Ronnie shook her head. "Never beat children."

"But we don't mean *beat* them," Louise offered, trying to explain. "Beating would bruise them, hurt them. Spanking is only a discipline, it doesn't really hurt them. Well, it may hurt but it doesn't bruise them, it doesn't leave marks."

Ronnie continued to look at her in disbelieving shock.

"Don't your people ever spank their children?" Louise asked, her voice now a bit acrid.

"No."

"Well, you must have perfect children." The hint of sarcasm in Louise's tone was an indication that her second glass of sherry on top of all the other wine she'd consumed that evening was dissolving her usual civility and diplomatic demeanor.

"No one in my village would ever hit a child," Ronnie continued in shock. "A parent who would do this would be shaming the child in front of the entire tribe."

"But how do you make your children mind, make them behave?" Louise asked incredulously. "Surely you must discipline them."

Ronnie did not understand the word "discipline" or she might have said, discipline was taught from the cradle on. Instead she responded to the idea of making children behave properly. "The children are taught what is right and what is wrong. They are taught it dishonors their parents to do wrong. They bring shame on themselves and their family when they do wrong."

"Well, that certainly is interesting," said Louise not knowing if she could believe it or not. Indian children must run absolutely wild, she thought. But then, of course, they were wild. Whatever was she thinking? As wild as Indians, wasn't that the expression? She giggled spasmodically to herself.

"I must go now and check children." Ronnie rose. She was very uncomfortable with everything that had transpired since entering the room this evening. Already her head was aching wondering what Jack would think. She had openly confronted his favorite sister. There had been harsh words. Now she was confused and upset with the white world's concept of raising children. She must talk to Jack about all of it, she told herself while trying to stave off the overwhelming sense of being smothered, palpably drowned in strangeness and animosity. She didn't want to offend his family but the concept of hitting a child, any child, much less your own child was totally abhorrent to her and more than she could cope with anymore this evening. Then, she was suddenly struck with the sickening fear that she hadn't understood anything at all correctly. She had misunderstood everything perhaps, she had spoken out and disgraced her husband and made a complete fool of herself. She vacillated between indignation and feeling foolish and small. Suddenly she desperately wished only to leave and find solitude. "I say good night now," she said, "I…" She wanted to apologize but she just didn't have the words. Everything was becoming a jumble of chaos in her head.

"Are you feeling all right, my dear?" Marie asked in concern.

Ronnie only nodded as she left the room quickly. She would go to the nursery, check on her children, and take the baby for his last feeding.

Just then Richie and Clarissa came in and said a formal farewell to his mother for the season.

"We'll be taking off early tomorrow morning," he grinned and hugged Marie.

"God bless you and keep both of you safe," Marie said softly, just as she had been saying every year, only this year her blessing included her daughter-in-law.

"We'll be fine, Ma," he said and they left. Neither was in favor of long good-byes.

Louise poured her third sherry and then sat down on the settee beside her mother.

"I wonder if John realizes what he's got there," she said dryly. Her mother looked at her in the flickering candlelight and cocked an eyebrow in a questioning way. "Well, I mean, never spank a child?! How on earth will she ever raise decent, civilized children?"

"You have seen their children, does Gray appear to be uncivilized to you?"

"He's very young," Louise murmured, slurring slightly.

"I'm sure he's still intimidated by everything he sees," chimed in Helen who had returned, Thor was talking business and was not ready to leave.

"Perhaps," nodded Marie.

"And that business about being raped? Well, that was bad enough but then being turned into a… a… well, you heard what she said," Helen added.

"I believe the word you are looking for is *whore*."

Helen cringed slightly at the word. "I really can't imagine how my brother ended up marrying a woman who had been a… a…"

"Whore," Marie again supplied the word. "You can say the word in private company, Helen, it will not soil you."

Helen flushed.

"It did not sound to me like she wanted to be a whore. Did she not say she was only ten or so? She was only a child," Marie reasoned.

"That's not the point, Mother," Helen said, her speech becoming just the slightest bit strident. "Whether she wanted to or not, she was still used by God only knows how many men… I know she'd been married before, and to an Indian at that. John was aware of that, I presume. And he knew he wasn't getting any lily-white virgin but still," she grimaced, "and now… why she's the mother of his children!"

"I am not trying to be dense, Helen, but I fail to see the point. She is not a whore now. She is a model wife and mother."

"But she was certainly rather badly damaged goods, wouldn't you say?" Helen asked with almost a snort of condemnation.

"Damaged goods?" Marie looked keenly at her daughter. "If you had been taken as a child, raped, and forced to serve as a whore, do you think that you should then be denied ever living a decent life with husband, home, and family?"

"Mother, don't get upset. I just meant… well, I really don't understand it, that's all. John could have married anyone, don't you think? He's terribly attractive even if I do say so myself and he has money of his own from *Grand-père*, as we all do. He's civilized and can be charming in his own way. Why would he choose to marry her?"

"Perhaps because he loves her," Marie responded.

Now Helen did snort. "Love or lust?"

"A good healthy dose of both, I should hope."

"Mother!"

"Do you love Thor?"

"Of course I do, what kind of question is that?" She looked over to the door.

"Yes, it is a wife's duty to love her husband and you are a very dutiful wife, Helen, but do you ever lust for Thor?" Marie saw her daughter's mouth fall open. "Never mind, do not answer that."

"I should think not," Helen responded testily. "Now, I see Thor coming back so it really is time to leave. Good night, Mother," she leaned over and kissed Marie's cheek. "Louise." she nodded to her sister and left.

The house had become more quiet as they heard the others leaving. Marie saw Jacques nod to her and go into his office. John and Jamie had gone up the stairs. Louise was trying to sober up and think more clearly. Marie looked at her daughter, slid an arm through hers and walked her to her suite. Upon arriving, Marie lit several candles.

"Mother, please don't be angry but Helen does make a point. Our brother is what we call a *catch;* he could have married almost anyone."

Marie turned and looked at her middle daughter.

"Louise, I am going to tell you something I have told no one else. Only your pa-pa knows." They settled on the edge of the bed. "When I was only thirteen I was working for a childless couple who owned a tavern in a small village in France. I was completely on my own in the world, no one to care for me, no one to take care of me. The woman had taken me in and was like a mother to me but she died of the fever and soon after, the tavern-keeper forced himself on me. If I let myself think about it, I can still smell his filthy breath. I was barely thirteen, not even Charity's age, I had nowhere to run, no one to help me, I felt trapped and so he continued to use me. Then, he began selling me to his customers. That made me a tavern whore."

The blood had drained from Louise's face as she sat motionless, staring at her mother, hardly believing what she was hearing.

"You cannot imagine the degradation and humiliation I felt and I pray you never do. The things he forced me to do were bad enough, but the things he made me feel about myself were far worse. In a short time, I could stand it no longer, I had to make it stop. I had to either kill him, kill myself, or run away and take a chance on dying on the road, or worse. I chose to run away. I chose life. God was with me and I found a position as a servant where I was well treated. Your pa-pa was the first man to give me a sense of having any worth as a human being. He became my champion and in the years to come, he was my friend and he fell in love with me for who I am. Thank God, he did not think as your sister does or neither of you would exist." Marie sat looking at her daughter, this daughter who looked so like herself.

"Mother... I..." Louise stopped to swallow away the dryness in her throat suddenly feeling very sober. "I don't know what to say. You never told us."

"It is not a story a mother wishes to tell her children."

Louise sat dumbly working her mouth open and closed, as if to speak but finding no words. Her eyes were unfocused as all her thoughts turned inward, as she tried to digest what she had just been told. Finally, she was able to speak.

"Mother, I'm ashamed of what I said. I'm sorry. I'm sorry," her voice was no more than a whisper. "Please forgive me?"

Marie smiled then and opened her arms to her grown daughter who fell on her knees with her head in her mother's lap. Louise's arms wrapped around Marie's small waist.

"Of course, I forgive you," she said as she caressed her daughter's back. "Louise, it took me many years to stop questioning how your father could possibly love me. Do not give Ronnie any reason to question how John can love her. I can understand how he can love her. She has an inner strength, yet she is gentle, and she is very intelligent, make no mistake just because her ways are different and she is still learning our language. And let us not forget, she is also very attractive. I can imagine that there are many men who could fall in love with her."

Louise lifted her head and nodded. "I won't say anymore. You can count on that."

§

In the guest bedroom where Richie and Clarissa were spending the night before their departure, Richie was shaking his head.

"I must say I'm surprised Ronnie told all of you. That should only be between him and her. She's such an honest person. There's no pretense about her. But she doesn't understand our world. She doesn't realize how our society can chew on this kind of gossip. I'm glad we're leaving. I don't want to be part of the discussion that's bound to rise up for some time to come."

Clarissa nodded and snuggled up to her husband.

§

Caroline waited until the children were in bed and she and Phillip were alone. She hesitated at first and then realized that everyone else would know and if Phillip later heard from them he might question why she had not told him herself. Finally, in the dark as they lie in bed she relayed the conversation of the drawing room. She couldn't see Phillip's expression in the dark, but when she was finished he was so quiet she thought for a moment that he had fallen asleep.

"Are you still awake?" she asked softly.

"Yes." There was another long silence. "I was just thinking," he said at last.

"About?"

"Remember I told you about the girl up at the lumber camp?"

"Yes."

"That's what I was thinking about."

"Whatever made you think of that?"

"Because I think it's odd. Don't you think it's odd? She was raped and hung herself and it took John ten years to get over it and when he does he marries another girl who was raped. Doesn't that seem a little ironic?"

"Oh, I don't know. You said that girl in the camp… what was her name? Anyway, you said she was very beautiful."

"Yes."

"And Ronnie is also very beautiful. What it tells me is if you are a beautiful woman and without protection in this world you are very likely to be raped."

Phillip thought about this. "I guess there's no disputing that, most men are only a step up from animals. We've raped and pillaged since biblical days. Look what I did to you."

"Phillip," she turned to him softly and ran her fingers through his thick curly hair, "you didn't rape me. What we did, we did together. I loved you so much I would have done anything for you, married or not. And I love you even more now. And," she grinned in the darkness, "I think I've grown much better at it now, don't you?"

"Nawww, you're terrible," he teased burrowing into her neck with kisses. Throaty giggles erupted from her generous mouth.

"Do you still think I'm beautiful?" she asked shyly.

"Like a blazing sun rising over pearls," he murmured running his hand up her smooth, milky white thigh. They stopped talking then and concentrated on other things.

§

"I think our eldest son has married a very unusual woman," Marie said calmly as she crawled into the big featherbed she and Jacques shared. "The girl was only ten years old when she was raped and brutalized. Ten years old, Jacques, can you imagine? Only ten and she sees her father slain, her brother tortured and she is forced to whore for the white men and yet she had it in her heart to save our John's life. You would think the very sight of us would make her skin crawl from the memories."

"Hmmm… and you think a woman who was raped and turned whore is worthy of being our son's wife?" he asked calmly.

"Why of course she is," Marie's voice rose in sudden defense and then she realized what her husband was doing. "Have I told you lately how very, very much I love you?"

"I cannot remember you telling me so… today," he teased and caressed her. "And have I told you how very, very much I love you?"

"Jacques," she became very serious, "do you know… truly know, how very happy you have made me, *mon amour*? My life with you has been everything and more than I could have ever dreamed. I was reminded tonight of how much you have done for me. To heal me. Without you, I do not think I would have been a whole person and only a whole person can survive the storms of this life." She had risen up onto her elbow, the night candle was lighting Jacques' face, his silver moustache turning gold in the reflected light. "We have had our storms and I doubt not that we may have more, but you are always there for me, to protect me, to uplift me, to help me through. You really have been my knight-in-shining-armor." She leaned over and kissed him lingeringly.

When their lips parted, he reached out to stroke her cheek and pushed a wisp of hair behind her ear. "Back in France, just before the *lettre de cache* seeking my arrest was issued, my father had begun talking of finding a bride for me." He saw her look of surprise even in the dim light. He had never told her this before. "It is the way of the aristocracy, *ma cœur*, it is business but I bristled at the very thought. I was not raised to accept an arranged marriage but I have no doubt eventually I would have been forced into one simply because I had become my father's heir." She saw him swallow. "I never would have found anyone like you, Marie. In a way that *lettre de cache* was a blessing. I told my father this when they came here to visit. I told him that warrant was the author of my happiness for I cannot imagine any life without you as being much of a life at all."

"Oh, Jacques, *mon amour*," she sighed and bent in to kiss the warm flesh over his beating heart. She felt his hands caressing her and she rose up to throw off her nightgown.

Some time later they were both pleasantly spent.

"For two weary grandparents," he sighed, "we do not too badly."

She giggled softly beside him. "We do much better than 'not too badly,' *mon cher*, much better," she smiled in satisfaction, raised up a little to give him one last kiss, and then burrowed in beside him to sleep. "Sleep well, *mon amour*."

"Sleep well, *ma cœur*," he replied as he gathered her into him, wrapping his arms around her and pulling his thighs up until they met against the backs of hers. Her rounded bottom was soft and warm against his belly and groin. He buried his nose into the smooth flesh at the back of her neck and took a deep breath letting it out in a sigh of contentment. She had her own delicious scent more powerful and pleasing than any perfume and it made him feel young and vital, yet peaceful and relaxed.

To the sound of Marie's soft rhythmical breathing, Jacques drifted off to sleep.

§

John was thoughtful as he climbed the stairs to his old bedroom. Mother might have had the best intentions with her stories about the Indians but… had they hurt more than helped? Had they made Ronnie uncomfortable feeling she was being singled out and seen as different? Seen as one of *them* as opposed to being one of *us*? He had tried to read her reaction. Tried to gauge her mood. She had seemed all right but then, she could hide her feelings so well sometimes it was maddening. Then, was it his imagination or had everyone disappeared for the night rather quickly and simultaneously? He'd gone out to the privy and suddenly everyone was leaving and instinctively he could not help but wonder if something had happened.

John opened the door to his old bedroom quietly, expecting to find his wife in bed. Instead, he saw her sitting cross-legged upon the floor in front of the fire. A blanket was wrapped around her and she was rocking slightly and softly singing in a low, quiet guttural voice. He closed the door behind him and turned back to her, thinking at first she was nursing the baby. He was going to ask why she wasn't in the rocking chair his mother had brought in for her but then he noticed their infant son was in his basket fast asleep.

"Ronnie? Ronnie, sweetheart, what is it? Why are you on the floor?" he asked quietly as he approached her. She didn't answer. She didn't even acknowledge his presence. She just kept rocking and softly singing in her old language. John didn't know what to think. Suddenly, he felt a queer sensation move through his stomach as his heartbeat began to increase. She'd never done anything like this before, at least not since they'd been together. The closest he'd ever seen her like this was when she had been mourning Gray Wolf. What the devil had happened? Or was she praying?

He decided to remove his boots and did. Then, he slipped out of his jacket, hanging it over the back of a chair before he loosened his cravat and dropped it on the bureau. He sat down near her before the hearth and waited patiently for a long time until at last she stopped singing and was quiet.

"Ronnie?" he asked gently again but she made no response. "Please tell me what you're doing?"

"I am sitting," she replied, her gaze never leaving the fire.

"Yes… but, why are you sitting on the floor like this?"

"This is where we sit. You know this. You have been to our village, you have sat before our fires, you have been in our huts."

"But we aren't in a hut now, sweetheart. This is a house. We have comfortable furniture."

"This is how I am comfortable," she retorted quickly but still not looking at him.

"Ronnie, what happened?"

"I am not a white woman. I have a white ancestor of many, many years ago who I know only by stories. I will never be a white woman."

"I'm not expecting you to become a white woman."

"I will never belong in white man's world."

"Ronnie?" he reached out then and brought her shoulders around to face him. "Look at me. I don't expect you to be a white, I don't expect you to be an Indian. I only expect you to be yourself. I love you… you, dammit, you, the woman. Not because you're white, not because you're Indian. Do you understand? Our world is the two of us together and the children, no matter where we are, that is all that is important. That is all that is important." He saw the tears then as they rose up out of her eyes, crested her lower lids and ran down her cheeks.

"I shame you, Jack, because I am not white but I shame myself trying to be white. I deny my own people."

"Oh, Ronnie," he pulled her to him bestowing healing kisses. "You don't shame me. What on earth has given you that silly idea? I had to love someone very much to be willing to marry and it is you I love, you I married." He held her then as she wept quietly. "This is my fault. You've seen me tip-toeing around the narrow minds and I apologize for it. I've hurt you."

"No-no," she protested. "But I see how your sisters look at …me…"

"My sisters? You mean it's more than Izzy?" he asked quickly.

"I am not good enough for you. You come from very…" she struggled within herself searching for the right word. "I do not know word in English. Family much important. They expect you to marry someone more important than me."

"More important?"

"A white woman… more better than me."

"Stop it! Ronnie… no one is *better* than you. Don't you know that? You are the best thing that has happened to me in ten lonely years. We are a family and I love you. God, how I love you… with all my heart."

"Jack," she reached out and put her hand across his mouth. "I say things tonight. Things I should not say. I was angry and…"

"Hush," he gave her a smile as he took her hand from his mouth. "So you got angry and gave them a little back, is that it? It's all right, darling, it's all right. They can take it. I'd say it serves them right. You haven't shamed me." He was laughing as he continued to hold her, rocking her almost like a child. "I hope you told them off but good." Then he grew serious and made her look at him. "You could never shame me, do you understand? Do you?"

She nodded weakly and he kissed away her tears. "I love you. God in Heaven knows, I love you so much. I love you and I wouldn't change a single thing about you, do you hear me? Not one single, solitary thing. Nothing. Not one little thing." He felt her shiver and went to pull the blanket about her more tightly when he realized she was completely naked beneath it. "What the…"

"I did not bring my Indian clothes and I could not stand…" her voice trailed off but he understood. She hadn't wanted *white woman* clothing on her.

"Do you think you can stand me?" he asked as he bent in and kissed her naked shoulder. She said nothing but became pliant in his arms as he continued to kiss her, his breath very warm upon her skin. "Would you rather make love right here on the floor?" he whispered and her response was to pull him down on top of her right there in front of the fire.

Later they made their way into the huge feather bed. As they lay in each other's arms, sated and content, Ronnie spoke again.

"Your sisters and mother tell me whites beat their children with something called a *spanking*. Will you beat our children?"

"A spanking is not a beating, sweetheart, you misunderstood. I'd never spank the children while they are as young as Sunshine, but in the years to come, if Gray or Sunshine or little Matt do not do as they've been told, and will not listen to reason, I might have to spank them."

"Jack, I cannot stop you from punishing your own children but you must promise me you will never beat Gray Wolf's Son. He is a Mohawk warrior and it would shame him unbearably if you were to beat him."

"Ronnie, a spanking is not a beating."

"You hit child?"

"Yes, on their bottom, like this," and with that he pulled her to him and smacked her exposed buttocks.

She gasped.

"It may sting a little but it doesn't harm them."

"Jack, you must not hit Gray Wolf's Son."

"Ronnie…"

"You must beat me instead."

"Ronnie, don't be ridiculous! I'm not going to beat you. I made a promise to you at our wedding, I told you I'd never beat you."

"But you must not hit Gray. If that is what you think he deserves then, you must hit me instead."

"You don't spank a child just to hit someone, you do it to punish them for breaking rules because sometimes that's the only way they will listen or that's the only way to protect them.

"He will know if he does wrong his mother will get beating. Please Jack, please… you must promise me this."

"All right," he sighed, "you win. I won't spank Gray. I guess I'll just have to think of other ways to discipline him when he needs it. Now, set your mind at rest and go to sleep."

Ronnie felt a great burden of concern fall away from her. "Thank you, my husband," she sighed in relief and wrapped her arms around him while drawing her slender leg up over his thigh.

Chapter 4

Isabelle watched for an opportunity to be alone with her big brother John. Things had been strained between them ever since that first day and had gotten worse after her open confrontation with his half-breed wife. It didn't surprise Isabelle that the woman had obviously told John all about it. Now, he'd been giving her the cold shoulder for days and she really couldn't stand it any longer. She put on a huge smile, mustered all her charm and endearing sweetness and sought him out. It didn't take long for her to find him in the tack room of the stable repairing some harnesses.

"Good morning," she said breezily, beaming at him.

He looked up briefly and returned to his task. "Good morning," he said a little stiffly. It wasn't like John to treat her this way and she hated it.

"John, I can't bear this any longer," she blurted out in one breath. "I'm sorry. I apologize. I know I've been a selfish little ninny but you just have to forgive me."

"Why?" he looked up again.

"Because that's what big brothers are supposed to do," she grinned impishly. "You're older and smarter and so you have to forgive we who are younger and less smart. And then when I'm older and wiser and smarter I will have to do the same to those younger than me," she continued to beam at him.

He felt his mouth involuntarily curving into a smile even though he tried to knit his brows and remain stern. He looked at her and at that moment she crossed her eyes at him and he burst out in a laugh.

"Does that mean I'm finally forgiven?" She looked so cute standing there that he couldn't help but open his arms and she immediately rushed in. "Oh, John, I am sorry. I really am so glad to have you home again and I don't want to spoil it. I just didn't know how to… well, you know. It was a bit of a shock. I guess I don't deal well with really big surprises. I'm sorry. I really am. I can't stand you being upset with me like this."

"I don't care for it myself, brat," he said affectionately, "but I won't have Ronnie hurt. You have to understand that. She's my wife. She means the world to me and I won't have her insulted and hurt… especially by my own blood."

"I know, I am sorry. Truly, I am… especially after learning what all she's been through."

"What do you mean?" He pulled back to look at Isabelle's face.

"Well, you know…" she replied evasively. "Surely she told you."

"As a matter of fact, Ronnie hasn't said much other than you two evidently had words. She seemed to think I'd be upset, but I told her you deserved whatever you got."

Isabelle pulled another little pout but her mind was racing. If Ronnie hadn't told John everything then she probably was lying after all. Hadn't she been right? The wretched half-breed would say anything to make them all feel sorry for her. They really were nothing but liars, these savages. "When did you first meet Ronnie?"

"When?" he asked in puzzlement.

"Yes, how long have you known her?" she asked with a face full of innocent curiosity.

"Actually," John began to speak more easily, "I first met Ronnie when she was only a child. I think she was about ten and I remember thinking she wasn't much older than you."

"Really? You were thinking of me?" she looked genuinely pleased.

"Yes."

"Well, how did you meet her? Did you go to her village?"

"No, she wasn't in a village. She was…" he stopped himself and looked away. "Look, it's not a story for your ears and it's none of your business anyway."

"John!" a flicker of hurt crossed her face and he immediately wished he hadn't sounded so harsh.

"I'm sorry, Izzy, it's just that… well, it's not a pleasant story and certainly not for one as young and innocent as you."

"I'm not a child anymore," she said soberly. She was quiet for a few minutes watching him work on the leather straps in his hands. She could feel her heart pounding as she dared to bring up the subject. "She told us some white men had burned her little brother, is that true?"

"Yes, it is," he replied bluntly, his brow creasing as he looked at her.

"But why would they do that?"

"Because they were scum, that's why. Filth. Human garbage. The kind of people you don't even want to hear about." The force of his reply made Isabelle tense slightly and step back. John looked at her sharply. "How did that bit of information come up anyway?" he asked. "It's hardly polite tea time subject matter."

Isabelle shrugged, not the easy one shouldered Gallic shrug her father so often employed but a nervous pinched two shoulder tensing. "She just mentioned that her brother had a scar from being burned. That they used to hate the whites but that they don't anymore." Isabelle's mouth had grown so dry her tongue felt like it was curling up on itself. John was frowning at her again. She felt his eyes boring into her. "She said a lot of things and it was all very hard for me to believe," she said quietly, a tremor in her voice.

"In other words, you called her a liar," John's tone was harsh as he grabbed her by her upper arms and Isabelle felt a sick wave roll through her stomach. She didn't want John angry with her again, she'd just wanted some substantiation of that horrible story. She wanted to know that she and everyone else in her family wasn't being played for a fool. She looked up into his face, wide eyed with a kind of helpless fear. He was so much bigger than her and his face looked so fierce he didn't even look like John to her.

"I'm sorry," she squeaked out.

"Look, I don't know how much Ronnie told you but whatever it was, it was the truth. She's the most honest person I know, how dare you call her a liar?! How dare you?! That's a far greater insult to an Indian than it could ever be to you or me. They don't have writing or written contracts. All they have is their word and we're the ones that are always breaking our word to them!" He was shaking her now.

"I'm sorry," she cried out. "I'm sorry."

"When Ronnie was ten years old, whites brutalized her so badly she could have died, did she tell you that? And yes, they tortured her brother. I discovered... ah, I am a doctor. I treated her. She has every reason to hate every white man in the world but she doesn't."

Tears were running down Isabelle's cheeks now. Ronnie's story was true then. She had been raped and made into a whore and... oh, mercy, it was too horrible by half and then not to be believed was even worse. She had insulted the woman terribly.

John was shaking his tiny framed sister like a rag-doll until he realized her teeth were clicking together and she was crying. He immediately let her go, ashamed of his own temper.

"I'm sorry," she was sobbing. He shook his head. He wasn't angry with her anymore and he searched for his handkerchief and gave it to her.

"It's Ronnie you should be telling that," he said in a much more subdued tone.

Isabelle buried her face in his handkerchief. She cried even harder for a few moments and then stopped and blew her nose soundly. Then she wiped her eyes.

"You're right. And I will. I just hope she can forgive me," she added hiccuping for breath.

"I'm sure she will," John replied and suddenly realized that this might be a good thing after all was said and done. Isabelle had lived her whole life in a pampered protected world and the real world just wasn't like that. Reality could be brutal enough without the unnecessary hostility she had created. Having to apologize would be good for her. At least he could hope.

"John, I… I have to go back to the house now," she stammered and ran out of the tack room and back toward the house.

Isabelle didn't see Ronnie until some time later but when she did she asked to speak to her alone. They sought privacy in the garden.

"I…" Isabelle cleared her throat as they walked along the flowerbeds. Humble pie had never been a very palatable dish. "I just want you to know, I realize I was wrong to call you a liar. I'm sorry and I'm sorry for what happened to you although I had nothing to do with it."

Her face completely expressionless, Ronnie looked calmly at the smaller girl.

"Well… anyway, I don't want to quarrel with you any more and I hope you can forgive me." As apologies went, it was not the most gracious the world had ever heard but Ronnie gave a small nod of acceptance. Isabelle turned then to absentmindedly touch one of the hyacinths coming into bloom. The flower gardens at this end of the grounds were fully matured and well tended. And they provided a riot of color and scents throughout the summer.

"You must understand," Isabelle added, "it's really not that I care that you married John. It's nothing personal. If he's happy with you that is his business. But I am betrothed to a very important man in Boston. It's what he thinks that I'm concerned about. Most people don't… accept your kind of marriage very well these days. No matter what it was like in the old days." She was still concerned with what Hamilton would think if he found out, but she'd made up her mind to deal with that when and if the situation arose. There was nothing else she could do. She had no wish to alienate her oldest brother who had always spoiled her, and cause everyone else to be upset with her. Acting a little spoiled and frivolous had always been gently indulged but Isabelle had no stomach for becoming a pariah within her family.

"I do not think I understand," Ronnie ventured. "What does our marriage mean to you?"

"Hamilton… my fiancé, my intended husband, could call off the wedding and refuse to marry me when he finds out about you."

"Why would he do this? It was not you who married me." Ronnie was genuinely surprised.

"Isn't there anyone, any group of people your people dislike so much that they would be very angry if you should marry one of them?"

Ronnie thought for a moment. "Huron dogs," she muttered at last.

"What?"

"Huron… our sworn enemy for," she gestured toward the horizon, "all time."

"And so what would happen if… say… Gray grew up and married a Huron maiden?"

"Would never do this!" Ronnie gasped.

"Why not?"

"He is Mohawk warrior."

"But let's just say after you and John raise him, he meets this lovely girl and falls in love with her and after they marry he finds out she's a Huron."

Ronnie was shaking her head.

"Now, just for the sake of argument, let's just say it happens. What would your people say?"

"He would not be accepted back into tribe," she almost groaned.

"You mean he would become an outcast?" Isabelle almost smiled, it made her point better than she had hoped. "No one would speak to him?"

"More… he would not be allowed to live in village any more."

"There, you see? Is that so very different?"

"Have I made Jack an *outcast*?" Ronnie looked at the girl with a kind of wild terror in her eyes. "His family does not turn their back on him… but do the rest of the whites?"

"No, not really but with John it's different, he's a soldier after all. I'm speaking of my fiancé, his world might turn their backs on him."

"But he does not marry me."

"No, of course not, but my brother did."

Ronnie stood rooted to the ground as her mind assimilated the example. What if she had married a Huron? How would the tribe treat Wani? And she couldn't understand. If she had married a Huron, she would be an outcast, it would have nothing to do with Wani. Finally, she spoke. "It should have nothing to do with you. I am sorry if your world does not understand this."

Isabelle looked at the taller woman in frustration. She didn't understand at all, but then why should she? She was nothing but a savage. Isabelle turned and walked off.

John had waited as long as he dared to give Ronnie a chance to become comfortable staying with his family before he told her he must leave her for a couple of days. It was only a short time before they would have to leave and begin the long journey back to their frontier outpost. His pilgrimage up to the logging camp could be put off no longer.

"Phillip?" he spoke to his brother late one evening. "You've said nothing of the Olafsons."

His younger brother looked at him seriously for once. "I thought I'd let you bring the subject up when you were ready to."

"Is the old logging camp as it was?"

"Yes, everything is more or less the same. The Olafson children are all married now of course, raising families of their own... but then, they had a pretty good start on that before... before you left. Sonya lives for her grandchildren. She's well. The camp has sprawled a bit. We've had no repeat of the... troubles. But the stockade remains."

"I need to go up there," John said quietly.

"You do?" Phillip's surprise was evident.

"Yes."

"All right."

"Do you have any business to take you there?"

"I can always find some."

"Good. Can we leave tomorrow?"

"Of course."

"Thanks, little brother," John looked at Phillip with eyes filled with gratitude. Gratitude for not asking any questions, for not pressing to get reasons, for just going along willingly in trust. Phillip's thoughtful expression softened, he nodded and said nothing.

It was late spring and warm but John was too busy noticing all the little differences to pay any attention to the beautiful weather. The road was wider but deeply rutted with wheel tracks. The farm where so long ago he and Phillip had sought shelter on a rainy night was plowed and planted and neat, with a prosperous look about it. A wood frame house had been erected on a new site. The old cabin looked like it had fallen to other uses. The barn looked fairly new as well. There were children playing in the front yard and John wondered briefly what had become of that sad plain little mouse who had so graciously scrubbed his muddy clothes that night so many years ago. There were other farms along the road now; many, in fact. The increasing population was evident.

They arrived at the logging settlement the second day near dusk, but it was still light enough for John to take a good survey of the place. It had changed little but yet it had changed as any place might be expected to change in over ten years. It was quiet until the dogs set to barking, being the alarm of their arrival. Folks were in for their suppers by now. And more new cabins dotted the landscape. After being hailed at the gate, they were warmly admitted and walked their horses into the grounds and straight to the sprawling Olafson home.

John had barely left his saddle when Sven Junior passed through the cabin door and was treading across the porch and down the steps. He gave them a friendly greeting, focusing on Phillip whom he was used to seeing. When he finally turned to look straight at John, he registered the slightest moment of honest surprise.

"John!" The larger man grasped the eldest Power brother in a firm arm grip and handshake. "It has been too many years. Good it is to see you." They were sincere words.

"Sven," John acknowledged with equal warmth. "I'm home for a brief visit and thought I'd come up and say hello."

"Still in the military then?"

John nodded.

"Well, glad I am you are here! You are more than welcome… anytime. Come now, come in. Mama will be happy to set two more places at the table."

They all went indoors.

Supper at the Olafsons was still a gathering for most of the family and John was able to see them all again that night. Snotra with a home and family of her own, kept her own kitchen, but Skadi, newly married and expecting her first child, welcomed any excuse to eat at her mother's table. John was momentarily quiet comparing the young Skadi to the sister he had known so long ago. The awkward young girl had grown into a very attractive young woman, some would say a beauty, but nothing so startlingly breathtaking as Freyja. John smiled at her and congratulated her on her expectancy.

They stayed up rather late, talking. The business of the logging camp filtered through the general conversation but mostly the talk was of the people, enlightening John on what had happened to everyone, marriages, births, a few deaths. The only people of the camp John didn't know were those who had been born since he had left and a few spouses, wives mostly, of those who had grown up or worked here. He, in return, shared the news, briefly and with little detail, that he was now married and had brought his wife and children home to meet his family.

"Glad I am to hear that, John," offered Sven Junior and John was given congratulations all around. None of the Olafsons had ever expected John to wait ten years before finding another woman to marry. Sonya herself had been deeply concerned as year after year, Phillip relayed that as far as they knew John was still in the military on the frontier, still unmarried, still alone. They were genuinely happy for him now. And so the evening hours had disappeared but through it all the one name that was never mentioned, the one person of whom no one spoke was Freyja.

Before going on to bed, John caught a glimpse of the vase in the parlor, still setting in its place of honor. Unable to stop himself he went over and took from the shelf looking fondly at the beautiful full figured young woman painted upon it from the legend of Sigurd and Brynhild. *You shouldn't have given up,* he thought to himself with a sad half smile, *you, too, should have chosen life.*

John awoke very early the next morning because he wanted to. He had trained his body to do that in the military. He simply had to concentrate on when he wanted to rise and somehow, he awoke very close to that time no matter when he'd gone to sleep.

It was still dark as John quietly dressed and, holding his boots in his hand, left the bed he had shared with his brother. He silently made his way through the house, the faint pre-dawn light allowing him to make out the furniture and avoid any noisy collisions. Once on the porch, he threw the dog a scrap he'd found in the kitchen. Then, he buttoned his jacket against the early morning chill and sat down to pull on his boots. He tugged on the comfortably broken in foot gear, stood, briefly touched his pocket to hear the reassuring crinkle of parchment and took off on foot to the stockade gate.

Sliding the bar back himself, he opened the gate which swung with ease and with only a faint creaking. The meadow which now held a little graveyard was not far, within easy walking distance actually, and John had no need to saddle a horse.

By the time he reached her grave site, dawn was so near the sky was turning vivid shades of peach and orange and it was quite light. He mistook her grave at first, looking for and expecting to find the wooden cross which first had been driven into the ground to mark her final resting place. Instead, he discovered, after carefully looking over each site, an almost white marble marker, shaped like a stone tablet, on which was chiseled:

Freyja Olafson
1697 - 1714
Beloved daughter
and sister

She had not lived long enough to become a wife or a mother.

As John looked at the grave in the cool muted morning haze, he felt a lump growing in his throat but not for him. No, not for him this time, this time the lump, the sadness, the sorrow were all for her.

Beautiful Freyja, John thought to himself, *my beautiful little Nordic goddess. You were so young... too young to realize how precious life is. I don't blame you for not knowing any better but if you would have just waited, we would have found you. I would have brought you back. I would have found you and it would have been all right.*

John's body trembled suddenly with a little shudder. He reached into his pocket and took out the folded parchment, unfolding it carefully, and exposing a long lock of shiny blonde hair. He looked at the lock he'd taken from her body the day they found her, touching it almost reverently with his finger.

I had to forgive myself, Freyja, and I had to forgive you. It took me a long time to move beyond that anger but I have now. I'm at peace and I've come to say good-bye. I hope and pray you are at peace, too.

Then, John bent down on one knee and with his knife he dug a small, deep, neat hole over her grave and gently let the lock of hair coil into its bottom. Carefully, he filled the hole with the loose earth and patted it down, caressing the ground.

"Good-bye, Freyja," he spoke out loud. "May God watch over you forever and ever. Amen." Then he stood and was still for a moment. He felt a slight breeze, heard the rustle of the leaves in the tree tops and the early morning song of the nearby birds. He knew she wasn't there, it was only her body that was there. It was only her *remains*, as they say. She had left a long time ago. Her spirit had departed when she had broken her own neck. But it gave him comfort to think that somehow she could connect to this spot and would know that he had been there.

John turned slowly and began the walk back to the stockade. As he walked his thoughts turned to his wife and their son, and their daughter and Gray Wolf's Son and how very alive they all were. And how good it was. He was suddenly very, very happy that he had the will to survive and his pace quickened. He was more than happy, he was grateful and ecstatic that his Ronnie had the will to survive and the tenacity to overcome whatever fate threw into her path. They had the raw, stubborn courage to continue on. The frontier was not for the faint of heart, the timid, or the weak. You had to take it head on with both hands and fight to tame it. But together, he and Ronnie could overcome and carry on, building a future that was full of promise.

John wanted very much to get back to his wife and to their life on the frontier.

Chapter 5

John and Phillip reigned up their horses to listen when they heard the bell from several miles away. It wasn't the high pitched, clang of the school bell that called students in to class. It was the slow, deep bell of their settlement church. If it were clanging faster, it would be an alarm but instead, it was reverberating an extremely slow, mournful dirge that went on and on.

Something had happened!

Both brothers ribbed their horses forcefully and headed for the settlement of

Chartes Landing without another word. As they galloped through the main street they slowed and stopped in front of their mother's general store, threw open the door which had its own little jingly bell. Lyndyn, their mother's clerk, looked over and the expression upon his face told John, whatever had happened was personal.

"What is it, Lyndyn?" John asked.

"It's your father, John. I'm so sorry."

"Father." Both brothers cried out at once.

Turning on their heels, they left. Leaping back onto their horses, they sped for home. It wasn't far. Soon the large, imposing, white frame house came into view. They rode for the stables and had dismounted before the stable-hand could grab their reins.

Bursting in through the front door they found their old housekeeper, Jane, weeping so pitifully, she had no concern with whether they had scraped their boots before coming in or not.

"Master John! Master Phillip!" she gasped looking up from her handkerchief with red swollen eyes. "Thank God you're home. I am so sorry. So sorry. Lord, have mercy. Look to your mother. She hasn't eaten in two days."

"What has happened?" John asked, demanding clarity.

"Your father, sir, had just taken his exercise with the foil. Suddenly he grabbed his chest and dropped to the ground. Doctor Ajax said it was his heart."

"Where's mother?"

"Locked away in her room. She said we would hold off on the funeral until you boys were home. Guess it will be tomorrow now." And with that she burst into another fit of sobbing.

"Please ask Margot to make a strong pot of tea and a small tray of Mother's favorite food. Send it up when it's ready."

"Y..yes, M…Master John."

They took the large staircase two and three steps at a time. Phillip keeping up with John but breathing harder with the effort.

At the top of the steps, sitting outside the master bedroom, they found Richard with a look of profound sadness on his face. He looked up as the younger men approached.

"First, I lost my son. Now I have lost my best, my dearest and closest friend. I could not bear it if we lost your mother as well. Get her to eat, John, you are a doctor, you know how important it is."

John nodded and turned to the door.

"Mother? It's John and Phillip. We just returned. We heard. Mother? I'm coming in." He tried the doorknob and found the door locked. "Mother? Mother, can you hear me? Mother, I have to see you. I have to know you are all right. Mother?" He waited and could hear nothing. "Mother," he shook the knob. "Mother? Open this door immediately or I'll kick it down!"

They heard movement, a sound almost like a whimper. The key was turning in the lock. John opened the door just in time to see Marie retreat to the gloom of the heavily draped room. He gestured for Phillip to wait.

"Give me a few minutes, Phillip," he said to his brother softly. "Don't want her to feel out numbered."

Phillip stepped back. John walked into the room and quietly closed the door.

"Mother?" John said softly, unprepared for the sound of the voice he heard reply.

"I am glad you are home. We can have the funeral now and get this whole mess over with."

"You sound angry," he said in surprise.

"Of course I am angry," she snapped. "Do you not think I have a right to be angry? All these years he told me how he would keep me safe and always be there for me. All these years of telling me how much he loved me but then saying how he hoped he went first because he did not wish to live without me? It is not right, it is not fair! He was still young. How could he leave me all alone like this? You are a doctor. Tell me, how could he die like this without even a warning, a sign….a….how do you say?…. A symptom? How could he?"

"Mother," he approached softly. "I'm sure Father had no wish to leave you now." He tried to take his mother in his arms but she evaded him and turned away. "He was not ancient, but at fifty-nine, he was no longer young. These things can happen without any warning. Did Doc Ajax ever say anything in his check-ups?"

He saw her shake her head. "Nothing. Unless he, like his father, swore the doctor to secrecy. So I am angry. And now you know why I wish to talk to no one, see no one. I will put myself through the funeral. That is all."

"Very well. I understand. You do not have to talk to anyone. But you must eat. Margot has made up a tray and I will sit here to see that you eat. You do not have to talk and I will be very quiet…… agreed?"

Marie looked at her eldest son. He looked so like his father in appearance. And she knew he would not leave her in peace if she did not agree. She nodded. John went to the door and took the tray that was waiting.

"Phillip, she needs some time. Why don't you go see your wife, you too are in shock."

Phillip nodded. A dazed look had descended upon him. He knew he wanted to feel Caroline in his arms and have his family around him. He never imagined they would lose Father like this. So unexpected. So soon. He had appeared in the best of health. They said he had been fencing, for pity's sake, taking exercise as he always did.

Marie ate enough to satisfy John. He called for his black bag and mixed up a mild sedative. Some years back she had fought off an opium addiction so he knew not to give her anything too strong.

When she was comfortably in bed, he left the room and shut the door.

"Uncle Richard," he slipped his mother's door key into his pocket as he nodded to the big man sitting guard. "She's eaten and is resting now and she can't lock herself in again. Why don't you go lie down as well. There's time before supper. I'll give you a little laudanum to ease your pain."

Richard nodded and accepted the assist to get up out of the chair. He groaned deeply. "My heart broke in two when they told me Raphael died. But your father and mother got me through the worst of the pain. Now my heart is broken again and your mother's as well. Who will get us through this time?" he asked as John administered the sedative and removed Richard's boots. "I may have been the taller one but your father was a giant of a man among men. God threw away the pattern after he made him, John. And the world is much poorer for his passing," he sighed. "We are all poorer for losing him."

"Uncle Richard, try to rest now."

Richard stretched out and eased into sleep. John quietly left the room.

John wanted to find his wife. He had been home for an hour and he had yet to seek her out. He felt instinctively that she would be outdoors, enjoying the natural surroundings and watching their children at play.

He was right. He found Ronnie in the gardens.

"Jack," she sprang up when she saw him. "I very sorry about your father."

They wrapped their arms around each other and just stood holding each other for a time. With Ronnie in his arms, he was beginning to allow himself to feel his own sense of loss.

"Thank you, sweetheart, I guess I still don't believe it. I just put Mother to bed and had Uncle Richard lie down as well."

Sunshine toddled over and wrapped one arm around his leg and grabbed on to her mother with the other.

"He looked so good. So healthy. Fit. Well. Strong." John shook his head in disbelief. "How is everyone else doing? How are you and the children doing?"

"We good, Jack, just sad for you."

"How have my sisters been doing?"

"You need talk to Louise. Her grief double now. Lose two most important men. Helen is strong."

"And Izzy?" he asked pointedly.

Ronnie looked down. She did not want to say what she really thought of Izzy.

"That bad, huh?" John looked at his wife. "You are a model of discretion, sweetheart."

Ronnie looked up at her husband.

"That is a compliment, Ronnie," he said softly and gave her another long, meaningful embrace. "There is much I need to do starting with a message to

Commander Greeley. I've got to let him know what has happened. It's going to delay our leaving," he pulled back to look into his wife's face. "I hope you are all right with that."

"Of course. Do what you must do. You eldest son."

"In a way I envy Richie. In his mind Father will be alive until late this fall."

Ronnie stroked the back of John's head and neck. "I am so much sorry."

"Every child lives knowing this day will come. I'm grateful Father appeared to be so well right up to the end. It's a terrible shock to everyone but it's better than the alternative." He couldn't help thinking of Alana and how pitifully she had wasted away. Whether his mother realized it or not, this was the better way.

John left Ronnie in the gardens with the children. He went to the ground floor suite where he found Louise. She opened the door to his knock and almost collapsed into his arms, clinging to him like a child and sobbing uncontrollably.

"Oh, John, thank God you're here, thank God. It's too much, it's too much! It feels like the world is crumbling all around us. Like God is punishing us. Why? What are we going to do? Don't leave us, please, don't leave us."

"Sh-sh-sh," he hugged her like the big brother he was. "Sit down, Lu-lu." He pushed her lightly into a chair, gently detaching her hands from his clothing. "I'm going to give you something to help you get hold of yourself... to help calm you." He opened his bag and proceeded to mix up the same mild sedative he'd given to his mother. "I'm not going anywhere at the moment. I'm here, Lu-lu, I'm here. Now drink this." He handed her a glass. "You feel like you're in a darkness and you can't find your way out but you will. You will. You're stronger than you think. You have to be. You have five wonderful children, Rafe and Father live on in them and they need you to be strong. You represent their world. You can't let their world collapse, can you? We're all here together and we have to pull together so everyone can crawl out of the dark."

"You're right," she gulped. "You're right, but don't leave us, John. You know the right thing to do. Have you seen Mother? She won't talk to anyone. Did she talk to you?"

He patted his sister's head and stroked her back as he took the empty glass from her and nodded. "Mother is trying to deal with this shock in her own way, Lu-lu. We have to give her some space. You know how you felt when you first heard that Rafe was dead. I imagine that's a little like Mother feels right now only Mother doesn't have a mother and father to help her through it."

"Mother can't be a child," Louise said more softly.

"That's right, now do you think you can go to your children. Let them know you love them. They lost their father too. They need to know they still have a mother who cares about them and who will be there for them. They may be terrified that they're going to lose you as well."

"You're right, John. They lost their father too. Rafe was such a good father.

He loved us all so much." She looked up at her brother. "I need to see the children and let them know everything will be all right."

"That's good, Lu-lu. Go to your children and give them extra hugs."

"Thank you, John, for coming home. For being here, for knowing what to do." The sedative was having a calming affect.

He nodded, helped her out of the chair, gave her another hug, and saw her out the door making her way to the nursery. John took a deep breath. Next he needed to check on Izzy. He took his bag with him. She might need a sedative as well. Poor Izzy, setting aside his personal feelings concerning how she had been treating his wife, he realized Izzy being the youngest had just lost her father at a very tender age. They had all had their father to lean on when they were twenty and twenty-one. They'd all had him in their lives when they were twenty-five. But not Izzy. He was gone now forever and Father had doted on Izzy, gave her privileges and spoiled her like none of the other girls. John suddenly realized this may be the hardest of all on Izzy and he found he was dreading this meeting.

He rapped on Isabelle's door.

"Come." He heard her voice say and he opened the door.

He couldn't tell what she had been doing but she was dry-eyed and standing by the window.

"Hello John."

"How are you doing?" he asked softly.

She shrugged. "All right I suppose. I'm just so tired of all this gloom and doom. I want us all to be happy again."

"It takes time," John muttered, shocked at her lack of feeling. "I'm home now and I have been checking on everyone. Do you need anything?"

"I need to get married so I can move into my own home. Is this going to put the wedding off even longer?"

"I don't know," John replied, taken aback by her manner which was almost too calm and rather cold. "I shouldn't think so but that is up to Mother."

"Have you seen Mother? No one else has seen her. She's been locked away in her room, refusing to come out. Refusing to talk."

"Izzy, she just lost the love of her life. She's..."

"When is the funeral? Now that you and Phillip are back are we going to have the funeral? It's been more than three days."

"Yes. The funeral is tomorrow. I'm sorry we didn't get home sooner."

She shrugged at that. "I suppose Father won't be walking me down the aisle like he did Helen and Louise. Who's going to walk me down the aisle? Will you, John?" she asked looking up at him hopefully.

"I doubt that I can, Izzy," he answered quietly. "I'll be back on the frontier. I'm sure Phillip will walk you down the aisle."

She pursed her lips. "I don't even know where I'm getting married. Father was going to bring the whole family to Boston so we could have the wedding there and all of Hamilton's family and friends and business associates could attend. But I don't know if Mother will agree. You have to talk to Mother, John, convince her that it's the best thing to do. To keep Father's plan even if he can't be there. Will you?"

John had the feeling that he was being led into another trap. He knew people dealt with grief in different ways. Some tried to deny the reality. Was that what Izzy was doing or was she really so bloody cold and self-centered all she could think of was herself?

"Izzy, I told you when I first returned I was not going to get embroiled in your personal arguments. I'm still not. As far as I'm concerned you can get married right here in Chartes Landing. It was good enough for your sisters. If Mother wants to do something else, that's up to her but I will give you a small piece of brotherly advice."

Isabelle looked as if she could chew nails. "What's that?"

"Don't even mention your wedding to Mother for at least one whole month. Try to pretend you care about other people's feelings, not just yourself!"

"John!" she exclaimed in protest as though she was being thoroughly misjudged.

"It appears you are doing fine. I have others to see," and he took up his black bag and left.

John made a stop at the nursery next. Sarah, their head nursemaid, was red-eyed from weeping but seemed to have things well in hand as the littlest ones were napping. He told her the funeral would be tomorrow and anyone seven or older would be allowed to attend.

"Do you need anything, Sarah?" he asked quietly.

"No, Master John, except to tell you how very sorry I am. We're all going to miss him terribly. Master Power was a real gentleman, in every way."

"Thank you, Sarah, I appreciate that. Where is…… Rachel is it?"

"Oh, yes, sir, she's taken the older ones out on a nature walk."

"A nature walk?"

"Yes, Master John."

"Very good. Ah… if I don't catch up with her, please relay the news about the funeral."

"Yes, sir."

John left the very familiar walls of the nursery. Funny. The nursery looked considerably less vast than it did when he was unbreeched and in dresses. They all wore dresses, boys and girls alike. He hadn't worn his first pair of breeches until he was seven years old. He smiled. That was the age to which he and his brothers looked forward. They couldn't wait to turn seven so they could wear breeches just like Papa. It was a rite of passage.

Being in the nursery had brought on a plethora of memories. Things he had forgotten. As a very small boy, he remembered Father used to come every day and play with them. Sometimes he was a dragon. Often he was the horse on all fours that gave them rides and as they got bigger he trotted about with them hanging from his back. He'd wear them out before nap time which the nurse-maids appreciated. As they grew older and were breeched, he spent hours with them teaching them to ride a real horse, to fence, to load a musket, to shoot.

John felt the tears running down his cheeks and stopped on the backstairs to sit and weep. His father had never demanded anything of him, had let him find his own way, had accepted his career choices. He was the eldest but Jacques Power had never said John had to take over any particular family business. The only thing Father had ever asked was that John write home more often.

Now that John was a father he realized how precious that communication was and he had communicated so little. John wept in the knowledge that communication was now impossible. His father was gone. He wept quietly for some time and then drew out his handkerchief and blew his nose with a mental promise not to repeat this regret with his mother. He would write faithfully from this time forward.

Pulling himself together, John descended the remaining steps just as Jane Sims passed the downstairs door.

"Jane," John tried to avert his red eyes, "I'm rather making the rounds. You are my next stop. May I ask, how are you getting on?" The woman's eyes were almost swollen shut.

"What don't kill us, makes us stronger. Ain't that what they say?"

"Well, if they don't," he gave her a weak smile, "I'd say it was true any-way."

"Your ma be strong enough, Master John. She don't need no more strength-ening."

"What are you trying to say, Jane?"

"She needs you, Master John. She won't never say so herself but you're the clear thinking, level headed child she needs now. Stay. Please. Come home for good."

"I've asked to extend my leave but the military is my career, Jane, and this is no longer the frontier. Now, let us talk about you. Have you been able to sleep? Would you like something mild to help you sleep?"

She shook her head. "All I need to sleep well is to know you'll be here to watch over your ma and the rest of us."

It was useless to reply so John turned and headed to the stable in search of his youngest brother, James. Jane's husband Donald had passed on several years back. He must have been close to seventy, thought John. He had been their gardener and general all-around handyman ever since Father built the house. Ironic. Donald Sims had dragged around a lame leg his whole life and lived well into his sixties and Father who could fence like a musketeer didn't even make it to sixty.

James seemed to spend a good deal of time with the gardens and the fences, trimming, pruning, fertilizing, mending, and planting. They said in fall he helped Father supervise the apple harvest and knew what needed to be done after to make regular and fermented cider, and vinegar, and market the apples. He was courting right now, John smiled briefly, some gal by the name of... what was it Mother said... Throckmorton? John wished him luck.

John had been fortunate enough to find love... again. Phillip and Richie both seemed happily matched. Hopefully Jamie would find a good gal. And Louise? John deeply hoped she would find someone to love and be loved by. Maybe she couldn't expect to find the passion everyone had said she'd had with Raphael but that was young love. He thought of Switzerland and how he and Alana had crammed a lifetime of passion into a few precious months. But with five children, what Louise needed now was a steady hand from a decent man, some one to help share the parental load of guidance and discipline as the children grew older and left the nursery. Then John felt guilty. He was older than Louise and he had found passion again... and on the frontier of all places. Still, Louise was an heiress. He thought what that really meant. That could bring out the fortune hunters. John suddenly realized how vulnerable his sister might be. Father would never have allow her to be misused.

John hadn't seen James anywhere outside near the house and decided to ask the stable-hand if he knew where John might find his brother. He was told James had saddled a horse to ride out through the orchards, so John saddled a horse as well.

He found James acres from the house, walking his horse amidst the apple trees at the far end of the orchard along the river.

James looked up as John approached. "You're back."

"Yes. Phillip and I heard the bell. It's been one helluva shock." He walked his horse up along side James' animal. "No warning at all was there? Just a few days ago I was reassuring Father that both he and Mother appeared in good health with many years yet to enjoy."

"So what brings you out here?"

"Oh, I've more or less been making the rounds as big brother and doctor. See how everyone is doing. It helps to share the grief, Jamie, and everything told to big brother is held confidential by the doctor."

"Umph," James grunted. "This family doesn't seem to know how to share grief. Helen took off for her own house, Mother is locked in her room, Louise is a blubbering mess, Izzy is the same self-serving little brat she's always been, Richie is well out of it and now you and Phillip are home... bet he took off for his own place too. And Uncle Richard, poor Richard... I think I feel the worst for him."

"Why's that?" John asked calmly.

"You weren't here to see what he went through with Rafe's death. You never met Rafe did you?"

John shook his head.

"Handsome devil," James said as the horses walked and he kept an eye on each tree as they passed. "If I were a girl I would have been madly in love with him myself. And nice… the nicest fellow you ever could meet. I mean the king of nice. Friendly. Helpful. Never heard him raise his voice, treated our sister like a queen, never had a bad word to say against anyone, and Richie swears he never cheated on Louise in all his treks. And it would have been so easy. In fact, it must'a been especially hard not to since he had perfect manners with everyone and I guess some of those tribes actually expect you to bed their women, huh? Cheez, he was a… what they call a *paragon*. And he gets an arrow right in the neck. Richie said he bled out in maybe a minute. There was nothing to be done about it. And here's poor Uncle Richard, he ain't never going to have another son like that. Even if he got some girl with child tomorrow, he's not going to live long enough to see the kid grow up… well, most likely.

"It crushed him but still Mama and Papa were there to help him through. His two best friends. And now? His best friend is dead and his next best friend is locked in her room not speaking to anyone," at this James sounded very hurt.

"That's changed," John said quickly, feeling the key in his pocket. "The door is now unlocked but she is resting. Everyone deals with grief in his or her own way," John was wondering how James was dealing with it. "Some people get angry, some seem to deny anything has happened at all, some, like Louise, get very emotional, some get all stoic and hide it. A few years back I saw my wife grieve for her first husband, Indian style."

"Yeh, what was that like?"

"It was… something to behold. No one could have witnessed that without feeling something very profound. She sat out in the open by his slain body, chopped off her hair and wailed out her grief to the universe. She wailed herself into exhaustion but when she was done and the funeral pyre was nothing but cold ashes, she could continue with life and slowly come back to normal. That was her way of grieving, Jamie, what's yours?"

The horses walked along in the silence. John looked over at his youngest brother and saw him weeping.

"I just want my papa back," he sobbed quietly.

John leaned over from the saddle and put his hand on his brother's knee. He pat him purposefully.

"Never be ashamed of honest tears, little brother. The only tears which are shameful are the fake ones.

John rode back in with James and after assuring him things would get better again, he went off to see the church pastor. The time for the funeral was set. John proceeded next to Doctor Ajax's offices.

"Hello John," Archibald Ajax greeted the slightly younger man as he walked in.

"Hello Archibald," John said shaking the other's hand. "Where's my father's body?"

"It's setting in sawdust and ice waiting for the funeral. I am so sorry for your loss, John. Your father was much admired in this community and we're all going to miss him mightily."

"Thank you. Please tell me you didn't do an autopsy on his body."

"No, John, of course not. I'd never do that without the family's permission. It was pretty obvious. His fencing partner that day saw him clutch his chest, then complain of severe pains down his left side and difficulty breathing. They sent for me and your mother but by the time either of us got there, he was gone. His heart always sounded strong to me but you know how these things can go. Comes out of the blue and they're gone."

John nodded.

"How is your mother doing?"

"She's angry."

"Angry at what?" Ajax asked in surprise.

"Angry at Father for leaving her. You know, anger is not a completely un-heard of reaction. I went to a symposium on grief in Paris. At the time they were debating the healthfulness of the stoic response to grief."

"Really?" Ajax was always interested in hearing about the experiences he could never afford to have within the greater and more learned medical com-munity of Europe.

"Yes. Many have been taught that the stoic approach, which is almost a de-nial of natural emotions, is the only way to handle grief. I believe they said this was more the norm in the colder countries, Scandinavia, England, Scotland, the German states. Whereas in southern Europe, Spain, the Italian States, Greece, the Holy Lands, people are more verbal and physical, they scream, they cry, they wail, they beat their chests, rip their clothes. And so the debate was which is the best."

"And... ?" Ajax prodded.

"Well, of course there was no consensus of agreement but personally I think each must handle it his own way without society imposing just one given stan-dard. In my own family I can see it all. Mother is angry; Louise is emotionally distraught; Izzy appears to be denying it. James seems to be feeling lost. Helen appears to be attempting the stoic approach. I personally feel a few tears of honest grief even for a man is healthy. Oh, just so you know... I gave Mother and Louise each a mild sedative and Richard a dose of laudanum."

"And what about you, John?

"Not to worry. I've shed a few healthy tears but there's too much to do. We were going to leave for the frontier tomorrow. I've sent a communique to my commander explaining the circumstances here but I cannot overstay for long."

"You're a calm and wise head. Your family needs that right now. But once you leave they need to be able to support each other through the adjustment. I'll see you at the funeral tomorrow. What time?"

"Eleven at the church."

"Very well. John, make sure I see you before you leave. And again… I'm sorry for all of us. Your father was a truly good man and he will be greatly missed."

John stood at the door for a moment.

"What is it?" Ajax asked.

"I'd like to see him," John replied softly.

"Of course." And he led the way to the laboratory in his cellar.

Chapter 6

The church was over-flowing. Phillip had closed the mill. Marie sent word to close the store. Every business in the small community was closed. Everyone attended the funeral with the exception of small children and whoever was designated or volunteered to watch over them. Jacques-Jean Charte Power was *the* founding father of Chartes Landing. Without him it wouldn't exist.

Richard gave a very touching eulogy. He was the one person who had known Jacques his entire life, since early childhood, going back to when they were both barely out of the nursery. Richard was the best friend who had asked to flee France with Jacques, to share the dangers and risk the adventures of the unknown. Richard kept his emotions in check as he spoke eloquently about the early days and Jacques' character and how one could not have wished for a better business partner or a better friend.

William Boot spoke next, briefly, recalling the care and concern Jacques had shown for him when he had lost his first wife, how Jacques and Marie had taken his motherless children into their own nursery. Jacques Power had been someone who cared about all the people who came to live in Chartes Landing, who encouraged the fair treatment of indentured servants and who had established an ordinance against slavery within their settlement. And William bore witness that no one could find a better, more caring, or more fair-minded employer.

John was the last to speak. He had to reach deep down and rely on his professional training and military discipline not to crumble into an emotional vortex after all the things he had heard said. He looked out at his wife, his mother, and all his siblings watching him. He was the eldest, the first born but he was also the son who had been home the least. It was no secret that for the past thirteen years, John Power had not been around. They knew this, and most in his audience knew this and so John addressed this very fact.

He was in many ways, the prodigal son he told them. He had not squandered an inheritance but he had squandered a father's love and yet when he returned, when he was finally able, he was greeted not with recriminations, not with judgments, not with guilt but with more of his father's love. He could only hope and pray to be as good a father as his had been. And he knew his siblings could attest to the same. While Jacques Power always provided exceedingly well for his family, while he was a true friend, a caring employer, and a deeply loving husband, he always had time for his children, made time for his children, and took time for his children.

"He taught his sons everything we needed to know to be good men; he taught his daughters, by example, everything they needed to know to take the measure of a good husband and if we ever fail, it will be our fault not his."

From the church everyone moved on to the neat little graveyard Jacques had designed for the community. He had also designed a modest mausoleum in anticipation of events to come. Most family plots had at least one or two babies per couple who had died or at least one child taken early in life but under the Power name there was none. Jacques and Marie had had a truly blessed young family.

Next to the mausoleum was a plot where Raphael Bonchance had been laid to rest, and next to him a spot Richard had already prepared for himself.

As the casket was interred, John was at his mother's side and he saw her finally dissolve into tears. At last. Some anger might remain for a little while but she was weeping out her grief now, it was a healthy sign. He drew her closer on one side, Ronnie was pensively quiet on John's other. Richard was on Marie's other side. His tears flowing like twin rivers.

As the pastor said his last words, John looked around at his brothers and sisters. Louise was blind with tears and being supported by Lyndyn with her three oldest children standing tall but silently weeping. Helen was trying very hard not to cry but was not entirely successful while Thor stood beside her, stoic and strong, an arm about her shoulders, their three oldest children standing in front of them, also trying not to cry.

Phillip, Caroline, and their girls were all weeping quietly. James stood straight and tall, his head down. John could tell his cheeks were wet. And then there was Isabelle. She was perfectly coiffed and attired with a little white linen handkerchief edged in black satin, dabbing behind the veil at a bone dry cheek. She was only going through the motions and John was concerned.

The family went back to the house and half the town showed up with food. Tables were set up on the lawns, chairs were set out and John issued some requests for liquid refreshments. There was tea and lemonade, regular and hard cider. Someone brought a keg of small beer and Margo made a large pot of coffee. There were casseroles of every kind, along with ham, thin sliced roast beef, and turkey. Something called *potato salad* brought by the wife of one of the mill men. They had Boston style baked beans thanks to a recipe Isabelle had brought back from one of her visits. It seemed almost everyone had brought a dessert which meant the children had to be watched carefully or there would be an epidemic of bellyaches come evening.

As John walked about greeting those he knew, he heard story upon story about his father. Stories he'd never heard before. How Jacques helped this family or that through a time of bad luck, how he'd kept that one or this one on the payroll through a lengthy recovery from an accident and paid all the doctor's fees. How he'd built the school and insisted every child, male and female, be allowed to attend until they could at least read, write, and cipher simple math even if their parents could not afford to contribute to the teacher's pay.

John recalled what he had observed during his time with his *grand-père* in France and realized his father had benevolently run the settlement much like his own father had run his estates. And he had looked out for "his people" quietly and without fanfare. The Old World attitude of *noblesse oblige* came to mind. Was it any wonder he had been so well loved and admired?

"So what are your plans, John?" Phillip asked a bit too casually.

The three brothers were standing under one of the big old trees that had loomed majestic in the backyard ever since they could remember. It was Saturday, the day after the funeral. At the moment all the Power family enterprises were closed but all the notices had said work would resume as usual the following Monday.

"Yeah, John, what *are* your plans?" James looked at his big brother.

"Right now I'm just waiting for the reading of Father's will," John replied, and took another gulp of his morning coffee which he'd put into a military cup without a saucer.

"Father has a will?" James asked.

"Of course he has a will," John replied. "Every responsible man has a will drawn up to take care of his family."

"Where is it?" he looked between his older brothers.

"With his lawyer in New York Towne," answered Phillip who had plucked a long grass stem and was chewing on it.

"He sent word, he's coming here today on the early packet," John explained.

"I can't believe Mother had the presence of mind to notify him of Father's passing," said Phillip.

"She didn't," replied John. "I believe it was Lyndyn who brought it to Doc Ajax's attention and with Mother's permission he found the name of the firm in the file in Father's desk."

"Who? Lyndyn?!" exclaimed Phillip, obviously upset at the thought of Lyndyn going through their father's desk.

"No, Doc Ajax," answered John.

"What file?" James asked.

"Yeah, what file?" Phillip echoed, accepting that the family doctor might search their father's desk.

"The file I imagine every good provider has that's labeled 'To Be Opened Upon My Death.'"

"Oh," Phillip nodded. "Speaking of which…. Have you two noticed Lyndyn's been spending a good deal of time lately, hanging around our sister?"

"I haven't noticed," replied James.

"You don't notice anything. He seemed to be glued to her all day yesterday."

John looked at Phillip. "What? Are you worried he's swooping in on the wealthy heiress?"

"Well, you never know. Louise is a good-looking woman but she also has *Grand-père's* legacy and whatever Rafe left her and who knows what Father's will is going to leave her…"

"I'm going to stop you right there before you say something you'll regret. The family has known Lyndyn for years. He's a decent soul, took care of his mother and sister and has been faithful to our mother in running that store…"

"So has Caroline," Phillip interjected before he could stop himself.

John raised an eyebrow. "As far as I'm concerned, if our poor widowed sister with five children to raise can find comfort and emotional support from a good man like Lyndyn, I'm glad for it and so should you be." Then he added, "I'm getting another cup of coffee." And he walked back into the house.

They were all gathered in the dining room. The adults and their spouses were seated. This included select members of the staff and friends who had been invited by the lawyer. The grandchildren, age twelve and older, which included Phillip's three eldest daughters, Charity, Faith, and Hope; Helen's eldest son Thomas; and Louise's eldest daughter Rebecca, stood solemnly near their parents for this very important, very grown-up meeting presided over by Sir Reginald Coats-Filmore Swittington Esquire.

Sir Reginald represented the firm of Beadington, Beadington, Coats, and Coats-Filmore Attorneys at Law all of which sounded a great deal more impressive than the man looked. The primary offices of said firm were in London and the pale faced, circumspect little man was only the second son of Sir Reginald Coats-Filmore's third youngest daughter. As such Sir Reginald Swittington had been begrudgingly admitted into the law firm, sponsored as he was by his grandfather, but with absolutely no prestige.

Destined to clerk for his grandfather and his uncle until the older men died, he had instead volunteered to go to the colonies and represent the firm in a tiny, one room office above a haberdashery in New York Towne.

Colonials were not keen on lawyers and avoided them whenever possible. They had seen lawyers descend like birds of prey upon widows and orphans in England and wipe out most of the family holdings. They had witnessed lawyers stoke the fires of contention between combatant clients embroiling them in long, drawn-out litigations which ended with most of the reparations going into the firm's coffers rather than to the aggrieved. The people of the colonies wanted none of that. It was considered prudent for every man in the colonies to seek out a rudimentary knowledge of the law for himself and then write up his own contracts in simple clear terms… that is if a simple, honorable handshake wouldn't do. There was a reason for the popular saying *"every village should have a lawyer but woe to the town that has two."*

Sir Reginald's fingers were almost permanently tattooed by ink before he could afford his own clerk to do all the tedious copying his scant business required.

In spectacles and a somewhat out-of-style wig, he sat at Jacques' place at the table; it seemed appropriate as he was at that moment speaking for Jacques. This was his Last Will and Testament.

Sir Reginald spoke first to the grandchildren. Jacques had established a trust fund for each one to be awarded upon their twenty-first birthday allowing for them to launch the career of their choice or buy land, a home, a farm, as they desired. The only caveat was that the money was to be used for tangible assets, not to pay accumulated debts so they had best not accumulate them, and it was not to be squandered on riotous living. Not wanting to demotivate anyone from working for their own dream, the sums were not vast and would make no one wealthy but they would assist in the struggle for that dream.

"Does anyone have any questions so far?" Sir Reginald asked, looking up from his papers and over the rims of his spectacles.

"Yes, sir, I have one." It was Charity, the eldest grandchild. Phillip wondered whether he should be embarrassed. Caroline looked to her daughter with interest wondering what was on her mind.

"Yes, what is that?" Sir Reginald looked at the girl.

"Well, sir," the girl began, trying to keep from shaking, "if the money being held in trust is all equal then won't those of us who are older receive a lesser amount than those who are just babies now since there will be more years to accrue value before they come of age?"

Phillip found himself scowling at his daughter's audacity whereas Caroline felt rather proud.

"Looks like we have a banker in our midst," Sir Reginald commented lightly. "You won't have to worry about that, my dear. Your grandfather worked everything out wherein each grandchild shall receive an equal amount at the age of twenty-one… and this does include future grandchildren. Born of his children. Now, if any leave their trust intact beyond that time, it will, of course, grow bigger. Any other questions?" he asked in a tone that said he did not expect any.

Having understood, the grandchildren were excused from the room and the doors were closed again.

"Next," continued Sir Reginald as he cleared his throat, "there are a number of bequests to long-time employees, friends, and family retainers. Modest lump sums *in memoria*." At this he read through a list starting with Jane Sims who began discreetly sobbing, followed by Sarah their faithful nursemaid, Margot their long-time cook, William Boot, Doctor Ajax, and a few others. When he finished they were also excused.

"This next becomes a little more complicated," he continued when the doors had been shut again. "As you may know, by British law, everything in a marriage belongs to the husband to do with as he wishes with the exception of any legally protected dowry and since Marie Power brought no dowry to the marriage, it is a moot point." The little lawyer paused and looked around the room at the remaining faces. "It was Jacques-Jean Power's intent to leave everything - all lands, holdings, assets, and business interests to his widow, Marie Power. He did not wish however, to so burden her with all these responsibilities.

"Therefore, be it known that this house, its furnishings, all outbuildings and livestock, accompanying fields and lands up to and including the original site of the original cabin and her oven, I bequeath to my beloved wife Marie.

"Be it also known that the store known as the Chartes Landing Emporium, it's stock and land and income, I bequeath to Marie. It has always been hers and hers alone to do with as she wishes.

"Also, all interest accrued on the Swiss bank account established by my father shall be transferred into her name, free and clear. For her to draw upon as she desires."

"Also, any other assets not specifically bequeath elsewhere shall belong to Marie."

John stole a look at his mother and saw the tears flowing down her cheeks.

"To my son Phillip, I bequeath the lumber business and the saw mill in equal partnership with my daughter Helen along with a parcel of land for each of you purchased at your grandfather's request years ago;

"To my son Richard, I bequeath my interest in the trading posts which shall become an equal partnership with my daughter Louise, along with a parcel of land for each of you purchased at your grandfather's request years ago;

"To my son James, I bequeath the apple orchards, the cider mill, and the press and bottling business along with a parcel of land purchased at your grandfather's request years ago;

"To my daughter Isabelle, I bequeath an annuity established to insure her from penury along with a parcel of land purchased at your grandfather's request years ago;

"And to my son John, I leave a parcel of land purchased per your grandfather's request, land I hope you and your family can be happy on, the land upon which you were born. Furthermore, I leave you with the heaviest burden of all, a burden of Honor.

"John, I charge you with looking after your mother, insuring the appropriate over-sight of various assets and investments Sir Reginald Swittington Esquire and Monsieur Denis Dufee of Dufee Shipping shall make known to you.

"Also, you shall administer various bank accounts for your mother, insuring their good status.

"Also, if any dispute should arise within the equal partnerships established by this will, you shall be the deciding vote.

"Life's blessings and tragedies, your travels, education, and experiences have broadened you more than any of your siblings. I have complete faith and trust in you and your sense of Honor. Find a way to make it all work, John, for you, your wife and children, and now as the head of the Power family.

"My final words to all of you. I love you. You all have made my life rich and rewarding beyond measure. I place my trust in you all to love each other and teach your children well. We shall meet each other again in Paradise."

"And finally, to my dear, faithful, and beloved friend Richard Bonchance, I bequeath the guilt-free companionship of my wife; if you can bring each other happiness or comfort in any way, know that you have my blessing."

"And he signs it with his signet ring and a final note that his ring should be left with Marie."

The lawyer stopped speaking and the dining room fell into complete silence.

Each person was trying to process what it all meant.

Isabelle looked down at her lap. They had never wanted for anything but it seemed Father was far wealthier than she had realized. Heavens! Even dividing everything up, Mother was still a very wealthy woman. Hamilton's family had best know her whole family in its own right belonged in high society.

Phillip looked at Helen. He was now the official final authority in the lumber camp and the mill. He couldn't imagine Helen ever taking an interest as long as she received her share of the profits. He'd have a freehand… but then there was Thor. That's why Papa had set him in partnership with Helen… because she was Thor's wife. It really put Thor on equal footing with Phillip and he wondered how that was going to work. Well, if they ever did butt heads, he was sure John would see things his own brother's way.

Louise knew that between what Rafe and Grandfather had left her, and officially being partners with Richie, she would never have to worry about money. Why, Uncle Richard had even told her he planned to leave her everything he had been going to leave Rafe. But money wasn't everything was it? She'd give it all up if she could just have Rafe back. The tears began rolling down her cheeks again.

James was happy, or as happy as one could be considering the circumstances. Papa knew he loved the land, growing things and working with the apples. Maybe he'd expand to a second cash crop. Or maybe start breeding horses. He'd have to think about that. Papa trusted him.

Helen looked at her husband. Had Papa just put Uncle Richard in Mama's bed? Good heavens! Papa had just told the whole world they had his blessing. Richard might be a little crippled from arthritis but…… oh, that was just too disgusting to think about!

Richard looked toward Marie. She was trying so hard to stay calm but he could tell she needed someone to hold her, she needed a shoulder to cry on and he had always been willing to give her his.

John looked at Ronnie sitting by his side. What had Father done? John had to believe this was written before they knew he was married. Before they had met Ronnie? Had Father not realized how unhappy Ronnie was here?

"Sir Reginald?" John spoke quietly to the man sitting to his left. "Might I ask when was the last time Father updated his will?"

"Of course. It was two weeks ago, I can look up the exact date if you like."

"No, that isn't necessary," John replied. "Did Father have some sort of premonition of his passing?"

"No, I don't believe so. He came to the office quite regularly, whenever the family changed, when his assets shifted. He believed in having everything in order. Knowing his own father had died suddenly in his sleep was, I believe, a very motivating factor."

"And he didn't seem any different this last time?"

"No, not at all, he was the same cheerful, positive person he always was. He did say his eldest son had come home and he could now rest easy. He knew who had the strength to take over as head of the family if anything should happen to him."

John looked down at the dining table, slowly running his fingers along the edge. "I need to speak with you more privately before you return to New York."

"Of course. Perhaps we can use your father's office."

"Yes. Shall we say in an hour? I need some time to digest this. It's all been quite a shock."

The little man nodded.

John ushered Ronnie into Jacques' office and closed the door.

"Ronnie, sweetheart, how much of this did you understand?" he asked, taking her hands in his.

"It is your father's final words. He was chief, sachem, leader of family and tribe." She gestured toward the village. "Now he choose you to be sachem, must lead family, must lead tribe," she replied without judgment.

"But what about the frontier, your mother and brother? Gray growing up as a Mohawk?"

"You have more family here. They need you. I can take the children and go back."

"No!" John instantly rejected the very idea of Ronnie and the children leaving him. "We stay together, Ronnie, for better or worst, remember? I'll think of something."

Ronnie looked at her husband, so very glad he had rejected her offer to leave. She threw her arms around him and clung to him for a few moments. "I love you, Jack," she whispered. "I will do whatever you wish, whatever you say."

John opened the door just as Sarah approached holding their baby obviously on the brink of throwing a mighty howl.

"Feeding time, ma'am, this little fellow is hungry."

"Yes, yes, I take outdoors where more quiet." She knew she could find a quiet private spot somewhere in the gardens. Jack did not like her baring herself in front of other men.

John gave Sarah a thank you and saw his wife out the garden doors. Then he decided to take the temperature of the family and see to his mother.

Marie had pulled herself together enough to oversee a light tea for everyone. There was still so much food and she had never believed in waste. She told Margot to set up a buffet in the now empty dining room and they could let everyone take a plate as they wished. Even she found she could eat a little.

These are not the bad times, Marie thought to herself, *with people around, things to do. It is the quiet times, the loneliness of our empty bed at night. Did you not say you only slept well when I was there by your side... oh, Jacques, I feel the same I miss you so I do not know if I can stand it. How can I go on?*

"Mother?" It was John.

"What? Oh," she gasped a bit. "Sorry, I was just remembering. Did I ever tell you when your father asked me to marry him, he told me later that he was afraid I might have rejected him?"

John shook his head.

"Can you imagine? Reject him? I asked him how he could think that and he said it was because he had nothing to offer me. He came from a world where titles and estates, mansions and servants were all part of a man's worth when he asked a woman to marry. And there we were, the three of us, sharing this little crooked log cabin in the middle of the wilderness, your father making his way by trapping and gutting animals for their fur... you know when we first landed and began to clear the land, I had to tell both him and Richard to wrap their hands in rags to protect them from raw blisters? That was the peasant world I came from. I had no expectations of an easy life, I only knew I loved him so fiercely I would do anything for him. He told me he had nothing to give me but his heart and his name but he hoped someday to give me so much more. And look what all he built. Could any family ask for more? Could any woman ask for more? But I would gladly give it all away this instant just to have him back." She sighed but she wasn't crying.

"John, your father was the wisest man I have ever known. He knew you had the strength, courage, and intelligence to oversee this family and keep it together. I am sorry that this is going to give you greater challenges and burdens but you will grow wise." She put her arms around him then, this son who looked so very like his father. She kissed him lightly on the mouth, a mother's kiss, and then holding his head in her hands she gave him a father's kiss, one on each tan cheek. "*Je t'aime mon fils*, I love you my son, *je t'aime*," she said softly in the old language, the language he and all his siblings had learned equally in the nursery. "*Confiance en Dieu*. Trust in God."

Marie moved on then, like a willow wisp, gliding out and into the dining room to make certain the grandchildren were not over indulging in sweets or giving Sarah and Rachel a hard time.

John watched her go and wondered if that was how Ronnie loved him, *so fiercely she would do anything for him*. He trusted in their love but was cognizant of not wanting to strain it too far.

It was time to meet with Sir Reginald.

"You are probably more aware of all my father's holdings and concerns than any of us in the family. He provided very well for us; barring foolishness, money was never an issue. I suppose he felt it best to quietly go about his business without burdening anyone else. The lumber mill, the trading posts, the cider mill, these were all visible and a good training ground but everything else… ? I for one had no idea. So now I put the question to you, Sir Reginald, can I oversee these things from my post at the frontier?"

Sir Reginald sat in the wing backed chair, his hands grasped together resting on his belly, his focus on his hands. John knew he was thinking. The other suddenly took in a long steady breath and exhaled. He cleared his throat.

"May I call you John?"

"Of course."

"John, for a time the various investments could coast along without a lot of attention. Mister Power certainly didn't have to give them daily attention but matters closer to home are a bit different. Your father was very concerned that someone be able to defuse any small arguments before they grew like a snowball into a damaging avalanche. He told me specifically that while he didn't see anyone as a specific problem still he recognized that there was a tendency amidst a few of your siblings to… shall we say, plead for Mother's favor?"

John grunted. Unfortunately he knew Izzy had already been a thorn in Mother's side concerning the wedding.

"He wished to spare her that, giving her the opportunity to simply say *go ask your brother*. But I believe his biggest concern was for your health."

"Me?"

"Well, yes, John, things are a bit more dangerous on the frontier, wouldn't you agree? And you a soldier who must fight when called upon. If anything were to happen to you, who would you choose to head up the family and spare your mother the burden? She's no youngster anymore herself."

"Mother's from good solid stock and I expect her to live for many years yet," John said a trifle defensively; in reality he knew nothing of Mother's *stock*. "But I see your point." He sat silently for a moment in thought. "I suppose Phillip. He grew up fast, took on more and more responsibility..."

"And would he now be willing to step back from all that to oversee everything? I'm afraid your father didn't think so. You are the one who can let your siblings continue doing as they are, as they have chosen to do. Allow them to adjust into their new relationships, and be fair-minded in helping to settle any disputes. You can hardly do that from the frontier."

"Hmm."

"Without your presence, do you not think it would be likely that your mother would be harassed, albeit lovingly, but harassed none the less to take sides and intercede? Apparently, your father thought so."

"Well, Sir Reginald," John stood and put forth his hand, "it does appear that we are going to be seeing much more of each other as we work together."

"My pleasure, John," the small man took John's hand for a hearty shake and then bowed. "I am at your service, sir."

John returned the bow. "Please stay another day as our guest. I will feel a bit more clear headed in the morning and I imagine we need to go over the actual investments."

"Yes, of course, as you like."

John sat back and rubbed his forehead. Sir Reginald had made the case quite well for father's last wishes. Certainly Mother deserved his support. But what was he going to do for Ronnie? Did she know when she came to him for help, when she lived at the white man's fort and fell in love with him that someday... someday she might have to live in the white man's world?

John rubbed the back of his neck, he could feel the tension. He'd just have to take it one day at a time. She would have to trust him to look out for her and take it one day at a time with him.

A tap at the door announced Isabelle.

"Well," she semi-sighed as she flounced in and landed in the same chair Sir Reginald had just vacated. "So, you said you weren't going to get involved but it looks like you are right in the middle whether you like it or not."

"What is your issue, Izzy?"

"What it has always been, my wedding. I miss father as much as anyone but

I have been mentally preparing myself for leaving home and leaving Chartes Landing for some time. I think it is sensible to accept that my brothers and sisters and my parents are all soon to become letters to me. I can still write to Mama and Papa, and Mama will write back. Papa never will but I can imagine him reading my letters anyway and it will still feel pretty much the same. Is there anything wrong with that?"

Something in John's gut was telling him this was not healthy.

"Izzy, have you had yourself a good cry?" It was getting on toward a week since Jacques' death.

"What? And why would I want to do that? Have you seen Jane... or Sarah... or Louise, even Mama. Their eyes are all red and swollen, they look like they've been beaten about the head. I don't need to cry, John. It doesn't mean I'm not sad inside but why wallow in it?"

"Everyone needs to cry, honey, even I have cried. I miss my father more than I could have imagined and I'm not ashamed of red eyes. It's normal."

"Well, I prefer to think more on the positive side. Now, Hamilton would really like to have the wedding in Boston. My family can all come to Boston, and I want you to give me away, John, and I don't need the people in this settlement..."

"Who have known you all your life."

"But they aren't really my friends and they don't really care if the last Power girl is finally getting married."

"All right," John sighed, "I'll speak with Mother." There was no use in arguing the point, it was her wedding. "But Izzy, look at me, as your big brother, as head of the family, and most importantly, as a doctor, I'm telling you to let those feelings out and cry."

"Oh, John," she half giggled, "don't be silly." And off she went.

Chapter 7

In the end Isabelle got her way. Marie had decided that the change in location and all the changes it would bring about might help everyone *cope*, was that not the word she had learned? Yes, it would make it easier to cope with the biggest change which was Jacques not being there.

To Isabelle's surprise, Marie also saw no reason to postpone the wedding any longer. They would plan for an early autumn wedding when the trees were still full of spectacularly colored leaves. True, they were in mourning, they were a house and family in mourning but life had to win, she told John. Life had to go on. She knew Jacques had been finding excuses... just a little... to keep putting off the wedding because he dreaded "losing" his last daughter.

How stupidly ironic that he should be lost to them first. And that Izzy should go on as if she hadn't even noticed.

Marie commissioned the wedding dresses from the same esteemed designer who had designed dresses for her other daughters. Miss Lilly, a Huguenot now living in New York Towne, had once been an acclaimed member of the Dress Designers Guild, the only female guild in France established under the good graces of his Majesty Louis XIV. But Miss Lilly like so many hundreds of thousands had fled for her life and her sanity.

Isabelle stood confidently in her shift as Miss Lilly took her measurements.

"You are a little angel, *ma petite,* such a dainty little figure, it will be a pleasure to dress you. As before I will send three renderings, each especially designed to compliment your face and figure. And such a beautiful face but not like your mama, perhaps your…"

"They say I look exactly like my *grand-mère*, and I have her coloring. She too was very tiny and pale with pale blonde hair and gray eyes."

"Ah, so, the blood it reproduces itself, yes? So, you will select your favorite design and send it back to me, I will let you know when to return for the final fitting. And now the mother of the bride-to-be, if you please." Isabelle began to put on her frock and Marie stood for measurements next as Miss Lilly scribbled a few notes.

"I will not wear black at my daughter's wedding and gray has never been a good color for me. I thought something made of this." She handed Miss Lilly a swatch of reddish brown silk with the most beautiful iridescent sheen woven right in.

"This is perfect for you," the designer nodded. "Madame Marie," she lightly scolded as she took Marie's measurements, "you are not eating, *n'est-ce pas?* You are wasting away by inches."

Marie had been fine and completely in control when suddenly she began to weep.

"But what is this?" the designer looked to the daughters, "did I say something wrong? Forgive me, I am so sorry. I was only teasing but your ma-ma, she has lost weight. Your waist is a full inch smaller, madame."

Helen looked a bit embarrassed. Ronnie had no idea what was wrong.

"It is nothing," Isabelle said in French.

"Our father died last month and you just used one of his favorite expressions," Helen explained. "We are all trying to press on despite our pain."

"Oh, forgive me, Madame Marie, I had no idea. Perhaps a cup of tea?"

Miss Lilly snapped her fingers and an apprentice brought in a tea cart. Everyone was offered a cup.

Ronnie had begun to trust the nursery staff with her children. They brought little Matthew to her for feeding, and supervised Sunshine and Gray. Gray had found playmates among Louise's youngest children and took lessons in his letters and numbers along with everyone else. But a two day excursion to New York Towne was something else. John had insisted on accompanying the ladies and they had brought only Matthew along. At the moment, father and son were patiently waiting outside on the street, at the bottom of the stairway to Miss Lilly's studio.

"While Madame Marie has her tea, perhaps I can measure you, Madame Ronnie," Miss Lilly said graciously.

Ronnie still had all her clothes on and suddenly clutched at her breasts. They were tightening as her milk let down and were becoming quite uncomfortable. She could hear Matthew crying in the street. "Oh, please, my baby…" and she hurried to the door. When she returned she had Matthew in her arms. She unlaced her blouse top and proceeded to give Matthew his lunch.

"Such a handsome baby," trilled Miss Lilly. She had never had any children and had passed the age for hoping and entered the age for accepting she never would. "You have an excellent figure, Madame Ronnie, but this will reduce the size of your bosom perhaps just a little?" she laughed and proceeded to finish measuring Marie instead.

Wedding preparations also necessitated a trip to Boston. On this occasion only Marie, Isabelle, and John went and they stayed as the house guests of Hamilton's parents, the Carters. The Carters lived in a pleasant home on a wooded lot on Beacon Street overlooking the Boston Commons where sheep grazed. Marie appreciated the opportunity to get to know her daughter's future in-laws. This, too, was a new experience. It was a bit odd to think of her daughter marrying into a family with whom they had no real acquaintance. Marie knew everyone at Chartes Landing. But Jacques had assured her that he had had the Carters "investigated" and they appeared to be of sound reputation.

Rutherford and Henrietta Carter were extremely proper and welcoming but Marie thought them a bit stiff, and perhaps more than a little snobbish. Not to her or to John or Isabelle but toward the rest of the world in general.

They, in turn, found Marie a bit colloquial but her French accent was beyond charming and she spoke well and could be understood. She was also well-read and intelligent and apparently had money of her own as Isabelle had said her mother owned the only general store in town. John, of course, was the kind of handsome male that graced any gathering. He spoke French like an aristocrat, had the physique of a Greek god, was a doctor, an officer in His Majesty's army and quite wealthy in his own right. Mistress Carter was very disappointed when she discovered John was married for she could think of at least seven young women within their social circle who were over the age of seventeen and under the age of twenty-five who would have leapt at the chance to meet him. And of course, his father who was also Isabelle's father had actually founded a town of his own. They appeared to be the kind of family to whom it never hurt one to be connected.

"So, we were thinking the United Church of Christ might be an excellent choice, it has plenty of room and is in a convenient setting. Have you interviewed any churches yet?" Henrietta Carter asked.

"No," Marie smiled, "we were hoping you could recommend. Have you a Huguenot church?"

They were gathered around the dinner table having a succulent roast leg of lamb served up with an excellent mint jelly.

"Oh, that would be the French Church of Boston on School Street," replied Henrietta.

"There is a Huguenot Fort somewhere farther into the interior. That would be due west by southwest," Rutherford Carter spoke rather randomly. "Had a massacre there, caused them to abandon it. Then, more of you Huguenots arrived and rebuilt the fort but that was quite some time ago," he elaborated. "Not that you'd be wanting to hold a wedding in a fort," he laughed, a dry, stilted laugh.

"No, of course not," Henrietta looked at her husband with mild disdain. "I'm sure the French Church will be fine although I understand their membership has been dwindling. Well, I can assure you, it doesn't matter to us. We told Hamilton, it doesn't matter to us at all, son, as long as they are Christians and not Catholics. So, is your husband away on business? We had been hoping to meet him, we've heard so much about him."

The room went quiet.

John looked at Isabelle who had been engaged in muted conversation with Hamilton. She looked up with the same startled, wide-eyed expression one often sees on gentle hunted animals.

"Isabelle," Marie gasped in hurt, "have you not told them?"

"Told us what?" Hamilton said, suddenly blanching pale, fearing scandal. *Had Isabelle's father run off with a mistress? Oh, Lord. He is French. They all end up with mistresses. Well, if so, could it be kept quiet?*

"Izzy," John said in an unmistakable tone of authority, "don't you think it's time you told Hamilton and his parents why I am to walk you down the aisle?"

"Oh," uttered Henrietta as this in itself was a revelation previously unknown.

Isabelle reached for her water glass to take a sip but she began shaking so violently the water was literally thrown out of the glass onto her, her plate, and around her place at the table. Hamilton jumped up and took the glass and put it safely down.

"Isabelle, what is it? What is wrong, my dearest. Tell me, whatever it is we will fix it. Tell me."

"I'm afraid this is something you cannot fix, Hamilton," John spoke mildly. "Tell him, Izzy. It's time you said it and faced it. It's time you had a good cry and accepted it."

"I say, must you… I mean she… can't *you* tell us?"

"Trust me, Hamilton, I know what I'm doing. Isabelle, tell him. Tell him why Father will not be walking you down the aisle as he did your sisters."

Isabelle collapsed against Hamilton. She had begun sobbing in full gasping sobs like a child in the nursery.

"What is it, Isabelle, sweetness, tell me? Did he run off with a mistress?"

Isabelle pulled back and looked at Hamilton, horror, confusion, grief, and suffering all racing across her face. "No," she groaned, tears flowing from her eyes, "it's worse, much, much worse."

"What could be worse?" he asked and then thought fleetingly of sodomy.

"My papa's dead," she sobbed. "Oh, Hamilton. He's dead. He's dead and I'll never see him again."

Was that all, thought Hamilton, so relieved at the utter banality of it he had to catch himself from being dismissive. "That's right, sweetheart," he produced a clean white handkerchief. "You have a good cry." Then he carried Isabelle effortlessly into the salon where he continued to pet on her while the butler brought a fresh glass of water.

"I am sorry you had to witness this but Isabelle has been in complete denial ever since it happened," John spoke calmly. "It isn't healthy."

"Oh, my," Henrietta exclaimed. "How long has it been?"

"It's been a month now. Father used to fence every day to keep fit. He had just finished a bout when he clutched his chest. It was his heart. And it was totally unexpected. But Isabelle wouldn't accept it, wouldn't say it, wouldn't cry, acted as if somehow it wasn't true. I'm not surprised she didn't tell Hamilton. The moment she said it, it became real and she couldn't deny it anymore."

"Well, Heavens, I am so sorry for your loss. We had no idea. Is she going to be all right?" Henrietta asked craning her neck to see the young people in the salon.

"You don't think her mind has been…" Rutherford couldn't even finish his question.

"She should go through the normal grieving process now. She should be fine," John said confidently, "but for her sensitivities, I'm afraid she will be a little raw, like it happened last week rather than last month."

"She was our last," said Marie, who had been quiet and quickly flicked two tears from her cheeks. "Our youngest and I am afraid she has been a bit spoiled. My husband indulged her greatly. Losing him has been extremely hard for her to accept. It has been hard for all of us."

"I understand, my dear. I understand completely," Henrietta said. "Mister Carter, I do believe we are all in need of a medicinal tot of spirits."

"Yes, yes, of course." He rose and using a key attached to his fob, he opened a cabinet within which a considerable selection of various "medicinal" spirits was concealed.

With Isabelle on the road to a healthy acceptance of her father's death only one hurdle remained. Inevitably some hard choices had to be made regarding Isabelle's guest list and it all came down to one decision. If she wanted John to walk her down the aisle, indeed if she wanted him at her wedding at all, she must accept Ronnie's presence. And with Ronnie came their baby but neither four year old Gray nor his two year old sister, Sunshine, needed to be in attendance. They were too young to care but old enough to stay behind in the nursery. Ronnie had made the proposal as an olive branch of compromise. Isabelle agreed. Without Gray tagging along, no one would think of Ronnie as an Indian. Isabelle blithely avoided saying anything to Hamilton, deciding if the matter ever came up in the future, she would simply feign innocence with complete lack of prejudice. *Why, I never even thought about it, darling, it simply didn't seem important.* And everyone was satisfied.

Several days after their return from Boston, John sought out his mother and found her in her store. It had been too long, she said. She had neglected her responsibilities.

John walked into the Chartes Landing Emporium and saw her in the office. "Mother?" he called as he knocked on the frame of the open door.

"Yes, John?" she looked up with concern. She was not expecting him. "Is anything wrong?" she asked, removing her reading glasses.

"No-no, I just wanted to ask you a question."

"Yes?"

"Did you ever go horseback riding with father?"

Immediately Marie thought of the Sundays in New York Towne when Jacques would take her out riding. Her eyes teared up as she remembered pressing against his back. She cleared her throat. "Not for many years. We usually took the trap or carriage. Why do you ask?"

"I want to take Ronnie out to look at the property Father left us. She can ride but..."

"Yes?"

"What would be proper for her to wear? I mean she doesn't ride sidesaddle, she rides Indian style, like a man, you know, one leg on each side."

Marie smiled. "Of course, unless I was sitting in front of your father and he was holding me, that was the only way I could ride as well. ...So... what to wear? ...Hmm... do you know where our town seamstress lives?"

"No, but let's face it, Chartes Landing isn't that big. I'm sure I could find her."

"Of course. Let me help." She took a quill and wrote quickly upon a piece of paper.

"Here give her this. Ronnie was just measured for the wedding, so I put down her waist and hip measurements as well. Important information for a seamstress. And you can describe how tall she is better than anyone, I am certain, yes?"

"Thank you," he said and kissed his mother's cheek.

As John walked from his mother's store he saw Doctor Ajax flagging him down. John paused and waited for the man to come up the intersecting street.

"…John… a word."

"Of course. And how are you this fine day?" John asked. "Out seeing patients?"

"More or less, but I was hoping to come across you. Have you a minute?"

"Of course." John looked at the other man with curiosity.

"Do you know what your plans are yet?" Ajax held his black bag and sidled over to a bench in front of the shoemaker's shop. It was early and the shop was not yet open. He set down his bag.

John scratched his ear thoughtfully. "No, not exactly. I'm waiting to hear from my post commander. I've updated him on the situation and asked for a year's leave of absence."

"I'm sure you'll get it," Ajax took out his handkerchief and wiped his brow. Despite the early hour, the day was getting warm and the Englishman's face was flushed out quite florid. "I have been thinking. Your father left me that money. A damn nice thing for him to do, I must say."

John nodded.

"I would really like to take a sabbatical myself," Ajax went on. "Go to Europe. See what I can learn. Never had the means before but thanks to your father, I do now. Well, I wouldn't want to leave my patients without a physician."

John was listening attentively without expression.

"If… if you are going to be here a year, could you see yourself looking to the community needs? I could leave on the next ship and be back here by late spring." He looked expectantly at John.

John stood thinking. He saw no reason it should hurt anything if he was going to be in Chartes Landing anyway. It might be good for him to get back to practicing a variety of medicine. He really hadn't done that since… He thought back and realized it was not since Huffsmeier's clinic. Since then he had been mostly absorbed in treating battle wounds, hangovers, and the clap.

John looked at Ajax and nodded. "I don't see why not but I do want to hear back to be certain before you leave. While I cannot imagine that I would be denied, still I would like to know for sure that my commander agrees to a full year. He might say six months."

"Fair enough. Fair enough. I shall wait. In the meanwhile, we might go over a few of my chronic cases. This is quite wonderful, John. I really appreciate it." The man was grinning ear to ear. "I can't tell you what this means. I never imagined I'd ever have the means. And now the opportunity." He reached out and shook John's hand.

"Do you speak French?"

"I shall have to refresh," Ajax admitted. "And I have a patient who is teaching me German."

"Yes? I would say that might be equally useful. Once you have been to Paris, you might find working side-by-side with some doctors in the German states to be very enlightening. And in Switzerland. I can give you the name of one who was doing advanced work with the microscope... if he's still alive." John offered. "He is the one who first introduced me to 'the world we cannot see'. I'd love to know what progress he's made."

"That would be marvelous. I would truly appreciate it." John noticed that Ajax was quite suddenly looking ten years younger. "Well," he grabbed up his bag again, "I have my work cut out for me."

"Oh," John gestured. "Do you happen to know where the seamstress shoppe is?"

Three days later John presented Ronnie with a riding skirt, split like the pantaloons men wore a hundred years earlier. Matthew was too big for a back carrier and so Ronnie fashioned a sling that held him in front of her. Together, she and John rode out of town.

John brought his service weapons, canteens, and a saddlebag full of diapers on one side and food on the other. He had checked with the surveyor's office just to be certain but he was pretty sure he knew the way. With the cleared road, it was only a day's ride. Fourteen years ago he had ridden out with his father and a group of volunteers to find out what happened to one of his father's old employees who had struck out with his new bride and her children to homestead along the Delaware River. It was before John had left for medical training and that's when his father had almost been sliced to death by an unhappy Indian. But John remembered they had stopped for the night at the site of the Indian village where the local tribe had taken his mother for safety and where he, John, had been born. His father had pointed out the very spot. This was the land his father had purchased for him at his grandfather's request. A thousand acres of trees, natural springs, game, and meadows, all he had to do was get it surveyed and put up his markers.

As they rode, John noticed the changes in the landscape. The growing farms of fields and pastures had grown far beyond the first Indian village. And the farther they rode, John noticed a change in his wife. She looked happier, more relaxed. She'd been through a lot since leaving the fort. Rude strangers, family drama, Father's death and funeral, and Izzy's wedding. She had not complained once. John fully appreciated how much his wife must love him. And it warmed his heart. Somehow he had struck gold again so to speak and he couldn't feel more blessed.

It was getting on toward twilight when they came to the site. The forest had completely taken over but John recognized it by the rock formations at the large creek that ran near by. He reined up his horse and dismounted. Then he helped Ronnie dismount. Matthew had already had his supper "in the saddle" and was happily sleeping in the fresh air. Ronnie fashioned a bed and laid him in it, then covered him with mosquito netting. Marie had convinced her it was more effective than bear grease and less messy and Ronnie found that to be true.

John soon had a fire started. He had unsaddled the horses, brought them to the creek to drink and then tethered and hobbled them where they could graze. He staked out a kind of tent to shelter their bedrolls. It augured to be a clear night but it was getting cool.

Ronnie was warming up their supper and trying to boil water for tea. He came up behind her and she stood. Wrapping his arms around her, he tried to think of how he could tell her what he was thinking, feeling. Feelings weren't always easy to express, or to define.

"Ronnie," he nuzzled close on her neck. "I am so very proud of the way you …have… well, in the military we'd say *mustered through* or *toughed it out* but I don't suppose that means a lot to you, does it?"

She turned to look in his eyes and gave a little shake to her head.

"I know you've been through a helluva lot since we left the fort. I never expected you to have to go through all this. I just want you to know that I realize it has been challenging for you and I appreciate and recognize how difficult it has been. I am very proud of the way you have endured it all." He gave her a long kiss.

"Jack, I am very proud to be your wife. I will always stand behind you."

"No, darling, I want you to stand *with* me, you and me together, not you behind."

She smiled. "Stand *with* you. You are my man and my love. Now you are sachem of your tribe, I am proud to be the sachem's wife." She opened the neck of his shirt and ran her fingers over the plains of his chest. She had become used to the small area of blond, curly hair upon his thorax and now considered it with affection. She stroked the rise of his pectorals. "In my old village you would be expected to take a second wife now," she pulled his shirt from his breeches and moved across the ripples of his abdomen, "and I would have to listen to you please her in the furs." Her teeth lightly tugged his flesh. "I am very glad this is not your way. I would have to smile but I would want to carve out her heart with my knife."

He knew Ronnie came from a people who did just that. Carved out hearts and even ate them raw. She had once saved him from what might have been just such a fate. "I'll remember that and never look at another woman," he chuckled.

She ran her finger just inside his lower lip, and then she repeated the move with her tongue. "We eat now and then you please me in the furs," she said in her husky voice.

He grabbed her lightly and undid the pantaloon breeches from her hips.

"You have me half undressed," he said hoarsely, "and food is not what I want at this moment."

Apparently Ronnie had felt inhibited in their bedroom near the nursery in the big house because John witnessed an explosive return to the native as he held her in his arms. Her cries of pleasure and passion were a very powerful motivator to drive him to new lengths of endurance. And when at last he finally exploded within her, she echoed a strange long warble and lie exhausted beneath him. It took several minutes for either of them to have the breath to speak. Then she saw to Matthew, making sure he was within the protection of the tarp and netting, covered up and snug. As she lay back beside John, he heard her say, "I think tonight we have started another life, my husband. Maybe girl, maybe another son. Time will tell."

He drew her in close and kissed her forehead, cheek, nose, and chin, repeatedly. "God, woman, I love you," he finally said and they snuggled down together as the night grew chilly.

Baby Matthew woke early in demand of his breakfast. Ronnie rose up out of their blankets, naked and not seeming to even notice the chill of the morning. John watched her change their son, then bring him to lie between them as she gave her breast to him. When Matthew had finished with the first breast Ronnie turned her back to John to give the baby the other. John crawled over her and without disturbing his son he took the emptied breast into his own mouth. It was warm and silky with just a few drops of milk to flavor it and John licked and sucked until he heard Ronnie moan with pleasure and he knew he had to have her again. With their son calmly draining her pap, she opened to John and he slid into her. Her physical restrictions fueled her desire and just as the baby was nodding off to sleep, Ronnie quietly surged and trembled and took John with her. They all slept peacefully for another hour.

The birds were singing, the sun was shining and all was right with the world. They had eaten their breakfast, packed up their belongings, and were walking their horses as they explored.

"This is all ours, sweetheart, for acres and acres. What do you think? Do you think you could be happy living here?" He looked over at her and was surprised to see she was not smiling.

"Just… us… all alone?" she said so softly he almost didn't hear her.

"I thought that was what you wanted, to get away from all the people," he looked confused.

"I like people. Nice people. People who understand Indian way. You mother, you Uncle Richard…"

"*Your* mother… it's *your*," he corrected.

"Your mother, your uncle, your sister Louise, good people."

"Sweetheart, now I'm confused. I thought you'd be pleased."

"I do not understand, Jack. How can you be sachem of tribe if you no live with tribe?"

"It's not exactly the same thing and since it's only a one day ride I could go in regularly to take care of business."

"And I would be all alone, no women?" she said in a small voice. "Even at fort I have the commander's wife to pass time with while you do soldier business."

They were standing on a ridge. John did not know it but it was the same ridge his father and Richard had lain on watching the newly constructed Indian village as they tried to figure out where his mother was. John looked out and around, everywhere he looked he saw trees and more trees. There was the creek flowing westward, there were birds and squirrels and he thought Ronnie would be thrilled with it all. Then he remembered. The stories his parents told about how the "big brave" had thought his mother was being punished because Father had brought her out into the wilderness and left her "alone." Alone to an Indian was ostracism, punishment, not the normal way to live.

"I think I understand now," he said as he looked back at his wife and softly stroked her hair. "So maybe someday we can build a house here and we will have workers, staff to help run the place, and a passel of children running around and a few neighbors, just the *good* people, right? But for now, I guess staying near Mother and having help in the nursery and Margot to cook and Jane to clean, and Uncle Richard to tell stories to the children is best."

Her face lit up again and she smiled. "Maybe this be place we come to hunt, to spend time alone together, and make babies?"

"Darling, that sounds good to me."

Chapter 8

The wedding was over. It had been exhausting, but all the work had been a diversion. Miss Lilly had outdone herself again and designed a complete trousseau for the bride who was moving into Boston's nascent high society. Isabelle had left home to start her new life.

It was another sleepless night for Marie, who found herself tossing and turning and finally could stay in bed no longer. She remembered the forgetfulness laudanum had once given her and thought of asking Doctor Ajax for a very small bottle. Who was to tell him she had been forbidden? Then, she remembered what she had put Jacques through, all the suffering, the wasted time, the fears and rejection and he had never stopped loving her. She chastised herself for even considering the drug and found herself near tears again.

She put on her night wrap and quietly went downstairs looking for Jacques' cognac. Better to get quietly drunk and face her punishment the next day, heaving her guts out with a crushing hangover. Bringing the decanter and glass up the stairs she noticed light coming from Richard's room. The door was not completely shut. Good. She wouldn't have to drink alone. Richard had never turned down a glass of Jacques' cognac. Padding softly down the hall she saw him sitting on the settee before the fire. He'd lost weight since Rafe's death and was looking more like the old Richard. She knocked which caused the door to open wider.

"Richard? I cannot sleep either. Would you like to join me?" She held up the decanter.

"Marie," he acknowledged her presence. "When did you begin drinking cognac?" He stood and found his water glass, presenting it to her. He was moving much easier these days between regular visits to the Swedish sauna house and sessions with Thor's stepmother Ingrid with her magic massages. Marie, Jane, and Margot all saw to it that he ate healthfully for his age. And not trekking in the wilds and sleeping on the ground did much to facilitate his improvements as well.

"I do not… at least I never sought to drink it before. Perhaps I thought it would make me feel closer…" she didn't finish the sentence but poured Richard a liberal glass and a smaller one for herself. She took a seat on the settee and he joined her. "I must apologize to you," she said softly and he looked at her. "I thought I knew what loss was." She took a sip of the cognac and closed her eyes. It was strong but the lingering taste after she swallowed reminded her of Jacques' kisses. "I thought I had lost so much in my youth; I thought I knew loss but I did not. I had Jacques." She drank again and let the liquid roll around in her mouth before she swallowed.

"Never have I felt such… emptiness. The incurable ache. Only now can I appreciate what you have been going through, how deep the wound at losing Rafe." She took another swallow, she could already feel it going to her head. "And now we have both lost Jacques. Oh, Richard, how have you done it? Everyday I feel like my insides have all been spilled out onto the ground, the emptiness is so complete, only to discover the next day I feel like I am losing my insides all over again, ripped out and laid raw."

"Like Prometheus," he muttered.

She looked at him in puzzlement.

"A schoolboy story. A Greek god who dared give fire to humans, so he was punished by being chained to a rock where each day his liver was eaten out by an eagle, but each night it grew back because he was immortal."

"Oh," she said and took another swallow. "Thank God we are not immortal. At least I know at some point this must end." She sat quietly for a time watching the flames. She drained her glass. "And if this is what John went through… twice… no wonder the poor boy hid away for ten years. I should apologize to him as well. I cannot fault him. I cannot blame him. What can you possibly write to someone when you feel like this?" Richard also finished his drink and she poured them both another. There was a soft blur to her senses now and it was somehow soothing.

She sipped.

"I have tried to pretend Jacques has only gone to New York Towne. I spent nights alone in our bed when he was off somewhere… but it does not work. I cannot forget that he is never coming back. I cannot stop remembering that he has left me forever…" She sipped some more. "He said 'until death parts us'… his vows, our vows, they were only good until death parted us… and now he has left me all alone." She sipped some more.

Richard said nothing as he watched her, she was still such a lovely woman and her heart was as broken as his. He wanted to wrap his arms around her, embrace her, caress her, kiss her but… he could not take advantage of her like this. They were two broken hearts.

They sat for a long time, she watching the fire, he watching her. He got up, poked at the burning logs, and threw two more on the coals. He returned to his seat.

Marie poured more cognac. She continued to drink. She was beginning to feel as though she was floating while so many memories played out in her mind. Jacques, her Jacques, her love, her life, where was he now when she needed him so desperately?

"He's gone," she said out loud breaking the silence.

"He's gone," Richard echoed.

"He's gone," she repeated. "And my beloved bequeathed me *things* and he bequeathed you… me." She sat quietly staring at the fires. "What do you think he meant by that?" She set her empty glass down and stood, weaving just a little as she went to the bedroom door and shut it tightly. "He gave us his blessing did he not… for companionship, and he told us to love each other?" Standing before him she opened her wrap. The thin fabric of her nightgown did little to hide her in the firelight.

"I cannot take the alone-ness for another night," she cried out softly as she looked at him. "I need to be held, Richard, please, please hold me."

"Marie," he groaned without moving, "Do you know what you are asking? I am not strong enough to just *hold* you tonight."

"I know," she said softly. "And if I forget for a time that you are not Jacques, you must forgive me." She closed her eyes and pushed her gown from her shoulders. As it slipped down her arms and pooled to the floor Richard rose from the settee and carried her naked into his bed.

It was a bittersweet experience for both of them. They spoke not a word. He had wanted her for what seemed like forever and now she gave herself up to him freely, generously, passionately but he knew as her eyes remained shut, he was Jacques to her. And he enjoyed the pleasures of her body and the passions of her heart only because his best friend was now dead.

From the moment he touched her naked flesh he was as a man who had been living half starved his whole life. She was so soft, a tender, delicate creature but also a jungle cat of sharp claws and sharper teeth, at once pliant and giving, yet unyielding and demanding. He had her while her low moans and rapid gasps were a siren sound to drive a man mad and which drove him beyond the limits of his endurance. He felt himself dissolving metaphysically from one form to another. He had been heavy base lead now turned to brilliant gold, lifted until he knew the sharp smash of glass being reduced back to powdered sand and forged molten into a hard unyielding shape again all within the crucible of her. A sizzling fire that consumed but did not burn. As his heartbeat thudded in his ears he wondered briefly if this was not how Jacques would have preferred to meet his end. And he knew that he could happily die at that moment in her arms.

Later, in complete exhaustion she snuggled in to him, her flawless derrière nestled warm and comforting against his groin, her arms pulling him around to hold her, his one hand filled by her soft, full breast, he felt guilty and yet, so satisfied and alive. Her quiet regular breathing told him sleep had come to her at last. He remembered he had once told Jacques a woman was a woman in the dark, implying they were all much the same. Jacques had disagreed and now Richard realized how very right his friend had been!

He had bedded countless women. Was it because he loved her so that this had been an experience unlike any he had ever had before? Or was she so incredibly unique? She held back nothing, she gave everything and if he must be Jacques to her, he could accept that... for now. He knew she loved him as a friend, someday perhaps she would open her eyes and see him as her lover. But did this not presuppose he had served her well enough to receive another invitation?

Shortly after dawn Marie awoke and rose from the bed. Richard opened his eyes. She collected her gown and pulled on her wrap, tying it tightly around her. Taking a peak out the door she padded off quickly to her room. She never once turned to look at him, Richard observed. Did she feel guilt? Shame? Or was she just perpetuating the illusion that she had somehow spent the night with Jacques?

Chapter 9

Chartes Landing - Four Years Earlier

"Janey," Richard stood in the foyer and called out to the faithful house-keeper. It only took a moment for her to appear, hustling rapidly from another room.

"Yes, Master Richard. Is something wrong?"

"To the contrary," Richard smiled in his teasing way. "I have been asked to deliver a message. Pack an overnight bag and put on your best big city bonnet. You are to accompany Monsieur Jacques and me, as we send off Masters Richie and Raphael for another season."

"But why? You know I don't care much for the water." she frowned and began to wring her hands.

Richard gave his best Gallic shrug. "I know not, Janey, perhaps they felt you were due a change of scenery. Has it not been over a year since Monsieur Sims passed?"

"Yes, but I'm just fine, sir, truly, I don't need no trip for diversion."

"Janey," Richard said more softly, "I do not believe it is a request. It is the master's orders."

"Oh dear, oh dear." She pat her coif and smoothed her apron.

"We leave in a half hour, now hurry, hurry."

They left in Richard's boat. Jane sat stiff and still, making herself small and eyeing the water with distrust. Most of the conversation was monopolized by Raphael and young Richie as they spoke of the kind of goods they thought they should bring.

The daylight hours were getting longer but still night fell quite early. Once they arrived in New York, the five went to The Pork 'n' Porridge for a hot meal and a room. That night, Jacques asked for another bed to be brought into his room. Richard and Rafe shared one, Jacques and Richie the other. Jane was in a shared room with another woman and Jacques did not know it but Jane had brought along her own sheet to lay upon her half of the bed where she slept fully clothed. The Thompkins would have been offended if they knew Jane did not consider *their* standard of *clean* to be up to *her* standard of *clean*. Sheets at even the best inns were rarely changed but once a week and you might not be the first one to sleep on them.

The next day Richard went with the young men to help them get stocked up for their trading trek while Jacques cheerfully guided Jane to accompany him to the Harbor Master's offices.

Stepping into the familiar office, Jacques held the door for the faithful housekeeper. It seemed like only a few years ago that he had had the good fortune to happen upon her and her husband, but that had been the year of the hurricane, the year of John's birth. That was almost thirty years ago Jacques realized as he went to the board posting the recent arrivals.

"I am seeking indentures, have you had any ships come in with them?" Jacques asked not seeing any notes or indications on the board. Indentures, unlike slaves, could be on any ship in any quantity.

"Waste of time," said the Harbormaster briskly, "usually gone before we can make note. Slavers is different. Selling on the wharf is frowned upon. The auctioneers expect the whole lot to be brought in so they can sell them on the block midtown. Looking for their commissions, I expect."

"I am not interested in slaves, monsieur. What would you suggest?" Jacques frowned. Things were constantly changing. Nothing stood still and New York Towne had become an extremely busy port with very few graces... like common courtesy for example.

"Just stay close and watch for new arrivals is the best I can advise," the man said brusquely and turned his attention to his papers.

Jacques bowed slightly to the man and escorted Jane out the door.

"What kind of indentures are you looking for, sir?" Jane asked as she pulled her bonnet down more tightly over her coif. The wind off the sea was quite stiff.

Jacques made certain his own hat was snug as he took her arm and led her along the wharf front. It was crowded and they found themselves bobbing and weaving to avoid collisions.

"This is the surprise, my dear Jane," he smiled broadly. "Do you realize you have been with us almost thirty years?"

"Yes, sir." She looked at him with bird-like eyes.

"Please do not misunderstand. We have no desire to see you leave us. No-no, Madame Marie and I expect you to consider our home your home for the rest of your life."

"Thank you, sir," she sniffed slightly, waiting for the *but*.

"However..."

There it is. "However," "but," same thing.

"...we do feel it is only prudent on our part to begin training someone to take over in the eventuality that you might want to start slowing down a little."

Might as well say when I croak.

"You have always been an excellent housekeeper, Jane. You have taken care of us... well, like a mother, is this not so? And who is better qualified to train up someone to follow in your footsteps but you?"

So tightly were her stomach muscles tensed that Jane was at a loss for words.

"Make no mistake you will continue to be the *head* housekeeper but it is time for you to have a trainee under you. We have had girls before but they were young and they married and moved on. This time we look for someone perhaps a little more mature. Perhaps a couple, like you and Donald were? We must depend on the help of Providence, I am afraid, for a housekeeper like you does not come along every day." Jacques was very sincere and he hoped he had soothed the woman's feelings.

"Time goes on, Jane, and we all get older. I have slowed down, Monsieur Richard has slowed down, I just want to make sure you have the opportunity to slow down a little as well… if you want. At the same time I do not want to lose the great benefits you have given us with your most excellent care." He saw her stiffened shoulders relax a little and she looked at him again. "Yes, yes, benefits. Have I not told you? After the things my son shared with me about the unseen world around us, the tiny things called *micro-organisms* that can only be seen with the micro-scope, I am convinced your superb standards of cleanliness have saved my family from diseases and sickness. Yes, I am convinced of it."

Jane actually gave him a small smile.

"I never knew you felt that way, sir."

"Yes-yes, and you can imagine how important it is for me to know that you are training someone who will take the same care of us."

"I do remember the girl we called Dulsey. T'were Miss Helen what took her."

"That is right, I had forgotten her," he continued. "So now you must help me keep a look out. If a ship has indentures they usually post some kind of sign. There are fresh ships arriving almost every hour."

"I think we should perhaps watch especially for a Dutch ship, sir," Jane offered, warming to the task. "The Dutch women do know how to clean. German women too, but I hear they travel mostly in families and don't indenture themselves very often."

They stayed by the docks all day moving from here to there as they saw new ships arrive. None of them were Dutch and none of the indentures pleased Jane.

As Jane fell asleep that night she thought again about what Master Power had said. He was right. She needed to begin training someone. It would take a long time and goodness, it might take several years just to find someone worth the training.

They were up at dawn, ate a good breakfast, took box lunches with them and parted company again. Jacques and Jane went their way starting at the east docks where the fishing fleet had already departed and there was room for new arrivals to unload. Richard went with Rafe and Richie to see them off at the west docks. The trio waited for their trade goods to be delivered after which they carefully loaded up their square-sailed boat. The sun was shining brightly as the young men sailed off up the Hudson, waving a fond farewell for another eight or nine months.

Richard caught up with Jacques and Jane just as the *Zeemeermin* pulled into dock. Jacques guessed it was Dutch and from the gaudily painted carving on the prow of a big busted woman with bright pink nipples and the lower body of a fish, he also guessed *zeemeermin* meant mermaid, or something like it.

Gulls were screeching as they flew about pulling fish from the water and pouncing upon any crumb carelessly dropped on land. The men were used to the sounds of the birds and the noises of the humans shouting back and forth to each other. For Jane, however, it had been a long time since she had been in such apparent chaos and it was hard for her to keep focused.

As soon as the gangplank was lowered Jacques stepped forth and asked about indentures.

"*Yah-yah*," a stocky little dutch man with a brimless hat replied. And so, they waited.

A crowd of passengers came up on deck. Jacques, Jane, and Richard were the first in line at the gang plank and had an excellent view as the individuals came forth. Jacques spotted the plump woman dressed in an impossibly clean, starched apron and cap as soon as her feet hit the deck and he noticed a younger version of herself following closely at her side. When the deckhand unhooked the thick rope that ran across the opening from the gangplank, Jacques immediately headed toward these two women.

"Do you speak English?" he inquired.

"*Yah, mijheer*," came the reply with a curtsy from both of them.

"You are together?"

"Mine daughter Phoebe, *mijheer*, and my name Nora. Much we would like to be staying together, *yah?*"

"My name is Power and this is my Head Housekeeper Jane Sims," he replied. "I am looking to add to my household staff. Jane would you be so kind as to talk with Nora and Phoebe and tell me what you think, while I speak with the Captain."

"Very good, sir," Jane replied and turned her bird-like eyes on the women. "And how would you proceed to clean out a fireplace?" she asked the young one without preamble.

"Oh," the girl squeaked when she realized Jane was looking directly at her.

"Ashes sweep to pan and go to ashes bucket, *yah?*"

Immediately the mother said something in Dutch which sounded very much like a scolding.

"What would you do?" asked Jane of the older woman.

"Damp cloth is good to keeping dust down. Hang cloth over opening before to sweep. Shovel as much ashes as I can into bucket, only sweep last small bit. Make less dust."

Jane was impressed but she didn't say so. She continued with several more questions before Jacques returned.

"So tell me, Jane, what is your expert opinion?" he asked and Richard stifled a grin.

Jane took a couple of steps away and turned her back to the women. "The mum knows what she's about, sir, but the young one ain't got the sense of a sardine."

"Mmm, still I would hate to separate family from each other. She is very young, only thirteen I am told. If you discover you cannot train the daughter, perhaps we could use her elsewhere."

"Yes, sir." And the expression on Jane's face said she didn't think the girl worth the bother.

Jacques bought the contracts.

Nora's contract was for seven years and she began working directly under Jane, who soon found the woman a trustworthy soul when it came to the gentle art of housekeeping. Not that there was anything gentle about beating rugs with a carpet beater until your arm felt like it would fall off.

Phoebe's contract was for ten years and she began working it off as a scullery maid under Jane's dubious eye. More than once Jane would have gladly taken the carpet beater to the young girl's backside rather than to the carpets if the Powers were not opposed to physical punishments. But when young Phoebe left a filthy trail of ashes, cinders, and clinkers spilling from the ash bucket as she wandered through the house, Jane was absolutely apoplectic.

"I can't deal with her, ma'am! Lord knows I've tried! The ninny has the attention span of a flea and nothing in her head to think with but air. She makes for more work than she does and she'll be the death of me. I can't see any way out but to rid ourselves of her. Take her back to New York Towne and sell her to some poor unsuspecting soul," Jane huffed to Marie who was reading in the library.

Marie remembered what it was like to be thirteen and alone in the world and while she had never been so inept still she could not bring herself to separate mother and daughter.

"Jane, please, calm yourself. You will make yourself ill. I will not sanction separating the two."

"We can't sell her here in Chartes Landing, ma'am. Even if you was to find someone who couldn't tell just by lookin' at her that she's a witless chit, you'd be making an enemy for life if you stuck 'em with the likes of her," Jane fumed.

"I understand your feelings, Jane. Now please send both mother and daughter to me. I wish to speak with them."

"Yes, ma'am."

Marie sat patiently waiting in the library. She saw no reason to disturb

Jacques with this domestic issue if she could come up with a solution herself. In mere moments there was a soft tap on the door.

"Come, come," she said and watched mother, neat as a pin, and daughter, soiled, stained, and disheveled, walk in looking apprehensive. "Nora. Phoebe," she acknowledged them. They curtsied. "Nora, I have been hearing nothing but good things concerning your work. And I want you to know I appreciate it. Please have a seat." Nora sat and as Phoebe was about to sit, Marie stopped her. "Phoebe, you cannot assume that just because I offered a seat to your mother, that I am offering one to you. Would you turn around please?"

The girl halted, looked surprised, and turned with her back to Marie.

"Do you know you have something that looks like food on the back of your skirt?"

Nora jumped up as the girl spun a bit like a dog chasing its tail, trying to see. There was a barrage of Dutch during which Nora pulled Phoebe's skirts around and gathered them over the sticky food, capturing it from soiling anything else. "I am so sorry, Mistress Power," Nora said.

"There is no harm done, but Phoebe, you puzzle me. Now, if you can keep the mess away from my upholstery, then you also have permission to sit… carefully."

The girl sat.

"Phoebe, do you like it here?"

"Oh, sure, mistress, it is…" began Nora.

"No, Nora, please. I wish your daughter to speak for herself. Phoebe, do you understand my English?"

"*Yah*," the girl nodded.

"Good. Now I want you, not your ma-ma, to answer; do you like it here?"

The girl looked at Marie, then looked down and shrugged.

"A shrug as a reply tells me that perhaps you are not so happy here, yes?" Marie again cautioned Nora not to speak.

"I want not to leave home," the girl said sullenly.

"Ah, I see, did you have friends you left behind?"

Phoebe nodded.

"I understand. It was sad to leave them, yes? But I also know your mother decided the best thing for you and for her was to come to the New World and work to build a better future. When I was your age, I would have done anything to have a ma-ma who loved me and cared about my future but my ma-ma died when I was only three. If your ma-ma thought coming here was the right thing to do, then you must trust her. Trust that she is wanting what is best for you.

"Monsieur Power and I both worked very hard to build the home we have here. I came here with nothing and my first day in the New World I was robbed of the few coins I had saved. I tell you this because I want you to know, no one gave us anything. We worked very, very hard and struggled through much but it was worth it, yes? We have been rewarded for our efforts.

"Now, you heard me tell your ma-ma that we are pleased with her work but I am also hearing that Mistress Jane is not pleased with *your* work. She tells me you are not attentive, you are sloppy and messy when the whole point of your job is to make things clean. Your behavior just now seems to say the same thing. Would you make my chair that I worked very hard for all sticky just through carelessness?"

The girl sat staring into her lap holding her crumpled skirt.

"Phoebe, perhaps I should tell you how things could be. We own the contract for your work. We could take you back to New York Towne and re-sell your contract… and keep your ma-ma here. It would be our right to do so. The next person who bought your contract could take you perhaps to their farm on the frontier where you would fear Indian attacks. Where you would have to work in the fields and face crop failure meaning there would not be enough to eat. And do you think they would feed you as they might feed their own children if the food was scarce? They might beat you… it is also within your owner's rights to do so. And because your ma-ma was not there to care about your well being, you could get sick and die. That is how it could be.

"Now you must tell me… if you have a worker who will not work, who does not care about doing a good job, why should you keep them?"

Phoebe looked up at Marie, fear registering in her eyes. "Please send me not away, mistress."

"I do not want to, Phoebe, but you must do much better than you have been. Do you understand? You must *want* to do well. You must listen to your instruction and work hard. I am giving you a second chance to apply yourself and stay in our safe home near your ma-ma. Do not disappoint me."

The girl shook her head vigorously.

"Good, now go and change your skirt. Wash your face, comb your hair, and put on a fresh apron." Marie dismissed the girl and turned to Nora. "You are excused as well, Nora. You may go back to your duties."

The two mothers looked each other in the eye.

"Thank you, mistress."

Marie nodded.

There was no doubt that Phoebe's attitude changed. She was much more attentive to what she was told. She was more pleasant, better groomed, and she was truly trying her best. The difficulty seemed to be that she just wasn't any good at spotting dirt like her mother or Jane. After a good six months trial, they settled her into helping the laundress. She did what she was told under close supervision. And when the weather was foul or there was little to no laundry to process, Phoebe liked to help in the kitchen.

It was soon discovered that the girl had a knack for baking and most especially for baking sweets. Marie was very pleased to hear it but Nora noticed her daughter soon needed all her clothing adjusted, and she let out her seams to accommodate her growing waist line.

"What are you doing *mijn dochter*, eating as much as you serve?" Nora asked in Dutch. "Keep this up and you never find a husband."

"*Moeder*, by the time my contract is over, I will be twenty-three. What man will want me then? My best years will be gone."

"*Nee-nee,*" Nora cried, "Mistress Marie is a good woman. If you are good baker and you find good man there is no reason you could not marry and continue to do baking, huh? Marry, have children. But if you turn into huge doughnut, what man will even look!"

"I want man who wants woman with a little meat on her bones, *yah!*" Phoebe said saucily and went back to the kitchen.

Chapter 10

It was early November 1725. A new year would soon arrive. Marie stood looking at the dining room table and began counting on her fingers. Christmas would mark seven months since Jacques passed but she knew in her heart that he would have wished nothing so much as the family gathering as it always had for the holidays. And planning a Christmas feast was a project to occupy her mind. She remembered the time when she had asked Donald Sims to construct yet another leaf to accommodate their growing numbers. The children had always been allowed to "graduate" from the children's table and join the adults once they had passed their twelfth birthday. The grandchildren were growing up and even with the losses, the table was becoming too crowded.

Marie counted fifteen family now that Richie and Clarissa had returned, not including her and Richard which made seventeen and she fully intended for Jamie's Cynthia to join them – eighteen, and she was going to invite Lyndyn – nineteen. And Jane, of course, she had always shared their Christmas feast – twenty. With John and Ronnie still here, Marie held out no hope of convincing Isabelle and Hamilton to visit for Christmas but this year she again would invite Silas and Netty Weaver, Caroline's parents. There was a good possibility they would not come but if they did, that made the count twenty- two. It was impossible to think of squeezing eleven people at a table side build for eight.

Caroline's parents had been invited to dinners before but Marie discovered they did not feel comfortable dining with "management." However, Marie also knew they had a younger daughter who had married this past spring and left for the frontier while their oldest son was now in the military and their younger one had left home to discover what he wanted to do in life. Reasons, justifications, and sympathies aside, Marie knew the Weaver household would be bereft of children and cheer this year and she hoped they would accept her earnest invitation for a dignified Christmas dinner in a home still in mourning.

William Boot and his exotic wife Ingrid, the masseuse, had begun keeping Christmas on their own several years back when their children began courting. With Thor's sister and brother, Rega and Ansel, now both married with growing families of their own, the Boots had a crowded table on holidays. Thor, Helen, and their children always went to the Boots for the New Year's dinner.

"Jane," Marie called the elderly housekeeper who was always hovering near at hand. "What is the new boy's name again? Tom… Tom… Tom Kenny, is that not right?"

"Yes, ma'am." Jane's face grew a little stiff and suspicious. Tom Kenny was an indentured who had in a sense taken Donald's place as all around fixer and handyman but he had unexpectedly proved himself good at furniture making. He was hardly "new" but so far, he'd kept to himself and not been in the main house.

"Please send word I would like to see him as soon as possible."

"Yes, ma'am."

Marie was aware that Tom Kenny had a soft accent but from where, she did not know; English, Irish, Scottish, Welsh, they were all much the same to her ear. She had never inquired and now, unless it came up naturally in conversation, it seemed almost rude to ask. He was the last indentured Jacques had brought home and that was over a year ago, she realized, yet she had seen little of him in all that time and still thought of him as "the new boy." When he came to the house, she immediately led him into the dining room.

"Tom," she said clearly, "I have a very important project I wish done. If you can do it, I will leave it in your hands, but if not, then you must say so and we will find another." She smiled. He returned the smile and nodded.

"I find my table is becoming too small and crowded. We already have added several leaves and now I would like to have a small table built, same height, same width, and matched carving. Big enough to seat seven people, three on each side and one on the end and to fit very snug up against this end of the big table." She pointed to her end. "When needed we would attach it and when not needed, it would stand alone over there… just a beautiful side table."

He paused to examine the carving along the table's edge and on the pedestal feet. "Hmm," he nodded, "should be nae trouble, nae trouble a'tall. Ye'll have yerself a table fit fer a baronial hall, mum. Ye must be plannin' a rare big feast. By my count ye can already seat eight maybe nine per side easily, that's eighteen-twenty total. Add three more 'n' yer table sits twenty-four or even twenty-six."

"A good number, is it not, Tom?" She asked lightly trying to avoid his blue-eyed stare.

"Beggin' yer pardon, mum, but it's Tom-Kenny."

"Yes, yes," Marie responded just a trifle confused and despite her efforts she found herself caught up in his brilliant blue eyes which were looking at her with almost an air of amusement. "But we are generally not so formal as to always use the last name of... ...our... help."

"Yes, mistress," he nodded again, "and Tom-Kenny be what folks has always called me. Now, Llywelyn, that be my *last* name." The corners of his mouth twitched slightly as though he might have laughed with amusement but for a fear she might take it wrong.

"Oh... I see, well... I am sorry. I did not know." For some reason she felt a sweat break out on her scalp. How could she have a servant for over a year and not know his last name? "Then... Tom-Kenny, do you think you can have the table done and ready by... by Christmas." She broke her gaze from his. "Can I count on it for Christmas?"

"Oh, aye, mistress, ye can always count on me." And after what seemed like an uncomfortably long stare he bowed, turned, and left.

Marie stood in her dining room trying to explain the rapid beat of her heart and the weakness she felt in her body. The boy couldn't be any older than her Jamie. And he was not especially good looking except as all healthy, well nourished young people are good looking. He was lean and well muscled with strong, broad shoulders. And when he'd stepped into the house and pulled his woolen cap from his head, she'd seen his light blond curls tumble about his face and for one brief and yet inexplicably long moment she had seen Jacques just as he had been when working at their cabin site. And now she could hardly breathe and her hands were shaking.

"Nora," she called out to the passing housekeeper. "If anyone should ask, I have gone to my room to lie down for a bit."

"Yes, mistress."

Marie was told Tom-Kenny had returned with his measuring rod and taken precise measure of a number of things regarding the table. He had also spent considerable time sketching, she was told. Then he had left again and she had heard nothing from him since. It was now the first day of December and she was becoming a little concerned. Grabbing her shawl she went out to the workshop beside the tool shed.

As she pulled open the door, Tom-Kenny looked up, smiled, and stood up straight but there was nothing hurried or subservient about his actions. He was alone and the workshop was pleasantly warm and smelled cleanly of fresh wood. A small iron stove in the corner held a fire fed by wood scraps and shavings.

"Good day to ye, mistress," he bowed slightly.

"Good day. How is my table project coming along? I have heard no progress reports," she added.

"Aye. Come, see fer yourself," he invited as he walked up to her, took her elbow and guided her to where he had been standing. "Feel," he encouraged softly as he took her hand and ran her fingers along the satiny smooth grain on the surface of the wood.

As he stood over her from behind, his right hand guiding her right, his breath falling softly on her neck, she thought for a moment she might faint. He was the same height as Jacques. His hand traveled upward along her arm, a slow caress ending along her neck. His fingers lingered as he pushed a loose curl out of the way and a tear rolled down her cheek. He kissed the spot on her neck beneath her ear and her knees went weak. She moaned softly feeling herself drawn into a whirlwind without reason or thought.

"Ye must'a been a child bride for ye be much too young and beautiful to be now left so alone." His finger lifted her chin up towards him, just as Jacques used to do. He kissed the tear from her cheek and she felt his tongue run along her lower lip. She thought she smelled Jacques' cognac.

"Who are you?" she caught her breath.

"I am yours, *mon cœur*," he whispered.

"Jacques?" Marie whimpered and against reason she threw her arms around his neck and kissed him deeply. Her fingers ran through the curls on his head. "Oh, Jacques, *mon amour*, Jacques, Jacques. Say it is true."

Tom-Kenny's hand was pulling up her skirt, past her stockings, and he felt her become pliant beneath his hand.

"Marie, *mon cœur, mon amour, ma fleur, mon petit chou...*"

Marie's eyes flew open. Jacques had never ever called her *his little cabbage*. She gasped and pushed away.

"What are you doing?" she asked but this time her question had the ring of indignation. She pushed her skirts down. "How could you pretend to be my husband? You must think me mad to believe he has returned from the grave."

He stood still, not moving away but looking very sad and holding her with those piercing blue eyes. "I pretend nothing, m'lady, and ye be no maiden t' nae be knowin' what's what, right enough. I only ken my heart and my cock want ye something fierce. T' is a sin t' waste what God gives us. Ye a lonely widow, me a lonely man who wishes only t' service ye well. I could be dead tomorrow. In a year ye could be wed to another. Today is today and all we have."

He could tell by the look on her face that on some level she agreed but she still held reservation as well as an air of displeasure. He had not sufficiently overloaded her senses to block out reason. He stepped in to her again and bent to her neck. It seemed a vulnerable spot. He kissed her, ran his tongue over the tender flesh and felt her weaken and tremble. His hand now held her breast, his thumb brushed her nipple. He continued to kiss her neck as his hand once again pulled up her skirts, past her knees, past the tops of her stockings. His hand slipped under and his fingers found their goal. He was not without skill as he watched her begin to squirm and struggle with desire and hope.

"I… want you… inside me," she gasped at last with closed eyes.

He needed no second invitation.

When it was over Marie stood quickly and brushed vigorously to sweep the wood shavings from her clothes. He joined her in the effort and tried to claim another kiss. She pushed him away.

"I must go," she said suddenly and flew to the door.

Through the open door he saw her running to the house and he smiled.

Richard saw her too. From his bedroom windows he could just see the tool shed and workshop and it did not please him to see Marie running in almost a panic back to the house. He went to his open door and listened. She did not cry out, she sounded no alarm. What the devil could have happened in that workshop to make her wish to run from it so? Unfortunately, Richard could well imagine what might have happened.

He and Marie had never spoken of their night together. And she had never come to him again. But he knew her heart still ached for Jacques. She was so very lonely in the midst of a house full of people. And there was something about that last servant Jacques had come home with that Richard did not like. He was too bold and not at all subordinate in his attitude. And those damn light blond curls were too much like Jacques' had been twenty-five years ago. Richard recognized that Marie was very vulnerable… and a very wealthy widow.

The table was delivered a week before Christmas. The surface shined and by way of a hidden latching mechanism, it joined to the other perfectly. Marie was very pleased but when she turned to Tom-Kenny to thank him, the lustful look he was giving her did not please.

"I think we need to talk," she said with a small scowl when no one was within hearing.

"I agree," he grinned. "But I nae ken as I ever heard it called *talk* before."

"I am serious. And I do mean talk."

"Ye can come to the workshop…"

"No." She cut in quickly.

"Where than?"

"I… I know not at the moment. I must think. I have much to do for the holiday. I will let you know," she said quickly as Nora entered the room. Tom-Kenny left.

That night Marie retired early. She pled fatigue but she only wanted to get away so she could ponder the mysterious spell with which Tom-Kenny could hold her. It was irrational. She knew Jacques was dead. Why did it sometimes feel he might live through this young man. Her mind said neither of them was married nor promised to another. She was no virgin whose maidenhead needed protecting. He was obviously well schooled and practiced in the subject. What were they hurting? What harm was there? But he was young enough to be her child. He must understand there was no future for them. It was only physical, only temporary, only until she could learn to live with her loss. In the past, had not men used her without any emotional attachment? Could not she now use a man without emotional attachment?

She fell asleep as she often did, thinking of Jacques. And he came to her, as he sometimes did in her dreams. It was her one solace, her reprieve from reality, to have him there again beside her. To hold her and love her, to assure her and make love to her. Marie felt the bliss of knowing his touch again, feeling the powerful charge of their flesh molding together. He sucked her breasts as she ran her fingers through his cool curls and felt the ache to have him within her. She felt warm flesh beneath her hands, muscles stretched taut beneath her fingers. She wrapped her legs around his hips. She was almost there and it was so real. She strained and cried out, her heart beating like it would leap from her chest as she rode the crest to the exquisite ending.

Marie awoke. Against all logic she held flesh and blood in her arms. Abandoning reason she whispered hoarsely. "Jacques?"

"If that is who ye want me t' be," came the reply.

"Tom-Kenny!" She scrambled to pull away from him and cover herself. "This is wrong."

"Why?"

"You are younger than most of my children."

"I dinna see you as my mother," he grinned.

"But I am only using you," she said in shame. "You need to find a girl your own age, love each other, have a family."

"I nae thought o'er much of children," he shrugged.

"No, this, this cannot be," she shook her head.

"Do ye not realize the passion ye can drive a man to? Yer sweet to the touch and to the taste. Ye have the skin and body of a woman half yer age and the honeypot between yer thighs? Well, that drowns a man for sure."

"You must not speak that way," she said weakly and pulled away leaving the bed. Her gown was on the floor. She scooped it up and put it on. "I know not how you got in but you must leave…" she looked at him. "now. And no one can see you. Do you understand? My sons would tear you to pieces."

"Then they should not know." He fixed her with his fierce blue eyes and she turned away. He crawled from the bed naked and walked silently to her side. Taking her hand he brought it to him and put it on his rock hard erect flesh. "Would ye leave me this way then? Ye had yer satisfaction, would ye not allow me mine?" he whispered into her ear.

"Fine," she agreed, her sense of fairness in play. "How… how do you wish me?"

"Oh, Mistress, I wish to have ye every way possible but I do not think I can last that long in one night," he smiled salaciously and pressed her down on the bed.

Marie obliged and was soon lost in wanton reveling as she called upon her memories with Jacques.

Marie sat in the library trying to establish the seating for Christmas dinner. As she expected, Isabelle had written she and Hamilton would be spending Christmas with his family. But Silas and Netty Weaver had agreed to accept Marie's invitation. Their eldest daughter and three oldest grandchildren would be filling much of one side of Marie's holiday table. She would seat the older couple next to their grandchildren.

Jamie had assured her Cynthia was coming and Marie decided to seat the girl at her right hand so she could get to know her better. Lyndyn seemed pleased to accept his invitation and Marie would seat him next to Louise.

Marie insisted Jacques' place at the head of the table always be set complete with dishes, utensils, and a napkin as well as a glass of wine. She allowed no one to sit there and no one argued the point. As the eldest, John sat on Jacques' right hand with Ronnie beside him. It was the seat Phillip had occupied all the years John was gone, and undoubtedly Phillip would occupy it again when John and Ronnie left.

There were twenty-one to be seated, not including herself, that made ten on one side, eleven on the other. She tried to think of one more person to even things out. There were three ten year old grandchildren and she couldn't play favorites. Age and pecking order was very seriously considered amongst them. Sarah preferred to celebrate in the kitchen under Margo's jurisdiction with the rest of the staff. If he were still alive, Donald Sims would have filled it, she thought, which led her to think of Tom-Kenny. Immediately she rejected the idea, it was absurd. There was no justifying it. And how would that be anyway? Him sitting there with lust all over his face, undressing her with his eyes.

And then she thought of Miss Lilly. She had worked on Isabelle's trousseau just this past late summer. She had no family of which Marie was aware. She would invite the master designer as a holiday house guest and if Miss Lilly was pleased to accept the invitation Marie would have her table balanced.

Marie sipped her well watered wine and sat back in her chair. This was their first Christmas without Jacques. The first in her children's lives. The first for her since they arrived in America except for that horrible winter he and Richard were trapped wintering in an Indian village. She recalled the Christmases with the Wingates. She had worn her heart on her sleeve for the man. Tears began to form and she made herself think of something else. This was the first Christmas they would have John here since he left for Europe when he was just twenty. She thought about the words of comfort Jacques had given her.

"He is a young man going out into the world, the same age I was when I told my own mother good-bye. But there is a great difference mon cœur, *you have other children to fuss over and our son can always return to us."*

She had sat on Jacques' lap and he had held her and it was true, their son had come home at least for a time. But John would leave again and Jacques was no longer here to comfort her. Suddenly Marie craved the mindless miasma of sex and the forgetfulness it could bring. She grabbed up her shawl and went to the workshop in search of Tom-Kenny.

A letter arrived from Miss Lilly. She was overjoyed to accept Marie's kind invitation and wrote that the packet boat's last sailing before Christmas Day would be on Saturday and she had already secured her passage.

Even with the distractions of the holidays and another guest to prepare for, Marie found herself seeking out Tom-Kenny almost everyday and he was coming to her bed every night. It was like an addiction and like all addicts she was becoming careless. While John was busy, Ronnie noticed Marie's sojourns to the wood shed and the flush on her face when she returned. Ronnie thought nothing of it. Often older widows sought out the young bucks for the solace and comfort they could find in pleasures.

Richard also took notice of the almost slavish way Marie always found some excuse to disappear in the middle of the day. He would not say anything yet. He had no desire to shame her. God knew he had sought mindless comfort in meaningless sex almost all of his life. His one true moment of profound love-making was the night Marie had come to him and ironically it was not himself he had been to her.

But he did not trust this Tom-Kenny fellow. They knew nothing about him. Richard needed to find a way to separate him from Marie. Loosen his hold and his influence over her before something disastrous happened. Like a child? No, Richard was reasonably certain Marie was no longer fertile, though you would not know it by looking at the woman. No, of more concern was that the young weasel might talk her into giving him his freedom, or half of everything she had, or everything she had by law if she married the lout.

It was "men's night" at the Swedish steam bath. Richard had talked John into accompanying him for his weekly visit.

"Madame Ingrid has worked miracles with the muscles of my injured leg. I almost feel like I am thirty again. Almost but who am I kidding, huh? I am an old warhorse now," he said with humor as they sat on the wooden shelves forming steps up to the top and hottest part of the bath.

"You're still full of piss and vinegar, Uncle Richard. I hope you always will be," John chuckled. "And submitting to this torture, you also think helps?" he sat comfortably on the lowest level, sweat glistening from every pore.

"John, wait until you are my age, then you can ask yourself if it helps. The warmth drives all the arthritic pain away. You might remember that for your patients."

They sat amiably for a time in the quiet steam. There was a group of towns-men, who were murmuring amongst themselves, perched on the wooden "steps" built into the other side of the small room. John and Richard, both large men, were left to have the opposite side for themselves.

"I have something I have been wanting to suggest to you," Richard said at last.

"What's that?" John took a cup of cold water and poured it over his head.

"The new fellow, Tom-Kenny I believe is his name, has proved himself a good...... no, an excellent furniture maker. I believe his talents would be much more valued up in say, Boston. I have heard that often when an indenture has exceeding special talents he can be set out to earn for his master. Let us con-sider, to hold the fellow here doing general handyman work is a waste when there may be ten others of sufficient skill to do the same."

"What are you suggesting, Uncle Richard, that I should sell his contract?"

"Not necessarily, he could provide a source of revenue. You might hire him out to a fine furniture making house and the wages he could earn would far ex-ceed the cost of getting a new general handyman, eh? Wages which would be-long to you or more correctly to your ma-ma."

John looked at Richard. "That's rather ingenious."

Richard smiled.

"But why Boston, I should think there are furniture makers in New York Towne?"

Richard shrugged. "Perhaps, but the population is only little more than half. Boston is our largest city. I read it is now 12,000 strong and strikes me as filled with more *hoity-toity* types who will pay very fancy prices for nice things."

John smiled thinking of his sister Izzy. "I shall look into it after the New Year. Would you like to come with me?"

"I leave it in your most capable hands, John. I think I would serve better staying to keep an eye on things here."

John nodded and threw another cup of water over his head.

Miss Lilly arrived and Marie wouldn't think of putting her into the smaller sewing/sick room so she was installed in the last remaining large guest room which was right next to the master bedroom. With her routine disrupted by the rigors of travel and the unfamiliar although very comfortable surroundings of her strange bedroom, the midnight hour found Miss Lilly still wide awake. Even with the heavy draperies at the window, the room was growing quite chilly. She was debating whether to leave the comfortable warmth of her bed to throw another log upon the fire when she heard faint but distinct sounds. Drawn by natural curiosity, she left the bed, slipped on her dressing gown and opened her door.

The hall was a bit warmer and the thick Turkey carpet beneath her feet felt very soft. She discerned that the sounds were coming from the master bedroom. The bedroom of a widow. The walls and doors were sturdy and thick but still…

She paused at the door and bent to the keyhole. She heard the unmistakable sounds of love-making. Miss Lilly smiled, pleased to learn Madam Marie was only a widow, not a corpse. She heard a soft cry.

"Jacques, oh, Jacques, *mon amour.*" Ah, was that not her husband's name? Then she heard a familiar voice reply.

"I'm here *mon cœur.*"

Miss Lilly started. She would know that voice anywhere and the bad French. Had she not taught him that endearment and many more as well? If she were a man she would breakdown the door and challenge him to a duel but she was not and so she must work more craftily.

Christmas dinner was rather sedate but extremely elegant. Jacques' place was perfectly set, as a memorial, a magnificent sprig of holly complete with bright red berries laying across his plate. After John said grace, Marie, looking very lovely even in her gown of mourning black, raised her glass and everyone again grew quiet.

"To Jacques," she looked down to the other end of the long table and in her mind's eye she saw him, "my husband, my beloved, my heart, my knight-in-shining-armor, you are forever present in our minds and our hearts."

Everyone else raised their glass. "To Father!" "To Papa!" "To Jacques!" "To Master Jacques!" "To Grandfather!" "To Grand-papa!" The salutes echoed around the table.

Marie remembered looking across the long table at him last Christmas and how his smile had warmed her. She also remembered how they had all been grieving for Raphael. She looked at Louise and saw her smile at Lyndyn. Next, she looked to Richard and he smiled at her.

She raised her glass again. "And to Raphael who also remains in our hearts."

Again the salute went around the table.

"And now let us see what Margo brings us from her kitchen," Marie said brightly. Margo was in her early seventies now. Her daughter did most of the work but Margo had the energy and the heart to supervise.

Through-out the evening, the conversation was animated but not boisterous and Miss Lilly proved an outstanding dinner guest with many tales to tell of her life in connection with Louis's court and life within the guild. She shared her reason for fleeing.

"Every day grew more stressful, *mes amies*. Rather than looking forward to new business as I should have, every tap on my door had me fearing the *gen d'armes* had come to take me away to prison for being a Huguenot. I could not eat, I could not sleep. My loyal patrons loved me but truly it was not within their power to protect me so finally I fled to England... London."

"London? But then what brought you to the colonies?" asked Louise.

"Ah, it is a cautionary tale which I will discreetly share with so many young ears here to listen." She glanced at the seated grandchildren. "I was most fortunate and found patronage immediately among some bankers and wealthy merchants' wives. People always think one wants only the patronage of the nobility but the truth, *mes amies*, is the nobility are notoriously poor debtors. The merchant's wife, she pays her bills on time."

There was a titter of laughter and nodding heads all around.

"So there I am in London, building up my business and through some strokes of good fortune I built it rather rapidly. I was doing well, I was happy, I was productive... but I was lonely." She looked at Marie. "Then into my life comes a young man of such extraordinary charm, I must confess, my brain took ...a... I believe the English say 'a leave of absence.' Despite the difference in our ages, I had such hopes, such dreams, it was not too late for the family I wanted." She paused and took a sip of wine. "But before I knew what was happening my money was gone, my business on the edge of bankruptcy and his charm? It disappeared along with my money. His physical attentions became very unpleasant and at last I fled for the sake of my well-being."

"Oh, how terrible!" Louise spoke.

"Yes. The sad thing is he had a considerable talent for fine furniture crafting. If he would have applied himself he could have had a very successful business of his own.'

"And what was the name of this prey-er upon women?" Richard rumbled quietly. He was seated at Marie's left hand and next to Miss Lilly. He spoke so only their end of the table could hear.

"His name, monsieur, was Llywelyn, Tom-Kenny Llywelyn."

Marie gasped softly.

They ate, they drank, they told old stories. The young people were excused to pursue their own amusements. Then Caroline got on the harpsichord while Lyndyn turned pages for her and soon everyone was singing favorite caroles.

The hour grew late.

Silas and Netty Weaver were the first to say good-night and leave. Then Phillip and Caroline gathered all their daughters which seemed to empty the house. Jamie left to escort Cynthia home, while John and Ronnie proceeded to the staircase. Ronnie went up to check the children in the nursery but Richard stopped John and asked for a word. Marie convinced Helen to leave her two youngest who were fast asleep in the nursery for the night and she and Thor took only their two oldest home with them. Louise sent Rebecca to bed and saw Lyndyn to the door.

"I'm so glad you came," she said as she helped him with his coat and hat.

"I was very happy to be here. You have a wonderful family, you know."

"Yes, I know. They have been so supportive. It's been hard," she said softly. "I loved Rafe very much but I've finally come to accept that he's gone and there's nothing anyone can do about it."

"Louise, would you mind if some Sunday afternoon perhaps, I… I came to call on you?"

"I wouldn't mind at all, Lyndyn, in fact, I think I'd like that."

"Would next Sunday be too soon?" he asked timidly.

"Not too soon at all. Why don't you plan on joining us for Sunday dinner?" she smiled and sent him on his way.

Marie had fresh sheets put on her bed and insisted Richie and Clarissa sleep there. It was too late, too dark, and too cold for them to ride all the way home and then return for tomorrow when everyone would be exchanging gifts.

"I will be perfectly comfortable in the sewing room," Marie said when they tried to object. Saying good-night, she retired knowing she had warned Tom-Kenny not to come into the house the week between Christmas and New Year. After hearing Miss Lilly's tale, Marie was left feeling cold and glad she would not see him for a time.

Meanwhile Richard and John went into Jacques' old office.

"What is it Richard, you look like you want to run someone through," John said as he poured them each a small cognac for a nightcap.

"No, I was never the swordsman, that was your pa-pa, may he rest in peace. I much prefer the damage a tomahawk can do. You heard the story Miss Lilly told of the no good she had to flee from?"

"Yes." John stifled a yawn.

"I asked her his name and I am certain only our end of the table heard it, but you should know. It is Tom-Kenny Llywelyn."

John stiffened. "Are you sure?"

"A fine furniture maker, she said. And a man who preys on women. I have noticed he's been seeking out your mother lately. Finding ways to spend time with her."

"Really, why didn't you tell me?"

"Your mother's business is her own," he shrugged, "until some predatory whoreson shows himself upon the scene, that is."

"Right. Tomorrow I think I'll have a word with Mister Llywelyn."

It was the day after Christmas and John knew the packet boats were running again. He expected one coming from the south to pull in at some point in the late morning. At nine o'clock, dressed with his sword and pistol at his belt he found Tom-Kenny in his workshop reeking of cognac and rubbing sleep from his eyes.

"Oh, Master John, sir, I weren't expectin' company ya ken? Forgive my appearance."

"Drink enough of my father's good cognac and it will knock you on your arse," John said without humor.

Tom-Kenny grinned sheepishly but didn't deny it.

"I want you to pack together all of your belongings, we're taking a little trip."

"To where, sir, might I ask?"

"To Boston."

"Boston! And what might we be doin' there, sir?"

"That is really none of your concern. As my indentured you go where I tell you." John had ceased even trying to be amiable.

"Beggin' yer pardon but I ken I be part of the goods and chattel what belongs t' the house and your mother. Does she know about this?"

John removed several sheets of paper from his inside pocket. "This is a copy of my father's will. The pertinent part states clearly that I, as head of our family, have administrative power over anything I feel needs my attention. And I have decided that we are going to hire you out to a Boston furniture maker for the duration of your contract which is something more than five years."

"Again I ask, sir, does yer mother know about this? I'd like t' speak with her."

"My mother is more than happy to see you go especially after hearing how you treated a friend of hers in London."

"What?" Caught off guard, Tom-Kenny began to look like a trapped animal. "I'm sure there's been a misunderstandin'..."

"If you ever come near my mother again, I'll have you flogged within an inch of your miserable life," John cut in tightly, using his best British officer tone. "Now pack together your things, you will not be returning."

Richard went looking for Marie and on a hunch he headed toward the site of the old cabin. He found her, wrapped in the first fur Jacques had given her and perched on the big rock, looking out to the harbor. When she heard him approaching, she turned to see who it was then turned back and remained silent. He too remained silent as he sat down beside her.

The day was fair despite the cold and they sat like that for a long time. Finally he heard her say, "I feel like a fool."

"Sooner or later we all do foolish things, Marie, but doing a foolish thing does not make you a fool."

"Does everyone know?"

"No… no, even John does not know everything, only that the man is a threat, a *prédateur.*"

"When I think of what he did to Miss Lilly… I am so ashamed."

"You have nothing of which to be ashamed."

"I was so… so… how do you say *crédule,* do you know?"

"They say 'gullible.'"

"Yes, that is right. I was gullible. He seemed to cast a spell, Richard. All I could see was Jacques. But in truth, he looks not at all like Jacques." She gave a tight, humorless laugh. "We old widows are ripe for the plucking, are we not?"

"Marie," he scolded softly. "You are not old." He shifted and reached out to smooth a curl from her cheek. "In my eyes you will never be old."

She looked up at him then and saw love and kindness in his eyes.

"Richard," she breathed softly. "I know you have deep feelings for me. I have not come to you again in these past months because I wished not to just use you while I try to understand my own feelings. I did not mind using… it was mindless… meaningless… all the while I saw only Jacques."

"I know. I understand."

She leaned over and kissed him gently on the mouth.

Chapter 11

1726

Nora and Phoebe were as sad as anyone when Jacques Power died. He was a good man, they told each other and Nora even wept a few tears. She had developed a little crush on the man and his charming, gallant ways. He had always treated her with respect, like a person not a slave.

"Always the good they are taken from us too soon. Why do the good die young?" she asked her daughter.

"*Moeder,* he was not that young."

"You are only seventeen. Wait until you are older, you will have a different idea of what is young. I feel so sad for the mistress, she will be lost without him. Such a tragedy."

Nora continued to mourn with Marie until one morning in early spring, she happened to see Marie leave Mister Richard's room in her bed dress.

"Hardly to believe my eyes, I can," she whispered to her daughter in Dutch. "Her husband barely cold and she in another man's bed."

"Maybe she was not. Maybe he is sick and she was checking on him."

"Have you seen him sick?" Nora asked sharply. "The man has been acting much too happy. Now I know why. He *neuken* the mistress."

"*Moeder*, such language! I cannot believe you use!" Phoebe almost giggled. "Maybe he help her forget being so sad. It has been a year now. Life must go on."

Nora looked at Phoebe. It *had* been almost a year.

"Nothing," she raised a finger to her daughter's face, "do you say to anyone about this."

"Never. I do not wish to be sold to a farm in the wilderness," Phoebe said as she walked away. *Besides,* she thought to herself, *I have found a lumberman whose sausage knows how to make my doughnut happy.*

John was sitting in his father's office making some notes on a patient. John had been granted an official year's leave of absence which would soon come to an end. Tom-Kenny Llywelyn was safely settled with a Boston furniture making house and the owner had been appropriately warned of his questionable character and need for close supervision. The revenue from his earnings went directly into Marie's bank account on a quarterly basis. Setting that whole Llywelyn situation aside, nothing unusual had happened, no crisis, no quarrels, and Mother seemed to be doing well enough watching over her store which Lyndyn and Caroline ran together. He didn't see any reason he couldn't go back to his post as soon as Doctor Ajax returned to the settlement. Ronnie had been most supportive and he now wanted to get her back out to the frontier so she could visit with her family. Matthew was fourteen months already, Sunshine was two and a half, Gray was five and a half and getting tall. Ronnie had been right about them starting a new life during their first visit to their property. She'd just given birth to their second son, Mark, but Indians never saw any impediment to traveling with an infant.

"John. Good. I caught you," Marie said as she entered the office and sat down. If John didn't speak she could well believe it was Jacques' ghost sitting there. "I need to talk with you about something so you can tell me what you think."

"Of course, Mother, what is it?"

"The girl Phoebe."

"The chubby one who bakes?" he said with recognition.

"Yes. I am afraid she is going to get even chubbier."

He looked at his mother expecting more of an explanation.

"Her mother tells me she is *enceinte*."

"Who is the father?" John frowned.

"I am told it is one of the lumbermen, an Eric Vandercleft," Marie said with a weary sigh. "The girl is soon to be eighteen and she will have a baby for which to care. Her contract was very long, ten years. She has worked off almost half of that. Would it be such a terrible thing to simply forgive the rest and set her free?"

John sat for a moment thinking and tapping his index finger on the desk. Finally he spoke. "It would set a bad precedent."

Marie looked at him.

"What if after you did this every indentured female believed if they got themselves with child they would be let out of their contract?"

Marie considered this scenario and realized it could be a problem. Even if they did not forgive the contract of the next woman, there could be resentment and unhappiness because they did it for one girl.

"You are right. But I want the contract reduced to the standard seven years, yes?"

"That is reasonable. By serving seven years very few would even realize you'd given her a three year wedding present," John leaned back in the chair. "So when is the wedding?"

"That is another thing I wish to talk about. The father-to-be is reluctant, it would seem. The mother says he has not been around since Phoebe told him she suspected."

"I shall talk to Phillip."

"I think he works for Thor."

"Then I shall talk to Thor. People must be held to their responsibilities. Don't worry about it. We'll take care of it. Mother, I've been meaning to talk with you myself. I'm tying up some loose strings with Sir Reginald. Ronnie and I are planning on heading back out to the frontier soon. I'm just waiting for Ajax to return."

"Oh, John, must you go? You could resign could you not?" She looked at him in such a wistful way he felt a little guilty.

"It's not just me, Mother. Ronnie has family there and in less than two years, Gray will be seven and from what I understand this is a big step. His mother will turn him over to the male head of the family which is her cousin, Yellow Rock. It's a rite of passage ritual and from then on he will be trained up as a warrior, no longer under the wing of his mother."

"At seven? How sad," Marie grimaced.

"From then on he stays with the tribe and if he ever wants to see his mother, he'll have to make the effort."

"I cannot imagine losing you and your brothers when you turned seven. Her heart will ache for Gray."

"It is their way."

She nodded but looked at him sagely. "Somehow I do not think that makes it any easier for a mother to bear. So when is Ajax returning?"

"Soon. I expect him at any time. His last letter told me he had already booked passage on a ship out of Liverpool planning to arrive now within weeks."

"So soon," she gasped.

"It has been a year, Mother. And everything here seems to be running along pretty smoothly."

"When will we see you again?" she asked sadly.

"If all continues as planned, we'll come back when Gray turns seven. After he's been turned over to the tribe I think perhaps Ronnie will need the diversion."

"Almost two years."

"More like eighteen months."

Marie smiled wanly and gave a small dismissive shrug. "John, just please write often. To hear from you will give me a sense of peace… that is not exactly the right word. I need to hear that you are still *connected* to us and all is well."

"I promise I will write."

"Good."

John went to the mill the next morning to ask Thor about Eric Vandercleft.

"Strange you should ask about him, John. He asked to leave the mill this year and transfer to the lumberjacks. They left for the season two weeks ago and went up to the logging camp."

"I didn't realize you were still doing that."

"The young ones don't mind coming here for their winters. At the mill they continue to earn for their family and it brings them closer to the cat-house," Thor grunted a smile. "Mind my asking what your interest is in Eric?"

"Apparently he's been a little free and lose with the daughter of our housekeeper and now she's with child. The housekeeper's all upset and went to Mother, Mother came to me. He should have stuck with the whores."

"Well, he doesn't work for me anymore. I'll see you around." Thor went back to his work with a dismissive attitude.

John looked around for Phillip and saw him through the glass window of the office. Phillip waved when he saw John and opened the office door inviting his brother inside, away from the noise of the saws.

"You're out bright and early. What brings you to the mill?" Phillip asked with a half-smile.

"Good morning," John said easily and stepping into the office, he closed the door behind him. "Mother came to me yesterday and told me Nora's daughter is expecting a baby and by all accounts Eric Vandercleft is the father. Thor just told me this Vandercleft transferred from the mill to your lumberjacks this spring and has left Chartes Landing. Do you know much of him?"

"Oh, Christ," Phillip looked angry. "I wondered why he developed a sudden desire to start climbing trees. Looks like I'll be riding up to the camp tomorrow. Want to come with?"

"I will if you need me to but frankly, if he's not inclined to do the right thing, what can we do about it?"

"I can fire him!" Phillip snapped.

"You could," John replied, "but I don't see that this would help Phoebe and her child."

"And what would you suggest?"

"Don't you think it might be better to get the couple in a room together. I mean right now we have Phoebe talking through her mother, our mother, me and you… to him. I say let's get him back down here on some pretense and get them together to talk."

Phillip smoldered. "What pretense?"

"Well, I'm rather hoping you could help me with that," John smiled, "but if you go up there with that look on your face he's going to know you know."

Phillip grunted then sighed in a mixture of disgust and acceptance.

"I suppose I could send a message that there's been an accident and we need him back at the mill. He is the last man to join the lumberjacks."

John shook his head slightly. "Considering that when Phoebe told him, he tucked tail and ran to the lumber camp, I'm of the opinion sight unseen that if you just send a message he'll jack rabbit out of the area and none of us will ever see him again." John stood gazing out the office window onto the mill floor but he really wasn't seeing it. He was focused on the problem instead.

Phillip sat looking at John's back.

"We don't have a sheriff or a constable or a fort authority…" John came to the realization that as a bona fide British officer he represented the highest authority in the settlement. "Damn." He turned back to Phillip. "I guess I need to put on my uniform when I accompany you."

"Good, we'll leave tomorrow morning," Phillip nodded.

When John and Phillip arrived at the camp they stayed within the stockade until the men came back from their day's work, hot, tired, dirty, and hungry. Eric Vandercleft was looking forward to a dip in the river and a hot meal, instead he was faced with the two Power brothers, one - his boss' boss, the other - a fully uniformed colonial British officer.

Vandercleft was a surprise to John. Not a very large man, half a head shorter than either brother and quite minute appearing within the group of tall, brawny lumberjacks.

"Eric!" Phillip called. Both brothers saw the look of a frightened rabbit upon the young man's face. Reluctantly he walked to the brothers. "From the look on your face, I'd say you know why we're here. Let's go somewhere we can talk privately."

They went to a spot behind the tool shed. The Olafsons made certain no one bothered them while Mother Sonja informed Sven Junior of the reason for their visit.

"When a man takes his pecker out and swives an innocent young girl, he must accept responsibility for what happens," John said in a level voice of authority.

"Innocent?! Believe me she weren't that innocent, sir," Vandercleft said boldly. "Bengt Solinson had her first, bragged about takin' her maidenhead. I know Charlie Simmons bragged and joked about her. I ain't sure how many besides. I was only the last poor sucker and she tries to pin the baby on me. I have no wish to get married and I sure ain't raising another man's spawn." Vandercleft was shaking but adamant.

John looked at Phillip who looked at him. They both were thinking the same thing. Phoebe didn't exactly sound like a model of virtue and if she had been sleeping around, how could they know who was the father? On the other hand, Vandercleft could just be trying to blacken her reputation in his own defense.

"If that's true, I can fully understand how you feel. However, that is only your side of the story. You need to come back to Chartes Landing with us so we can talk with you both and any other participants. Phillip will explain to your boss here."

"That's fine with me, sir, but I ain't taken no responsibility for her. Damn slut couldn't get her skirt up fast enough."

"I caution you against making disparaging remarks about the girl," John growled. "Nothing's been proven yet. When was the first time you had intercourse with her?" John asked very clinically.

"The first time?" The young man thought for a moment. "It were the day after Easter. She was makin' some disrespectful jokes, almost made me go soft."

John doubted that but it gave him a reference. He was beginning to doubt that Vandercleft could be the father. If his timing was accurate, Phoebe could only be less than two months. That wasn't even time to be absolutely certain she was with child. Mentally he kicked himself, he should have examined the girl before coming here.

"Phillip, stay with him. Let him wash. I'm going to talk to Sven about finding a secure room."

The three men traveled back to Chartes Landing and immediately went to Ajax's office.

"I'll stay here with Vandercleft, you go find Phoebe," John said.

Phillip left.

"Have a seat," John offered as he opened windows and aired out the office which had been sitting closed up in the growing heat of the last few days. "Are you absolutely certain about the first time you…?"

"Oh, sure. Remember as clear as day. It weren't that long ago."

"No, it wasn't. Is there anyone else who might remember you bragging perhaps about swiving her?" John saw Vandercleft screw up his face in what passed for concentration. "It's important."

"Well, I might have said something to Billy. Billy Timkin. He was always joking about how a man would have a hard time reaching her cunt unless he had a long one 'cause of her being so fat."

John tried to hide his distaste. "Look, if Phoebe corroborates the time you first were intimate there will be no need to bring in witnesses. But it is very important that when she gets here you say nothing about the date, understand?"

Vandercleft nodded but looked a little confused. "What does co-arbarate mean?"

"Corroborate? It means to affirm, agreed with… but if you say anything someone could say you were putting words in her mouth. So keep your mouth shut."

The minutes passed slowly. John removed his sword and uniform coat in exchange for a more "civilian" look. He put on a standard somber coat he kept at the office. Finally Phillip arrived with Phoebe and Marie. Phoebe looked scared senseless and as Phillip closed the door behind them Marie spoke.

"Phoebe was afraid to come alone, the only female, and I cannot say I blame her. Nora wanted to come but I forbid her to leave the house. I thought perhaps you are meeting here because you do not want the interference, so I came."

"That's fine, Mother. Have a seat please. Phoebe, please tell me when you and Eric here became… um, lovers."

Phoebe looked at Marie who gave her a small smile and reassuring nod. Then she looked at Eric who was staring at the floor. Then she looked up at John.

"The days, they run one into another, I cannot keep up," she shrugged.

"Take your time, Phoebe," he said calmly. "Remember, I am a doctor and these things are important for your health. Now, it's spring, we just came out of winter. There was Lent and then Easter."

"Ah, *yah-yah*, I remember now. It was Easter. I have my Easter bonnet and Eric admired it and one thing led to another and that was our first time."

"Very good," John said mildly. "Now I need to give you an examination. Please come this way and Mistress Power will stay right with you."

Phoebe immediately looked to Marie who was rising up from her chair. The three went into the exam room where Marie helped Phoebe loosen her clothing before she lay on the exam table.

In a very professional manner, John palpated Phoebe's belly through her shift. The girl's extra layers of fat didn't make it easy but he detected a head and a rear. He resisted doing the typical physician grunt. He looked in her eyes, had her open her mouth and finally, he examined her large breasts which appeared to be quite tender and sensitive.

"When was your last menstrual cycle?" he asked and she looked dumbly at Marie.

"The Curse," Marie prodded. "Your monthly flow?"

"Oh, *yah…*" Phoebe flushed. "I do not know. I forget."

"It's been a while, I wager," he said and motioned to Marie to help the girl dress while he went into the larger room to wait. They came out and took seats.

"Phoebe, are you sure about your Easter bonnet?"

"Oh, *yah*. I was very happy he had noticed."

"Very well, then I must tell you Eric is not the father."

Phoebe's mouth dropped open and the blood began to rise in her cheeks. "How can you say this?" she asked as Eric Vandercleft smiled broadly in relief.

"Because Easter was only a month ago. You are already in your second trimester at least. It is impossible to say for certain unless you can tell me the date of your last menstrual cycle but you are at least five, possibly six months along, maybe even seven. You should be having this baby before summer ends."

Phoebe didn't seem to know how to take the news. On the one hand she would suffer the discomforts of pregnancy a much shorter time than she had thought. On the other hand she would have a small infant to care for sooner than she thought. And it was then impossible to name the father for before Eric she had often slept with two or three during the same time. What would she do now?

Phillip drove the carriage that took them all back to the Power home after they had dropped Vandercleft off at the mill, a free man. Phoebe ran to her mother and John and Marie spoke privately.

"I did not realize the girl was… so loose," Marie said quietly.

"So what do you want to do?"

"Do? There is nothing to do, Mother Nature had this in hand."

"But…"

"John, I will not throw the girl out because she has one child. But I will talk with her. We do not want a second without a proper father."

Chapter 12

The house was growing more empty. Isabelle was gone. John, Ronnie, and their children had departed. James had been camping out on his property overseeing the construction of his house and would soon be wed. That left only Marie, Richard, and Louise with her children. And one little bastard boy born without a father to the housekeeper's daughter. The poor little mite was healthy, well tempered, and certainly not to blame for his unorthodox entry into the world. And Marie had a sobering talk with the new mother clearly stating a second bastard would not be tolerated and Phoebe would find herself sold to a frontier farm.

Thank God for the children, Marie thought. They had filled the nursery and now they filled the house with a robust, healthy energy. Caroline continued to bring her children over every day that she spent in the store so they could be watched and share play and lessons with their cousins. And Caroline was beginning to show that another baby was on the way. They prayed for a boy. Phillip wanted a son so very badly.

Rebecca Bonchance would soon be thirteen. She had been allowed the old "girls' room" when Izzy moved out. Rebecca always ate dinner with the adults now. She had her father's dark coloring and Richard said she looked a great deal like Raphael's mother, a beautiful if tragic figure from his past. Sebastian Bonchance would be eleven in December and was the undisputed lord of the nursery. He had a way about him that often made Louise tear up. Michael was eight and favored his mother in looks, Jeannette at five was just an adorable rascal and her little brother Frances followed her everywhere. These younger ones missed Ronnie's children.

Marie had become much more brazen about her visits to Richard's room. At their age, they didn't often make love and she could open her eyes now when they did. But they talked a lot and he loved to hold her.

"Between the apples, courting, and building, we hardly ever see Jamie anymore. If it were not for your grandchildren, this house would be so quiet," she said one night as they sat before the fire. Autumn had come early and the heat felt good. Richard had his arm around her, keeping her close.

"They are your grandchildren as well, do not forget."

"You are right they are your grandchildren and my grandchildren, *our* grandchildren. In a way," she reflected softly, "it is almost as if we have been married all these years."

"A very chaste marriage," he grinned and could not resist stroking her cheek.

"We share a lot of memories. We three shared so much together."

"Yes, we did."

"Losing the memories is almost as bad as losing the person," she said very introspectively. Richard was like a very comfortable pair of old shoes that never pinched, never raised up blisters, never made your feet hurt. Was she being unfair to him? "I still love him, Richard," she said out loud. "You know I always will. There are times when I almost forget that he is gone. I catch myself expecting to see him in his office or coming up the walkway." She was quiet for a time. "Jacques told me once that he thought if I had gone to New France you would have followed me, would you have?"

"Yes," he replied without any hesitation. "I would have never let you go off on your own. Never. You were so young, so small, so defenseless but so brave. And you owned my heart already. I knew I could not compete with Jacques. He was the handsome young god, the graceful, gallant one. He had the pretty speeches and that magic about him but... if he had not been there, if he had allowed you to go off on your own, I would have pursued you until I wore you down and won you for myself."

"What, you? The man incapable of settling down?" she smiled.

"For years, I told myself I was not made for marriage, that I was incapable of being faithful, that I did not want to be *domesticated* and *civilized* but it was only sour grapes." There was a long silence before he choked out: "But he was my best and closest friend."

Richard always shaved now and Marie ran her hand down his cheek and reminded herself that Richard felt Jacques' loss just as much as she perhaps, if in a different way. She crawled up into his lap facing him.

"I do love you, Richard," she said softly. She looked up into his eyes. "Not just as a brother; I have long loved you as a brother, you know this. But now I find I also love you the other way and I think that is good. I think this is why Jacques gave us his blessing. He knew. He knew in the wake of his leaving us we would need each other. I do need you. And I do love *you*."

In a fevered response, he all but ripped her gown from her shoulders and buried his face on her breasts. She cradled his head. He was straining as she moved on him with maddening restraint. He wanted to climb up into her and live there forever.

"I have been wanting to hear that for years," he panted and took command of the rhythm which finally culminated in an explosion of feeling for both of them.

"Ah, *mon Dieu!*" he cried.

"Oh, Richard!" he heard her sigh after she had groaned her satisfaction and he thought his heart was going to burst.

They took a few minutes to regain their breath while Marie sat comfortably on his lap. Then she left his lap and stood. "Come, put another log on the fire and join me in bed."

He too rose.

"So tell me," she said, pulling the bed covers up around them. "What do you think of Lyndyn as a stepfather to your grandchildren?"

He looked at her. "What is this?"

"Oh, come, have you not seen it? He is surprisingly sturdy and Louise seems to be leaning on him more and more. And since he seems to enjoy the leaning, I would say… it will happen eventually. He has shared Sunday afternoons with her all winter. Have you not noticed him at our Sunday dinners? I am remembering that while Lyndyn was taking care of his mother and sister, he always used to ask me about Louise. Until you came home with tall, gorgeous, gallant Raphael. Then Lyndyn stopped asking. He saw his sister married. He took care of his mother until she died and still I never heard of Lyndyn linked with any girl. I think he has always been in love with Louise."

"Perhaps you are right."

She turned to look into Richard's eyes. "She will never stop loving Raphael, Richard, just as you and I will never stop loving Jacques. But she is young, too young to stop living. It has been almost two years. She needs a good man… just as I do." She leaned over and kissed him tenderly.

"You are right," he said in acceptance.

"Tomorrow is Sunday. I love Sundays. After church, Helen and Thor will bring their children, Phillip and Caroline will bring theirs and the house will again be bursting at the seams. It is good."

Richard was going to say something but stopped himself. He might be wrong or things might work themselves out. Why put a cloud into Marie's sky but he did not think Phillip was keen on Lyndyn joining the family. Richard suspected Phillip, and perhaps Caroline as well, expected Marie to turn the store over to them and them alone someday. And if Lyndyn was married into the family, that was less likely to happen.

"I want to see my daughter happy again but I must admit, I like not the thought of losing the grandchildren from the house. And frankly, Louise has never run a home. Lyndyn lives simply in his mother's old home but I doubt that he could afford to get a housekeeper, cook, maid, and nursemaid. If they do wish to marry, I am going to suggest Lyndyn simply move into Louise's suite."

She looked up at Richard.

"What?" she asked.

"Every man has his pride."

"And would his pride be less offended if Louise was paying for all these things herself. She has the means but one would hope her money could be kept for the children."

Richard shrugged. "You will have to talk with them and see how they feel… that is if they ever speak of marriage. We are putting the cart before the horse I think."

"You are right," Marie yawned. "It is late and I am tired. Come, *mon cher*, let us go to sleep."

Archibald Ajax had returned from Europe on time as promised. He was bubbling over with all the medical theories and practices being argued and debated in Europe. He and John had had several very long conversations exchanging information before John and Ronnie left. Archibald had done most of the talking as he shared the advances he had learned about and at the end, John updating him on his patients. During this, Ajax had spent a lot of time at the Power home. Then John took his wife and children and returned to the frontier. Ajax found he now missed seeing so much of the family, especially the young widow, Louise Bonchance.

Then Phillip extended an invitation to his home for dinner and Ajax discovered Louise to be there as well. She seemed to be putting her grief behind her, he observed, she no longer wore mourning black and her eyes sparkled in conversation.

After dinner he had invited her to take a digestive stroll with him. Phillip and Caroline both had encouraged her to accept. She was acutely aware that this was the first time she had been alone with the good doctor. He had delivered her children but even then they were never alone.

"Are you warm enough?" he asked with the greatest of courtesy.

"I'm quite comfortable, thank you. It's a lovely evening."

"I was unaware that your brother had invited you and I was exceedingly pleased to find you here." He looked over at her. "It appears you are making an effort to put your grief behind you."

"I'm trying, Doctor Ajax."

"Please… call me Archie." She looked up at him. "I'm not talking to you now as your doctor but as a… friend who'd like to see more of you."

"Oh."

"Would you object?"

"To what?" she asked, a bit puzzled.

"To my calling on you socially," he smiled.

"Why no, I think not. I'm just a little surprised, is all."

"Why is that?"

Louise's mind was racing. She didn't want to say *because I'm thirty-one and have five children.* "Oh, I don't know. I guess because I haven't felt very visible."

He chuckled. "Not visible? Why, you have the ability to light up the room when you walk in."

She blushed.

"It's true! That clerk of your mother's, Lyndyn, is it? He seems quite under your spell. And," he stopped so they stood face to face, "as a gentleman, I must ask straight out… is there any agreement between you?"

"Agreement?"

"Any promises between you?"

"No, no nothing like that. We are friends."

"I'm glad to hear it. Then, I may call upon you?"

"I would be most pleased, Archie," she smiled and they turned to go back into the house.

Sunday arrived a gray and dismal day. It was raining and had been raining since before dawn. Marie gave orders for fires to be maintained in all the common rooms to drive out the damp and candles and lamps to be lit early. The house was reasonably cheery as her guests began to arrive, trying not to get too wet in the process.

The table Llywelyn had constructed had been detached once John and Ronnie left and set to the side as Marie had planned. If she were not so practical minded she would have had the thing taken out and burned for the memories and shame seeing it caused her. She still could not explain her behavior to herself but Richard seemed to feel there was nothing for which she should feel shame. It was a common behavior among the Indians.

Marie greeted Phillip and Caroline warmly as the children flowed into the house but as the older woman looked to her daughter-in-law, she grew concerned.

"*Mon chère* Caroline, are you feeling unwell?"

"It is nothing, Mother Marie."

"Which means it is something," Marie frowned.

"Nothing really, the baby was just doing cartwheels in my stomach all night."

"Phillip, I do not want your wife coming into the store tomorrow. She is working too hard." Then turning to Caroline she added. "You are not seventeen anymore and you need more rest, yes?"

Caroline smiled weakly. "Yes, Mother Marie."

Pulling her son aside, Marie whispered. "You make a very good living, *mon fils*, your wife does not need to work. She needs rest."

He nodded.

Richie and Clarissa had not yet returned. Marie did not expect them for another month or more. It meant they all fit around the main table with room to spare and so she had again invited Doctor Ajax to join them.

"I must say it is a most welcome thing to be in your home on a day like today," Ajax said as he allowed Nora to slip his coat from his back after which she gave it a good shaking out on the roofed portico. "A good day for ducks, we used to say."

Marie smiled as she took her guest's arm and led him to the fire in the drawing room.

"I am so glad you are a little early, Archibald. If I may impose upon you for a favor…?"

"It's no imposition. I'm at your service, Marie. What do you need?" He looked both concerned with whatever was on her mind and pleased that he might be of help.

"It is Jane Sims. I am worried about her."

"John mentioned your housekeeper."

She nodded. "She is very strong minded, as you know, I think. I have tried to make her slow down and rest more but she tells me she will get all the rest she needs when we put her into her coffin. But today she has not been able to leave her bed. Would you mind taking a look at her?"

"Of course."

"Sebastian," she called to her grandson when she saw him lingering nearby. *"Montrez Monsieur le docteur jusqu'à la chambre de Jane, s'il vous plaît."*

"Oui, Grand-mère," the boy responded. Raphael and Louise had often spoken in French together and thus the children had picked it up rather naturally. Since Raphael's death, Marie liked to help them continue to practice it.

Young Sebastian led the doctor up the main staircase and then continued up the attic stairs. Stopping at the first door, he pointed. "This is it," he said, switching automatically to English which he knew was the doctor's language. Children have a sense for this.

Ajax rapped lightly, heard a weak response and opened the door. The room was larger than the others on the third floor, a modest but comfortable bedroom/sitting room with three dormer windows and on the floor several large "rag" rugs braided and stitched into huge ovals. The pleasantly cheery curtains which hung at the windows had not been opened for the day. Donald and Jane had occupied this room for over thirty years. They were the first servants to live on this floor and Donald was the only man ever to do so. Now it was looked upon as the "head housekeeper's room." It was neat and clean but darkened by the closed curtains and lying in the bed under a mound of quilts was Jane.

"Hello, Jane," Ajax smiled warmly. The soft patter of rain could be heard on the roof above. "Mistress Marie tells me you are feeling a bit poorly so she has sent me to check on you." He proceeded to take hold of her wrist and count her pulse with the aid of his new Swiss pocket watch.

"It's nothing, really. I'll be right as rain if I just have a small rest."

"Hmm." Ajax checked her eyes, looked down her throat, and palpated her abdomen. "Anything hurt?" he asked.

"No, sir."

"How old are you now, Jane?"

"I'll be sixty… one soon."

"When was the last time you sat down and ate a real meal?" He stared her straight in the eye.

"Don't know. Don't have time." She turned her head from his gaze.

"Are you telling me Mistress Marie is such a difficult taskmistress that she does not allow you the time to sit down and have a proper meal each day?"

"Oh, no, sir, no. That's not what I meant."

"I am going to write instruction for you. And I shall tell Mistress Marie. At least once each day you are to have a proper sit down hot meal. And you are to keep your seat for at least one half hour. Every day you are to have at least two servings of vegetables, one of fruit, and either meat, fish, cheese, or eggs, understand? And bread with rich, creamy butter."

"Yes, sir."

"I happen to know Young Margot keeps just as good a kitchen as her mother did, God rest her soul, so you've no excuse now. I'll have them bring a tray up for you immediately."

When Marie saw Ajax descend the staircase, she left the rest of the family gathered in the drawing room and went over to meet him.

"I cannot see that there is anything seriously wrong," he said as she approached, "but she is not eating as she should. She didn't bother to deny it. I left her with written instruction which I have copied for you as well. I asked her age and she said she was sixty, soon to be sixty-one," he frowned. "Is that correct?"

Marie snorted a little laugh. "She has been sixty going on sixty-one for the past five years now and before that she was fifty-nine for a half-dozen or more."

"So how old is the woman?"

"She has to be well over seventy," Marie said quietly.

"I want a tray sent up to her following my instructions and assign someone to stay with her until she eats everything. At her age, many cannot smell as they used to nor is their taste as keen. The appetite dwindles. She needs food to give her energy. Going into winter underweight and with a sad spirit is not desirable."

"Very well," Marie nodded. "I shall return shortly." She headed to the kitchen.

When she returned she led everyone into the dining room. She noticed Ajax maneuvered to sit directly across from Louise with meek Lyndyn between Louise and Rebecca and fifteen year old Charity sat next to Ajax and directly across from Lyndyn. Charity began flirting outrageously with the doctor.

After Phillip said the blessing, the wine was poured and Marie gave a small silent salute to Jacques' place at the end of the table. For a few moments everyone else disappeared and she saw her Jacques just as he had been and smiling at her. Then everyone returned to her consciousness and she took a sip of her wine and asked Cynthia how her family was and how the plans for the wedding progressed.

"We're all ready Mother Marie, just waiting on Jamie," Cynthia responded turning a look to James. She was a very English looking lass, with a very fair complexion, small eyes, and a rather large jaw topped with honey blonde hair.

"The house is almost ready," James said quickly. "I told them to post the banns. The house will be in move-in shape by three weeks."

"Then it looks like we're to have another wedding," Marie smiled.

"May I say you look especially lovely today," Ajax spoke boldly across the table to Louise. "And assuming at least one of us is invited, may I escort you to your brother's wedding?"

Louise blushed. "Yes, of course. That would be lovely."

Marie raised her eyebrows. *So that's the way it is,* she thought and looked to poor Lyndyn who appeared to be in the middle of swallowing his tongue. *You are going to have to do better, Lyndyn. A faint heart never won a fair lady.*

Phillip and Thor, at the far end of the table, seemed incapable of not talking business leaving their wives out of the conversation of course. Thomas sitting beside one female cousin and facing three others across the table was looking more out-numbered than usual. He was fourteen now, a tall boy, thought Marie, close to his father's height already. She smiled. He looked capable of holding his own.

Marie noticed Caroline picking at her food. "*Ma chère* Caroline, is the food not to your liking, would you like something else?

Phillip turned to look at his wife.

"No, no, I'm fine. Thank you."

Then Helen spoke toward Ajax. "Doctor Ajax, I wonder if you would be so kind as to explain *ee-nock-u-lay-shun* to us. My sister Isabelle has written there seems to be quite the debate in Boston. One side is for it led by a preacher named Cotton Mather and his friend a Doctor Boylston. The other side led by a Scots Physician, Doctor William Douglass is opposed."

"Yes, of course," Ajax smiled. "It is a process by which one is purposely infected with the pox and develops a mild case of the disease."

The women gasped.

"Why on earth would anyone do that?" Richard growled.

"Because from then on one is immune from ever contracting the disease again. I was inoculated while in Europe. I was only mildly ill. I have a small pock-mark here," he pointed to his hairline, "and I'm told there is one on the back of my neck. That is all. Certainly far better than those who are taken ill by the disease naturally; and now I can always attend the sick without fear of catching the disease. There are mixed theories on why it is so but the fact remains, in Boston, in '21, when they had their last epidemic, hundreds died, hundreds were horribly scarred for life but out of the several hundred who had been inoculated, less than a dozen developed a bad case of the disease and only six died."

"In Boston?" Marie barely whispered.

"Yes. Actually they've had four such outbreaks in recent times. I'm afraid port cities are very vulnerable to being infected by diseases. Sailors and goods can bring diseases in easily." Ajax replied. "And the greater the population, the more easily the disease spreads. It's very contagious, I'm afraid."

"Another reason it is a blessing to live in Chartes Landing," Phillip said a bit boastfully and signed for everyone's wine glass to be refilled.

"But Isabelle now lives in Boston." Marie had turned white as a sheet.

"Forgive me, Mistress Marie. I did not mean to upset you," Ajax frowned, "but I would encourage her to seek out an inoculation before another epidemic occurs. Unfortunately, it seems inevitable."

"My sister writes Doctor Douglass argues in his pamphlets that it only causes the disease to be spread and it kills the healthy," Helen argued. "There are many preachers who are opposed as well on moral grounds."

"Excuse me, Doctor Ajax," young Thomas spoke. "I don't understand how purposely giving yourself a disease when you're perfectly healthy can be any less harmful than taking a chance on getting it naturally? I mean, you're still sick and subject to the same fevers and pox, aren't you? I've met some who have had it and had as little damage as you."

"I'm afraid the medical community itself is not in agreement on *why* it is so, however, the figures don't lie. It must be related to the unique method used to give the inoculation. You see, we actually borrow the infection from an already stricken person. After the stricken has broken out in pustules, some of the pus from those is collected and then we carefully open the vein of the healthy person and apply the pus there. Somehow being infected in this particular way just…"

"Doctor Ajax!" spoke out Lyndyn, "This is hardly dinner time conversation! I beg you to cease in the presence of the ladies." Louise, seated beside him, was looking positively ill and Caroline was faring no better.

"Oh, I am sorry," Ajax looked appropriately chagrined. "I'm afraid after spending a year with the academics I forget myself. We talked about everything as we ate. I do apologize everyone."

"That is all right, Doctor Ajax," Marie sought to sooth. "It was, after all, we who asked the questions. The information and the warning is appreciated." But she noticed Louise barely looked in the man's direction for the rest of the evening.

Ajax was lingering in the front hall. The men were gathered on the front porch to smoke and drink cognac while avoiding the rain. He didn't really feel a part of their conversation. Marie had ushered the ladies into the drawing room where tea and sherry was being served along with a variety of Phoebe's sweets. He didn't feel he belonged there either. He had certainly made a bad impression with Louise and expected she just might cancel their agreement for him to escort her to her brother's wedding. *Not too smart, Archie, blathering on about pus and pustules. Louise is a fine looking woman, a young widow of means but like most of the female variety she's not overly fond of medical talk with its blood and gore and suppuration.* He would have taken his leave if it were not for the rain, which at the moment was thundering down in drenching waves.

"Doctor Ajax," Charity swept into the front hall.

At the sound of her voice he spun around.

"Don't mind my aunts and my cousin," she said apologetically.

"Oh," he gave a grunt and smiled. "It's all right. Everyone everywhere is rather divided on the subject. I should not have become so graphic in describing the procedure."

"Well, you can't leave in this deluge and we can't have you standing in the hall. Come, it's comfortable and quiet in the library. Would you like a drink? Some cognac perhaps, or sherry… port… tea? We even can offer ale these days. Nora has taught them in the kitchen how they make ale in Holland."

"No," he smiled as he followed her into the library. "I am quite sated after that delicious meal. Mistress Marie presides over a fine table. It's a spoiler to a bachelor who has no kitchen of his own. I always appreciate her invitations."

"Have a seat, please," Charity offered, standing in front of the chair before the fireplace. He naturally then took his seat on the settee upon which she immediately joined him pulling her skirts daintily about her. "Please tell me more about inoculation. I promise I don't have a weak stomach."

Ajax proceeded to tell her how the process had been discovered several decades ago by an English-trained doctor who found it being used in Constantinople by the Turks. And how Doctor Boylston had so believed in it he had inoculated his own six year old son and two slaves who became mildly ill but then recovered nicely and proved impervious to any further contamination. Thus encouraged, he had inoculated around 250 during the epidemic of 1721 of which only six died, a vast improvement in percentage than amongst those not inoculated.

Charity listened with apparent fascination as he described the process of opening a vein and introducing the tiniest bit of matter gathered from the pus filled eruptions on a stricken patient.

"Just one pustule gives enough matter to inoculate several dozen men… or women," he spoke sincerely.

"So little is needed?" she asked in amazement.

"So little, what clings to the tip of a needle is all. We still don't completely understand but contracting the disease from the pus is never as harsh as contracting the disease by exposure to it through the air."

"Does my Uncle John know of this?" Charity's eyes were large and brown like her father's.

"It's one of the things we spoke of before he left."

"He could inoculate Aunt Ronnie and her whole village. I understand smallpox is devastating among the natives."

"But there is a danger. If one of theirs should die, John would be blamed," Ajax explained. "Don't forget one to three percent of those inoculated can be expected to die. And that's among the whites. We have no idea what that percentage might be among the Indians."

"Oh," she sighed in disappointment, "you're right. That could start another Indian war."

Ajax looked at the clock on the mantle and was surprised to see a half hour had passed.

"I do believe the rain has ceased for the moment so I really should take advantage of the break and leave." He stood. "It has been most agreeable talking with you, Charity. Are you really so interested in medicine?"

"Yes, yes, I am. I find it a very noble calling," her lashes swept downward before coming up again as she gazed into his eyes. "Grandmother has taught me a lot about the various herbs and their medicinal qualities."

"Extraordinary," he said. How could it be that in all his visits to the Power home, he had never noticed this girl before?

"What is?"she gazed at him.

"Oh. Nothing," he cleared his throat. "I must go take my leave of your grandmother." He bowed to her and left.

At two that morning, Caroline awoke with a groan that evolved into a cry of pain. She clutched her belly as Phillip lit another candle.

"Get Doctor Ajax," she whimpered when she saw the blood and Phillip jumped into his breeches.

He ran to the stable and rousted the stable-hand as Phillip himself threw a saddle on the nearest horse.

"Ride for the doctor," he cried and the stable-hand was instantly awake, mounting the horse.

Back in their room, Phillip found his wife now sitting on the floor in her own blood.

"Caroline. Caroline, oh my lord, oh darling. What can I do? How can I help?"

"I think I'm in labor. But it's way too early. Oh, Phillip… I'm losing our baby."

"Sh-sh, don't worry," he tried to sooth her as he held her. "Whatever happens is… as long as you are well… we will get through this. Do you understand? It will be all right."

"Oh, Phillip, it hurts so bad," she trembled as she gripped his arm.

"Ajax will be here soon." He held her as another pain ripped through her insides and she stiffened in his arms. "Where the hell is Ajax?" he all but screamed.

All the staff was awake now. The kitchen help was boiling up water. The chambermaid was bringing fresh linens and the wax treated pad to protect the bed. The housekeeper was bringing empty buckets and rags.

Caroline was crying in Phillip's arms.

Ajax arrived in time to clean up and make certain the placenta was delivered. The tiny body was much too young to survive outside the womb. The outside looked perfect but the insides were not completely formed he told them. Ajax washed the little one and wrapped it up to give to Caroline; it was the son for whom they had been praying.

She took the little bundle from Ajax and shared with Phillip.

"I want to name him *Gabriel*," she said, as tears flowed down her cheeks.

"Yes," Phillip gave a sob, holding the little hand that was no bigger than his thumbnail. "Gabriel. I like that. He is one with the angels now."

"Gabriel. My son. My poor sweet baby. My dear sweet baby," she sobbed. "Why weren't you safe inside me?"

They worked to get Caroline off the floor and comfortably back into the bed. Ajax double checked the placenta, making sure it was intact and completely removed from her womb.

"It's time to rest," he said and held out his arms to take the wee babe from her. She was not ready to give him up. She continued to hold him, cradled in her hands, a kind of stupor had descended upon her until Phillip took the child in his own hands. She gave Gabriel a last kiss and then allowed him to be taken.

Phillip reclined beside her and held her in his arms.

"I am so sorry," she whispered. "I lost our son. I couldn't hang on to him."

"Shh, shh. He was too good for this world so God decided not to wait but took him right away."

"Someday we'll see him," she almost smiled. "Someday when we're all together again in Paradise and he will know his name is Gabriel."

"Yes. Now sleep, my dearest. Rest and grow strong again." He kissed the top of her head.

When Phillip reappeared in the hall, Ajax had already had the babe spirited away to the undertaker. There would be a tiny funeral for a tiny child, the first of its kind in the Power mausoleum.

"Phillip, a word?" Ajax pulled him aside. "She will recover I have no doubt and near as I can tell she will still be able to bear children but I must warn you. She is an older mother now. She needs rest and you must abstain from intercourse for a time. I prescribe three months. And when you do resume, try not to… not to impregnate her right away… well, there are things you can do to prevent another child too quickly."

"I understand, doctor. I am fully aware."

"Good. She should have a full six months before risking another pregnancy, a year would be even better."

"I understand but why do you say *risk?*"

He shrugged. "Partly because no pregnancy is without its uncertainties, partly because she is now in her thirties. I'll be back tomorrow to check on her."

"Thank you."

Phillip did not sleep again that night. He could not stop questioning himself, asking himself if somehow he had put too much pressure on his wife. His desire to see her become his mother's successor at the store… had it compelled her to work harder than she should have? Had it cost them their son? It weighed heavily upon his conscience.

Phillip passed the sad news to Marie who saw to it the family was informed. A small funeral just for Phillip's immediate family was arranged. The first tiny coffin found its way into the family mausoleum.

Chapter 13

Frontier 1726

The four room, two bedroom frame house within the confines of the fort felt smaller than Ronnie remembered. They had been home two weeks and she told herself she was happy cooking her own food and wearing simpler clothing again but it was not as pleasant as she had expected. There was no one to cook while she played with her children. No one to sooth the fussing baby while she helped Gray with his letters, and the dirt and dust of the parade ground was not to be compared to the green lawns and numerous flowerbeds of her husband's childhood home. Dirt and dust was everywhere and unless she took the time to wash off all the surfaces and scrub the floors almost daily, the children soon were covered with it.

John was very busy catching up on his duties and Ronnie spent much time alone cooking and cleaning. She missed Marie, the other grandchildren, and even John's siblings. Without realizing it, Ronnie also missed the staff that kept the home and kitchen humming along without any attention on her part.

She longed to seek out her former village and visit her mother and brother. It had been over a year since she had seen them and she had another baby to show them but John had no time to escort her. Then one night he came home and told her he had arranged for Charlie One Claw, one of the company scouts, to take her and the children to the village a long day's ride from the fort.

"I know how much you want to see them again," he said quietly as they lie together in their bed, the baby's cradle hanging from the ceiling beam.

"It is so good of you to think of me and arrange this," she said just as quietly.

"It is a rare few minutes when I am not thinking of you," he smiled and nuzzled in to her, his hands relishing the lushness of her young body. "I want you to be happy," he looked in her eyes. "It makes me happy to know you are happy but I also want to know that you are safe. The commander tells me there's been some renegade activity lately so I am also assigning a dozen men to escort you."

"Do you think this is needed?"

"I see no reason to risk you," he murmured as he moved upon her and soon lost any thought beyond the moment.

The new day dawned clear and Ronnie was filled with excited anticipation. She had packed all that was necessary as well as gifts she had brought from Charts Landing. Twelve men, the scout, and she each rode a horse. Charlie One Claw rode with Gray Wolf's Son sitting in front of him while Ronnie had a carrier which fit in front of her across her horse's withers in which two and a half year old Sunshine rode on one side and toddler Matthew rode in the other. Infant Mark rode on Ronnie's back safely in his own carrier. To balance the weight Ronnie also had the bag of food in the side with Matthew.

After saying good-bye to John, they rode out under a clear blue sky. John was loath to see them leave without him but he had ordered the surgery scrubbed from ceiling to floor in readiness for inspection plus all the men were to be ready for the commander's general inspection. There was much to attend and he could not go with her.

Mid-morning the detail halted for a stretch break. Ronnie changed the infant and nursed him while Gray Wolf's Son, Sunshine, and Matthew received a snack and had an opportunity to run about near by. Everyone remounted.

At noon the soldiers would have eaten in the saddle but because of the needs of the children they stopped again. They were allowing themselves only a fifteen minute break but halfway through it, a group of renegades descended out of nowhere. Amidst yelps and trills, musket shots and flying arrows, Ronnie found herself at last surrounded and alone but still unharmed. Fighting like a mountain lioness trying to protect her cubs, Ronnie lashed out and laid open the arm of one of the attackers. She was finally brought to a halt when another caught Sunshine by her fine blonde hair and held a knife to her little neck. Ronnie immediately dropped her knife in surrender.

Wild eyed, she looked around her. At least half the soldiers were lying on the ground, dead or badly wounded. The rest had fled. Charlie One Claw had disappeared with Gray Wolf's Son. The baby was still safe on Ronnie's back in the carrier and Matthew was under her left arm while a terrified Sunshine was being lifted to her toes by her hair. A strong arm came up from behind Ronnie and grabbed her own hair, pulling her painfully backward.

"You stink of the white man now!" she heard a familiar voice say.

"Tonoaki!" she gasped.

He walked around to stand in front of her, grinning harshly just inches from her face. His handsome face covered in colored clay.

"Please, let us go. I have no quarrel with you. I go to see my mother in the village of our people."

"Our people?" he sneered. "These do not look like our people." He grabbed Matthew by the arm, the child's flesh looking very pale next to the brave's swarthy hand. Sunshine was crying and he turned suddenly and shouted for her to be quiet. She screamed even louder. "They do not even understand our tongue!" He motioned for the other to let the child go and she ran to her mother where she buried her sobs into Ronnie's riding skirts.

"Tonoaki, it is beneath you to make war on children. What do you want?"

"You will come with us," he said as he grabbed Matthew from her arms and roughly carried him off to insure her compliance.

Ronnie adjusted the wicker carrier on her horse's withers, then she set Sunshine up in the saddle and got on behind her. Without a word she followed Tonoaki who held her year old son.

Charlie One Claw drove his horse on as hard as he dared while keeping a tight grip on Gray Wolf's Son. The guards at the fort saw him coming and called for the gate to be opened. He pulled his lathered steed to a halt and dropped the five year old at the feet of the commander's wife who had come out to see what the commotion was about. Leaping from his horse, the scout ran into the surgery where he found the captain.

"We were attacked!" he almost shouted.

John blanched and as Charlie relayed what had happened, several other wounded men came riding in on their horses, some of which were also wounded.

Together they reported to Commander Greeley.

"Killing and maiming almost a dozen of my men insures we will hunt them without ceasing until they are caught," snapped Greeley. "This cannot be overlooked. What the devil did they do it for? The detail carried no supplies, no significant munitions."

The sergeant limped in bleeding from his leg and shoulder. "They took Captain Power's wife and children," he confirmed. "They were not hurt, sir, but they rode off with them and what horses they could grab. She tried to put up a fight but they threatened the children."

John had the sickening feeling it was personal.

John attended the wounded before the entire company of fifty British soldiers left, leaving a minimum number of able bodied and wounded behind to hold the fort. They marched to the site of the attack to collect the bodies of the fallen. They found three of the men still alive. John field-dressed their wounds and gave instruction for their care knowing at least one would not survive if he even made it back to the fort still breathing. A detail was sent back to the fort with the injured and the dead.

Surveying the ground, John could only feel relief that Ronnie and the children were not among the bodies. He saw the sun glint off of something in the grass. He walked over and picked up a small doll whose shiny button eye had caught the sun. His mother had given it to Sunshine.

It was getting dark and they bivouacked there for the night.

"Major," John walked into the commander's tent and set the doll down.

"What's this?"

"It's a doll my mother gave to my daughter. I don't think it fell out of my wife's pack by accident. I think my wife is saying she will try to leave a trail of bread crumbs, so to speak, to help us track her."

Greeley looked at John and then looked at the doll. "It's possible. Tomorrow I'm taking twenty men and a scout to the village. See if they can give us any help in locating these renegades. Fact is, this outlaw group risks stirring up a full fledged retaliation. I don't think the sachem will want that. Meanwhile we allow Charlie One Claw to track and use the men to fan out and look for any bread crumbs your wife may have left behind."

It was growing dark and Ronnie let a strip of lace from her sleeve fall to a bush as they rode along. Tonoaki led them down into a ravine and then up onto a plateau among some giant rocks. They halted at last.

Ronnie slid down from the saddle and was lifting Sunshine down when Tonoaki strode over with Matthew held roughly in a blanket scrap.

"Here, woman, tend to your brat. I will take this one," he grabbed Sunshine. "At least she should know enough not to piss herself."

Ronnie took hold of Matthew. "Is there water?" she asked as Sunshine began to whimper in fear.

Tonoaki pointed to a small stream that flowed from the rocks.

She went downstream to clean and wash the toddler, finally putting a fresh clout on him. She set him on the blanket from her horse and gave him jerky to gnaw on. Next she saw to her infant. After changing his swaddling, she put him to her breast. Tonoaki sat staring at her, his thoughts unreadable.

When the baby had fallen asleep, she strapped him safely on his carrier and allowed the toddler to suckle next. Tonoaki continued to stare.

"I do not understand why you attacked the soldiers," Ronnie said quietly but looking him in the eye. "Your numbers are small. You are no match for them. The fort will not forgive the killing of their men."

"I am an outlaw. I ask no forgiveness. I take what I want." He reached out and grabbed her neck. His grip was strong but without intent to harm. He moved his large hand down the slender column, feeling the smooth, softness of her skin as he continued down to her free breast, holding it, squeezing it, and then, bending in to suck it himself.

Ronnie didn't know what to do. Against her will she felt her body respond and she silently fought the familiar stimulation. The rest of his party sat around a fire, talking among themselves, tending to their wounds, their backs turned away. They did not care what he did. Finally, he pulled away.

"You are his woman now?"

"Yes, but I was not before…" she stopped herself from saying *before you beat me and drove me away.* "She is your daughter. We call her *Sunshine.*"

He looked at the blonde haired girl who was almost three years old. There was something in her face that reminded him of his own mother and he saw her eyes were no longer blue. Was it possible that she really was his? No one but the jealous slut Mist-On-Moon had accused Morning Light of adultery. All others had said she was a faithful wife. She had been his prize and he had lost her. Now she belonged to another.

He took the little girl and walked to the water.

Ronnie's heart pounded in fear of what he would do next. She could no longer see him. She tried not to think of what he might do. She told herself to stay calm and wait for what he actually did.

At last he returned. He had washed the colored clay from his face and had Sunshine on a tether. He led her to Ronnie who gave the child a travel cake and told her to sit, eat, and then go to sleep.

"I need to eat to keep my milk," Ronnie said boldly as she settled her toddler to her breast. "If you had not captured us, I would be at the village eating well."

Tonoaki grunted, went to the spit where his companions were roasting a wild turkey. He sliced off a hunk, brought it back to Ronnie and handed it to her. He licked his fingers and then ran them through her silken hair and breathed in the sweet smell of flowers.

"One more night," he said, his voice husky with desire. "Give me one more night."

"And what will you give me?" she asked looking directly at him while quickly eating the turkey. Amongst John's family, she had learned not to always look downward.

"Your life. Your children's lives. You can return to him in peace."

"I want his life as well." She said almost casually as she laid her toddler down to sleep.

He laughed. "You ask too much. I could take you right now, do with you as I want."

She looked him in the eye. "But that is not what you want, Tonoaki. You want me willing. You want me as I used to be… in our furs."

"Yes." He pulled her to her feet and grabbed hold of her, licking her neck and her cheek.

"Your word," she pulled away, her body stiff and unyielding. "He goes unharmed. We go unharmed. And I will give you what you want, I will give you this night."

"You have my word." He shuddered in almost a spasm of desire, wanting her beyond reason. The children were asleep and he led her to a separate spot within the rocks, a spot away from the others, a spot with privacy where he spread out his blankets. "Morning Light," he sighed and removed his breech cloth to reveal himself stiff and throbbing.

She reminded herself that she had been with him many times already and this time she was buying the lives of those she loved the most. She removed her clothing and allowed herself to be pulled down by his side. She did not fight him but was pliant and allowed his hands to roam over her body unchecked, feeling, caressing, holding, probing her softness. She forced her own hands to move over him, to repeat the things she used to do in pleasure, which now she did in barter. Finally, she rose up onto her knees and straddled his hips, coming down upon his stiffly rigid member. She moved sensually upon him, riding him slowly into a frenzy of need until he rolled her onto her back and drove himself into her forcefully, rapidly, repeatedly until he heard her cry out and he matched it with his own cry. But never did she kiss him. The kiss was only for Jack, that was theirs alone.

She lay with the large brave all night. She had promised him a night. After they had slept a time, he awoke and took her again like a man desperate to turn back the hands of time. To go back to when he held proud stature in his village, when he was looked upon with respect, when he had won the hand of the beautiful young widow every brave in the village wanted. Back when they lived happily and in harmony with a future. But no one can turn back time and Ronnie knew the emotion she felt as she lie in Tonoaki's arms was only pity. And there is no greater insult to a Mohawk warrior than pity.

It was almost dawn when she heard her infant whimper and she strove to rise out of Tonoaki's arms. He grabbed her hair and brought it to his nose, inhaling deeply of its scent.

"Please, our bargain is made," she said without warmth.

"The first ray of the sun has not yet arrived," he grunted as he held her fast and breathed in the scent of her skin. She was quiet and allowed him once again to lick her breasts and plumb her depths. She heard her infant begin to cry and she hastened to allow Tonoaki to take her one last time. When he finished and rose away from her, the first ray of sun hit him. She rose without a word and put on her riding skirt. The rest could wait until after her infant was fed.

Tonoaki gathered his men along with the captured horses and they left after he pointed in the direction of the fort. "Go that way," he grunted, then gave her a hard smile. "You will run into the search party he has tracking us." And with that he left her and her children to fend for themselves. She was grateful he had left her horse. Had he recognized it as Gray Wolf's horse and for this he had respect?

Ronnie finished nursing her baby, put fresh swaddling on him and strapped him into his carrier. She herself finished dressing before she woke Sunshine and gave her food from her carry bag. Tonoaki had left the wicker basket carrier that fit across her horse's withers. She saddled her horse. Matthew finally woke and was ready for his breakfast. Ronnie wished she hadn't put the saddle on so soon. Poor horse, it must carry them all.

Finally, everyone was fed and washed. Her canteen was filled from the stream where the water was most pure, bursting forth from the rocks. She put the canteen into Matthew's side of the carrier to balance Sunshine's weight. They left the rocks, traversed through the ravine and tried to retrace the path they had traveled. They went slowly. Ronnie was unsure and it helped when she actually recognized a spot or collected one of her "bread crumbs" as they went.

The sun was growing warm and the children were all dozing. Ronnie continued in the general direction. The sun was her only guide. They came upon a small meadow she recognized from the day before. As they emerged from the trees she turned around to look and several feet from where they were, she saw Mark's dirty swaddling. She got off the horse to pick it up. She shook it out. It was dry now and she packed it away.

She helped Sunshine down from the horse to pass her water. She tried to have Matthew do the same; he was only fifteen months but it was not too soon to train him to pass water standing by a bush or tree rather than soiling what he sat on. She had him on leading strings which were tough rawhide strips that kept him tethered to her. She dug in her bags to find more food. She was running low. Sunshine came up holding something in her hand. Ronnie looked and recognized the eatable berries. "Yes," she nodded, "these you may eat." And she went into the berry patch to gather some herself. It became a game as she picked.

"One for Sunshine, one for Matthew, one for Mama. two for Sunshine, two for Matthew, two for Mama." The children laughed and awaited the next berry to be popped into their little eager mouths like hatchlings in a nest.

When they had had enough she gave them water and drank deeply herself. As she was putting the cap onto the canteen she heard a deadly sound. It was a rattle, a warning. One of them had tread too closely to a rattlesnake. She looked to the ground. Matthew was close to her and she pulled him closer and shouted to Sunshine.

"Stop! Be still! Do not move!" She saw it then, coiled like a spring ready to snap, its head rising to strike at Sunshine. It was full grown, a large rattler at least the length of a man. For a moment Ronnie was frozen with fear, then by instinct she forcefully threw the canteen weighted by the water and jerked Sunshine back at the same time. The child fell backward as Ronnie dragged her to safety. The rattler struck the canteen and then slithered away.

Matthew was laughing, Sunshine was crying, and Ronnie was shaking with adrenaline.

"Bad snake," Sunshine cried. "Mama, bad snake."

"Yes, very bad snake." She hugged her daughter and then her toddler as well. "I think we go back on horse." Sunshine was clinging to her mother like a tick. "It is all right now. Bad snake go away. He will not come back," she said reassuringly. "You stay right here, Mama go get our water." But it took many minutes before the trembling child would let loose of her mother's leg.

Finally, Ronnie walked over to the canteen. As she lifted it up she saw that it was dripping. The fangs of the rattler had punctured the side and water was leaking out. Ronnie dropped the canteen. She feared the water remaining was no good. The snake bit through and most likely squirt its venom into the water. She could not give it to her children now, she thought. And the vessel was no longer fit to carry liquid. She thanked the Great Spirit they all had had a drink before this happened. She left the ruined canteen lay and went back to her children putting them on the horse. They crossed the meadow in what she hoped was the right direction and urged the horse on.

§

Charlie One Claw picked the soft linen cloth from the tree branch and smelled it. It smelled of the scent she wore. He grunted. At least he knew they were still on the trail. It was hard to track on rock and this patch of ground was very rocky.

"Captain?" he called to John. "It better we stop. Light is fading and I could miss sign. We camp for night."

John nodded and the command was given to make camp.

The next morning as soon as it was light John was awake and ready to go on. It was a frustration that they could not go faster. Most of his men were on foot whereas the renegades and Ronnie were on horseback. But the shear number of horses made them easier to track. After a quick breakfast of tea and hardtack they moved out, Charlie One Claw in the lead. They made their way along a small creek bed until the scout spotted a shod horse print on the bank. Indians did not put shoes on their horses, it was undoubtedly one of the captured ponies. He looked up onto the creek bank and saw evidence of many horses having passed through. He led the column across the creek and into a grove.

Charlie One Claw was able to follow the tracks for several miles through the trees and finally out onto a meadow. John ordered the men to stay in the trees and take a break, allowing the scout to search the meadow without the contamination of thirty soldiers beating down the grass.

The scout was puzzled. He expected another sign to tell him in what direction the group had gone when leaving the meadow. He looked searchingly and found the horse prints themselves a puzzlement. There was no evidence that the group had camped but instead of a clear line progressing through the meadow, tracks went back and forth in both directions. Then he found the canteen. No one threw away their water as a bread crumb. He showed it to John.

"What do you think made these holes?" John asked.

The scout shrugged. "Is size and space to be snake bite maybe."

"Snake bite?! That would make sense. The canteen's no good now," John said half to himself.

When Charlie One Claw finished studying the tracks he told John at least one rider went back into the grove.

"Could she have escaped them?" he asked Charlie One Claw

The Indian shrugged. He didn't think the tracks indicated a hurried pace of flight but he hesitated to say so to John. If the renegade band let her go after bringing her this far, he suspected she had made some kind of bargain with them. But what could she bargain? She had only herself and the children. Did she give them a child? Charlie One Claw grunted to himself. The woman he knew would never give up her child. Did she give them herself? If they wanted her body, they could take it as a spoil of warfare. The only thing he could think of was that she had made an agreement to work with them. Give them information, perhaps, on shipments of supplies. Arms. Ammunition. Is that why they had now sent her back to the fort?

"Band go this way," he pointed, "but your wife's horse go back toward fort I think."

"She escaped them," John said hopefully and picked a few men on horseback to go in search of Ronnie with him and Charlie One Claw while sending the other scout with his lieutenant to lead the remaining men on the trail of the renegades.

§

Ronnie had discovered no more of her "bread crumbs" to assure her of the path and feared they were only going farther into the forest. The sun had ceased to be of any help in giving her direction as an overcast of thick clouds blotted its very existence from view. She started to backtrack and became more disoriented. The children were whining for food and finally she stopped in a small clearing.

She got down from the horse, tethered it securely and split a travel cake between Sunshine and Matthew. After the incident with the snake she was leery of allowing the children down on the ground. The baby was crying fiercely and she took it from its carrier and changed its swaddling. Then she sat down to nurse.

As Baby Mark pulled on her pap, Ronnie looked out at the forest in every direction. She realized she was hopelessly lost. Is that what Tonoaki had intended when he had brought them so far and then just left her? She suspected it was. He wanted her to suffer but forcing his own daughter to suffer as well? A tear formed in Ronnie's eye. If Sunshine had been born a boy, Tonoaki might have stolen him away but as a girl, Sunshine was considered of no value. Since he had rejected her from the very start, they had formed no natural attachment. Ronnie was reminded of how Red Elk, her father, had loved her and called her his "Morning Light." She was certain Tonoaki was not even bothered to think of what might happen to his child.

The baby had finished nursing and was once again asleep in his carrier. Ronnie heard distant rumbling and grew concerned that it might rain. If it rained, their tracks would be wiped out and a tracking party would never find them. She was most concerned about having no weapons, nothing save a small cooking knife in her bag. If it was just herself, she would not care but she feared for her children. She began dragging dead-fall together. She would start a fire, perhaps a tracking party would see it. Perhaps they would see the smoke. At least it would discourage any animals.

§

"Where is she, Charlie?" John asked after he heard the rumble of thunder. The scout was peering hard at the ground.

"She lost," muttered the Indian. "Her path makes no sense. Tracks say she go deeper into forest, away from fort, away from village."

"They did it on purpose," John almost growled. "They confused her and then abandoned her with three small children. It's a sick game. For some reason they didn't have the stomach to kill her and the children outright so they figured the wilds would do it for them. But it wasn't a certainty so she could still have hope. The sick bastards!"

"This way," Charlie One Claw urged his horse on and they all followed.

§

Night was falling and Ronnie kept the fire burning brightly. It would protect them from animals. She split the last travel cake between her daughter and her toddler. She was concerned that without water her milk would cease to flow. The horse grazed on sparse grass and other tender vegetation. Tomorrow, she considered, she would allow the horse its head and hope that it would find water for them.

Ronnie had put the blanket down at the foot of a huge oak tree. The ground was not soft but the tree trunk protected their backs. To the side she had placed the saddle to hem in the children on one side while she took her place on their other side. In between their mother and the saddle, the children found little pockets among the roots in which to lie. She watched them as they drifted off to sleep and she sang an Indian lullaby, something she used to sing to Gray Wolf's Son. When she finished all was quiet except for the crackle of the fire, the hooting of owls, and the howls of a wolf.

As she lie there she could not help but think of what John would say when she told him what she had done. She must tell him. They must not have pleasures again until her moon time came for if it did not, she would know it was Tonoaki's child she carried. And what good would that do? If this child ended up being brown, could John accept it, love it as he did Sunshine?

It all weighed heavily on Ronnie's heart as she continued to add wood to the fire and doze in a fitful sleep.

They were a small valley away but they saw the fire, big, bold, and gleaming through the night. Afraid she would move, would disappear into the Indian forest when daylight came, John and his men traveled through the night walking ahead of their horses to keep them from breaking a leg.

John was unprepared for the indescribable relief he felt when he saw his wife move, waken, and call out to him. Banishing the sorrowful memories of another girl and another tree, he ran to scoop her into his arms and cover her with kisses. Her face was smudged with dirt, her hair was tangled, her clothes were soiled and torn ragged, and she smelled vaguely of baby urine and spit up but it mattered not. She was alive, thank God, they had found her, and now she was safe.

"You are unhurt?" he asked, wanting reassurance.

"We are unhurt, my husband, but very thirsty," she said softly.

They were given water and food and as they ate, the dawn rose and Ronnie told John it was Tonoaki who headed up the renegade band.

"Tonoaki! No wonder the bastard led you off to abandon you. Didn't have the guts to kill an unarmed woman and three children so he thought to let the wilds do it for him."

"It is a band of only eight that I could count. I cut one very badly on his arm but then one held a knife to Sunshine's throat and I must surrender. Tonoaki took Matthew and threatened to harm him if I did not follow them in peace."

"Considering what he did before, I'm very surprised he didn't beat you."

"I am no longer his wife."

John looked at Ronnie. There was a twisted logic in there somewhere he was sure. An unarmed woman… or man… you couldn't harm but your wife you could beat within an inch of her life and slice off her nose as well.

"He look much at Sunshine. I think he start to believe she is his daughter, regret what he did."

"I just bet he does," John stood and began to kick dirt at the fire. "I hope he isn't thinking of trying to take her."

"No, I do not think so. Daughters only good for marriage alliance. Tonoaki is outlaw now, can make no alliances. I ask him why he kill soldiers, he knows it will never be forgiven."

"What did he say?"

She shrugged. "He have no answer. Say he can do what he wants."

"He can dance on the end of a rope too," John said as he saddled Ronnie's horse and set the wicker carrier in place. "We're going to ride to the village and meet up with Greeley to report."

"Finally, I see my mother," she said and suddenly she was crying. John rushed to her side and took her back into his arms, holding her and assuring her everything would be all right. She clung to him, sobbing and broken for several minutes. Then he felt her put on the mantle of Indian stoicism again. "Jack, something I must tell you private."

John grabbed the first two men within reach and assigned them to watch the children while he and his wife "had a private word." He led her off to a distant thicket.

"What is it, Ronnie? You look… he did something you haven't told me, didn't he? Did he force you?" he asked, knowing that was the Indian way of saying *rape*.

She shook her head. "Not force… make me bargain."

"What kind of bargain?"

"Me for our children. He give me our children's lives if I give him one more night." She no longer could look at her husband.

"One more night? What did he mean 'one more night'?" John was in denial.

"One more night… as his wife," Ronnie struggled to say. She looked up at John's face and saw all the anger and hatred he was feeling. "I think this only reason he attack. What he want from beginning. It was worse than being forced. If he force, I could fight back," she said as her hands became fists. "With bargain I cannot fight him. One more night with me he said in exchange for our lives. I had to agree but all I feel is pity."

"Pity?!!" John all but shouted.

"At one time Tonoaki have good life, respect of his people, a home and family. Now he is outcast leading a small group of outlaws. He has lost everything and will never get it back. Yes, I pity."

John had never felt so enraged, a fury that was blinding him to everything else. "Get on your horse," he spit out. "Charlie," he called, "lead us to the village. We need to report to Commander Greeley as soon as possible. Men, fall in!" he shouted.

John said nothing more to anyone as they moved through the forests but he did a lot of thinking. He knew it wasn't fair to be angry with Ronnie. She had been in an unwinnable position. Her virtue for her children's lives. Was there really any contest? If some arsehole had told him he had a choice – watch his children die or submit to being buggered, wouldn't he do it? Of course he would and he could even force himself to pretend to enjoy it if that was part of the deal. But *pity* the bastard after? Never! That he could not understand. That was just too close to sainthood and he had never mistook Ronnie for a saint. She wasn't even a Christian.

Perhaps it was a little more realistic to consider that she had felt a little gratification maybe, thrill even, to know someone would go so far as to attack, kill, and maim a dozen men and make themselves a permanent outlaw… just for the reward of one more night spent deep between her thighs. Did she find that kind of savageness flattering? Did it impress her own wild heart? Perhaps submitting had not been such a hardship, not a pretense at all. She had been married to that savage after all, did his violent desires attract her, exhilarate her? Perhaps she had even liked their reunion. Had Tonoaki brought her to satisfaction like he used to? Had he made her cry out in pleasure? Had she actually wanted Tonoaki again? Was he somehow better than…? Why else would she feel pity for him now?

Darkness had come back to John.

Chapter 14

The reunion with her mother was nothing like Ronnie had planned. The presents she had brought from Chartes Landing had been stolen and tensions ran high through the entire village because of the attack on the soldiers. At the sachem's encouragement five warriors volunteered to scout for the British. Commander Greeley divided both his and John's men into two equal groups with instruction to go out in different directions taking into consideration those men under the lieutenant that John had sent to follow the trail through the ravine. With three patrols out searching, Tonoaki's band didn't have a chance of staying in the area undetected.

John had taught the men to fight "Indian style." No parading out in neat lines, marching to drums, and generally making themselves easy targets. Instead, they moved from bush to bush and hill to hill as quietly as a patrol of men can, and all the while looking for signs. Footprints, broken branches, trampled leaves. You didn't move a dozen or more horses through an area without leaving some sign.

Ronnie and her children were offered shelter in the long house of the sachem, her mother's husband. She had to get used to being called *Morning Light* again as well as sleeping on flea infested furs on hard sleeping platforms, cooking in the smoke of open fires, and applying bear grease to repel the mosquitoes and fleas. Marie had told her lice could be discouraged by frequent washing of one's hair with smashed yarrow but the children were always dirty now as they ran naked with the other children. Eating with dirty hands and getting dirt and other children's snot into their food.

Her mother, Singing Wind, had lost more teeth and was beginning to look very old. Her cheeks had sunken in and her hair was turning gray. She listened quietly as Ronnie told her everything that had happened with Tonoaki.

"Do you think you now carry his child, my daughter?" she asked solemnly.

"I do not know, Mother. He poured himself into me three times. I could not resist, it was part of the bargain. He held me with him so I could not wash. Now I fear." Ronnie could still see Jack's face as he had left the village. He had looked at her but his eyes had been different, their color was like frozen rain. He had nodded a good-bye but he had not embraced her, had not kissed her, had not looked at her as if he would miss her. He looked only like he wanted to kill. She understood; he wanted to kill Tonoaki for what he had made her do. She would feel the same. "My moon-time is not for two more weeks. What must I do to insure I bleed?"

"The tea only works if you drink right away, next day."

"I know. Is there not something else?" she clung to her mother's knees, desperation in her face.

Singing Wind looked at her daughter. "You still want the white man? Many braves here would not care whose child it was as long as they had you."

Ronnie knew what her mother was suggesting. "I love him, my mother. I love him as much as I loved Gray Wolf. And I took a solemn vow to be his mate until death."

"Then we wait for your moon-time. If you bleed, problem over."

Ronnie knew better. Even if there was no child, would Jack ever forgive her?

Ronnie asked her brother, Wani, and her cousin, Yellow Rock, to escort her to the fort to get Gray Wolf's Son. She wanted all her children with her but for this trip she left her youngest children with her mother. One of the women in the village agreed to nurse infant Mark. It was summer dusk as they approached the fort. The gate sentry called out for them to halt.

"It is all right," she cried out. "I am Captain Power's wife. I stay in village while my husband out with patrol. I want to see Mistress Greeley. She watch my son."

"Wait right there," a young private said from the tower. "Don't come no closer."

She, Wani, and Yellow Rock waited.

After a time Mistress Greeley poked her head over the tower wall.

"Is that you, Ronnie?"

"Yes. Yes. Mistress Greeley, how is Gray?"

"Oh, he's fine. Who is that with you?" the older woman asked peering into the growing gloom.

"This my brother, Wani, and Yellow Rock, my cousin. You meet at wedding. They bring me so I can see Gray, bring back with me."

"Oh, for pity sake, let the girl in. She's Captain Power's wife."

"Sorry ma'am, we have orders not to let anyone in except Army personnel." They heard a voice respond from above them.

"And their spouses, isn't that so?" the feisty commander's wife asked.

"Er… yes, ma'am."

"That is Captain Power's spouse, you numb skull!"

Finally, the door in the gate opened.

"Sorry, ma'am, just you. We can't let them in," another private said half apologetically.

Ronnie looked at her brother. "Make yourselves comfortable here. I will have food and water sent out to you."

Both braves nodded as if to say it was no surprise the whites had no manners. They were prepared to make camp for themselves.

After having food and water sent out for Wani and Yellow Rock, Ronnie joined Elinor Greeley for a light supper. Gray Wolf's Son was already in bed.

Conscious of feeling very dirty, Ronnie begged a few moments with soap and water. She scrubbed her face and hands before running a comb through her hair and joining the older woman at the table.

"So you must tell me, what is the news? I'm afraid my husband left here in such a hurry and I haven't heard a thing since. No one wants to talk."

Ronnie relayed everything she knew but left out the personal details.

"But why on earth did they kill our men just to take you and your children off into the wild and then abandon you?" Elinor Greeley asked in exasperation. "It makes no sense.

"True. But the leader was my former husband. The one I ran from when I came here."

"Oh, the one that beat you so severely?" she gasped.

"Yes."

"But he didn't beat you this time?"

"No, I no longer his wife."

Elinor looked very puzzled.

"There is no honor in killing an unarmed woman and small children so he abandon me with no weapons. Perhaps he wished the wilds to kill us."

"Oh, my dear, I am so sorry. And so far there has been no word from the patrols?"

"I expect fort to hear before we do but it is only one week."

"It seems so much longer," Elinor sighed and gave her guest a little smile. "I must tell you, Gray has been doing very well with his letters. He is reading already. And he has been such good company. I must admit I miss the commander when he isn't here. And it sounds like you won't be staying either."

"No, I must return to my children and visit with my mother."

"How is she doing?" the other asked only out of politeness.

Ronnie cast her eyes downward. "She... looks so much older than I remember her."

Elinor remembered seeing the woman at the wedding and judged her to be perhaps ten or fifteen years older than Elinor, herself.

"The Indian way of life was very hard, perhaps too hard," Ronnie said softly.

That night Ronnie was in her bed thinking. She felt guilty leaving Elinor Greeley all alone especially while her husband was out chasing troubles made by Ronnie's ex-husband. And to be truthful, Ronnie did not really look forward to spending much more time in the village. Life at her mother-in-law's home was much easier than life here at the fort but life here at the fort was easier than life in the Indian village. She had no home of her own in the village, her mother had no home of her own. She lived as second wife to the sachem, in his long house shared by other wives and many children. She wondered if Jack might agree to build another bedroom onto their house for her mother. She could come to visit them. Help with the children. And another week should tell if there was to be another baby in eight more moons.

She could not ask Jack to rear another child of the haughty, vengeful Indian. If Tonoaki had given her another child she must try to find a way to get rid of it. But how? Indians had such a different way of looking at some things. They never sought to get rid of a child. Even if the mother committed adultery, this was not the child's fault and while a warrior might cut off his unfaithful wife's nose, he would never think to… But wasn't that exactly what she had feared when she had run away from Tonoaki? She had feared he would kill her daughter, his daughter, *their* daughter, just because she looked white. But then Sunshine was only a girl and until a baby was born they did not know if it would be a girl or a boy.

Ronnie tossed in her bed. She wished Jack was home. She felt broken like a pottery bowl and she needed her husband to help her put the pieces back together again.

Morning came. Ronnie changed into her buckskins and arranged for more food and water to be sent out to her brother and cousin. Then she woke and fed Gray, dressed him in only a breech cloth but she took more books for him. They left with Wani and Yellow Rock for the village.

It was now almost four weeks since John and the patrols had left. Ronnie's moon time had not come and she knew beyond a shadow of doubt that she carried a child. She was even feeling ill in the mornings.

She walked to Okonhsa's hut and found the village wise woman tending a pot on the open fire outside her dwelling.

"A pleasant day to you, Okonhsa."

"Morning Light, it is good to see your grace and beauty return to our village. Will you stay?"

"I visit my mother. It has been too long."

"It *has* been too long." The woman's coarse broad face broke into a grin. "And I hear you now have four children."

"Yes." She hesitated. "Okonhsa, can we talk… inside?" she gestured to the hut.

"Of course, Morning Light. Always. We have no secrets. I can still remember you when you first arrived in our village, a frightened, sickly child so abused by the white but bold in taking your vengeance. It surprised me to hear you had married one."

"All whites are not alike, just as all Indians are not alike. Gray Wolf would have died for me whereas Tonoaki nearly killed me in jealousy because my white blood surfaced in our daughter."

The very stout older woman nodded an unspoken agreement as she led the way into her hut. Plants and flowers hung drying all over the inside of the hut while pottery jars filled with mysterious things lined a portion of the walls.

"Sit, Morning Light, and tell me, what troubles you?"

"You are right, I am troubled. I have heard whispers of a plant that can make one bleed and lose a child," Ronnie said very quietly. Okonhsa looked at her with startled surprise.

"Who tells you this?"

Ronnie shrugged. "Rumors, whispers, I do not remember."

"No woman seeks to get rid of her child."

"Okonhsa, please. Do you have knowledge of such a plant?"

"This plant you speak of, I have only heard it used as a poison, against a rival."

"A poison that in moderation does not kill but makes a woman bleed, is this not true?"

"Morning Light, this plant is very dangerous," the older woman said gravely. "Too little might only cripple the child, too much could cause the woman to bleed to death. I will have nothing to do with this. For what do you seek such a plant? Do you carry another child and not want it?"

Ronnie avoided the woman's probing question.

"Go home and rejoice that you are young and healthy and bring life into the world."

"Please, Okonhsa, help me find this plant?"

"No!" Okonhsa said firmly and turned her back to Ronnie which was the equivalent of shutting a door.

Morning Light's young brother, Wani, was soon to be sixteen. A sturdy, stocky young warrior who bore an ugly round scar on his left forearm. When the boy was only four, a trio of bushwhackers had held the end of a thick burning stick to his arm to force his ten year old sister to their will.

After their father's death, Wani had taken the role of being the male head of the family very seriously but it was token. He was far too young. Their shared tribulations had drawn the two close together. Morning Light now sought out her brother who had just returned from hunting.

"Wani?" She approached. "Please, walk with me, my brother."

"Morning Light," he acknowledged her. "You are still here? Your husband has not yet found Tonoaki? I would love to see that meeting after what he did to you…"

"What do you know of what he did to me?" she jerked around to look at him.

"He beat you. Everyone knows…" he paused. "But that is not what you were thinking, was it?" Wani's sharp mind jumped onward. He guided his beautiful sister out of the village gates to a quiet spot along the river. "What did he do to you this time?"

Morning Light bent her head in shame and began to cry despite her efforts not to weep. She did not know that her hormones were playing havoc with her self-control.

"What is it, my sister?" He swung around and took her firmly by her upper arms. "Why do you weep?"

"He was no better than the bushwhackers who burned you," she sobbed. "He forced me without forcing me."

"He threatened your children?" Wani's expression grew dark.

"The lives of my family in exchange for one night in his furs; it was worse than being forced. As part of the bargain, I could not fight him."

Wani emitted a low growl and punched the tree with his fist.

"Now I fear I am with his child. I fear what this child will do to my marriage." She saw the frown on her brother's face. "I love Jack, I truly love him, Wani, just as I loved Gray Wolf. You know how much I loved Gray Wolf."

Wani nodded. "We often say we wish to find a maiden to love us as you loved Gray Wolf. It is a story told often when we are sitting lonely around a campfire."

"I did not know that."

He nodded. "What can I do to help you, my sister?"

"I need you to take me to the next village. I need to speak to their wise woman."

"What of our wise woman?"

"She will not help me."

"To do what?"

"Do not ask, Wani. It is a woman's concern."

He considered. He did not know much about women's concerns. It was not appropriate for warriors to know much about women's matters. He would let it go.

"Does the white not love you as you love him?" He asked and saw her grow uncertain. "When do you wish to leave?" he asked. "Remember it will take two days to get there, two days to come back."

"Can we leave tomorrow?"

"Yes. Make your preparations."

Morning Light nibbled on travel cakes throughout most of their journey to keep from feeling sick. She took baby Mark with her to continue nursing. After they arrived in the neighboring village, Wani tended their horses while Morning Light sought out the village wise woman. While waiting, Wani found warriors his own age to spend the evening with before sleeping out by the community fire. Morning Light and her infant were offered the hospitality of the wise woman's hearth. In the morning, his sister left the hut carrying a handful of strange looking plants with tiny bright blue flowers wrapped in a large dark leaf. He did not recognize them as she quickly wrapped them into a cloth from her saddlebag.

When they returned to their village, the first thing Morning Light did was check on her other children.

"Did you get what you were seeking?" Singing Wind asked with suspicion.

"Yes."

"Daughter, please do not rush. Think about what you are risking. What would these children do without their mother?"

"It is safest if done early. Before I am two months is best," she whispered in the crowded long house. "I think I should go out into the forest to prepare what I need. I have been told what I must do and what to expect."

"It is days yet before you are two months. Can you not just rest a day? Think again about what you do. Pray to the Great Spirit to guide you. Please, you can wait just one more day. Why is it a bad thing to bring another child into the world? These are your children and this one," Singing Wind held a hand over her daughter's womb, "this one is also yours."

Morning Light nodded. "Very well, as you say, I will think deeply on it."

She spent the next day playing with her children and thinking about the one growing within her womb. Did Tonoaki really matter? It was her child. Her child.

The following morning, to Singing Wind's dismay, Morning Light took a small clay pot of hot coals, a cook pot, bowl, her bundle, and several other things. She prepared to leave the village.

"Wani, go with your sister…"

"I do not need anyone with me," she snapped and then felt another wave of nausea.

"…for protection!" Singing Wind insisted.

Wani nodded and followed his sister.

They walked into the forest until they found a spot where Morning Light felt comfortable. She gathered her firewood and started a fire. Wani left and found a spot at a distance. If she called he would hear and come but otherwise it would be as if he was not there.

Morning Light proceeded to do as the wise woman had told her. When everything was done, she set the liquid decoction aside to cool. She stared at it. It looked so insignificant, so benign. But with this liquid she could end the life of her child… and her own life as well if she drank too much.

The three patrols finally merged and found each other but they had not found the renegade band. What tracks they did find seemed to indicate the renegades had gone far into the mountains and into official French territory. The British soldiers could not follow unless they wanted to start another war.

"He's like a goddamn bad penny, always bound to show up," John muttered to Charlie One Claw. "Let the French deal with him, they deserve each other."

John had not told Charlie what the renegade had forced his wife to do. "Let's head back, Charlie. The men are beat and I miss my wife."

It was rather amazing how energized the men became when they heard they were heading for home. At least it was the home they knew, the familiar surroundings of the barracks. Those barracks seemed especially attractive after being on their feet for a month, climbing through briers, brambles, and bushes while bivouacking some place new every night.

Charlie One Claw rode on ahead and reached the Indian village first only to find himself besieged by several of the women. It was a hysterical Singing Wind who was sure she was going to lose her only daughter forever and Okonhsa, the wise woman, who vouched for the mother's fears.

The Indian scout rode back to find John.

"You hurry," he urged John. "Mother say you wife go off into forest to take poison."

"Why would she do that?" John blanched. *Not Ronnie,* he screamed silently. *Not Ronnie too!*

"Mother say she is afraid you will hate her and her new baby, take poison to get rid of child in belly. Very bad medicine," Charlie shook his head.

"New baby? Oh, God," John ribbed his horse and galloped across a meadow with Charlie. In medical school he had heard of women who had done all manner of things to get rid of an unwanted child. It usually ended badly. Why would she do this? Why? His conscience reminded him he had been too angry to say a proper good-bye when they had left.

John knew he should have stopped at the commander's tent first but he didn't; he tore through the village, Charlie at his heels, until he came to the sachem's log house. Singing Wind was outside waiting for him. She began talking rapidly.

She says you go that way," he gestured, "brother Wani go with her, take her some place that way."

"Come on, Charlie," John said as he grabbed his medical bag.

Charlie One Claw found the tracks easy to follow and led the way.

The sound of twigs snapping and footfall charging through the forest alerted Wani who was ready with his bow and arrows.

John crashed through the brush.

"Ronnie?!" he shouted, his heart was pounding in panic as he took in the scene. The fire. The pot. His wife sitting there, motionless, an empty bowl in front of her. "Ronnie, oh God, what have you done?!"

She sat with her head bent down. She was starting to feel sick.

"Your mother told Charlie you were cooking poison to take," he said in panic. "How much did you take? I can give you a purge. Ronnie, talk to me!"

She tried to stand but rolled on to her hip, grasped hold of a tree trunk and threw up. John knelt there feeling helpless and guilty but at the same time very glad to see her empty her stomach. He peered over her shoulder as he held her. He saw nothing to indicate a vile concoction. She turned. He let go of her. She wiped her mouth.

"Why?" he demanded, his voice filled with hurt. "Why would you do such a thing? Oh, God, how could you do such a thing? I love you and I need you. I don't want to go on in life without you, don't you know that? Ronnie, darling, forgive me for how I treated you when we left but to take poison...?"

"Jack," she reached out weakly. "Not to kill myself but to lose the baby."

"Why would you want to get rid of our baby?" he held her tightly.

"Maybe his baby."

"His? You mean Tonoaki? You tried to poison yourself because of that bastard?!"

"I did not take. In the end... I could not. I empty onto ground."

"Oh, thank God!" John felt like he could breathe again.

"I decide if you and your family not want brown-skinned baby, I will give to Robin Song. She has not been able to have child."

"You would give up your child because of my family?" He stood shaking his head, holding her. "I would not let you do that. Who says we don't want a brown-skinned child?"

"I see how your sisters see Gray differently than others."

"To hell with my sisters. Oh, Ronnie," John was near tears. "I was jealous. I admit it. I was jealous of that bastard."

The confused surprise was obvious on her face. "Of what?"

"I was afraid you... *liked* going to his furs again. You said you pitied him."

"But that is insult."

"I know that now. Charlie told me."

"Wani?" she called and the young warrior came running. "Thank you, my brother. I am well now that my husband is back. Please return these pots to our mother and tell her I am well and did not drink. She will understand."

He nodded and left without the look of animosity he generally had for John. Ronnie turned to John. "Please come with me to the river. I very much want to bathe."

"I could use a good washing myself," he nodded and followed her.

She brought them to a part of the river quite distant from the village. It felt private and peaceful. As John removed his belt and sword, jacket and boots, he was aware that he was still a bit shaken. The thought of losing Ronnie, a repeat of what he had endured twice already put a hollow in his belly and he grabbed hold of her as she began walking naked to the river.

She tried to read the look on his face and realized he was shaking.

"Jack?" she said softly.

He looked at the beauty of her standing before him. "Don't ever leave me... please," he gasped as he held her to him, so tightly she could hardly breath.

She relaxed in his embrace and after a time leaned back to look at his face.

"My heart is full of my love for you, Jack. I took vow, I never leave you."

"That includes harming yourself or doing something that might harm you."

She looked long into his clear gray eyes with the black rim around them.

"Will you forgive me?"

"Oh, Ronnie," he gasped, "of course, but you must never do anything like this again. Please… tell me."

"Never again. Whatever may come, my husband, we face it together."

"Yes. Together."

"Now let me help you with your shirt and breeches so we can bathe… together."

"Together," he nodded.

He took soap from his bag and walked naked into the river with her. She washed the dirt and dust from his yellow hair until it glistened in the sunlight. Then, she soaped and scrubbed the muscles of his torso until his pale skin and light chest hair was covered in little bubbles that reflected the light. As she moved over his body, her touch grew provocative and he took the soap from her and began to wash her. She laughed and dove beneath the water.

When she surfaced her hair was well rinsed and she bit on wild mint leaves she found along the river bank, rubbing them through her hair. They washed each other's backs and when John began soaping her front slowly, enjoying the slippery feel of her breasts, he thought of what Richie had said about being together in a cold river. The river wasn't that cold but he grabbed hold of Ronnie and when she gave him an extraordinarily sensuous kiss he felt himself grow into her just like his brother had said.

He found himself taking her right there in the water while she squirmed and thrashed and then begged him to go onto the shore.

"We'll get all dirty…" he warned.

"We can wash again…"

He lifted her from the water, placed her on the bracken along the river bank and intended to swive her until she begged for mercy. She exploded and convulsed repeatedly and he finally could hold back no longer. It was he who was ready to beg mercy.

Together they lie panting and finally he rose and pulled her up beside him, holding her slender frame against him.

"Tell me it was not like this with Tonoaki," he said softly.

She looked up at him. "No, Jack, no. It was *never* like this with Tonoaki. I never love him. But this last time… in fear I pretend and he did not know the difference. But I never kiss. The kiss is ours, only ours."

John smiled. "Well, I think everyone in the 'white world' does know about kissing."

She looked almost disappointed. She had thought only Jack's family knew the kiss.

"Come, we wash off again and then, my husband, maybe you take me home?"

Chapter 15

Marie was thrilled to receive a letter from John via the fort near Wilmington on the Delaware. She read it, re-read it, and then shared the news it contained with the family at the dinner table.

"So it would seem Ronnie tried to make a journey to the Indian village to visit her mother and her ex-husband kidnapped her and her three children. He led them deep into the wilds and then abandoned them with no food, no water, no weapons, and no clear understanding of where they were."

"That's horrible," Louise said softly.

"Three children?" Thomas spoke. "But don't they have four, *Grand-mère?*"

"*Oui,* but the scout had been able to escape with Gray. The fort commander sent the entire company out to search for her," Marie smiled, "which, of course, they did. And they found her unharmed but very lost."

"I'm surprised he didn't beat her again," said Helen, spooning a serving of cabbage onto Thomas' plate. Thomas, now fifteen, did not appreciate it and gave his mother an unnoticed scowl. "He seems to have a penchant for that sort of thing."

"Apparently he is not allowed to beat her because she is no longer his wife," Marie said knowing how ridiculous this sounded. "It is part of the code they live by. John was desperately afraid the man would kill her and the children but John writes he has learned they see no honor in killing an unarmed woman and her children so instead they were left in the middle of nowhere perhaps hoping the wilderness would do the dirty work."

"I think he knew the soldiers would find her," Charity said a little dreamily. "I think he still loves her and was hoping to get her back. He really didn't want to hurt her. I mean why else would they bother to kidnap her to begin with?"

"Oh, really, Charity, for heavens sake," Helen retorted. "Phillip, you are raising a hopeless romantic. It's those questionable novels you allow her to read."

"There's nothing wrong with being a little romantic," Caroline spoke up in defense of her daughter. "Life does not have to be all sharp edges and neat boxes."

"What is that supposed to mean?" asked Helen.

Phillip gave his wife a meaningful look.

"Oh, nothing. Nothing at all. Forget I said it, it's nonsense."

"I should say so," Helen replied. "'Sharp edges and neat boxes,' it really makes no sense."

"But Charity has a point," spoke up Thomas. "Why did they go to the trouble of kidnapping her in the first place? If they didn't mean to hurt her and they didn't plan to kill her. They didn't ransom her and she had no information to give them... what was the point?"

"Exactly!" Charity smiled at her cousin in appreciation of his support. "Maybe he did it to ask her to come back to him and when she refused, *then* he led her into the forest."

Marie looked at Richard and suddenly realized why else the Indian might have kidnapped Ronnie.

"Well, I must say," Marie spoke mildly but with authority as matriarch of the family. "I did not expect my report of John's letter to create such a conversation. I would say a change in topic is in order. Doctor Ajax, I am pleased to see you accepted Charity's invitation to dine with us again. How are things in your world?"

Ajax looked to his hostess and smiled. "Rather mundane, I should say. Stitching up lacerations and delivering babies. Rather ordinary stuff. Can't compare to chasing kidnappers through the wilds. Of course, as a physician *uneventful* really is the ideal. No epidemics, no heavy casualties, just small accidents and the ebb and flow of life."

"That is rather poetically said," Marie smiled and lifted her glass to him. "Perhaps my granddaughter's romanticism is rubbing off on you." She saw Charity blush bright pink.

"Speaking of epidemics," Ajax went on smoothly, "I hear there has been another smallpox outbreak in Boston. Has your daughter been inoculated, may I ask?"

Marie sighed. "I am afraid I have very little influence with my youngest daughter these days. I often wonder what Jacques would say."

"What about her husband?" Ajax asked.

"Ah, he may have even less influence than I. She has refused to have an inoculation. She argues it could kill her or, and I quote, 'worse, it could leave me with ugly pock-marks.' Now she is *enceinte* and uses the baby as an argument. I do worry."

"Chartes Landing has never had any exposure but all it takes is one person to arrive on the packet boat having been exposed and ill. I have thought of going up to Boston and obtaining the necessary means to inoculate but I am afraid it might not survive the length of the trip back here. However, if there is an outbreak in New York Towne, I shall go." He looked around the dining table. "If I did, would everyone be willing to be inoculated?"

"I would," Charity said immediately. Her mother frowned. Then Faith, Hope, Rebecca, and Thomas all echoed their willingness to be inoculated.

Louise looked at Lyndyn. "Would you?"

"I believe I would," he answered. "Caroline and I come in contact with the public everyday. We may be at the most risk."

"Good point, Lyndyn," Ajax nodded approvingly. "And if you catch it, you bring the disease home to your family." He looked at Caroline. "But if you have been inoculated you can no longer carry the disease to infect another."

"Doctor, you have given us something about which to think," Thor said rather formally, closing the discussion.

When dinner was over, Marie invited Ajax into Jacques's office for a private talk.

"Have a seat Archie, can I offer you some cognac or possibly port or sherry?"

"I believe I will take a glass of sherry, thank you."

Marie poured out two glasses and then sat behind Jacques' desk. She took a sip as did Ajax.

"I say, this is most excellent sherry," he smiled at her. "But obviously you have something on your mind. How can I be of service, Marie?"

"You must tell me," Marie decided to be direct, "is there something between you and my granddaughter?"

"Who?" he looked alternately startled, surprised, and confused.

"Charity."

"Marie! She's but a child."

"Yes."

"I am a couple of years older than John; I could easily be the girl's father."

"Yes."

"Well... I mean... well, I'm just very surprised you could even think such a thing."

"Come, come, now Archibald, you are a single, attractive, refined man and she is a very pretty young girl who appears to be quite taken with you. I know you are English and I am French but we cannot be that different in seeing how these things can be."

"Mistress Marie, I assure you I would never take advantage of a child," he said, sounding slightly offended. "But I can tell you she shows an extraordinary interest in medicine. And frankly, I have encouraged her in that regard. In fact, I was hoping to approach her parents in respect to establishing a formal apprenticeship, working and studying with me. At the very least, she could have a vocation as a midwife."

"That is most strange," Marie frowned. "I have not heard one word from her ever concerning having an interest in the healing arts. Instead, what I saw tonight was a young girl rather youthfully enthralled with you. Before you speak to Phillip and Caroline, let me probe Charity's feelings a little, eh?"

"Of course." Ajax finished his sherry and tried not to look uncomfortable.

"Quite frankly, it is to your daughter that I should like to pay court. Am I wrong in thinking you would have no objections to that?"

Marie smiled. "I have no objections but why are you so hesitant? You escorted her to Jamie's wedding so I take it your talk of pus and pustules was forgiven."

He saw her smiling and gave a nod to her humor. Then he went on more seriously. "I've lived in Chartes Landing many years now but I have never bothered to establish a fine residence. I still live above my offices. All her life, Louise has lived with all this," he gestured. "The finest house in the settlement, with servants and nannies, and… well, I know they say 'love conquers all' but it doesn't, you know. I can't expect Louise to step down to… well, I could never provide anything like this."

"Archie, I am truly surprised to hear you talk like this. Do you care for Louise?"

"I do, Marie, I have for a long time."

"And if she feels the same, can you see yourself joining our little community here under this roof? Louise has never run a home of her own. I genuinely doubt that she has any interest in it. It is my home but I have always enjoyed having family around me. I never took you for the timid type. If you want Louise's hand you must press your suit. It will be her decision, not mine but I expect she will anticipate continuing to live right here."

Shortly after this conversation Marie was able to take Charity aside.

"Come, my dear, come sit with me a moment. I wish to talk with you." Marie steered her granddaughter into the library. "Did you see any of your mama's ordeal?"

"No, *Grand-mère*. We were all asleep and knew nothing of what was happening. It is so sad."

"Yes, when you are in medicine, you must witness many sad things."

The girl nodded a bit absently.

"Death. Dying. Messy sickness. Brutal carnage. Amputations. Miscarriages."

The girl shivered and said, "It is a rather gruesome calling."

"Is this what you want to do?" with those clear, gold flecked eyes, Marie was watching the girl carefully.

"Hm, not me." The girl looked up at her grandmother. "Why would you think such a thing?"

"Why, indeed? Doctor Ajax seems to be under the impression that you have a passionate desire to work in medicine."

Charity flushed bright red. "I may have exaggerated my interest just a little." She could not look Marie in the eye.

"Yes, *ma petite*, perhaps you did. I understand, Doctor Ajax is a handsome older man, a man of knowledge with a certain power in his hands. Quite attractive to an impressionable young woman who is just awakening to her own powers."

"We're only friends."

"Yes, well, a good friendship should be founded on truth, not a pretense of interest in something so serious as a calling."

"Please don't tell Mother or Father."

Marie smiled sadly. "Your ma-ma and pa-pa have fresh wounds to heal. I see no reason to burden them with more concerns," she looked the girl in the eye, "as long as I do not find you acting inappropriately, yes?"

"Thank you, *Grand-mère*," and she kissed Marie on the cheek.

Several days later, Richard found Marie half-daydreaming, half-thinking in Jacques' study.

"Ah, here you are! I have planned a surprise and insist you come out with me on this beautiful day."

"What is it?" she asked as she stretched and looked up at him.

"Then it would be no surprise. Come, come," he leaned down and taking her hands in his he pulled her from the chair and led her out.

She really had nothing better to do and so she smiled and played along.

"We will need to ride," he said as he guided her toward the stables. "Do you wish a horse of your own or will you ride with me?"

"Can we not take the trap?"

"No-no, where we go it is a bit rough for the trap. You can sit in front of me and hold this basket, *n'est-ce pas?*"

"Very well."

The horse was already saddled and Richard mounted first after which the stable-hand gave Marie a boost up to sit in front of him.

"Oh, *mon Dieu*," she giggled. "It has been many years since I have ridden like this."

"I know but you still move like a woman half your age."

"In fact I do not ever remember riding like this. Jacques always set me up sideways in front of him. I only straddled the horse when I sat behind."

"So now you have a new experience." Richard smiled and held the reins with his arms around her. Richard continually strove to find ways to offer Marie some new experience unlike what she might have done with Jacques.

They cantered a bit, then slowed to a trot and finally to a walk as the terrain became more rough. They had passed the orchards growing along the river and went into land owned by the Powers but never really tamed.

"Where are we going *mon cher?*" Marie finally asked.

"We are almost there. It is a spot I have found, very private, where we can once again enjoy the river without the trappings of civilization." He slowed the horse as it walked around some thickets. Finally, they stopped. Richard got down, took the basket from Marie and placed it on the ground before helping her down from the saddle. He tied the horse to a sturdy sapling.

"Come this way," he said and carefully led her down a short bank to a tiny beach along the river bend.

"I had no idea this spot was here!"

"Right! Is it not perfect?" he grinned broadly.

"Oh, Richard, this really is too perfect," she turned full circle to observe their surroundings. "Do we dare go in naked like the old days?"

"But of course, why else would I have brought you here?" He grinned, put the picnic basket down, and spread a blanket. When he stood up again he gave her a grand, exaggerated bow. "Madame, may I have the pleasure of removing your clothes? That, I understand is a question often asked at the French court."

Marie giggled. "But of course, monsieur. I am always grateful for assistance." She gave him a deep curtsy.

They playfully removed each other's clothing and Richard led her out into the water. He dove beneath the water and when he resurfaced, he assured her of the stability of the bottom in this area.

"It slopes very gently, like a small valley," he told her.

When it become waist high on Marie, he urged her to put her arms securely about his neck and then her legs around his waist. Holding her, he continued into deeper water.

"Please, Richard, not too deep. You are so tall but already, it would be over my head."

He laughed and suddenly she felt him sliding into her.

"Oh!"

"I have been fantasizing about you in this river, all wet and slippery, riding on my *short sword*, ever since we arrived in this place years ago."

"Have you really?"

"Just like this."

"What a naughty thing to think about another man's wife." She grinned. "It does not feel so very short… Just remember," she gasped and giggled, "Remember I cannot swim."

"I know… which makes you cling even tighter."

Marie did hang onto Richard very tightly. The water was buoying her up as he moved her upon him.

"Ohh, *mon Dieu!*" he groaned and she felt him throbbing within her but short of her own satisfaction. He continued to hold her to him as they regained their breath. "You did not…?"

"No," she replied mildly.

"I am sorry."

She shrugged and then chuckled. "Another fantasy fulfilled *mon cher,* but was it as good as being in our bed?"

He set her down in the shallower water and she noticed a frown.

"There is no *our* bed, Marie. It is my bed which you visit when it pleases you."

She grasped his arm and studied his face. The effects of wear and weather and years had etched strong lines of character but so many years spent under a bushy beard had left his cheeks and chin remarkably resilient. His hair was steely gray now as were the trimmed brows over his bright, observant eyes. But now those eyes were looking sad… or was it hurt?

"Richard… I thought you agreed with our arrangement."

"Make no mistake. Pitiful wretch that I am, I will accept you anyway I may be allowed but it is a very hard thing to forever fight Jacques' ghost."

She looked up at the big man, trying to understand.

"He sits across from you every night."

She turned from him then as tears filled her eyes. "You want to sit in his chair?" Her voice was so small he barely heard her.

"No, Marie, no," he boomed. "I am very happy sitting right around the table corner from you. Close to you. But you could allow your eldest son to now sit at the head of the table, instead of seeing Jacques there at every meal."

She walked up onto the riverbank and she was weeping as she toweled herself dry with her petticoat. Richard came ashore and went to the picnic basket. He pulled out the wine and opened it, pouring them each a glass.

"I have upset you. I am sorry," he said contritely as he handed a glass to her.

She accepted the wine and drank it down. "No, I am the one who is sorry. I truly am. I am trying… but you are right, I am keeping his ghost alive. It is not fair to you. I take such baby steps… but it is all I seem to be able to do." She looked earnestly into his eyes. "I do love you, *mon cher* Richard."

"I understand; forget I said anything."

"You wish to marry."

He shook his head. "I do not need marriage. You are all I need but I do wish our relationship was not a secret. And I would like us to officially share a bed."

"Oh, Richard," she sighed, "I could not do that in front of the grandchildren. How can I tell them to remain chaste until marriage and then openly sleep with you without marriage? I cannot."

"Then we marry. It has been well over a year and Jacques did give us his blessing. It is time to stop the creeping about. I have always been very open about my life."

"Oh yes?" she said in mockery. "You kept your entire life away from us a secret. You hid Raphael away until he was grown, how can you say this?"

"That was because none of it meant anything to me, except Raphael… and him I brought to you…"

She cocked an eyebrow at him.

"…eventually." He smiled and kissed her deeply, the taste of wine was in her mouth. "I owe you a finish," he said softly and took her glass from her. Setting them both aside, he pushed her down on the blanket and looked her over with adoration. "*Mon Dieu*, you are beautiful," he said parting her thighs. Then in a quick change of mood. "Now you must excuse me," he said with comical formality, "while I ravish your lovely *chatte*." And his head disappeared from her view.

In only moments he re-struck the chord that had been left to fade away only minutes before in the water. With the bright blue sky above her, the sun warming her exposed flesh, the gentle breezes upon her and Richard doing things which felt so good, Marie was soon overwhelmed, tearing at the grass and sand beneath her out-stretched hands, and crying out in spasms of pleasure.

When she was completely sated, Richard returned to her side to bask in the warmth of her smile.

"This is… This is so… remarkable," she sighed deeply. "To lie here in the bright sunlight, completely open to the world without a thread to cover me. It is so freeing, so stimulating like I am part of the warm earth itself and the endless blue skies and the forests full of life. I have never felt this way before. I wonder if this is how Adam and Eve felt in Paradise before the Fall. Could this be what we will feel like when we die?"

"You have washed naked in the river before."

"Yes, but that is not the same. I also used to bathe outside in my tub when I wanted a warm bath… while you and Jacques were gone, but even then I was contained, not in touch with the earth itself, not laying flat, spread out like this."

"Marie, *mon amour*, you make my heart so very happy," Richard sighed as he traced her profile with his finger. He had given her another new experience.

The grandchildren had all been dismissed from the dinner table and bid to take their younger siblings in tow and go outdoors.

"Why?" Was the common response to which Marie only gave them a stare and said, "Ask not why. Because *Grand-mère* says so, that is why." When they had left, Marie looked at Lyndyn. "Would you mind waiting for Louise in the garden? Just some family business to attend, she won't be long."

"Of course," Lyndyn nodded politely and left.

Phillip and Caroline, Jamie and Cynthia, Helen and Thor, and Louise and Richard were all that remained. Marie didn't know why she could feel her heart beating faster but any prospect of change was bound to bring some emotional response and she really did not wish dissidence.

She looked at their faces. These here were only little children what seemed like just a few years ago. She took a deep breath.

"First, I wish to tell you that I am working on new seating arrangements for our Sunday dinners. This year will see three more grandchildren added to the 'grown-up table.' *Mon Dieu*, it seems only yesterday Helen, Louise, and Caroline were sporting grand bellies together, does it not?"

There was a murmured response.

"*Mes enfants*, everyday I am reminded of my own mortality. But I know my Jacques would want me to live this life while I am able. It has been fourteen months, two weeks, and five days since he departed. It is time we say farewell to his… ghost. He will always live in our hearts. I need keep a place set for him at this table no longer. Beginning next Sunday, Phillip, you, as the eldest son here shall take your place at the head of this table. When John returns the seat, of course, belongs to him as the official head of the family."

Caroline gave a small smile to her husband, pleased at the recognition he was receiving.

"Also, I want you all to know, Richard and I intend to be married. We will wait until Richie and Clarissa return home which should not be long now."

The room suddenly became very quiet.

"I have known Richard almost all of my life. Indeed, just as long as I knew your father. We both loved Jacques and we all loved each other in profound friendship. We share a life-time of memories and there is no one who could be more companionable to me now that Jacques is gone." She smiled at Richard and openly gave him her hand. "I hope all of you can be happy for us."

The awkward silence that followed caused Phillip to stand and make a production of seeing to it that everyone had at least a swallow left in his glass. That done, he held up his own glass.

"Here's to Mother and Uncle Richard," he pronounced, "may they live the autumn and winter of their lives in good health and joyful contentment."

Marie smiled as everyone uttered agreements and down went the wine.

Louise found Lyndyn in the garden and shared the news with him.

"Good for them," Lyndyn said as they strolled toward the orchards.

"Do you not think it is rather soon? Papa has only been gone a little over a year. My mother says she still loves him."

"It's a respectable length of time, Louise, and I'm certain she will always love your father just as some part of you will always love Raphael. But did I not hear that they have known each other for many years?"

"Yes, as long as she knew my father."

"Then they should know what to expect of each other and whether they can trust each other, so why should they put off the comfort they can give each other? They're not youngsters. Who knows how long they have left?"

Louise thought as she walked along, holding Lyndyn's arm. "It was very strange to hear Mother say it was time to say farewell to Papa's ghost. I thought Uncle Richard was just as upset by Papa's death as any of us." She was silent for a minute, thinking. "I guess if they can comfort each other that is a good thing, isn't it?"

"Louise, do you think you can see yourself saying farewell to Raphael's ghost?"

"What do you mean?" She turned to look at him.

"He's such a hard man to compete with. I mean, he was so good-looking and so perfect. And in your mind I know he'll never grow old, never get wrinkles or lose his hair, never get fat. I know you'll always love him but do you think you might be able to love me as well some day? Because I'm here and I'm alive and I can put my arms around you to comfort you, if you'll let me, and Louise, I do so love you. I have for years."

She stopped and looked into his face. "You have? You never told me."

"I knew how much you were grieving. I didn't think you wanted anything more than a friend."

"I guess I didn't," she agreed.

"And now?"

"Now… maybe I might be able to think of you as… as a friend who is also a suitor."

§

On the ride home, Helen said almost nothing because of the children but once they were off to bed she sought a private conversation with Thor.

"I really do not understand why Mother would want to get married again especially at her age. I mean Uncle Richard has always been part of the family and he still is. He lives right there. Why would they want to marry?"

Thor laughed. "Perhaps he wants to make an honest woman of her."

"Surely you are not implying that my mother has been… been having relations with Uncle Richard!"

"No, Helen, my dear, I am implying that they have found comfort with each other."

"And you think Uncle Richard wants that comfort to extend to the bed?"

Thor looked at his wife. "Yes, I do."

"But they're too old to have children"

Thor just sighed.

§

"I suppose, all things considered, that went very well," Marie said to Richard when they found a moment to be alone in the library. "I cannot believe it; they were in shock."

Richard kissed Marie and held her close. "They did all seem to have a dazed look, like a bear you have dropped a boulder on."

She giggled at the image. "I believe Helen has already convinced herself we will only sit in our bed in stocking caps and flannels, reading until we fall asleep. Why does everyone under the age of forty believe everyone over the age of fifty cannot possibly enjoy carnal lust?"

"And does my Marie enjoy *carnal lust?*" he asked as he grabbed her derriere.

"You very well know I do," she giggled and suddenly his hand was reaching beneath her skirts. "Oh, no, not here. What if one of the grandchildren should walk in?" She pushed him away.

"Ah," he sighed adopting a wistful look of longing. "So we wait until Richie returns."

"Your namesake."

"You have made me very happy today, *ma chère* Marie. So very happy." He took her back into his arms and kissed her again.

Marie had the feeling it wasn't going to be that easy and she was right. The next day Phillip and Jamie made a visit to the house to speak with her.

"What is it, *mes fils*, that brings you here in the middle of your day?" she asked as she poured each of them a hospitable glass of watered wine.

"We have concerns, Mother," Phillip began. "Are you aware that marriage will legally transfer ownership of everything you have to Richard?"

"Unless," Jamie added softly, "he signs legal paperwork stating he lays no claim…"

For a long fifteen seconds Marie looked from one son to the other. "I cannot believe this is a concern of yours. This is Richard, of whom we speak. Your pa-pa's dearest friend and mine. A man who has saved both our lives and our marriage, who built the trading post network and trekking routes and never failed to split the profits with your pa-pa even when Jacques no longer felt he was due them. A man who has lost his only son and heir and intends to leave everything he has to Raphael's widow… your sister and her children.

Jamie looked properly chagrined but not Phillip.

"Well, you see that's where things could get a bit muddled."

"How *muddled* exactly?" Marie asked calmly.

"Well," Phillip took a deep breath, "let's say, God in Heaven forbid, but just for argument's sake, let's say you should pass away first leaving everything in Richard's control, not that it wouldn't all be in his control from the moment you married. And then if he has made Louise and her children his only heir? Well, don't you see? Suddenly, everything you have including the store goes to her and if she marries Lyndyn then he owns it all. Hardly fair to the family is it? What you, Father, and Richard built suddenly all passes to a man who was just your apprentice?"

"As I recall, you have already received half of the logging business and the lumber mill," she said to Phillip. "And you," she looked at Jamie, "have all the orchards and the apple cider vinegar business. Plus, you each have land bought for you as *Pouvoir* heirs."

"Yes, but…" began Phillip.

"And your brother Richie has already inherited your father's half of the trading business and what Richard chooses to do with his half is Richard's business, not yours."

"I realize that Mother but…"

"No!" Marie held up a finger of warning and Phillip swallowed his words. "I cannot tell you how distasteful this whole conversation is to me. You," she looked fiercely at Phillip, "have five daughters for whom to make dowries which will pass into the control of the men they marry. I am very sorry Caroline lost your son, and perhaps God will bless you with another but if not, to whom will you leave your business, eh? And you," she turned her stare at Jamie. "You do not even have children as yet but if you wish to raise them with a good knowledge of hard work then they must see you working for your rewards. Build your own fortune to leave behind you and quibble not over the scraps of what your elders have built. Now leave me both of you. Say not another word and leave my sight. You have disgraced yourselves acting like spoilt children greedily fighting over biscuit crumbs in the nursery."

Phillip and Jamie silently withdrew and Marie sat for a long time considering all the reasons why she felt like crying.

For the sake of Louise and her children Marie put up a good show of humor through supper that night. Ajax had managed to wrangle another invitation as he was devoted to wooing Louise and he carried much of the conversation while Marie begged an early end to her day. Richard knew something was upsetting her. He brought cognac to her room and a bottle of wine. After three glasses of wine she told him of her conversation with her sons.

"Marie, you allow these things to upset you more than you should. I told you I saw no need to marry and if your sons are so afraid of a change, perhaps it is better we just continue as we have been."

"No, I am in good health and of sound mind. I will not be dictated to by my greedy *enfants*. If I wish to marry, then I shall do so. They have no right to bring a dark cloud into my world. Oh," she sighed, "*mon cher* Richard, I am embarrassed by my sons. I cannot think what Jacques would say."

"But if Jacques were alive," he said, taking her into his arms, "there would be no issue to discuss. Perhaps if I made it more clear… what my intent would be if I survived you. I have no desire to rob Caroline of her interest in the store. And when I said I intended to leave Louise everything I would have left Raphael, well, you and I had not spoken of marriage."

"No, Richard, no! It is morbid and unseemly. I hate that they are so absorbed in what they will inherit when I die. It hardly makes me feel loved."

"I had hoped that I made you feel loved." He kissed the back of her neck.

She turned to face him. "You do but I mean my children's love. Toward the end, a mother always wants to feel her children's love."

"I do not wish you to be upset by all this, *ma chère*. Let us leave the matter rest for a time. Richie has yet to return home."

"True. And I should write to John. I wish he was here. I would like to have his opinion." She sighed. "I thought life was supposed to become easier as you got older."

Richard laughed loudly. "Oh, my sweet Marie. Do you not know… the more people you add to your life, the more complicated it becomes."

"But they are grown, they are supposed to be sensible."

"Yes, but you are a mother and always a mother and want to take care of everyone." He poured her another glass of wine. "And I want to take care of you. You are my reason for living."

"I am very blessed," she responded softly and reached up to stroke his face.

"Phillip?!" Richard called out as he walked into the lumber mill office.

"Uncle Richard, what a surprise. What can I do for you?" Phillip stood and gestured to the only other chair in the room.

Richard closed the door.

"I understand you have concerns for your mother's property if we were to marry."

"Well," Phillip tried to smile amiably. "The whole idea of her marrying again was a bit of a shock. No offense intended."

"None taken. If I still had a mother I might feel the same way. But I do not. What I am concerned about is Marie. She has been very upset with her own sons and I do not wish to see her this way. I am prepared to sign just about anything you wish in order to set this issue aside. I make no secret of the fact that I intend to leave everything I currently have to Louise and Raphael's children. I wish no one to feel they have been treated unfairly. Draw up anything you wish, to say I have no claim, I make no claim upon anything that is Marie's. That includes her home, her business, her investments, her bank accounts. That should satisfy all of you, *n'est-ce pas?* I love your ma-ma more than I can say and sharing our lives for what time we have left is all I desire. She will continue to control her holdings and she may leave it to whomever she wishes. Will that take care of things?"

"Of course, Uncle Richard. Please don't think badly of us. I'll write to Sir Reginald."

Richard looked at Phillip a little sadly. "And perhaps it would be better not to mention this to your ma-ma."

Chapter 16

Molly Adler had led a very sheltered life in New York Towne. Some would say an outright boring life. When her mother was asked once at a church tea what plans she might be making for Molly's future, if a marriage match was in the making, her mother had replied:

"Marriage?! Good Lord, no. I didn't go through the pains of having the girl only to lose her just when she could be useful. She will take care of me in my old age. That is the plan for her."

"But surely," her companion responded, "the girl deserves a chance for a home and children of her own."

At this Mistress Adler laughed unkindly. "With a face like hers, Mister Adler would have to pay some sap to take her. A waste of good money. Besides, she'll never want for a home, ours will one day be hers."

Some time later smallpox swept through their neighborhood. Molly's mother and father both died and Molly herself was stricken but survived, thanks to her youthful good health. The scarring was barely noticeable and seemed to simply add character since she'd never had any beauty.

Suddenly Molly found herself completely alone except for her few church acquaintances. She also was now the owner of the family home and furnishings, a farm outside of New York Towne, a half interest in a saloon, ten slaves who kept things running at home and on the farm, and an enviable bank account.

Cecil Tingley habitually perused the obituaries in the town's leading weekly publication. He was an ordinary looking fellow, nothing special, with sandy brown hair and rather watery blue eyes, but his smile and his self-confidence could transform him into someone quite attractive.

Smallpox had brought on a number of deaths. Tingley saw the obituary for Mister and Mistress Adler. The space given indicated the man was of some means. Sole survivor, a daughter Molly. No other siblings, no other relatives. He had found himself an heiress.

Tingley made it his business to begin attending the same church Molly did. In time he discovered who she was, a drab little bird hiding behind her veils. In more time he saw to it that he was in her path. He gave her smiles, nods, tipped his hat until he noticed she began looking for him. Finally, he arranged an introduction.

Molly had no preparation, no experience, no teaching to assist her in dealing with the man or any man. She had no means to judge his sincerity or true nature. She only knew what she was told and he told her she had bewitched him. Through some feminine allure she had taken over his world, his consciousness, his dreams, his very willpower. He must have her as his own or perish in the cruel wake of rejection. Molly was beside herself with joy and youthful lust, with feelings of love and happiness and disbelief that this should actually be happening to her.

They must wait a respectful year to marry she said when he proposed. He seduced her in the hopes of moving forward the wedding date. It worked. She was completely under his spell and agreed that six months was long enough. Her parents had never been that good to her anyway. Molly even convinced herself that she was beautiful in Cecil's eyes and so she felt beautiful as long as she stayed away from mirrors.

It was a small, quiet wedding followed by a rather drunken wedding night. Tingley did his duty and consummated the marriage, legal and proper, but from that time forth his attentions waned somewhat and Molly told herself it was to be expected after all, they were married now. He settled into enjoying all that his marriage had brought to him. The servants, the home, the rich furnishings. He liked to dress well, eat well, and drink fine wines. He also liked to gamble.

The half interest in the saloon was the first thing he convinced her they should sell. It wasn't difficult. Ownership in a saloon was hardly a worthy investment for a lady of good society, now was it? He did not need her permission or agreement to sell any of her assets but it pleased him to make a show of consulting her and gaining her approval.

Then he made a rather large withdrawal from her bank account and made a show of purchasing an expensive piece of jewelry for their first wedding anniversary. She appreciated his sentiments but did not know where she would ever wear such a bold and rather gaudy piece as they gave no parties and had no social circle.

In their second year of marriage he decided to sell the farm and the slaves that worked it. The money went into his private bank account. When he next looked into selling the house, he learned that in accordance with her father's will, the house could never be sold as long as Molly lived there.

"We will soon be married two years," he said quietly one night as they ate dinner. "And since you have not proved fruitful," he sighed with an attitude of wistful regret, "I see no reason to keep up such a large house. I noticed a very nice home, a bit more modest in proportion and newer, which I think we should look into buying."

"Oh," she replied feeling guilty that somehow she had not conceived many children already.

"I want to take you out tomorrow to see it."

"Of course," Molly nodded agreeably.

The new house was, indeed, delightful with many large windows to let in the sunshine, four bedrooms, a small attic and a modest garden requiring only a part-time gardener

"I do believe we could be very happy here," Tingley said as he showed Molly around. "And we can do nicely with just a cook and a housekeeper, no need to have two maids and a gardener. I can hire a part-time boy."

"But we still would need a laundress, Cecil. We can't expect the house-keeper to do the wash as well."

"Ah, yes, a laundress," he smiled. "You women are so much better at keep-ing track of all these things. Then I shall only sell one maid and the gardener." And he kissed her lightly on her pock-marked brow.

That spring they moved into the new house. Less than half of the furnish-ings fit and so everything left behind was also sold as the house itself was sold. Paintings, statuary, gilded mirrors, clocks, desks, chairs, highboys, chests, cup-boards, tables, settees, garden furniture, fine bedroom sets, the horses in the stable, the large carriage.

Molly set about making sense of the garden, working in it herself as much as the part-time garden boy did. She took pride in seeing it transformed.

Then one evening, Cecil did not come home. At first Molly was worried thinking something dreadful must have happened to him. Then she became ashamed thinking he had been gambling perhaps, become inebriated and fallen into the bed of some trollop. Then she grew angry.

It was two days and still no word. Finally, she became hysterical and sought out the local authorities, fearful something horrendous had indeed happened and his body was floating in the river or dumped stiff and cold in some alley. The authorities could uncover no word of him. They took his description, they set out posters of him, they searched the alleys and sleazy establishments, the known gambling houses and whorehouses. He was nowhere to be found.

The days passed and Molly couldn't eat. She couldn't face the world with-out her darling Cecil. It was now the end of the month and she gave a purse to her trusted housekeeper and sent her to the butcher, the baker, the green gro-cery, and the fish market to pay their bills for the month.

The next day, the first day of the month, there was a knock on the front door. The housekeeper escorted in a stranger.

"This be a Master Postum, ma'am, he says he's the... landlord?"

"What can I help you with, sir?" asked Molly, her eyes still swollen from weeping.

'I'm here to collect the rent, Mistress Tingley." He stood hat in hand.

"Rent? What rent?"

"This be my house you are renting, the Mister paid two months up front but it be due for this month now."

"I don't understand," said Molly in confusion. "We bought this house, it is ours."

"No ma'am, it ain't. Your mister said you might be interested in buying but there was never nothing settled. You only be renting it now."

Molly got up and went to her purse. After paying off the merchants for the month she found herself a bit short.

"I'm afraid I must go to the bank. Do you have an office? I shall bring it 'round."

Mister Postum left and Molly donned her light half-cape and hat and walked to the bank. The manager saw her walk in and knew there was going to be trouble. Best he contain it in his office away from other customers.

"Good day, Mistress Tingley."

"Good day," she tried to smile.

"Come to my office," he invited and led her in, closing the door behind her. "Please have a seat. Now, what can I do for you today?"

"I haven't seen you for sometime," she said trying to remember the man's name. "My husband has been taking care of all our business but he's not at home at the moment and I seem to find myself a bit short. I need to make a small withdrawal for the month's expenses."

The manager looked decidedly uncomfortable. He cleared his throat.

"Mistress, did Mister Tingley not tell you… he came in last week and closed both your accounts."

"Both?" she frowned in puzzlement.

"Yes. The account you inherited from your father and then Mister Tingley had opened another account of his own. He withdrew everything and closed them down."

"What? But why?"

"I'm afraid you'll have to speak with your husband, ma'am."

"I haven't seen my husband in days, the authorities are searching for him. We're afraid something terrible may have happened. I simply must have some money, a small loan perhaps? After all, my family has done business with you for years."

"Of course, I can draw up a small loan based on… say, a lean against your carriage."

"We sold the carriage and the horses."

"Well, then… it's rather overkill but the deed to your house should be sufficient," he smiled.

"The deed? But we sold the house… two months ago," she flushed out, getting very warm. "I only just learned that we didn't buy another… I'm afraid I have no deed."

"I see, well, is there anything of substance you can offer as collateral?"

Molly sat taking very deep breaths as she realized Cecil had liquidated everything she had inherited from her parents.

"My jewelry, sir. I'm afraid it is all I have left."

"Fine. Please bring it in and I will see what I can do."

Molly left the bank and removed her cape. She loosened the buttons at her neck. She would have hired a cab but she did not even have sufficient funds for that. Thoughts raced through her mind. Ugly thoughts. Harsh thoughts. Confusing thoughts. Where was Cecil? Why had he disappeared? What had he done? Her whirlwind courtship. How could she have believed any man could really love her? Plain, homely, scar-faced Molly. How kind he had seemed, how attentive. How he had pursued her until the wedding was over. She had believed he loved her. With complete trust she had allowed him to take over everything. Husbands were given control of everything anyway but she had never questioned. She had forgotten her father's will had said the house would always be hers... *as long as she lived there*. That was why he had moved her out. Moved her into a rental, made her think he was buying it... all so he could sell her house too, and she had let him. She had gone along with everything. She had been such a stupid, trusting fool.

Molly was weeping as she walked up the steps to her front door.

Jozy had been the family housekeeper for many years. When she saw the young mistress weeping as she walked she thought they must have found the master in the East River.

"Oh, mistress, have they found the master?"

"No, Jozy, and I don't think they ever will. He has gone and he has taken everything I had."

She said no more but went straight to her room and to her jewelry box. For a moment she was afraid he had taken that as well. But no, it remained. She wrapped it in a flannel and put it under her arm. She would go to the jeweler.

"Jozy, come with me. I do not want to walk alone."

The women walked in silence and finally arrived at the finest jewelry house in New York Towne.

"I would like to see the manager," Molly requested.

The clerk smiled and hustled away.

In less than a minute a gray haired gentleman, impeccably dressed, came out from a back area. He saw Molly clutching a jewelry box with a desperate look on her face and was afraid he already knew what she wanted.

"Yes, ma'am, may I help you?"

"I would very much like to know the value of these," she stated without preamble.

"Of course." He took the box from her hands and set it upon his counter. He opened the box and spent some time going through the pieces with the aid of a powerful eyepiece. At last he looked at her.

"The rope of pearls and these earrings are the most valuable pieces. The two silver brooches are quite old and very nice. The lockets do show wear."

Molly listened. They were her mother's pieces.

"But what of this piece?" Molly asked as she picked up the large necklace Cecil had given her for their first anniversary.

"Just costume jewelry, I'm afraid. Worth a few pennies no more."

"What?"

"It's fake, madame, imitation. In time these glass pieces will begin to discolor."

Molly was speechless for a moment. "Might I have a glass of water? Please?"

"Yes, of course," the jeweler nodded to his clerk and soon a glass of water appeared.

Molly drank the water and then spoke. "I shall keep my mother's diamond earrings. What will you give me for all the rest?"

When Molly and Jozy left the jeweler's shoppe she had enough money to pay the rent for several months and then some, but what would she do when that ran out? How would they eat and where would they live?

For three days, Molly thought. She wasn't a stupid person, she told herself, just stupidly naive, trusting, unprepared to deal with the world that really existed. She had been kept ignorant and now she needed to make some hard decisions. She asked herself what happened to refined women down on their luck such as she? Her answer: they became housekeepers, governesses, or nurse-companions if they were lucky; laundresses, kitchen maids, or general maids if they were not. She grimaced at the prospects. Lowly servants trapped working for someone else for the rest of their lives. She pictured herself at fifty, scrubbing out a fireplace on her hands and arthritic knees. NO!

What had her father liked to say was the oldest profession in the world? A much easier life, if one was careful. She had discovered she liked the activity but being in a house was safer and managing a house was more profitable. Being one's own mistress. She had classy furnishings which she knew wouldn't fetch much on the market if she was selling them for food, but they would furnish an establishment quite nicely.

Taking Jozy with her, Molly began to walk around that area of New York Towne known as the 'red light district' looking for fresh young faces and talking to the 'ladies of the evening' who had no place to go. She invited them home with her. She arranged for a doctor to come and give everyone an examination and when they were declared disease free, they officially became part of Molly's House.

Then Bernadette arrived. Recently come from London, she giggled at the name.

"What do you find so funny?" Molly asked.

"Best you change the name of the house, mum, for in London everyone knows a Mollie House is for men to meet up with other men, if you get my meaning. You'll be attracting the wrong kind of man who wants no girl."

"Oh! Oh my, well, I guess we will just have to call it Jozy's House," and she laughed as the hapless housekeeper stood by.

A short time later Molly found herself dodging the church busy-bodies. She decided they needed a new location. Molly had recently heard of the peaceful settlement of Chartes Landing which had no establishment such as she hosted, but did have a lumber mill with a crew of many single lumbermen and lumber-jacks. She wanted to leave New York and all its bad memories behind, and so in the summer of 1726, Molly, her girls and her furniture moved to Chartes Landing.

Chapter 17

Frontier - April 1727

John reread the letter he received from Phillip and thought of it in conjunction with the one he had received from his mother. By all accounts it had been a very emotionally trying autumn and winter at Chartes Landing. Phillip and Caroline had lost their baby son. Old Jane Sims had died. And old Margo had been very ill.

On the more pleasant side, Jamie and Cynthia were finally married and moved into what mother had described as "a very fine house though not so large as the one your father built." And Jamie appeared intent on breeding horses. Richie and Clarissa had returned safely from another profitable trek; Mother and Richard had married; and Izzy and Hamilton had welcomed their first child, a boy named Hamilton Chadwick Grenville Carter II (of course) whom they referred to as "Baby Chad."

Then John frowned. He sensed what could only be a certain note of pride as Phillip relayed that they had convinced… no, John looked at the letter again. The word Phillip used was "encouraged" Uncle Richard to sign a prenuptial agreement to relinquish all claim to any of their mother's possessions. And Richard had asked them to keep it a secret. Now what the hell had brought that on, John wondered? It wasn't as if Uncle Richard was a fortune hunter. My God, the man was family already and their father's best friend. A more gener-ous and trustworthy soul, they did not know. It was an insult, yet one of which Phillip seemed very proud. And who was the "them" he had asked to keep it secret?

As for Mother and Richard getting married? John wished them all the happi-ness they could find together. It wasn't easy to find someone to share your life with, really share it. He ought to know.

John looked at the clock. He was officially off duty now and done for the day. He left his office and went home to Ronnie who was getting bigger everyday. It wouldn't be long now.

It was a short walk from the surgery to his house. Ronnie had persuaded him to build a bedroom for her mother so she could come and help with the children. He had seen to the building of two. They'd need them soon enough. Of course the house wasn't really his, it belonged to the fort and the fort belonged to the king but still who knew how long they would be living here.

John smiled as he observed the strips of flowerbeds looking so out of place in a fort but the commander's wife had insisted. Women did civilize things. The daffodils were faded but the tulips were springing up. Strong stemmed, colorful flowers, he liked tulips. It was spring, soon it would be Easter. He knew the fort chaplain was making some special plans for his Easter sermon. John felt a stab of conscience that he had never talked to Ronnie about Christianity. Initially, her vocabulary was so limited but now he thought it would probably be a good thing to have her take lessons with the chaplain. Chaplain Rigby would like that. Saving a soul and all. Give him something to do. John smiled. Ronnie was the purest soul he knew.

John walked into the house he and Ronnie called home. By the smells he could tell supper had been prepared. The table was set complete with napkins. Gray was in the parlor reading from his book to Sunshine and Matthew, Mark was swinging from a kind of pouch seat swing nearby.

Gray looked up at the tall man who was now his mother's mate.

"Hello children," John greeted with a broad smile, "how is everyone? Where is your mother?" John looked around.

"She told me to stay here and read to my brothers and sister," Gray said solemnly, obviously taking his duty very seriously. "Mother is in the bedroom."

John immediately went to the bedroom door. He opened it just far enough to see Ronnie soundlessly grunting out her baby as she clung to one of the four posters of their bed. Her mother and Elinor Greeley were with her.

"Captain, be so kind as to give your children their supper. All is well here. Now out!" Elinor commanded.

It was insane. He was a doctor but even so, Ronnie would accept only female assistance. Indelibly etched into Ronnie's beliefs was the tenet that a man had no purchase in a birth. John brought them more warm water, then brought the children to the supper table. He gave Gray and Sunshine their food and hand fed Matthew while Mark slept in his swing. For himself, he had no appetite but waited until Ronnie called for him.

At last Elinor came out beaming ear to ear but said nothing more than he should go to his wife while she watched the children.

John rushed in and saw her, in bed and smiling, radiant actually, as she displayed the naked little baby on the blanket with her. His pale skin was flushed red as he squirmed and finally latched on to his mother's breast. His hair was pale yellow like corn silk.

John leaned over and gave Ronnie a kiss on her forehead. "Another fine son," he smiled. "This one we shall call *Luke.*"

"Luke," she repeated. "Luke." She nodded. "I like."

There was really no way to tell who was the father. Luke looked exactly like Sunshine had looked when she was born. Blond hair, blue eyes with fair skin… which was exactly how Matthew and Mark had looked. And Ronnie knew Sunshine was Tonoaki's daughter. John was as aware of this as Ronnie but he did not speak of it. Neither of them spoke of it.

John embraced the child as his, every bit as much his as Matthew and Mark. In any event, the child was most certainly Ronnie's child and he loved Ronnie more than ever. She was a superb mother and yet she had brewed a poison and been sorely tempted to drink it, risking her own life to save him from any embarrassment over a dark skinned child. He still shuddered to think on it but at the same time, foolish as it was, it underlined the depth of her devotion to him.

Chapter 18

Isabelle sat at her vanity table looking at herself in the mirror while Percy, her lady's maid, brushed Isabelle's abundant pale gold locks. She scrutinized her face. It was two months since Baby Chad arrived. She'd lost all the pregnancy puffiness and her figure was returning although she had not yet regained her eighteen inch waistline.

Isabelle considered. The doctor had told Hamilton to wait three months before "reclaiming his marital prerogative." She had rolled her eyes at the time. It was just as much her prerogative as Hamilton's and she enjoyed it every bit as much. What she didn't enjoy was being stretched out of shape for at least six months, feeling like she was going to puke every time she smelled something cooking, and the pain of birthing itself.

She had told Hamilton she was not a breeding cow after all and he already had his son and heir. The way she saw it, she deserved at least two years before she should have to go through the whole process again but she assured him she was not suggesting two years of abstinence.

"Surely there must be something you gentlemen employ to keep from impregnating the womb," she said batting her lashes while unbuttoning the front of his britches. And while she teased and petted him, he had stammered that there were methods but none of them were very satisfactory. "Then I must go visit mother," she cooed as she sought to please her husband first with her hands and then with her mouth. "I shall show her the baby and see if there is something we ladies can do." By then Hamilton was so wrought up in the pleasure she was giving him, he would have agreed to chipping a ship out of ice and sailing to the north pole.

Hamilton had refused to allow her to leave on her own so she had waited a week while he tied up business affairs. Then mid-week he had come home with the news that he must stay awaiting the arrival of a government official whose ship was due in harbor soon.

"Soon?!" she had exclaimed. "How long is soon, Hamilton, dearest?"

"It's a very important meeting, my pet."

"How long?"

"Perhaps a week… or two."

"Two more weeks? Oh, my darling, my handsome prince, in two more weeks we will no longer be forbidden and I so long to feel you inside me again but we can do nothing without the wisdom. Let me go to my ma-ma, and ask her secret. She stopped having children after me but I know full well she and my pa-pa did not stop enjoying each other in bed. She knows something. Please, my love, I can take Brutus, he will make a fine bodyguard. And Percy is devoted to me. And Drusie is devoted to Baby Chad. Oh, please, and if you have not joined us in three weeks I shall return to your waiting arms," she wheedled and, of course, Hamilton agreed.

Now, as Isabelle stared into her mirror she knew their bags were packed and they were boarding ship tomorrow.

It was not like Isabelle to arrive without fanfare but the trip and passage had been arranged so quickly there had been no time to send notice of the ship. She was riding with the same mail pouch that would have announced her arrival time. But she had written to Marie the very first she had decided to come home.

Marie talked to Richard and he talked to Phillip and between the two of them they had someone down at the dock for the arrival of the packet boat from the north every day. Often it was Richard, sometimes Marie was with him and they always brought up any mail for the rest of the family.

One day the packet boat arrived in the midst of April showers. Marie saw the little figure, breath-taking in her very fashionable garb, standing and waving excitedly at them. Marie also noticed the very large negro man standing next to her daughter holding a ridiculously feminine umbrella over Isabelle's head while a negro woman held another umbrella over a second negro woman holding a bundle in her arms. Marie's stomach tightened and she could not wave.

They had brought the covered carriage. Marie had assumed Hamilton would be with them and the baby and of course luggage. Richard took no notice of the rain although Marie could tell it was affecting his arthritis. He helped Isabelle up into the carriage where Marie was waiting.

"Oh Ma-ma, it's so good to see you again," she said brightly and leaned over to give Marie a kiss on the cheek. That done she turned to the young negress carrying the bundle. "Give him to me, Drusie, then climb in so you can take him back."

The girl gave up her bundle and with Richard's assistance, she climbed in out of the rain and took back the baby.

"Uncle Richard, would you arrange a wagon to bring my luggage and Brutus and Percy can ride on it."

"I should say not!" Marie interrupted. "Richard will arrange for your luggage to be delivered but the people come with us out of the rain."

"They're only servants," Isabelle said dismissively.

"They are people. Come," she called to the two, "get in. There is room."

"They stood looking at her and then to Isabelle until they saw her nod her head in approval. When she did, they climbed into the carriage.

"And would you like to introduce everyone?" prodded Marie.

"Well, this is Drusie, she looks after Baby Chad. And this is Percy, my lady's maid, and Brutus is our bodyguard. Hamilton wouldn't think of allowing me out of his sight unless I had a bodyguard," she added proudly.

"How do you do, everyone," Marie nodded and they all nodded in varying degrees of humility. "My name is Marie Bonchance. I am Isabelle's mother. I would prefer you refer to me as Mistress Marie." She smiled warmly. "That is Mister Bonchance, my second husband whom you may call Master Richard."

"Oh, Mother, you don't have to explain family history to them."

Marie looked at her daughter and just then Richard returned.

Richard pointed the large negro to join the stable-hand up in the driver's seat and then sat next to Marie. On the ride home she had a chance to hold her newest grandson.

"He's beautiful, Izzy, and so big for his age," she smiled.

"You don't have to tell me how big he is, I felt it," Isabelle grimaced. "Of course, Hamilton is so pleased he can barely keep his buttons from popping off. We didn't think *Hammy* was suitable and Hamilton is just so formal and his daddy's name, so we started calling him Chad."

"I think it is perfect and so is he. Isabelle, you did well, *ma fille.*"

"Thank you." She beamed.

When they arrived home, Marie went quickly to seek out Louise in light of Isabelle having brought servants with her. Louise was prevailed upon to move temporarily to Richard's old room so her sister could have what they still called *Grand-père's suite* as it had been built years ago in anticipation of a visit from Jacques' parents. And so it had a small room on each side for a lady's maid and a valet who served the Duke and Duchess. Percy was assigned to one side room, Brutus to the other and Drusie was shown to the nursery where Sarah was delighted to get her hands on a babe again.

Nora headed up the work detail that moved Mistress Louise. The luggage arrived and one small trunk was sent to the nursery and the rest went into Isabelle's room.

"My-my," Marie observed with a laugh, "I do not think your grandparents had so much luggage and they stayed for two years."

Isabelle pursed her lips. She threw her outer wrap on the bed along with her hat. Her maid immediately picked up the damp wrap and sought to hang it for drying.

"Percy will tend to the unpacking," Isabelle said sweeping a hand through Marie's arm. "I am famished and a good strong cup of tea wouldn't be out of place," she smiled.

"Excellent, young Margo has set up a lovely spread for us in the dining room," Marie responded and then stopped and took a good look at her youngest daughter. "You look so well… and happy. I am guessing married life agrees with you."

"It does Ma-ma, but I do have something I must speak to you about… privately, after we eat."

"Of course."

Sebastian Bonchance, who was growing fast and was always hungry, heard there was food and came into the dining room.

"Ah, Sebastian, good. Go up to the nursery and tell Drusie she may leave the baby there and come down here for food."

"Mother!" Isabelle reacted.

"Oh, I know it is not usual that the servants eat with us but there have been special occasions in the past and this too is a special occasion. Come," she gestured to Brutus who after hefting in the luggage had just been hanging awkwardly about in the hall. "Come and eat." She gestured to Percy.

Phillip walked in. "Hello, just in time for food I see. Thought I'd check if the little mite arrived. Ah, there she is." He grabbed hold of his sister and gave her a swing around.

"Phillip stop!" she half laughed and then turned in annoyance. "Mother, please! Stop! One does not eat with…"

Everyone had become very quiet, watching and listening.

"With what?" Marie persisted.

"Mother, you don't understand. It's very difficult to hire decent help in Boston. You have no idea."

"They have no indentures coming to Boston?" Marie asked rather sharply.

"You don't understand. Indentures all want a trade, no one wants to do menial house chores anymore. For that you need to buy a… a… slave."

"So, you finally say it. You know your father worked to prohibit slavery in Chartes Landing. We have an ordinance. There is no slavery in Chartes Landing!" She turned from her daughter and looked at the three people Isabelle had brought with her. "There is no slavery in Chartes Landing," she repeated.

"Here, that is the law. You are free."

The three looked at Marie with confusion and then, as though she were mad. They looked at each other.

"What you saying, Mistress?" Brutus finally spoke, his voice low and rumbling.

"I mean that for what it is worth while you are in our community, you are a free man. You can go where you want when you want, do what you want. Do you understand *free*?"

The big man nodded his head.

"I am afraid that as soon as you leave Chartes Landing, however, you well may be tracked and pursued as a runaway slave but as long as you stay here, Isabelle cannot tell you what to do. "You will need to find work while you are here. Something you can do to earn money so you can pay for your own needs."

Drusie began to tremble. In Africa her mother had been captured with others of her tribe by the black slavers, a tribe that made their wealth by kidnapping other tribes and selling them at the slave markets on the west coast. Her mother had been sold to a slave ship where hundreds were loaded into the dark hold. The captain had stopped them when he saw her mother, he held her out to be his cabin slave and by the time they had landed in the islands she had his seed growing in her belly. She had eaten well on the voyage over. She had been able to walk on deck in the sunshine and bathe in buckets of cool salt water. The captain had not treated her badly and because she was the captain's no one else touched her. In the markets of the islands, Drusie's mother looked healthy and strong and was beginning to show her fertility. She brought a high price and her new master treated her well and gave her many more babies, some of whom he sold and some of whom he kept. He had kept Drusie. She was the last girl her mother had birthed and when the master died, the plantation was sold in pieces. Drusie was one of the pieces. She and her mother were to go to the Boston market but her mother died on the ship. Drusie had been purchased by Hamilton Carter and brought home to his wife. Because Drusie was half white and only dusky skinned, Mistress Carter had set her to nursery work and she liked it. She didn't want to go, take a chance, risk getting a harsh job with a harsh new master, fend for herself in this big strange world filled with white people. With Master and Mistress Carter, she was taken care of.

"I... I... no wanna go, Mistress. I like Baby Chad. I like work for Mistress Isabelle. Please don't make me go." She was becoming hysterical.

"Very well, if that is your choice then you shall be paid while you are here," Marie pronounced and looked at her daughter. "What is the going rate for a nursery maid? Whatever it is, you are to pay it. Meanwhile, Brutus and Percy, you think about what you have learned. You have the same decision to make. Stay here and be free or go back with the Carters as your owners. Just tell us what you decide to do. And whether you decide to stay with the Carters or not, you also shall be paid as a free person while you are here."

Marie looked at her daughter. She could tell she was angry but what choice did she have. How dare she bring slaves to her father's town where there was never to be any slavery?! Marie was angry as well.

Richard came up with a small plate of the foods he knew Marie liked and gave it to her. He was grinning ear to ear.

Sebastian sat next to his mother Louise and Aunt Isabelle.

The three blacks sat with each other and ate like they had not eaten all day. Marie noticed and considering her daughter's thoughtlessness for her "property" perhaps they had not.

Phillip chose to sit close to Marie and Richard. "You certainly know how to stir a crowd, Mother. Of course I can't believe the little rascal brought slaves to Chartes Landing. Father would be spinning in his grave."

"I appreciate your support, *mon fils*, but that is such a vulgar expression. I cannot imagine your pa-pa spinning anywhere."

The next day, tempers had cooled and Marie sat down with Isabelle in the library to have a private talk. Isabelle expressed her desire to continue sexual relations without the fear of pregnancy.

"Of course, *ma chère*, I understand completely. I had a very difficult time birthing you. I was in my mid-thirties by then. I had had seven children and your pa-pa told me he was more than happy with our nursery and desired no more children if I thought my health was in danger. I became aware of a plant, two actually, that the Indians rely upon for preventing conception. You brew them into a tea and take it the morning after. It has proved effective for me and for your sister."

"My sister! Which one?" For a moment she envisioned Louise as the naughty widow of Chartes Landing.

"Helen, of course. She came to me after Jean was born saying she thought she had had enough. Come, we will go to my garden. As development began to spread, I did not trust that I would always be able to find my precious plants in the wild any more so I began to grow them beside the kitchen garden." Marie led the way as they walked out to the gardens and finally pointed out a sizable patch beyond the herbs that looked like just so much ground cover.

"Here we are." She began pulling up every fifth plant by its roots and explained to Isabelle what she must do. "For now we will dry these for you to take with you. And just before you and Hamilton return, we shall transplant some fresh plants into soil for you to grow in your own garden, yes? Just remember as I was told… do not forget the next morning without fail."

"Oh, this is such a relief. Hamilton and I talked and we see no need to risk pregnancy again for two or three years. I am expected to do a lot of entertaining for his business dealings and it can be so exhausting."

Marie put her hand over her daughter's very small one. "Just remember, *ma fille*, children are a treasure you will not always be given an opportunity to acquire. When you are young and strong, collect your treasure because it becomes much, much harder as we glide through our thirties. And eventually God turns off the flow altogether."

Isabelle nodded, then bent to her mother and gave her cheek a kiss. "Thank you," she whispered.

Chapter 19

Ever since Doctor Archibald Ajax had officially declared his love and asked permission to court Louise, she had established a rather sensible schedule. On weeks where Sunday was an even number date Lyndyn was invited to Sunday dinner and to call any other day he wished. And on weeks where Sunday was an odd number date, Archie could do the same. And so she got to know her suitors better from the perspective of being potential mates.

For a woman who was over the age of thirty and thought herself so luckless, she was in an exquisite dilemma and took a great deal of ribbing for it, especially from her brothers. From her sisters it was a more serious consideration.

"It's been almost three years since Rafe died," said the ever practical Helen, "you really must make up your mind and put one of these poor fellows out of his misery."

"I know, I know," Louise replied. The women of the family were gathered around tea cups and sherry glasses. "They both say they love me. They both are willing to be stepfather to my five children. They both are long time family friends and have good characters. And they are both amiable to moving in and living right here."

"Yes, but which one are you most attracted to?" asked Caroline.

"Yes, which one makes you feel all melty inside?" asked Isabelle.

"Neither. I mean I was a melted puddle on the floor for Rafe but perhaps I cannot expect that ever again."

"Well, Ajax is the more attractive," said Caroline.

"He also has the better physique," nodded Isabelle.

"He has a greater education and community respect as well," added Helen.

"Yes, but Lyndyn has been asking about me since I was fifteen, Mama says."

"Louise," Marie spoke, "I would never want you to marry because you felt sorry for someone. You owe neither man anything but a decision."

"Have you ever kissed them?" asked Isabelle.

"Who?" Louise looked surprised.

"Either one," prodded Caroline.

"No, of course not. I didn't have to kiss Rafe to know I loved him madly."

"Well, that was Rafe," persisted Isabelle, "he was something very special, his magnetism drew you like a moth to a flame but not every man has as strong a… magnetism."

"I think you ought to kiss each one," Caroline said with daring.

"I agree," said Isabelle. "And tell them this is a test so they put their best efforts into it. The one who kisses you like a brother is the one you don't want in your bed."

"Izzy!" Helen admonished because she realized going to bed with Thor was too much like going to bed with a brother.

And Marie silently knew that going to bed with Richard was nothing like going to bed with a brother despite the many years she had thought of him as a brother.

"That's what you must do," Caroline said solemnly. "And this is Doctor Ajax's week. You should give him his test right now."

"Oh, my," Louise began to fan herself nervously. "What do you think, Mother, do I dare?"

"A kiss never hurt anyone's reputation," Marie said quietly and wondered which man would curl her daughter's toes. Or if either of them would.

Ajax was walking toward the garden doors. He had been talking seriously with the men and trying to convince Hamilton of the wisdom of getting inoculated against smallpox at the very next opportunity and insisting on Isabelle doing the same. He was afraid he hadn't really made any headway however and decided it was time to bid good-night to Louise and take his leave. He was surprised when she met him at the door.

"Archie, walk with me a bit," she said, trying to calm her beating heart.

"Of course, where would you like to walk?" he smiled and pat the hand she slipped through his arm.

"Just around the other side of the house. I want to ask you something." When they gained the privacy she needed she stopped and looked up at him. He really was quite good looking. "Archie, why do you love me?"

"Who can say why one falls in love?" he said lightly and took the opportunity to hold her about the waist.

"But I really can't stand blood and gore so I'll never be able to help you with your work."

"I don't expect you to help me with my work. Did you help Raphael with his work?"

"No-no, of course not."

"I want a home, Louise, a family. And I looked up one day and saw the prettiest girl in Chartes Landing was sobbing her eyes out for the loss of her husband. You know what the marriage bed is like… the physical act I mean. You are no stranger to what happens between a man and a woman. I want us to share that. I want to provide for you and your children, protect you and be there for you. Maybe even have a child or two of our own. And I dare to hope I can someday gain your love."

Louise swallowed hard. "Archie, I want you to kiss me. I must tell you, it is a test. I know what it was like with Rafe. I want to know what it will be like with you."

He smiled and drew her up close to him. "Give the horse a bit of a ride before you decide whether to buy it?" he chuckled and then he covered her mouth with his. His lips were rather hard and fierce, Rafe's had always been so soft and gentle. The good doctor was thrusting his tongue into her mouth almost harshly and suddenly she felt repulsed. With her hands against his chest she pushed away.

"I'm sorry, I… forgive me," she gasped before she turned and ran away in embarrassment.

Ajax wasn't a pessimist by nature but he felt reasonably certain he had failed the test. And so, he went home.

Hamilton was ready to return to Boston. The trip itself was going to take at least five days and that was assuming he could book passage in New York Towne on the next ship bound for Boston. Work beckoned. But Isabelle was insistent they could not leave yet.

"Why, my dearest darling? What more must you do? We have the little roots for your special tea."

"Hammy, my love, my sister is in the middle of deciding if she is going to marry the doctor or the shopkeeper. It's like a melodrama. I must know who she picks. It means so much to me," she fluttered and pushed him onto the bed. Then she whispered softly in his ear. "We are no longer forbidden."

Encouraged by Isabelle, Louise sent a message inviting Lyndyn over Monday evening. It was unusual and Lyndyn was afraid he knew why. He couldn't see bringing flowers when the Power home had the best flower gardens in the settlement but he did bring small toys for Louise's three youngest, a book in French for Sebastian, and a book of poetry for Rebecca.

"That is very kind of you, Lyndyn, but you spoil them," Louise smiled.

"It's only this once."

"But why this day?" she asked softly.

"Can we walk in the garden?" he asked as several of the children came walking through the front hall.

"Of course."

He took her arm and ushered her out the door and around the back of the house toward the river. The sun had almost set. When they had distanced themselves from the playing children he slowed their pace.

"Louise," he finally spoke. "I love you more than I seem to be able to express but I really can't take this any longer. The handsome doctor is winning your heart, I'm sure. I know I'm not really good enough for you, I don't know why I ever thought I had a chance so I've made a decision. I'm going to bow out gracefully."

"What?" She stopped suddenly.

"I've decided to leave Chartes Landing. I watched one man come in and sweep you off your feet. Not that I blame you. He was irresistible. But I can't continue to live here and watch you marry another dashing hero."

"But… but you can't leave."

"I have to… I have to… Louise, you're tearing my heart into pieces."

She gasped and was fighting the tears that had come to her eyes.

"Lyndyn… Lyndyn, will you kiss me?"

He looked at her in stunned surprise as if the thought of kissing her was a goal not to be even considered.

"I invited you over this evening to ask you to kiss me, Lyndyn. So kiss me and show me what you feel."

"Oh, Louise!" He stood still for a moment and then reached out with both hands to gently hold her lovely heart shaped face. He was trembling. "I have loved you since the first time I saw you," he said softly. "You were fourteen, wearing a pink and white pinafore and you came into the store with a message for your mother. I was just a scrawny sixteen year old apprentice, but you looked at me and you smiled." His lips grazed hers and tenderly he sucked at her lower lip and then the upper lip. Then hesitantly he kissed both lips.

Louise was trembling now as well. She reached up to caress his head and then they were kissing deeply. They drew apart, trying to catch their breath. He continued to nuzzle her neck and kiss the tender spot just beneath her ear and Louise felt her knees go weak.

"Oh, my!" she whispered and pulled back to look into his eyes. Was it a trick of the light or her eyes? Suddenly Lyndyn seemed rather… handsome. She began to shake her head slowly as he looked at her. "You are not going anywhere, Mister Lyndyn Peterson," she said softly.

"I'm not?"

"You simply can't because we're to be married."

"But Ajax?"

"I feel nothing like this with Archie. Please, Lyndyn, kiss me again."

Louise and Lyndyn decided to have a small, quiet wedding that very Saturday while Isabelle and Hamilton were still there. It was only family in attendance and everyone met Lyndyn's sister and brother-in-law for the first time. The service was early as the two couples planned to sail together to New York Towne on the packet boat which would arrive late morning. Isabelle and Hamilton implored the newly weds to come to Boston for their honeymoon. And Louise agreed but said they must stay at a hotel if they went, reminding her little sister that it was their honeymoon after all.

Before Isabelle left the house with her slaves, Marie insisted they be paid for the jobs they had fulfilled in Chartes Landing as free people. Hamilton paid them, there was no denying his mother-in-law, but he was naively surprised when Brutus refused to go with them.

"I be staying here, Master Carter, where I be free."

"What will you do?" Hamilton was nonplussed.

"I go to work at the lumber mill."

Marie looked at Richard. "The boys didn't mention that last Sunday."

"No, they didn't," he smiled. "Well, Brutus is big enough and strong enough, he ought to do well at the mill."

"You might think twice before bringing anymore slaves to Chartes Landing," Marie said with a smile. "You could lose more of your investments."

"We're not cruel to them, Mother, you know that," Isabelle pouted.

"I suppose that depends on your definition of cruelty, *ma fille*."

The packet boat dropped off two passengers and a letter for Marie. She tucked it aside as she and Richard and Louise's children, Helen and Thor and their children, Phillip and Caroline and their children and Jamie and Cynthia watched the boat fill up fast. They were almost afraid someone would get left behind. There was Lyndyn and Louise, Hamilton and Isabelle, Baby Chad, Percy and Drusie, all the luggage for both couples and two crates of plant starts for Isabelle's tea to crowd onto a boat that already held passengers from the south headed for points north. There was no lingering, the captain was trying to keep a schedule. They waved good-bye and the families did the same, watching until the boat left the bay and hit the open sea.

Helen, Thor, and their children went home in their carriage as did Phillip and his family with promises to see each other tomorrow, Sunday. Jamie and Cynthia had brought only a trap.

"So did you know who she would pick?" Richard asked as he walked with his arm around Marie back to their carriage. He helped her up onto the driver's seat while Louise's children piled into the seats behind.

"No, but then it was not I who kissed them," she laughed. "I suspect for Archie it would have been a marriage of convenience, whereas Lyndyn has truly loved that girl since he was a green apprentice. And that is the kind of thing that just might come through in a kiss, yes?"

Richard stepped up onto the driver's seat next to Marie and took the reins. "Then Ajax may be disappointed but not broken hearted, *n'est-ce pas?* Perhaps he will find another."

"I am sure he could, but I do not want it to be our Charity," she whispered.

"What?"

"The girl has been throwing herself at the man and now that Louise is out of the picture…"

"Do you want me to have a talk with him?"

"I already had a talk with him when I first noticed it and he assured me he saw her only as a child while she was flattering him with a counterfeit interest in medicine. He said he was thinking of going to Phillip and asking if they wished to set up an official apprenticeship. Said she could learn to become a midwife. When I talked with her, she had no sincere interest in medicine and did not want her parents to know we had talked."

"Perhaps she needs to visit her aunt in Boston."

"It is a possibility but Izzy spoke of the entertaining Hamilton expects her to do for his business dealings and God only knows who she might meet or what might happen."

"I am certain Izzy would not allow anything scandalous to happen but Marie, you cannot control everyone's happiness. Children must make their own mistakes, *n'est-ce pas?* It is how they learn, it is the heartbreak that builds character."

"You are right, Richard, you are right. Jacques used to tell me the same thing. I am a busy-body."

"You are not a busy-body with the gossip, you are just so caring. Which is why everyone loves you."

"Oh, yes? I just cost Hamilton his slave. How much do you think he paid for Brutus?"

Richard shrugged.

"Well, however much, it is gone now. I doubt that he 'loves' me for that." They had pulled up to the carriage house and the stable-hand helped Marie down while the children scrambled out on their own. "I am almost certain if Jacques had been alive she would never have dared to bring her slaves here.

"Children, children. Everyone must report to Sarah. Your nice church clothing must come off and play garb put on. Then you may play for a while before dinner," Marie reminded everyone.

Richard stepped down from his perch.

"Come, *ma chérie*, I need a large cognac," he said.

They settled comfortably into the library and while Richard sipped on cognac, Marie put on her spectacles and read her letter from John. When she finished she was going to re-read it and share the news with Richard but she noticed he had fallen asleep. Quietly, she grabbed a blanket and covered him so he could nap before dinner.

Sunday arrived and Marie welcomed Phillip and Caroline, Helen and Thor, Jamie and Cynthia, and all the grandchildren available which was fourteen in number. Without all of them the table would have been far too empty.

Phillip said the blessing and after the food had all been served up, Marie decided to share the news from her letter.

"I received another letter from John. Ronnie has had another baby. His name is Luke."

Phillip sniggered. "That makes Matthew, Mark, Luke, and John. Good Lord, what's next - Christ himself? Someone pass the bread, please."

"Phillip! What is the matter with you? In front of the children?" Marie frowned at her son. "John also writes he has been sending Ronnie to the fort chaplain for lessons in Christianity."

"Oh, that's good," Helen said as she put a large helping of parsnips on Sybelle's plate and Thomas inwardly smiled, very glad to no longer be seated next to his mother. Suddenly a long reach came across Sybelle and plopped a heap of parsnips on Thomas' plate. He scowled.

"Yes. The one sad note is that Ronnie's mother is in very poor health it seems. John writes that Ronnie asked him to build another bedroom onto their house so she could bring her mother to live with them. Evidently, Ronnie is no longer enthusiastic about staying in her old village. John says she told him life here was much easier than life at the fort but life at the fort is easier than life in the village. Ronnie has noticed her mother is looking very old and worn-out."

"Well, how old is she?" Caroline asked.

"That is the shocking thing. He writes she is the same age as the commander's wife who is thirty-seven now but Ronnie can see how much younger than her mother the white woman looks. It is undoubtedly a very hard life the natives live. No wonder they get married so young and start having babies. She will soon be turning Gray over to her brother," Marie mused, "so if her mother dies, and she recognizes how much more comfortable things are here, I do not think Ronnie would have much objection to living here…"

"But what about his military career?" Phillip's head shot up.

"What about it?" Marie answered quickly. "He is a doctor and the head of our family. He does not need a military career anymore. I would much rather see him here and safe."

"I didn't realize you worried about him that much Mother Marie."

"How can I not, Caroline? Just last summer that renegade band killed and injured almost a dozen men and they still have not been caught. Ronnie's ex-husband bears a grudge. Who knows when or where he might be waiting to try to kill John? Yes, I worry."

"Worry not too much, *ma chère*, or you make yourself ill," Richard said quietly as he put his hand over hers.

To change the subject and lighten the mood, Helen said, "I wonder how the newlyweds will like Boston."

"If they're like most newlyweds, they won't really see much of Boston," giggled Caroline and held up her glass for more wine.

"Why not, Mama?" asked her daughter Grace.

"Because newlyweds don't go out much," answered Caroline with a smirk. Then she found herself staring across the table at Rebecca and Sebastian. "I just noticed, Uncle Richard, Rebecca and Sebastian are growing into very handsome children. Didn't you say Rebecca takes after her father's mother, your first wife?"

"*Oui*, they are going to be very beautiful." He looked to the children. "Your *grand-mère* on your father's side was an exotic beauty, your *grand-mère* on your mother's side," he gestured to Marie, "is also a rare beauty. Your pa-pa was exceedingly handsome, your ma-ma, is also a beauty, and your *grand-père* on your ma-ma's side was outrageously handsome. The only ugly duckling in the mix is *moi!*" He laughed.

"Uncle Richard, that's not true!" protested Caroline. "Is it, Mother?"

"If Richard began life as a lanky, awkward youth who was at sixes and sevens with himself, he has long since grown into a very attractive mature man," Marie said, squeezing his hand.

"But just remember, *mes enfants*," Richard continued, looking at his grandchildren, "your father's true beauty was on the inside. His honor, his chivalry, his kindness to others, his ability to see good in almost everything – that was his true beauty. And I think your ma-ma has chosen another man who is much the same and he will also now be your father. His true beauty is on the inside."

"What a generous thing to say, *mon cher*," Marie said softly and gave him a look that warmed his heart.

"You're turning into a romantic, Uncle Richard," Phillip teased.

"No," the large man boomed. "I am just mellowing like a barrel of fine cognac."

They continued to eat. The grandchildren were on their best behavior which was "to be seen but not heard." It was a privilege to sit at the big table and even the very youngest knew this was a special treat.

"How's the horse-breeding business going, Jamie?" asked Thor as he sat back contentedly with his wine, his stomach pleasantly full.

"Very well, I just bought a little filly that pound for pound is the best horse flesh I've ever put eyes on. I plan on breeding her."

Marie stood and the men all stood. "That is our cue, ladies, if they are going to start talking horseflesh and pork bellies, then we shall take the children to the fresh air. Nora, please see that port and cognac is brought to wherever Master Richard wishes. We will serve desert in half an hour."

"Yes, ma'am."

With the rustle of silks, Marie, her daughter, and daughters-in-law shepherded the children out to other activities. Only Thomas begged leave to stay with his father to listen and learn. Thor nodded his approval.

In New York Towne the Petersons, Carters, and company had been forced to share a room with two beds, two cots, and one cradle. The slave women had the cots and the couples each had a bed. They all slept in their street clothes. When they finally transferred to the ship which took them to Boston, they had their own cabins but they were so small and cramped and lacking in privacy that everything anyone said or did could easily be heard by all the other cabins as well. And so they continued to sleep chastely.

At last in Boston, the couples parted ways. Louise and Lyndyn checked in to one of the nicest hotels in town and booked the Honeymoon Suite. The suite included a sumptuously draped alcove holding a permanent tub with a drain, they needed only to call for water.

They were served a fine dinner in the plushly appointed dining room although they barely registered what they were eating. Lyndyn was nervous. He kept wondering if he had been short-sighted not to have paid a visit to the new whorehouse that had come to Chartes Landing. At least he would have had a little practice, he thought. Louise looked so... so dewy-eyed and happy while he felt all thumbs and elbows. He didn't want to disappoint her but he could barely hold his own fork.

Supper was over and Lyndyn had had four glasses of wine.

"I'd like to go to our room now," Louise said sweetly. "I'd like to wash the dirt of travel off in that lovely large tub."

"Of course."

"Would you like to join me?"

Lyndyn felt any response wedge in his throat. He could only bob a quick nod and rise to assist her from her chair. They left the dining room and proceeded past the front desk toward the staircase.

"Perhaps it would be a good idea to tell them we need the tub filled with water," Louise said softly.

"Oh... of course."

That done, they went on up the stairs. Once inside, Lyndyn opened another bottle of wine and had only just poured the first glass when a knock on the door brought the water. Two maids rolling a cart from the dumb waiter brought a number of pails of hot and warm water which they emptied into the tub after they had plugged the drain. Lyndyn gave them each a coin and locked the door after them.

Louise dipped her fingers into the water. "It's very warm," she smiled and began undoing the laces on her bodice and removing her outer layers.

"Perhaps you'd like to go first and I can... ah, go after. That's what mother used to do with Clara and I when we were children."

"Lyndyn, I am not your sister," she said coming closer. "Do you realize our marriage is not yet official? It has been almost a week since the preacher said the words but we've not yet been able to… consummate it." She turned her back to him. "Would you help me with my laces?"

Lyndyn concentrated on undoing the fastenings to her petticoats and then the laces of her corset. She was down to her shift when she turned and began to undo his cravat. Soon he was down to his shirt, a garment that fell midway to his knees.

"Ah, my shoes and stockings," he said and quickly yanked them from his feet, then turning to Louise he sat her on the edge of the bed and slowly removed hers. As his hands moved over her calves, he felt himself being overwhelmed with lustful passion. He was hard and throbbing and found himself kissing her and pushing her shift up as she fell back upon the bed. He sought the primal connection and with a small assist from Louise, he found it.

Instinctively he moved within her and suddenly groaned.

"Oh, God…!" He collapsed upon her. "That was… incredible," he said as he pushed himself off her and onto the bed.

Louise looked at him and smiled indulgently. "Yes, it is. But next time, darling, you must slow down and wait for me." She saw Lyndyn give her a look of surprise. "Yes, we enjoy it too. Why would we do it if God did not make it pleasurable to us as well?"

"I thought… I thought women did it… to have children…"

"And this is why the kitchen maid goes down in the hay with the stable boy, because she is looking for a baby?"

Lyndyn smiled broadly in chagrin. "You're right! That was a rather stupid assumption on my part."

"Not stupid, just uninformed," she murmured and kissed him again. "And now, our bath awaits."

They put a "Do Not Disturb" sign on the door and for four days they only opened the door for Room Service and chamber pot collections.

"It's really incredible," Lyndyn murmured as they reclined on the bed.

"What is?"

"You'll laugh…"

"No I won't."

"It's just that… well, I've never seen a woman naked before… not a grown woman… Your body is like a living, breathing work of art," he said as he continued to run his hands over Louise's curves. "I never realized you felt the way you do… so soft, so… wonderful."

Louise smiled, feeling very beautiful under his attentions.

"A woman can see a man's body as a work of art as well… when he keeps himself lean, like you are, so she can see the muscles…"

Lyndyn had worked himself up to her mouth again and all conversation fell away.

Finally, after four days the couple decided to respond to Isabelle's many messages, each growing more demanding until the last had turned downright frantic.

"My little sister will not be ignored," Louise smiled as Lyndyn continued to place kisses up and down her body. "I suppose it would not hurt us to dress…"

"No," he protested. "No, I want you naked and in my bed…" he crawled up over her, "so I may drown myself in you again." He continued to kiss and nip and she giggled loudly.

"But she may think you have eaten me alive."

"Hmmm, it's true you bring out the wild beast in me."

"Oh, stop, stop," Louise dissolved into another peal of giggles. "No, really, we must at least send a message back."

He gave an exaggerated sigh as though this was a great sacrifice and under-taking. "Very well, if we must. You write your note and I'll throw on some clothes and go down to the front desk."

When Lyndyn arrived at the front desk he saw the desk clerk smirking at him.

"Mister Peterson, are you comfortable in the Honeymoon Suite? We haven't seen much of you and your bride. Is everything to your liking?"

Lyndyn looked at the clerk with a new found confidence he'd never felt before. "What is most to my liking won't be staying behind once we check out. But the accommodations are very nice, very nice indeed."

"Very good, sir," the clerk sobered. "What might we help you with now?"

"I wish to send a message. Do you have a runner?"

"Yes, of course." He picked up a bell with a very high tone and rang it. From the rear a youth sprang forward.

"I'd like this message delivered to that address," Lyndyn pointed and flipped the lad a coin. "Here's for your trouble," he smiled, handing the note over before he went back up the stairs.

Louise was dressed when he returned to their room.

"I told her we'd be over there in an hour and a half. Do get dressed now," she giggled as he was again kissing her neck. "I must make sense of my hair."

At that, he took the brush gently from her hand and began brushing her long, light brown locks so richly highlighted. "You have such lovely hair, all silken with streaks like liquid gold running through it."

"My mother's used to be this way before it started turning gray."

"I wouldn't know. I never saw your mother's hair all brushed out like this, she always had it up very neatly under a cap at the store."

"When my father had to go to New York Towne on business of some kind or another, she would let us come to their room while she readied herself for bed and applied her creams and always she would let us brush her hair for one hundred strokes. Then, when we finished she would gather us together in the nursery and read us a story or two, depending on how short they were. It's funny what you remember from your childhood."

Lyndyn listened as he brushed.

"Sometimes I am afraid my children's only memories will be of their mother weeping and hiding away in her room."

"But you had years before that. What did you do when Rafe was on his treks?"

She smiled into the mirror at him. "We read stories. They took turns brushing my hair. In autumn we'd have cocoa before my fire."

"Those are the memories they will have."

She looked in the mirror at him and smiled. Just then there was a knock on the door.

"Who could that be?" Louise frowned while Lyndyn went to the door. It was the lad he'd sent with their message.

"Beggin' yer pardon, sir, but I thought you should know. I delivered your message but the house has just been put under quarantine."

"Quarantine! Whatever for?"

"Health official was there. Said it was the pox, the smallpox."

"Did they say who?"

The boy shook his head.

"Thank you," Lyndyn said and flipped him another coin before he shut the door.

"Oh, Lyndyn… my sister," Louise had paled.

"It can't be her or Hamilton," he said firmly. "They've been weeks at Chartes Landing and we have no pox there. And if they had contracted the disease before they came, they would have shown some sign, some symptoms before they left. I imagine they will be put under watch and when they prove symptom free they will be allowed to move about again. More likely one of their slaves brought in the disease."

"But Drusie and Percy were there in Chartes Landing with us."

"Louise, don't you think they have others who stayed here in Boston running the house?"

"Oh… and who knows what they did while Hamilton and Isabelle were away?" Louise said rather round eyed. "I should send a letter to Mother."

Lyndyn took her hand away from the quill. "Darling, don't worry your mother. There is nothing any of us can do until the quarantine is lifted. Except… you could write another note telling Isabelle we have heard and shall stay here and await the lifting of the quarantine."

"You're right, you're right. I shall."

"I don't believe they will even be allowed to send out a message right now for fear of contamination."

"That's right. Oh, Lyndyn, I don't know what I would do without you."

From that point on a small cloud hung over their honeymoon. They spent a portion of the day walking about the town, investigating the markets, and seeking out what entertainments and diversions they might find. One particularly beautiful day, Lyndyn rented horses and they rode the enormous white sandy beaches around the cape. But always the thought of smallpox hung in Louise's mind. One day they paid a courtesy visit to the Senior Carters who were beside themselves with almost hysterical concern. Louise could not wait to leave their company.

The newly weds found solace in affection and diversion in the pleasures of the matrimonial bed but the care-free ambiance was now tainted.

Louise wrote another note. She had heard the longest incubation period was seventeen days. If no symptoms appeared in seventeen days then the quarantine must be lifted.

On day eighteen, the health inspector examined every member of the household and pronounced them free of disease. The quarantine was lifted and Isabelle sent a note begging Louise and Lyndyn to meet in the hotel lobby.

At the appointed hour, Louise and Lyndyn were waiting. They saw Isabelle bound from the horse-drawn cab and burst into the lobby.

"Louise… Lyndyn," she kissed them each on both cheeks. "That was truly the most disgusting experience. To be locked up in one's own home, an actual prisoner, and all the time wondering who was going to give you some horrible disease. We wouldn't allow anyone to serve us or handle Baby Chad except for Percy and Drusie. Thank God they were there. It was horrible!"

The trio went into the hotel restaurant and were shown to a table.

"Where's Hamilton?" Lyndyn asked as he helped both ladies to be seated.

"He made a mad dash for the office at dawn's light. Poor thing, he was beside himself thinking of the work piling up and he couldn't get it brought in for they would never have allowed it back out."

"How did it happen, Izzy?" Louise asked softly.

"Beau-jam… oh Lord, one can only wonder how some of them get their names. I've been threatening to change it and I think I shall. From now on he will be *Jonah* like the Jonah who was spewed forth from the belly of the whale. I feel like I've been in the belly of the whale.

"Anyway, while we were gone, Jonah our stable boy, went to visit his part-time whore girlfriend. Seems she'd had a customer in her bed just before him who then came down with the smallpox. When the health authorities traced it back to the whore and she confessed to Beau-j… ah, Jonah being there next, it got traced to our house and we were put under quarantine. Jonah is very lucky to not have caught it but I hope Hamilton will have him caned, and caned good for what he put us through."

"He didn't know his girlfriend had someone in her bed who was coming down with the disease," Louise reasoned, trying to sound urbane.

"But he did not have our permission to leave our property. He was sneaking off. And look how we suffered for it."

"Well, all I can say, Izzy, is I am so glad you, Hamilton, and Baby Chad are well. Have you thought anymore about getting the inoculation Doctor Ajax is always talking about?"

Isabelle waved her hand. "I have no intention of bringing that disease into my home.

"I was talking with some fellows a few days ago," said Lyndyn. "Seems they have two houses set up, one for women, one for men. Those who get inoculated go there to be cared for as they do get a mild form of the disease. They are tended to until they are well again. You don't have to bring it into your home. At least you might think of sending your servants for inoculation so they can't bring the disease home to you."

At this Isabelle showed interest. "Now that I will suggest to Hamilton."

Louise and Lyndyn only had a week left before they needed to make plans to go back home. Lyndyn made daily inquiries with the harbor master. As luck would have it, one of the French ships owned by the Dufee family was in the Boston harbor waiting their turn to be unloaded.

When Lyndyn spoke to the captain, he learned they were headed for Chartes Landing to fill their soon to be empty hold with lumber. Lyndyn asked to be sent a message when the ship actually made it to a spot on the docks.

Isabelle wanted very much to show off her house and furnishings and invited her sister and new brother-in-law to dinner the first night Hamilton could promise her he would be home.

As they sat down to eat, Hamilton thanked Lyndyn for the inoculation idea.

"Well, it was not really my idea," Lyndyn replied modestly.

"No-no, I mean about sending the servants, excellent idea, excellent. We have the kitchen one, the garden one and the stable one all in now for the inoculation. When they are allowed to come back, then we'll send Percy and when they send her back we'll finish off with Drusie."

Two months later Isabelle wrote to her sister that all the servants had come home from their inoculation experience. Drusie alone had several disfiguring pock-marks on her face.

"I cannot help wondering," wrote Isabelle, "if being part-white has not added to her consequence of being so scarred. If I were not convinced against this course of action for myself before, I most assuredly am now. The girl looks so grim I am thinking of taking her out of the nursery lest Baby Chad get nightmares."

Chapter 20

It was the first snow marking the beginning of the winter. Ronnie had been preparing herself for this a long time. She fixed a very special meal just for Gray Wolf's Son. It was a meal of all his favorites and only he would partake of it unless he invited her to share it with him. It was the last meal he and she would ever have together like this. It was his seventh winter.

Ronnie dressed in a new buckskin tunic and leggings. She gave her first born a new set of buckskins and furs to keep him through the winter. He was tall for his age and she had made them large enough so with luck, if he did not grow too quickly, he might be able to wear them a second and third winter in remembrance of her.

Mother and son were alone for this occasion. Singing Wind took the other children outside and then to the surgery to spend time with John. Ronnie served her eldest son with great respect and, of course, he asked her to join him.

"My son," she said looking at the grave young face before her, "it is a joy to see you growing so like your father. He was a mighty warrior who had many sides. He was a hunter of great success who could feed his family well and also give with great generosity to those who were old and weak within the tribe. He was a skilled warrior who could fight our enemies and had many victories. But he also knew how to be kind and compassionate. He was not afraid of looking weak in his tenderness. He was fair in judgment and very loving. And he was most pleasing to look upon.

"Tomorrow we begin the journey to take you to our cousin Yellow Rock who along with your uncle Wani will teach you to become a Mohawk warrior. I ask that you remember my words. Battle the enemy as your duty but once peace is established hold no hate in your heart. Be a great warrior like your father but remember your mother as well. I have some white blood and so you too must have some white blood. You have lived in the white man's world, you know the white man's tongue, you know the white man's dislike for us. But always remember not all white men think the same, just as not all natives think the same. You have a white child's education to lay along side your Mohawk education. Use this knowledge as a benefit for your tribe, to help them accept the white man's world along side their own.

"I have seen for myself. The white world grows ever larger. It is not to be conquered. If our people are like the number of beans in this pot, then John tells me the whites are like the number of grass blades in the meadow. So many it is impossible to count. When the blood of your fellow warriors runs hot ready to rush into battle, be the cooler head who can take the time to think through the possibilities. Blood need not always be spilled for honor to be achieved.

"Know as you leave my hearth, you take a piece of my heart with you forever. Be not a stranger to your brothers and sister. Be not a stranger to me."

Ronnie forced herself to remain dry-eyed for she could see the struggle in her son's face to not shed tears of his own.

Early the next day they departed for the Indian village. John accompanied his wife but they left their other children at the fort in the care of Elinor Greeley. Singing Wind was feeling too poorly to join them. Gray Wolf's Son rode straight and tall upon the pony that was John's gift to him to mark this important step in the young boy's life. Ronnie maintained her stoic demeanor. To dissolve into tears at any point would mar things and was somehow disrespectful.

John considered how much more difficult this whole occurrence must be for Ronnie because she did not live in the village anymore. The mothers of the village formally turned their sons over to the male dominated world as well but for some that simply meant their fathers. The boy still ate at his mother's hearth. For others, they undoubtedly caught glimpses of their boys as life went on in the village. A moment here, a passing word there, a visit perhaps, a stop by for a favorite dish of food but for Ronnie this would not happen. Yellow Rock would consider a two day round trip ride just to see one's mother a waste of time and womanishly sentimental unless that mother was dying.

If it had not been for a need to rest the horses, Ronnie would have pushed John to ride back to the fort that very night. Instead the horses were put in the community corral and given hay and water while John and Ronnie accepted Yellow Rock's hospitality.

Yellow Rock was twenty-four now and had finally found an acceptable maiden in the neighboring village to make his bride. Thus he had his own wigwam and when Singing Wind went to live with Ronnie, Wani had moved in with Yellow Rock and Little Dove. John and Ronnie were shown to a sleeping platform that kept them off the hard, cold ground. Wani had another and Gray Wolf's Son was given a third, while Yellow Rock and his mate had the fourth.

John appreciated the extra layers of fur Ronnie had put down, but still it was a hard bed though it was warm. Holding his wife in his arms, he was trying to get comfortable when he became aware of the sounds of coupling. Yellow Rock and Little Dove were being quiet about it but still it was hard to ignore. Politely, John shut his eyes and pretended to be asleep.

Very little was said on the long ride home. John respected Ronnie's solitude. She was crying. He caught glimpses of tear tracks down her cheeks when the sun reflected off them. Later John would realize that in his concern for his wife he had allowed his guard and vigilance to drop. He had failed to recognize any sign of their being stalked until it was too late.

Suddenly out of nowhere in the growing darkness, John and Ronnie found themselves surrounded and disarmed by an armed band of renegades. One taking particular delight in leaping upon John and knocking him off his horse to the ground. He didn't understand what they were yelling and screaming but just before he was clubbed with something heavy and lost consciousness, he heard Ronnie scream something.

When John regained his senses he was first aware of his inability to move. His head felt so heavy he struggled to raise his chin and look about him. He was tied, spreadeagled in an upright position, hanging from a tree. Each hand was tied to a far reaching limb and each foot was bound to a wide-set stake. He had been relieved of all his clothing and was naked in the blowing winds of late December. A fire blazed some ten or twelve feet in front of him, too far for him to feel any warmth from it. A half dozen men hunkered around it and then he saw Ronnie. She sat on the ground near the fire, her knees bent, her hands and feet tied behind her. She was arguing with one of them. John couldn't understand a word. Then one of the others said something and the one she was arguing with turned to look at John and John recognized Tonoaki.

"So he is awake," Tonoaki smirked. "Are you cold? To a true warrior, this is only a spring breeze but the cold will make you bleed slower and your agony will be prolonged."

John understood nothing of what was said but he saw Tonoaki come toward him, his knife glinting in the firelight. He stopped very close in front of John, a wild crazed look in the Indian's eyes. Tonoaki pierced John's naked thigh with the razor sharp tip, not deeply but just enough to pull up the skin and begin ripping it from the thin layer of fat beneath. It took a moment and then John felt the most incredible burning pain.

"STOP!" Ronnie screamed out in their tongue. "We had a bargain. I bought his life."

"I changed my mind."

"A warrior stands by his word."

The deranged outlaw snarled but he halted his flaying.

"Why do you hate him so, Tonoaki? He has done nothing to you. Nothing! You saw Sunshine, she is of your spirit! This man only cared for me when you drove me away. You beat me for no reason, you would have killed me and your own daughter if I had not run away. If this man had not healed my poor body and saved me from dying of the fevers, you could not have enjoyed my favors this last time. So why do you hate him? He only has your scraps, your left-overs. What you no longer wanted! But he has done nothing to deserve this. Even your band can see you have no honor if you cannot face him fairly in hand-to-hand combat."

"Shut your mouth, woman!"

"Or what? You will beat an unarmed Mohawk woman or will you kill me as well? Go ahead, Tonoaki, kill me! Is it me you really want dead? It should be easy enough, I have no weapon and my hands and feet are tied. Behind my back, no less! I cannot even kick you like an animal. And neither can he! We will make fine trophy stories to brag about as you sit around your campfire in your old age."

"Shut up before I cut out your tongue!"

"Oh, very good, Tonoaki! Now you threaten to mutilate Gray Wolf's widow. I can hear the songs they will sing of your bravery. He mutilated an unarmed, trussed up Mohawk daughter of the shaman's hearth, natural daughter of the sachem's second wife, so she could not sing of his dishonor! Such a brave warrior was Tonoaki! Such a legend! Compare him to the honor of Gray Wolf!"

Tonoaki and his band had never heard a woman mock a warrior like this before. She spoke like a warrior might and deep down inside each of them, they knew she was right. There was shame not bravery in what they were doing. The shame washed over him and he threw the knife which stuck in the hard ground just a finger's width from her knee.

"Mount up!" he cried and jumping on his own pony he galloped away into the night. His band followed him.

Ronnie squirmed into position and rolled to the ground so she could pick up the knife behind her back. She worked at cutting her bindings first from her wrists and then, from her feet. The rawhide was stiff and her fingers moved awkwardly within their constriction. Finally she was free. Quickly she went to John and cut the bindings at his feet and then cut one wrist free and finally the other. He staggered in the cold, trying to regain the feeling in his limbs and his hands. The wound on his thigh bled and burned. He was shivering violently as she brought him closer to the fire.

She gathered together his clothing. His shirt had been ripped to rags so she used it to bind his leg. Then, warming each piece she helped dress him. His breeches had been split but afforded some protection. She helped him into his vest and then his coat each having survived in basically one piece. His feet were warmed by the fire until she drew his boots onto them. Finally she wrapped a blanket around him.

"Sit by fire," she urged. "When you warm, we continue to fort." She wished she had something warm for him to drink. Searching through his saddlebag, she found a small cup and filled it with water. She placed it on the edge of the coals.

John was shaking so badly that for a time he didn't even try to speak. He knew it was a combination of shock, injury, and the cold. He tried to watch Ronnie heat the water but he was seeing double and his head ached beyond measure.

She came to him as they waited. She covered his mouth with hers and breathed the warm air from her lungs into his mouth. Her lips were cool but soft. Then she lifted her tunic and he felt the heat of her groin against his belly as she wrapped her long legs around him tightly. She pulled his hands up inside her tunic and warmed them on her breasts, then shoved them around to her back. With her arms wrapped around him, her warm chest pressed against his, they sat for a while.

John felt his shaking begin to subside. Her warmth was so comforting and her fur lined cloak made a pleasant tent.

"You have a very enticing way of warming a man," he rasped as he held her closely keeping his eyes shut. Her warmth felt so good, life saving, and reviving.

"I would not do this for just anyone." There was a smile in her voice. "Now you drink warm water." She stood up, pulled her clothing into place and re-wrapped the blanket around him. She tested the heat of the metal cup. It was almost too hot to pick up. "Jack, be careful. Do not burn lips on cup… or how can you kiss me again?"

The hot water felt wonderful going down. It warmed him from the inside and rested like a warm pool in his belly.

"Did they leave us the horses? I'm surprised."

"Only mine," Ronnie nodded. "Is Gray Wolf's horse. Tonoaki know this. Perhaps he afraid Gray Wolf's ghost haunt him if he disrespects his things or hurt his wife." Ronnie looked down at the ground.

"What did you say to them?" John asked shutting one eye to look at her. "He was starting to skin me… how did you get him to stop, to leave?"

"I…" Ronnie looked down again. "I speak like I think my father would speak if he here."

"It worked. You saved my life again, Ronnie." He reached out and drew her to him as best he could while keeping the blanket around him.

"Come, up on horse," she urged and she brought the horse to him and steadied it as he mounted, the blanket covering his nether regions. She saw him weave and struggle. "Wait, hold on." She jumped up to mount behind him and pulled him closely to her. It kept him steady.

With the weight of two riders, she allowed the horse to set its own pace. What should have taken only an hour took more like three and it was midnight when they sighted the fort. The sentry challenged them and then let them through. Ronnie wanted to check on the children but it was much too late so she steered John to his surgery and made him lie down keeping his head elevated. As she started a fire in the small stove she sent someone to the commander.

Greeley opened the door to the surgery and gave John a scrutinizing look as the younger man clutched the heavy blanket around him and tried to sit up. Ronnie stopped him.

"He no well, Commander."

"So I see, what happened?"

"We were attacked, sir," John said as Ronnie stood by. "It was that band of renegades headed up by the one called Tonoaki."

"The blanket?" Greeley inquired.

"They cut my clothes off me and had me strung up for skinning."

Greeley tried not to react except to scowl in concern. "Very well, Captain. Take it easy. How do you feel? You have a lump on your head the size of a goose egg."

John gingerly felt his head with his free hand. "I do have a king-size headache but thanks to Ronnie, nothing worse."

"Not true," Ronnie interrupted rather boldly. "Tonoaki begin to skin Jack. Has wound on thigh that must be bandaged. And he have trouble seeing."

"What's this?" Greeley demanded.

"Just a little double vision, sir. From that wallop on the head."

Greeley nodded. "You tend to your wounds. You can make a full report tomorrow. Corporal?" Greeley called to the guard that had shadowed him. Get the sergeant to help the captain and see what the mess has to offer. I doubt the captain or his wife have had any supper."

The corporal scurried off.

"Thank you, sir," John replied.

Greeley left. The room was beginning to warm and the sergeant who worked directly under John in his surgery came in sleepy-eyed but was instantly attentive. John sent Ronnie to their house for a fresh change of clothing. When she entered the surgery again she found John almost passed out from the pain of pouring alcohol on his thigh.

"God in heaven with all the saints!" he cried out, thumping the exam table and she rushed to help him. She uncorked a bottle of whiskey and he took a long pull. "I cannot imagine the pain of being skinned completely," he rasped grimly just to remind himself he could be feeling much worse.

"Take this," Ronnie said as she thrust a jar of ointment at the sergeant.

"What is it?" the man asked, sniffing at the jar.

"Is rendered fat with cooked garlic," she responded. "Protect wound."

The sergeant looked at his captain, unsure of what to do.

John grunted. "Do whatever she says. She's saved my life twice, I trust her to mend my wounds."

"Yes, sir."

After the sergeant spread a coating of fat on John's wound, Ronnie finished dressing his thigh.

"Help me get into my clothes," he cried softly. "I do feel a little dizzy when I move around."

"Jack, maybe you stay here."

"What?"

"More quiet for you. Children come home tomorrow, play, make noise. Maybe better you..."

John grabbed for her hand with one eye shut and pulled her closer.

"Nothing is going to help me feel better faster than having my family around me, Ronnie. I want to go home now." After they dressed him, he stood and staggered to the mirror to check his wound himself. "The commander is right, it is the size of a goose egg… or at least a chicken egg." It was painful but whatever they had used to club him had not broken his skin.

With Ronnie on one side and the sergeant on the other, they walked John home. Just before the sergeant took his leave, John told him to find an eye patch.

Ronnie settled John into bed and began a fire in their bedroom fireplace. She added fuel to the kitchen stove and checked on her mother. Singing Wind was sleeping fitfully. She had woken when Ronnie had come in to get John's clothes.

As the room began to warm, there was a knock on the front door. The food had arrived.

"Don't make the room too warm," John told her. "Remember, I cannot sleep tonight. I'll eat a bite and as soon as it is light I will go make my report to the commander. Come, sweetheart, you must eat something too."

"Why no sleep?"

"I'm not sure. Seems somebody somewhere came to the conclusion that when you get hit hard on the head, there is a better chance of nothing getting worse if you don't sleep."

"Not so with my people."

John smiled.

He tried to eat but nothing had any appeal except sweet. He downed a spoonful of mashed potato running in butter. Tried to chew a quarter of a slice of ham before pushing it aside to focus on a slice of apple pie which he washed down with a glass of water laced with red wine.

Ronnie watched. When a big and strong man did not eat, it was a sure sign of trouble. She knew his head was giving him great pain. Excusing herself she went out to the kitchen and after a few minutes of various noises she returned to the bedroom with a steaming cup of tea.

"Drink," she said softly.

"I really don't want any tea right now," John began.

"Medicine tea. Drink."

John gave her a one eyed look and decided it was easier to drink the tea than argue. As he drank there was another knock on the door. It was the sergeant and Ronnie admitted him to the bedroom.

"Your eye patch, sir."

"Yes, thank you." John put the patch in place. "Oh, that's much better. I shall switch it every day so each eye gets proper exercise. Please report back at dawn. I shall need assistance getting to the commander's office to make my report."

When the sergeant returned, Ronnie insisted on walking on John's other side.

"I wait for you, Jack."

"No-no, sweetheart, I'll be fine. The commander is having my breakfast brought in I'm sure, and yours is waiting for you with Mistress Greeley. You go now… and thank you." He kissed her slender hand.

John entered the commander's office limping and steadying himself on walls and furniture as he went to keep from staggering. He found a large serving tray waiting for him with scrambled eggs, hash, bread and hot tea but he didn't feel at all like eating. He sat and made his full report while his head continued to throb.

"So you did nothing and from what you say, you saw nothing that they did but they wanted to skin you alive anyway? Are you certain it wasn't just a threat to scare you?"

"Begging your pardon, sir, but when you come to and you're stretched out, spreadeagled, wearing nothing but your birthday suit and eight braves with knives are looking at you like you're the day's kill, I'd say it's not a fake threat. And that Tonoaki actually started carving on my leg. I'm missing a one by three inch strip of skin." He touched his thigh gingerly. "I have no idea what Ronnie said to him… but he stopped and she was talking non-stop even though when he turned it sounded like he was threatening her as well. She told me she was reminding all of them that what they were doing was shameful. Dishonorable even in their world. She must have hit a chord somewhere because just like that he jumped on his pony and was gone. Gave Ronnie back a knife so she could cut herself loose, cut me loose. Even left her horse."

"So it's personal. That Tonoaki seems to have a real hate going for you, John. Do you suppose he knew your wife was going to be taking the boy to their village?"

"I suspect so. He knew she would be turning him over to family when he turned seven. It's not rational but I don't doubt that he's been out there watching ever since winter began. By that line of reasoning, he was watching us deliver Gray Wolf's Son but didn't want to involve the boy, so he waited until we headed back."

"Looks like you can no longer leave the fort unless you have an armed escort. If he catches you alone, without Ronnie… well, I think we know what will happen. But why? What does your gut tell you?"

John shrugged. "I married his ex-wife. He drove her away, damn near killed her but somewhere in that sick mind, I think he thinks if she wasn't married to me she'd be back with him."

"And would she?"

John looked at the older man. "You may ask Ronnie herself, sir. She's an extremely honest and open person, she wouldn't mind. But," John chuckled despite the ache of his head, "would any woman be likely to go back to a man who just skinned her mate in front of her? I'd say that's rather sick in the head." John sat back in his chair with a grimace.

"Speaking of heads, you need to go home and take care of yours. You don't look so good, John."

"I don't feel so good, sir," John agreed, "but as a doctor I know I shouldn't be sleeping for twenty-four hours. After the fact, I plan on sleeping for the next two days straight."

"Hmmm." Greeley stood, forcing John to stand. "Go home to that wife of yours and see if she can give us anymore insights."

"Yes, sir." John began to stand and experiencing vertigo, collapsed back onto the chair.

"Corporal!" Greeley called to the soldier outside his door. The door flew open.

"Yes, sir?"

"Get some help," Greeley snapped. Almost immediately a second soldier poked his head through the doorway. "Assist Captain Power home."

"Yes, sir," they replied in unison as they each took an arm and began to walk John out of the office.

New Year's Day passed very quietly in the John Power household. John was still convalescing with bouts of double vision, vertigo, and blinding headaches. Of equal concern was the raw open wound upon his leg. John knew the skin was the body's protection, the barrier against all those micro-organisms he had learned about in Switzerland. The world we cannot see, he called them. Creatures so small they were visible only with a powerful microscope. He spoke to Ronnie about them, showed her, and explained the importance of sterilizing bandages.

Ronnie faithfully boiled the bandages to be put directly onto his raw flesh in garlic and witch hazel. When the cloth was cooled she wrapped his leg again. The warmth and moisture aided his body as it tried to rebuild the skin he was missing. She gave him willow bark tea and made an argument against drinking spirits.

"Spirits cannot be good for you, Jack," she said softly. "Spirits not good for anyone. They make dizzy. They can give bad headache. These you already have, drinking spirits can only add to problem, not cure it."

She made her argument so softly and so lovingly, he could not help but bow to her wishes and drink only the teas she made along with modest doses of laudanum.

As John spent his time in bed, Ronnie was left to deal with her mother who was feeling poorly but still trying to help with the children. The rapidly aging

Indian woman found energy in being with her grandchildren even though her smile was almost toothless and she had to be encouraged to eat. Luke was almost nine months old, Mark was a year and a half, Matthew was two and a half and Sunshine was four.

Ronnie smiled as she watched the two oldest listen to Singing Wind tell them stories in her language. Mark was at the most difficult age as he had no patience to sit. He was walking and trying to get into everything but had little to no understanding of words. It was hard for Ronnie not to think of the large, well-staffed nursery back at Chartes Landing. It had lots of room to run and jump even when the icy snows blew outdoors.

Ronnie changed the swaddling on baby Luke. She and Jack had not shared pleasures since they had left to take Gray Wolf's Son to the village. She decided when they did she would take the morning-after tea to prevent Jack's spirit from starting another child. He had such a strong spirit, she smiled to herself. Jack had given her three strong sons even while she nursed. Unlike Tonoaki who had complained when she nursed Gray Wolf's Son saying it kept her from conceiving his child. Tonoaki had a weak spirit, she concluded, and in the end he had produced only a girl.

Ronnie recognized that she had no nursery with staff to help her like at Jack's family home. Right now she had enough to keep up with. Perhaps in a year or two… or three, they could try for a daughter.

It was time to nurse little Luke and Ronnie begged her mother to settle the others for their afternoon nap. Singing Wind began crooning to the little ones. Ronnie settled little Luke to her breast. The babe looked up at his mother and Ronnie cried out and almost wept for joy. Luke's iris' were turning gray with black around the edge just like Jack's. Luke was indeed Jack's son. She should have known. Tonoaki's spirit was too weak to produce a son. She smiled with gladness and joy and gratitude. Then she did weep as she thought of how close she had come to aborting him.

When his belly was pleasantly full, Luke nodded off for his nap. Ronnie carried the baby to his cradle and saw her mother dozing on the large bed shoved against the wall with the other children sleeping between her and it. She would wait to tell her mother and was reminded that it was in part Singing Wind's plea and counsel that had stopped Ronnie from drinking the dangerous decoction.

She couldn't wait to tell Jack.

He was in their bed but she saw his eyes open when she entered.

"Ronnie?" he gave her a brave smile.

"Oh, Jack, Jack, I have such good news." She sat on the side of the bed.

Looking with one eye, he could see the tear tracks down her cheeks.

"Good news doesn't usually make you cry," he murmured, taking hold of her hand.

"I know but it is such happy news my joy is overflowing. I love you, my husband, so very much!"

"Well, that is good news," he smiled again and kissed her hand.

"You tease. That is not the news. This you should know already."

"So what is your happy news?" he half-whispered, reaching out to stroke her soft cheek.

"Luke's eyes are changing, Jack. They are turning gray with black around just like yours! Luke is indeed your son, the son of your spirit, the son of your loins."

John was still for a moment considering. So Ronnie had already been pregnant when that bastard had forced her to lie with him. He might have raped her but he hadn't got her with child. John felt something within him lighten. Something he hadn't realized had been weighing him down. Luke was his son, really his son just like Matthew and Mark; and Tonoaki could go to hell without ever having a son!

John sat up straighter and swung his legs out of bed. "I've lain in this bed long enough. I want some real food to eat and I will sit at the table to eat it. After all, you have given me something to celebrate," he said as he stood and wrapped his arms around Ronnie while closing his eyes to still the vertigo.

She set him back onto the edge of their bed. "Your slippers, Jack." She pulled a heavy pair of wool stockings onto his feet and then his house slippers. "And your robe," she added as she helped him into it. "And now your eye patch." With her assistance he rose again and walked out to the kitchen table. "I have some apple juice," she said as she poured a glass. "You wait here I go to commissary for food."

Ronnie slipped on her fur lined cloak and was back in fifteen minutes with turkey, chicken, ham, a variety of vegetables, fresh bread, butter, a bowl of mashed potatoes and gravy, and a pumpkin tort. It was food from the holiday meal. The mess sergeant had been so pleased to hear Captain Power was asking for food that he had his kitchen boy go along to help Mistress Power carry everything.

John ate sparingly, but he ate. He was on the mend.

Chapter 21

In the year 1728, the first Jewish synagogue in America was built in New York Towne and horses and carriages were banned from the Commons in Boston. It was the year Puritan Preacher Cotton Mather died, the preacher who history would remember most for two very controversial issues. The first was his role in the Salem Witch Trials, a black mark on New England history and a proceeding to which his own father, the well known and much accomplished Increase Mather, had been publicly opposed. The second was Cotton's participation in the long ongoing controversy over the theories of inoculation against disease. Unfortunately, it was also the year smallpox came to Chartes Landing.

It was very early spring when Doctor Ajax diagnosed the disease in a visitor fresh off a ship up from the West Indies who had come to see his distant relative, Ned Murray. Immediately Murray's house was put under strict quarantine. Two weeks later, Ned himself came down with the disease and since no one else lived in the house, Ajax established it as the hospital house. He sent the word out to every household in the settlement and even into the countryside, that this was their opportunity to accept inoculation and forever be immune to the fearful disease.

Madame Tingley sent two of her working girls, her cook and her housekeeper to Ajax to get inoculated. They shared a room to themselves in the hospital house.

Richard and Marie discussed it. Richard was dead set against and Marie agreed that at their age, if the disease had not come down on them already perhaps they had more to fear from purposely infecting themselves.

Lyndyn made his case for going in for the inoculation and then residing in the hospital house until he recovered. As he had said some time before, he was vulnerable to bringing the disease home since he had so much commerce with the public. Louise debated at supper whether she should have Sebastian who was now thirteen and a half and Michael who was ten and a half go with Lyndyn.

The boys seemed to view it as an adventure and soon to be sixteen year old Rebecca was hoping a women's house would be established.

Marie looked over at Richard, then cleared her throat.

"Louise, *ma chère*, before you make any final decision I wish a word with you privately after supper."

"Of course, Mother," Louise agreed.

Marie had heard Thor and Helen were absolutely against it but Thomas was very soon to be sixteen and had a mind of his own which was in a rebellious state. He argued cavalierly with his parents that if he should die it would be of his own doing but they would still have another son in Joseph. And if he should not die, he would be free of fear of the disease for the rest of his life.

After supper Marie squeezed Richard's hand then led the way to Jacques' old office. Louise took Lyndyn's arm and followed. Once inside they each found a seat and Richard closed the door. He began to pour out small servings of cognac but Louise held up her hand.

"None for me, Uncle Richard, I've never liked the stuff."

"Is there something else I can get you?" Richard asked.

"No, just an explanation. This is all rather mysterious."

"Louise," Marie began. She had taken her seat in Jacques' old chair behind the desk. "I am afraid we have a family secret which has never been shared with you before but the time has come." She looked to Richard.

"It is my fault that it has remained a secret," Richard continued. "Your father and mother knew, as I know, but no one else, not even my son, Raphael."

Lyndyn's hand reached over to embrace Louise's hand in a gesture of support.

"As I have told you, Raphael's mother was an exotically beautiful woman; she was also a quarter Cherokee," Richard said softly. "That made Raphael an eighth. I am certain it is this mixture from where he got his extraordinary beauty."

Louise looked at Lyndyn, her mother, then back to Richard with a shrug as if to say *what of it?* "I don't understand, why bring this up now? I'm not Izzy and even if I were, the man is dead. We're not married any more."

"But your children are alive," Marie put in. "It is time you knew because your children are part Indian."

"Oh, Mother, that's ridiculous. And if they marry someone with no native blood then their children will be all of what? One-thirty-second. What is that like half a drop? No one cares. Even Izzy's stupid Bostonian Blue Bloods would probably find it more exotically intriguing than objectionable in the future years to come. As the Indians fade away I can just imagine a time when it will become *en vogue* to claim to be part native, especially if you are born in America."

"Louise, you do not seem to understand the concern," Marie said calmly.

"No, I guess I don't."

"We all know that smallpox is devastating to the natives. This is something you must consider before you agree to purposely infect your children who carry native blood."

They all heard Louise gasp.

"Oh! Oh, my lord! Are you saying... you are saying... that they are more likely to die?!"

Richard had come up behind Marie and his big hands rested on her small shoulders.

"I know not," Marie shook her head. "I know not how this works. Would they be more likely to die if they are inoculated? Or not inoculated? Or does their white blood make them less likely to die? I have not the answers. I can only say as a parent you should have all the facts before making any decision on your children's behalf. I envy you not. There seems to be so much more danger in the world today than there was when you were children."

At Sunday dinner Phillip informed the family that after discussion, he and Caroline agreed that he should get the inoculation as he was often dealing with the ships and sailors as the lumber was shipped out. Caroline said if there was a women's house established she would also get the inoculation once they knew Phillip was well. She cited the same reasoning as Lyndyn. She, too, worked with exposure to the public all day long. Then Charity who was now seventeen stated she also intended to get inoculated just as Doctor Ajax advocated if a women's house was established. Meanwhile Thor and Helen remained in stern opposition while son Thomas sat scowling his frustration.

Richie and Clarissa had already departed for the season but Jamie said he and Cynthia lived a rural life and saw no point in tempting fate. Besides, he added, Cynthia might be with child but they weren't entirely certain as yet.

At some point in the conversation, one of them asked Louise if she intended on sending Sebastian with Lyndyn.

"I really can't say," she said evasively.

"Can't say what?" Helen prodded. "Either you mean to or you don't."

"I'm not sure. I need to speak first with Doctor Ajax."

"What more is the man going to tell you? You know he's all for it," Phillip called down from the head of the table.

"I'll thank you to stop trying to bully me," Louise said sharply and her siblings went quiet.

"I received a letter from John," Marie spoke out.

"What's he been up to? It's been a while," asked Louise, grateful for the shift in topic away from her children.

"I am afraid the news has not been pleasant," Marie continued. "Gray has gone to his people as Ronnie told us he would but John was in some kind of confrontation with renegades and he was clubbed on the head. He's been experiencing incapacitating headaches and vertigo ever since. John is currently on medical leave and they were planning on coming here as soon as he can travel but I wrote back immediately and suggested he not bring Ronnie and the children until this smallpox scare is over."

"But wouldn't it be better if they came, *Grand-mère*," asked Charity, "they could all be inoculated."

"That sounds good, *ma petite,* except we have no idea how dangerous it might be for Ronnie and the children. She is an Indian, after all. Is the inoculation more risky for them? The disease itself seems to be much more deadly to them. Then… is it more risky for the children? And the children are so young, really too young even if they were full blood whites. None of us are prepared to see such little ones get inoculated."

"You're right, *Grand-mère*, I forgot," Charity sobered.

"Frankly, I am very concerned with these wretched headaches John writes of. I recall when I was clubbed on the head, I experienced much of what John writes but within less than a month I was much better. John has been suffering now for several months."

The room erupted, everyone talking at once.

"Mother!"

"When were you clubbed on the head?"

"*Grand-mère*, who clubbed you on the head?"

"When did this happen?"

"Why have you never told us?"

"Oh, have I never told you the story?" She looked innocently around the table at the questioning faces. "It happened long before any of you were born. I will tell you all about it when I return but right now you must excuse me." She turned to Richard. "*Mon cher*, will you come with me to find Ajax? I simply must speak with him."

Richard drove the trap to Ajax's office. Slowly but steadily they climbed the steps to his second story residence and knocked on the door. Ajax answered wearing breeches and a shirt open at the neck. He looked sleepy-eyed but surprised.

"Is anything wrong?" he asked, quickly throwing the door open wide.

"No-no," Marie said quickly. "I apologize for disturbing you but I have heard from John and I have some questions. May we…?"

"Oh, please, come in. Excuse my appearance." He grabbed his vest. "It's a trifle cramped but it's usually only me," he graciously pointed them to what chairs there were, an eclectic grouping comprised of one upholstered easy chair, one hard wood kitchen chair, and one settee. His little apartment was clean if rather Spartan. It lacked anything beyond the bare necessities. On a small shelf Marie noticed a collection of medical books, one written in French, one she guessed was German and the others were all English. A copy of the Bible acted as a book stop on one end while a stack of journals stopped the other end.

"Thank you," Marie replied graciously and took a seat along with Richard on the settee. "Archie, first I want you to know I have not invited you or anyone outside of the family for Sunday dinners of late until this whole inoculation issue is settled. I feel the children need to think through their own decisions without any outside pressure. Each, after all, must live with his choice, eh?"

"Of course, Marie, I understand."

"Do you?" She looked at him with those changeable eyes, eyes which at the moment looked almost green. "Forgive me but I think not. You have no family, you have no children. Think for a moment of having a little person enter your life. A piece of you, blood of your blood and you are emotionally invested in this little person and watching them grow and learn… for three years, ten years, perhaps twenty or thirty years. Long ago you realized you would give your life for this person, do anything to protect them and keep them safe. Then suddenly you are being asked to gamble with this person's life… how do you do it?"

Ajax nodded. "Perhaps it is less difficult to be logical if you are not emotionally involved."

"Of course it is, but still logic gives no guarantees, does it? Anyway, the grown adults of my family are each coming to their own personal decisions with no pressure either way. And we all shall have to live with the results. But this is not why I came here."

"Why exactly did you come?" He sounded tired.

"I have two reasons. Tell me what you know or have heard or read about how inoculation might be expected to affect the Indians or more specifically the breed of white and native mix? Surely some attempts have been made, something has been written?"

"You think of your son's children," he said and stood up. He took a bottle of wine from the sideboard and poured them each a glass. "As a medical doctor, John should get inoculated, of that I am absolutely certain and wholeheartedly recommend. As for Ronnie and their children, I have no idea how this process would effect them. To the shame of the colonialists both British and French in decades past, what was recorded as 'inoculations' was in reality simply the gifting of infected blankets to the tribes. The purpose was simply to cause an epidemic which would wipe the natives out."

Ajax saw the look of shock on Marie's face.

"It has been very effective. There are hundreds of tribes and they each survive the diseases of the white man at different rates. A tribe or two have been completely wiped out. They exist no more. Some others have lost as much as seventy percent of their people. With the Cherokee, more like fifty percent. But there has not been a native tribe that has not seen at least thirty to forty percent mortality in the wake of what was called *inoculation*. But to my knowledge the true process of inoculation which I advocate, has never been tried at all. Still," he sighed wearily, "if they die so easily from the disease, I would not be inclined to attempt inoculation on anyone of them I loved."

Marie swallowed her wine and held her glass out for more.

"I must tell you something, Archie, in confidence," she said.

He refilled her glass. "Of course."

Marie and Richard briefly explained Raphael's Indian heritage.

Ajax sat thoughtfully. "So you say the children are only one-sixteenth? My instincts are telling me this would hold no weight one way or the other. Do not worry. I would, in fact, be more concerned with John's children who are half and half."

"Not quite half and half," boomed Richard, "Ronnie has a bit of white herself."

Ajax shrugged. "Frankly, I don't know what I would do if I were their father." It was quiet for a moment, then Ajax asked, "What is the second thing?"

"Oh, yes-yes. I suppose I am a mother looking for some reassurance in an uncertain world. John writes he was clubbed on the head in an incident. That was December and yet John is still suffering from very bad headaches, bouts of double vision, and touches of dizziness even now, months later. His commander has put him on medical leave and he was planning on coming home to recuperate but I warned him off until we are certain we are smallpox free." She looked intently at Ajax. "You say nothing, Archie, and that is scaring me."

Ajax turned slightly from her gaze. "Oh, come now, Marie. I cannot diagnose long-distance. I must see him in person, ask him questions. It could be something serious or it could be nothing."

"Sick headaches and double vision is not *nothing*. So what might it be? Tell me the truth," she demanded.

"Really I cannot say without further facts. His body could be mending itself and all will be well. Now if you will excuse me I must go to the hospital house and check on my patients."

"Forgive us, we did not mean to detain you," Richard rose from his seat. "Let us give you a ride."

"Oh, thank you but not necessary, it's just a short walk."

"Who has been staying with them?" Marie asked.

"A woman I found who has had the pox already, her name is Molly Tingley.

"Molly Tingley? I do not think I have ever met the woman. Is she married?" Marie asked rather innocently.

"Ah, she runs a public house… popular with the men," Ajax answered as he shut his door and they progressed down the stairway.

"What is its name?" Marie persisted.

"I believe she calls it *Jozy's*."

"That is odd is it not?" Marie observed as they took their leave. "If her name is Molly, why call her own tavern *Jozy's?*"

Richard took his wife by the elbow and helped her into the trap. "I believe it is not exactly a public house. It is a place where men go to find relaxation with young women."

"A whorehouse?" Marie looked at Richard and smiled. "I did not realize Chartes Landing had become so sophisticated. Well, I certainly hope you feel no need to find *relaxation* there."

"No, *mon amour*, I get more than enough relaxation at home." And he squeezed her bottom.

Chapter 22

A week after Ned Murray was stricken, Doctor Ajax had his first female victim. Old Maudy Smyth was a washer woman and cleaning lady who keeled over like her legs had been struck out from under her as she tried to hang her latest batch of laundry on the wash lines. Doctor Ajax was called in and found she was complaining of a terrible headache and she was running a high fever. Immediately he placed her, her house and her laundry under quarantine. He discovered that Maudy had come to clean at Ned Murray's place and had lent a compassionate hand when she saw his guest was so ill. Now she was ill. Maudy lived in a small cottage of her own and Ajax commandeered it to be the "Women's Hospital." As soon as the pustules broke out on Maudy, the hard working doctor could offer inoculation to all the Chartes Landing females in addition to the men.

Phillip and Lyndyn were sent home. They were no longer contagious, they looked and felt well and one was hard pressed to find a pock mark on either of them. It was a joyful gathering at the Power house Sunday dinner.

"So what was it like?" Marie asked.

"I'm sure it's a little different for everyone," Phillip responded. "It was no walk in the meadow but altogether, not too bad. The first several days were nothing, we played cards. Then I noticed a headache which grew in intensity, then the fever came along with vomiting and… well, purging. Ajax said he saw a few eruptions along my hair line. You lose track of time. I know I slept a lot but three weeks and it is all over.

"I guess I'm going to get inoculated tomorrow and shall not be seeing you for… three weeks," said Caroline rather quietly.

"I'm going in with you as well, Mother," said Charity.

"We want to go too," spoke Faith and Hope almost in unison." At which thirteen year old Grace and nine year old Patience joined in.

"This is not a party," Caroline said quickly, "I do this only because I do have constant contact with strangers. You girls have no reason to risk this."

"But Rebecca says all of them are going," Hope replied, "even five year old Frances."

"Is this true, Louise?" Helen asked in shocked surprise.

"I'm still considering it. Nothing is certain as yet," Louise responded and scowled at Rebecca. "Daughter, you are spreading false rumors."

"But Mother, you said…"

"I said I was *thinking* about it. It is a big step."

"But Papa Lyndyn is fine."

Louise looked at Lyndyn. "Yes, he is. Praise the Lord. And I have ten more gray hairs from awaiting the result."

"What do you think *Grand-mère?*" Rebecca looked to Marie.

"I think your parents must each make up their minds what they believe is best for their children based on the facts they know. Now, who is the best student of mathematics? Is that you Thomas? Or you Sebastian? Or is it possibly Charity?"

"Truthfully," Charity answered, "Faith is much better than any of the boys."

"Ah....a female mathematician in the family," Marie smiled. "Then go at once and get slate and chalk from the schoolroom. Quickly."

They all continued eating as Faith disappeared and soon returned with slate and chalk.

"Very good," Marie said, "Now begin to add. Your ma-ma and Pa-pa plus you five girls makes seven- write seven. Good. Now your Aunt Louise and Uncle Lyndyn plus their five children makes another seven, yes? Write another seven. Your Aunt Helen and Uncle Thor plus their four makes another six. Then there is me and your Uncle Richard plus Nora and Phoebe and her little one, that is another five. Do not forget Sarah and her assistant, young and old Margot, the handyman and the stable boy. That is another six. And Uncle Jamie and Aunt Cynthia, Uncle Richie and Aunt Clarissa, that is four more."

"What about Aunt Izzy, Uncle Hamilton and Baby Chad?" asked Hope.

"No, we will not count them because they live in another community," answered Marie. "What is the total?"

"That totals thirty-five," said Faith.

"Right, some big mathematician was needed for simple addition I can do in my head," Thomas teased.

"Oh, but now we get to the interesting part," Marie continued. "Statistics gathered on inoculations say three percent can be expected to die. So, Faith, what is three percent of thirty-five?"

The young girl quickly set about her work and came up with a figure. "It is 1.05."

"So who is the one person within our little group that we would be willing to see die?" Marie asked of a table that had become very quiet. After a few moments she continued. "Of course percentages are most accurate in very large groups, when we are talking hundreds or thousands."

"But *Grand-mère*, you said you and Uncle Richard were not going to get inoculated, neither is Uncle Jamie or Aunt Cynthia, Uncle Richie and Aunt Clarissa, Uncle Thor, Aunt Helen and none of their children... that is twelve and I heard Margot and Nora talking, none of them is going. That is five more including the baby. I must subtract seventeen from our total which becomes eighteen and three percent of that is only half a person. We cannot cut a person in half."

"Very true which makes my point. Mathematic percentages are not guarantees but indicators. Within our tiny group we may have no deaths at all… or is it not possible we could have several? And this takes not into account how many may be left scarred. Now my children, this is what your parents must consider before you rush in with the enthusiasm of youth."

That evening there were many separate discussions all evolving around the same basic subject matter. Caroline was resolved to volunteer for the inoculation because of business. Phillip had come through it so well. With her mother accepting the procedure, Charity was determined as well. Her young heart wanted to show Doctor Ajax how much she believed in and supported him. She had told him she would be among the first to be inoculated if it became a possibility and he had been proud of her. And so she was keeping her word. Faith and Hope said they too wanted to go. Caroline reminded them that at fifteen parental permission was needed and she and Phillip had not yet made up their minds.

Thomas continued without ceasing to assert his belief that he was old enough to make such a decision for himself and against their better judgment Thor and Helen finally agreed to allow him to go.

Louise was up all night as her children were determined to join their cousins. She found herself vacillating wildly. At moments she was of a mind to let all of them go, then she would decide against allowing any of them to go. Next she thought to only allow the eldest to go, then she thought perhaps only the youngest who might get over it easier. Perhaps she should allow only the boys and keep the girls from possible disfigurement. She thought of how beautiful Raphael had been and saw Sebastian growing into his father's likeness and could not bear to think of his face being mottled with pock-mark craters. Then she looked to Lyndyn and her brother Phillip who had suffered no scarring and knew the scarring was more likely if Sebastian got smallpox the conventional way. She threw her hands in the air and thought once again they all might as well get the treatment.

By morning, an exhausted Louise with dark circles under her eyes told Lyndyn she had decided to allow ten year old Michael and almost seven year old Jeannette to go first to see how they fared. If all went well then the others could follow.

"Oh, does that seem cruel? Like I am sacrificing the young as an experiment for their older siblings. I can't. I just can't decide," she cried out and collapsed into Lyndyn's arms.

"Louise, sweetheart, no one says you must decide today. No one is holding a musket to your head. Would you rather allow fate to decide?"

"Fate?"

"I must be off to the store. We'll talk of it tonight when I come home. Go to bed my love, you're exhausted." And he kissed her forehead and led her to their bed.

When Louise awoke, she sought out her children and spent the rest of the day with them. She was aware that Caroline and Phillip had brought all their children to Marie. Marie told Louise that Phillip had then taken Caroline with Charity and Faith who had insisted on going to be inoculated as well, over to Doctor Ajax's office.

"And Hope?" Louise asked.

"Caroline would only allow one of the twins to go and they drew sticks. Faith drew the long stick," Marie replied. "Helen brought Thomas by to give me a hug. We shall not see any of them for three weeks."

Louise nodded.

"And what about you, *ma cher*, what have you decided?"

"Mother, I can't. I don't know what to do. I was up all last night trying to decide but I just could not. I wish I had the wisdom of Solomon."

Marie put a loving arm around her daughter. "Louise, perhaps a decision that is so difficult to make... should not be made, *n'est-ce pas?*"

"I don't know what that means. The children are all underage, I cannot allow them to run off willy-nilly deciding for themselves."

"No-no, I only meant that Doctor Ajax is a man of medicine and he strongly advocates the latest in medicine. It is what I would expect but what if he were not here constantly advocating? They call it a medical *practice* not medical certainty. Practices and philosophies are always changing. Would we all be in such a quandary over what to do just because three people we know not came down with smallpox for the first time ever in Chartes Landing? Doctor Ajax would quarantine them off, as he has, and that would be the end of it."

Louise poured herself another cup of tea and grew calmer.

Marie left to help Lyndyn at the store since Caroline was now under quarantine. When Lyndyn returned home for the night he had a pair of dice with him and after supper, he called Louise and the children into their suite and shut the door.

"Here is what we are going to do," he told them. "We are going to let God decide."

"Whatever do you mean, Lyndyn?" Louise asked.

"First we will pray and ask God's guidance, then each child will roll a die. If the die comes up with an odd number, they will go to Doctor Ajax. If the number is even, they stay home." He looked at his wife. "Agreed?"

"Agreed," she nodded softly.

"Children, do you understand? No fussing. We ask God for direction and we all accept what He allows, agreed?"

Everyone from fifteen year old Rebecca to five year old Frances nodded their agreement.

Lyndyn prayed earnestly out loud asking God's blessing and guidance in this huge decision.

"Lord, only you know if giving each child the inoculation is the right thing to do. Only you know if it will help them or harm them. Only you know if by not getting it they may someday be in danger of getting the disease itself and suffering far worse. Please guide us Lord God. We are unsure of our own wisdom as parents and we seek your wisdom through Christ our Lord. Amen."

"Amens" were repeated by everyone, even little Frances.

"Rebecca," Lyndyn gave her a die. "Here you go. Now shake it in this cup and in your heart you must ask God's guidance before you drop it onto the table and accept that it is His wish for you."

Rebecca nodded solemnly and took the cup and die, shook it and rolled it out onto the table.

"Two!" Louise gasped. "You will stay home!"

"Yes, Mama," the girl said obediently.

"Sebastian, you are next," Louise said.

The boy took the cup and die piece and shook it an inordinately long time before spilling the die onto the table.

"Four!" pronounced Lyndyn and looked at his wife who could not help but smile in relief.

"God wants me to stay at home as well," said Sebastian, trying not to sound disappointed.

Michael was next.

"One!" squealed the ten year old. "Does this mean God approves my going?"

"Yes," Louise replied tightly, "we must believe this is so."

He passed the cup and die to his seven year old sister. "Here Jenny, it's your turn." Jeannette barely shook the cup. The die bounced out and it was a four.

"What does that mean, Mama?"

"It means you are staying home with me."

"And now Frances," Lyndyn encouraged as Jeanette put the die back into the cup and handed it to her little brother.

He shook the cup and the die rolled out bouncing almost to the table's edge but stopping on four.

"Another four," Louise said quickly. "You will also stay home with your sisters and brother and me."

It was settled. Michael felt very special being the only one who was going to get an inoculation just like Papa Lyndyn. Lyndyn led a little prayer of thanks for God's guidance and then the door to the suite was opened.

The children went out to share the news with their cousins Hope, Grace, and Patience, Phillip's girls who would be staying at Grandma's until their mother came home again. Louise told Marie and Richard what they had done. Richard said nothing but was inwardly relieved and grateful that only one of Raphael's children was being put at risk. If inoculation continued to be advised, they could always get it in the future when they were older if an epidemic was imminent.

The next day Lyndyn brought Michael to Doctor Ajax and explained to the boy that while his mother would not be allowed to visit him, Lyndyn himself would come every day.

In keeping with the perversity of time which passes quickly when one is enjoying themselves and so slowly when one is enduring a hardship or waiting, the days crept by. Phillip went twice a day to see how "his ladies" were doing. Having been inoculated, he was told he was not at risk but Ajax did encourage no mouth to mouth kissing and a thorough hand washing before Phillip left the premises. There were only five other women in the women's hospital house and two of them were from Jozy's. Molly was still assisting Ajax in nursing. She had insisted the remaining two of her working girls be inoculated while the already recovered cook, housekeeper, and first two girls helped out in both hospital houses.

Lyndyn was allowed in to visit with Michael and Thomas. Having been inoculated a day sooner, Thomas became ill sooner but still he tried to be a "big brother" to Michael. Richard, not having been inoculated, was not allowed into the men's hospital house but he went each day and stood outside a window waving and drawing funny pictures for the boys. Richard brought Marie, Louise, and Helen with him until the boys became more ill and fevered. Then Richard saw it upset both Marie and Louise too much not to be able to go inside and give comfort. Still Richard and stoic Helen continued to visit and stand at the window just as encouragement.

After washing well and even changing his coat, Phillip would go to the family house and report how his quarantined ladies were progressing. It took some time for Caroline, Charity, and Faith to really become ill. But suddenly, all three were very ill. Phillip kept telling himself and everyone else that everything would be all right. He and Lyndyn had been ill for many days of vomiting and purging, he recalled. And how many days had they lay sleeping in misery?

But it was much harder for Phillip to watch the misery of his wife and daughters. Caroline's beautiful porcelain skin was covered in rashes, as was Faith's but neither broke out in the pustules like Charity. Then Faith and Caroline began to run exceedingly high fevers.

Phillip became frantic. It wasn't supposed to be this way. He and Lyndyn had run fevers but not nearly so high nor for so long. Charity's hands, neck, and face were covered in the ugliest blistery pustules but finally her fever broke. Caroline and Faith, however, continued in delirium.

Phillip didn't leave their bedsides. He kept moving from one to another until late one night Caroline opened her beautiful blue eyes, now blood shot, cried out for Phillip and then was silent.

Frantic, he called for Ajax, insisting he come look at her. Ajax was there, very concerned with the reaction the Power women were experiencing. They were the worst cases of inoculation reaction he had seen. The doctor felt for a pulse and finding none he knew Caroline Power was dead.

In stunned disbelief, Phillip sat by his wife's side willing her to answer his attempts to rouse her.

"She's gone, Phillip," Ajax said and went to the next bed to put more cold towels on Faith's head.

Phillip's reaction was near violence.

"No! Why? Why, Ajax? Why is this happening? What went wrong?"

"Phillip, please, you know there is a risk. I told you of the risk. Nothing 'went wrong.' It just happens."

"But Lyndyn and I were fine."

"I know. But we need to watch Faith and Charity now." Ajax tried to calm the grieving man and shift his attention. "Your daughters need your prayers."

Phillip stayed. He was in shock and never ceased praying. Then at three in the morning, Faith also slipped away.

Ajax sent a verbal message to Richard requesting someone come to Maudy's house to get Phillip. Lyndyn arrived and Ajax had the unpleasant task of telling him both Caroline and Faith had passed away. Phillip was now under a mild sedation and needed to be taken home and put to bed. Charity was beginning to improve and did not need her father to watch over her anymore. In fact, it was better he not be there because no one was going to tell Charity her sister and mother had died. It would be a terrible shock and right now Charity did not need such sad news.

Lyndyn understood. He oversaw Phillip giving his hands a good wash with lye soap and guided him outdoors into the trap. He stopped at Phillip's house to pick up a change of clothes and then Lyndyn had the miserable task of taking Phillip back to the family home and telling everyone that Caroline and Faith were dead.

Lyndyn administered another dose of the sedative as Ajax had instructed and he and Richard got Phillip into bed in the sick/sewing room.

"Lyndyn, how is Charity doing?" Marie asked anxiously.

"Her fever is down and she's sleeping. She will need to sleep a lot. The doc said she doesn't know anything yet and he doesn't want her to."

Marie was too shocked to cry. She went into Richard's arms for comfort. "Never has one of my children or grandchildren been ill when I could not comfort them. I am so frustrated. Lyndyn," she called out, "are you sure Charity,

Thomas, and Michael are doing well?"

"So far both the boys seem to be doing just as Phillip and I did. Charity has been… different but she is on the mend now."

Over the next two days, Charity's fever dropped to nothing but she was kept sleeping with small doses of laudanum. Finally she woke and asked for water. After water she was able to take some broth. She saw the beds next to her were now empty.

"What's happened to Mother and Faith? Did they go home already? When can I go home?" she asked weakly.

"Your blisters will scab over and when the scabs drop off, you will be free to go home," Molly answered. "Do you think you can manage some soft food. Pudding perhaps? Mashed potatoes? Some cooked oats with a little sugar and cinnamon perhaps?"

"Cooked oats sounds good," Charity replied as she looked at her hands. "Mother and Faith didn't blister like me. Can I have a mirror, Molly? I'd like to…"

"No mirrors. Sorry, honey. Doctor's rule. And keep your hands away from your face."

Charity obeyed but she wasn't happy. As she waited for her oats she looked down the front of her gown, then under the sheet at her legs and feet. She didn't see any other pustules but a rash was evident at her groin. The oats finally came courtesy of Molly's cook who was now working in the house kitchen. Charity ate but felt restless afterward.

She brightened when she saw Ajax coming.

"How are we feeling today?" he asked with a small smile.

"I'm feeling much better, thank you. I even ate, didn't I, Molly? I'll probably have to use the chamber pot next. I'm surprised Mother and Faith were able to go home so soon. I guess they must have had a much lighter dose than I." She held out her hands, looking at the blisters. "Molly says I have to stay here until these scab over and the scabs fall off, is that right?"

"Yes, Charity. That is right. You are contagious until your blisters dry up. Now, just because you are feeling better doesn't mean you don't still need your rest so lie back and try to get some more sleep."

"Thank you, Doctor Ajax. And from now on I'll be immune to smallpox, right?" She asked quietly with a smile.

"That's right, my dear, that's right," he nodded. "And if there is ever a need, you will be able to help care for the sick just like Molly."

"Good to know," she replied and suddenly feeling very fatigued, she reclined and pulled up the sheet.

The days passed and Charity watched the blisters on her hands begin to shrink, then dry and scab over. Finally the scabs began to fall off. When no one was looking, she began to sneak explorative trips to her face. She felt several scabs on her forehead but her cheeks felt smooth. She heaved a sigh of relief.

As Charity waited through the last days, which seemed the longest of all, she couldn't help wondering why her mother never came to visit, nor Faith. They would be immune now, like Papa and Uncle Lyndyn. She supposed that her mother was busy at the store but still, *Grand-mère* could always work at the store. The young girl tried to remember the last time she had seen her mother. They had all been fevered. She recalled vomiting, feeling so terribly wretched and then almost passing out in sleep. But Mother... someone had said "her fever's much too high." Who had said that?

Charity felt her gut tighten and a feeling come upon her that was a mixture of fear, dread, apprehension, and horror. Every time Papa came to visit he avoided answering questions about Mother...

"How is Mother doing?" she had asked

"We can't wait to get you home," had been Papa's reply.

And he never looked happy. If Mother and Faith were well and she, Charity, was recovering, Papa should be very happy. But Charity now realized he was not.

Suddenly it became clear. Mother and Faith hadn't made a fast recovery... they had died.

Ajax came to give her a final examination and tell her someone was coming, most likely her father to fetch her home.

"Doctor Ajax, please tell me the truth. Mother and Faith didn't make it, did they?"

Ajax maintained a professional demeanor but there was no sense lying to the child any more.

"No, Charity, they didn't. I am so very sorry."

"I knew it," she said softly. "Once I started thinking about it, I realized if she was well, she would have come to see me. I knew she wouldn't have forgotten about me if she were alive."

"Of course not, she would have been here every day," Ajax agreed with gentle compassion.

"And Faith... Hope is going to be lost without her twin... oh, poor Hope. How are Thomas and Michael doing?"

Ajax nodded his head with positive energy. "Thomas leaves today, I can release Michael tomorrow."

"What about the others you've inoculated?"

"Some were more ill than others but everyone is making a recovery."

"No one else died?"

"No."

"We were the three percent."

"What?"

"Nothing." Charity felt numb.

In the weeks that followed, the Power family tried to adjust to a new normal. Louise welcomed home her young son with so many tears of joy, Michael was confused until he heard Aunt Caroline and Cousin Faith had died. He and his siblings were beginning to understand why the decision to go or stay had been such a difficult one and why their parents had depended on a prayerful agreement with God.

Helen and Thor were more solemnly grateful but no less so. Helen grew closer to her sister as they shared the overwhelming feeling of each having been spared her son. They both looked to their older brother who had lost his son in a different manner and now had lost both his wife and a daughter. Louise also had lost a mate and knew for a time there was nothing any of them could say to ease Phillip's pain. Much like childbirth, the pain must simply be endured.

They saw very little of Phillip who left his children with his mother and left the business with Thor. Marie made sure he came to the house to eat often enough so as not to starve but she knew he had begun drinking heavily.

Marie had also lost a mate but not one nearly so young. It broke her heart to see her son struggling. Was he thinking what she was thinking? She wondered. What she kept thinking but would only express to Richard in the intimate privacy of their bed was that Caroline and Faith would still be with them if they had not allowed themselves to be purposefully infected with the worst, most dangerous disease of their time. There was no epidemic in Chartes Landing. The disease had been caught and properly isolated. Ned Murray and Maudy Smith had gone through it and survived. Only the visitor from the West Indies had died.

That was normal. In a full blown epidemic, adults had a sixty-six percent chance of survival or two out of three which is when a ninety-seven to three percent chance looked most excellent. But not when there was no threat.

"Marie, *mon amour*, you must never say that out loud. I have no doubt that Phillip runs that very thought through his mind all day and night, but say it not. It is like blaming the dead for their death."

"I wish John was here," Marie sighed deeply. "Phillip and he used to be very close. Phillip needs someone to confide in. John has also had his losses. I will write to him tomorrow. It is safe for him to come home now."

"We must give Phillip some time and some space," Richard said softly as he pulled her close.

"I have no problem with the children remaining here, in fact it is undoubtedly better for them but I do worry that Phillip is all alone, all by himself in that big house."

Richard smiled ruefully in the dark. "I do not think it would be any better if the house were small."

"Of course not, you know what I mean." Marie was quiet for a while and then she grunted to herself.

"What is it?"

"We must watch Hope as well. She has taken Faith's death very hard. Have you noticed she keeps going to the cemetery? And the child looks too thin to me. I do not think she is eating. And Charity? The child had such a sweet, well shaped nose. It will never be the same."

"In time people will forget what it was and think only that it is what it was always meant to be. And strangers will not know the difference."

"I wonder what Archie thinks when he looks at her. If she had not been so infatuated with the man, so determined to support his argument…"

"But we must be glad she survived and did so well."

Marie sighed. "Richard, I know not how you were with Jacques but you have always been such a voice of reason with me. You are wonderful. Now let us go to sleep."

A minute later Marie whispered loudly. "Are you asleep?"

"Not anymore."

"I just had a thought. I am going to take the girls into the store. It will give them something to focus on."

"Mmm"

"It is just what Charity and Hope need. Something to keep their minds occupied and we need the help. No sense in having strangers apprentice when I have grandchildren who are of age."

"Mmm-hmm."

"I am sorry, go to sleep… good night."

Chapter 23

Ronnie watched her husband as he read. John was having a relatively good day when his mother's letter arrived. He still wore his eye patch to combat his double vision.

She could tell by the signs on his face that the news was not happy. She nursed Luke and remained quiet, waiting for her husband to speak. He finished the letter, then went back and read some more. Finally, he looked up.

John sat for a moment with his eyes closed, digesting what he had just read and how best to share it with Ronnie. He looked over at her.

"Ronnie, my mother writes it is safe for us to return home now. They never had a smallpox epidemic. Only two people caught the disease from a visitor from the West Indies, they lived, he died."

She watched him, her eyes never leaving his face. She knew there was more and she waited.

"Doctor Ajax saw it as an opportunity to inoculate everyone against the disease." As he spoke, John realized Ronnie did not understand what inoculation meant. He took a moment to explain before he continued. "Apparently Ajax convinced about two dozen people in the settlement and seven of them were from my family. Most everyone came through it all right except for Phillip's wife, Caroline, and one of their twin daughters, Faith… they died."

"Caroline," she echoed softly, "with beautiful hair like copper waterfall."

"Yes. And you remember the twins, long copper hair just like their mother and very light skin?"

"I remember. Pretty girls."

John nodded. "Mother writes that Hope, the other twin, is not doing well. She's not eating. On more than one occasion, they've found her sleeping at her sister's grave or sitting alone and talking to her."

"Twins not like other siblings, Jack. Identical twins have very special magic. My people believe they can hear each other's thoughts if they want to. Know when each other are happy or sad, in danger or sick. Feel each other's pain."

John nodded. "Apparently. Hope told them when Faith died. It was hours before Phillip made it home and told them but she knew. Mother also writes my brother Phillip isn't doing well and seems to think I could… well, Mother seems to think I could be a comfort to him because I know what it's like. At one time we were very close, when we were young."

Ronnie nodded solemnly. They were silent for a time, thinking thoughts that should not be said out loud.

"She also writes that she talked to Thor's stepmother about my problems. Ingrid Boot believes she can *alleviate*… that means help to remedy… the double vision and headaches with massage and adjustments."

Ronnie gave him a smile of encouragement. She wanted Jack to be well again but she did not think she wanted him to be a soldier anymore. She rose to put baby Luke in his bed. She checked on the other children and then on her mother.

Singing Wind lay on her bed. "Morning Light," she acknowledged when she saw her daughter.

"Mother. Can I get you anything? You did not eat."

"You call family to me. I wish to say good-bye."

Ronnie fell to her knees beside her mother's bed.

"No, Mother, do not say this. You are just tired. Rest and be well."

Singing Wind put her hand on her daughter's arm.

"Rest will not cure me. I am weary and in pain…"

"What pain? Why did you not tell us? Tell Jack, he can help."

"No… no one can help, it is time. My usefulness is at an end. I am ready to go and leave all the pain of this world behind."

Tears blinded Ronnie as she looked into her mother's face. She shook her head.

"Who will stop me the next time I am ready to do something unwise?"

Singing Wind looked to her daughter in puzzlement.

"Luke," Ronnie said. "If not for you I might have…"

"But now you grow wise… and strong. You have mate who loves you. Leave here where Tonoaki plagues you. I will tell Gray Wolf. He will be glad for you."

Speaking the name of the dead was something Ronnie had had to do in her efforts to save John but now it upset her to hear her mother speak so. It signaled that Singing Wind was giving up on this life and planned to see the spirits soon.

"Mother, what of your mate?"

"I will see Red Elk soon. Five Beavers will not mind. He is sachem and cannot be bothered with passing of second wife. Tell him and Little Smoke I do not expect to see them for many, many years." She smiled and drifted into sleep.

Ronnie left her mother's bedroom and went to her husband.

"Jack?"

"Yes, sweetheart?"

"I would be most grateful if you send Charlie One Claw to village with message for Wani, Yellow Rock, and Gray Wolf's Son."

"What's wrong?"

"It is time they see Singing Wind before she passes to spirit world."

Charlie One Claw left the next morning and Ronnie began preparing food. With the help of several of the soldiers she had her mother's bed moved into the parlor and most of the parlor furniture moved into the bedroom. She left an easy chair for Jack and spread furs and cushions on the floor before the fireplace.

When her son, her brother, and her cousin arrived, Ronnie, in her buckskins, was able to welcome them into what might have passed as a wigwam. She had coached Jack in words of welcome and greeting which he spoke commendably well. She gave them all hospitable respect and served them food as they visited with Singing Wind who was very pleased to see them but was not able to get out of bed. When Singing Wind dozed off, Ronnie told them what had happened to her and Jack as they traveled home after delivering Gray Wolf's Son to them. She explained John's eye patch, a solution for his double vision from the vicious blow Tonoaki had given him. She described how Tonoaki had begun to skin Jack for no reason without even first offering him hand to hand combat. Everything he had done was an affront to the honor of the tribe.

"Tonoaki has gone crazy in the head," Yellow Rock said solemnly.

"The band that rides with him cannot be any better," Ronnie said and she decided to tell her male kin what Tonoaki had done to her when he had abducted her. "It was worse than forcing me for I could not fight. He bent me to his will by threatening my babies. My mother knew this and for all these past months we did not know if Luke was of Tonoaki's spirit or Jack's. But now we know. His eyes have started to turn and are just like his father's, just like Jack's.

"And remember when I was found by the river, not conscious? It was when I was another's wife and expecting Gray Wolf's Son. I had no memory of what had happened to me.

Yellow Rock nodded.

"One day when I was Tonoaki's mate we were by the river and something he did caused the memory to come back to me. And I remembered he had been there at the river that early morning and had overpowered and forced me and left me not conscious.

Yellow Rock listened but said nothing more.

The hour had grown late and each brave bed down on a spot before the fireplace.

In the morning, Ronnie rose and tended to breakfast. As the braves awoke she gave them a familiar berry drink and pointed them to the latrine. All returned and still Singing Wind was not awake.

John checked her pulse. She was still breathing.

All sat around in the parlor while Ronnie again served food.

"I am going to tell them we plan to go back to your home so you can heal," she said to John. Then in her native tongue she spoke to her relations again. "I wish to tell you something else. Jack is too injured to be soldier now but is still *doctor*, white man's shaman. In short time we are going to travel back to Jack's people where he is head of family and community, like sachem. They want him to come back, I think he wants to return, and I am happy to go with him. I will have the honor to be the sachem's only wife for as long as I live. If we go I do not know when I see you again." She looked sadly at Gray Wolf's Son. He was still just a little boy only seven and a half years old. "I know my son is going to be a fine Mohawk warrior but if some day in future he should want to come visit and learn more of the white man's world, I ask you to let him come, Yellow Rock my cousin, it is the future. Bring the message to Charlie One Claw at fort and fort will send message to us. We will arrange details. Also, let him keep and practice white man's speech and written words. Again, my cousin, it is the future. This learning will be important in times to come."

Yellow Rock looked to Wani and to Gray Wolf's Son and nodded. Then he reached out and put his forehead to Ronnie's. "You are becoming a wise woman, my cousin." She embraced him, then turned and embraced Wani, and finally embraced Gray Wolf's Son.

John checked on Singing Wind again and they all took up a vigil around her bed.

Ronnie began to sing a song of departing and Yellow Rock and Wani joined in. The haunting refrains drifted out onto the parade grounds where several of the soldiers cast questioning looks at Charlie.

"It song saying good-bye to mother. Old woman is dying," he told them.

They took the body across the river and built a funeral pyre. Singing Wind was wrapped in a beautiful robe she had made several years before, in anticipation of her death. John and Ronnie brought Sunshine and Matthew so they could be reminded that they were at their grandmother's funeral. The three Mohawk warriors paid a silent tribute and when all was reduced to ash, they headed back to their village.

At the last passing of the season, Singing Wind had turned thirty-nine years old.

Deep in the Indian forest, Tonoaki heard someone call his name. The others of his band were asleep. He rose silently from his pallet.

"Tonoaki," he heard a strange and compelling voice call.

"Who is it? Where are you? Show yourself." he whispered.

"Tonoaki."

"What do you want?" In the moonlight, he saw a form. "Who is there?"

"Tonoaki."

"Show yourself. Who are you?"

"Who are you, Tonoaki? An outlaw, a thief, a renegade, an outcast. You have no tribe, you have no home. Far have you fallen."

"Wha…" Tonoaki could feel his heart increase its beat as he drew breath more quickly.

"You possessed the greatest treasure when *Ohronkene Hahser* agreed to be your mate but you knew not how to appreciate her."

"Who are you?" Tonoaki cried out as he stumbled through the dark trying to find the figure that kept eluding him.

"You know who I am. You won her by deceiving her and then you beat her and falsely accused her."

"No… I tried to be a good husband. I loved her but she did not love me; she never loved me."

"A wife need only honor her husband, she is not compelled to love him. It is for him to nurture love within her. She might have loved you if you had not forced yourself upon her when she belonged to another."

"How do you know that?!" He was sweating now and searching the shadows for his accuser.

"I know you, Tonoaki. You have no honor. You forced yourself upon her again and made a bargain. Her cooperative spirit in exchange for the lives of her mate and children. How well did you honor that bargain? You tried to kill her mate."

"No, I only wished her to hurt as I hurt," he said twisting in each direction, grasping at air, stumbling through the underbrush. "I wished to punish her for not giving me love like she had for *Atakenhrohkwa Okwaho!*"

"You were never good enough, Tonoaki. You could never match *Atakenhrohkwa Okwaho.* He beat you at everything. Even the white man is better at earning her love than you. That is why you wish to hurt him. You are a coward and you have no honor!"

"Nooo…" Tonoaki crashed through the brush and stumbled in the darkness. "Come out here and face me! Show yourself! I challenge you to fight me. I will kill…" Tonoaki lost his footing and fell over a precipice, tumbling down and down.

In the morning his fellow outlaws found him. His neck was broken.

John wrote to his mother explaining Ronnie's mother had died and announcing that they were packing up to return to Chartes Landing. He told her he was still on medical leave. What he did not say was that he did not anticipate ever re-turning to life as a soldier. He had a final meeting with Greeley and offered the man his resignation.

"John, you're on leave. No need to rush anything. Give yourself a chance to heal. You're a damn fine officer and the best post doctor this army's ever seen. We're all going to miss you. As my right arm I'm especially going to miss you. Keep me informed. I expect you to fully recover and who knows… you may get bored with civilian life."

"Once I return, I don't know that my family will ever allow me to leave again," John replied with a wry smile. "But I appreciate the sentiments, sir. And surprisingly, my wife is actually looking forward to returning to that civil-ian life."

"Well, I'm going to hold this," Greeley pointed to the letter of resignation. "Officially you're on medical leave. I'm not going to push this through until you're sure that's what you want."

John told Ronnie to pack up everything she wanted to keep as they might never be returning. The day before their departure she went to the site of her mother's funeral pyre to say a final farewell. The next morning as they pre-pared to leave she could tell her husband was nervous about leaving the con-fines of the fort. They had some miles to travel by horseback until they reached the boat landing which would start them on their journey. Greeley had ordered a dozen men to escort them.

"Jack," she called, coming up to him as they prepared to mount. "My mother came to me in a dream last night. She said not to be concerned, Tonoaki is dead."

John's head snapped up. He had never encouraged or discouraged his wife in any of her native ways. He'd always liked that line from Shakespeare, *"There are more things in Heaven and Earth, Horatio, than are dreamt of in your philosophy."* He believed that. He had witnessed native healing that defied his science. Seen stock placed in dreams that was not misguided. Who was he to say what was possible or impossible?

"I knew the day felt brighter," he said and smiled at her as he helped her into the saddle. He secured Luke in the wicker travel basket hanging over her horse's withers. Mark went on the other side.

Charlie One Claw was going with them, at least as far as the boat landing. He took Matthew up on the horse with him. While to Little Sunshine's delight, she was swung up on a perch in front of her "Papa." John held the child as she clapped her hands in glee. He smiled, she was totally without fear.

Ronnie thought wistfully of Gray Wolf's Son but said nothing. She would pray to her gods and John's God that someday her first born would return to her if only to learn of the white man's ways. Life among the whites was in some ways easier but in many ways more complicated. She allowed herself a moment to think of Gray Wolf. He had saved her life when others would have killed her simply because they thought she carried the white man's disease. He had loved her and cared for her all those years when she was but a child. He had been a warrior who lived to kill. Theirs had been a simple life and a simple passion and she had loved him to the full-up of her being. John was a more complicated man. A warrior but not a warrior; a doctor, a healer; a leader of his people; a man who had lived several lives already, who had loved several women. Now he loved her and she loved him just as fiercely, but for John, life was more than just raising children, hunting food, and killing enemies. She must learn so she could keep pace with him and maintain his admiration and interest. She hoped to learn from her mother-in-law who had been so happily married for over thirty years. To have such a life and such a love with such a man was to be greatly cherished.

Chapter 24

arie stood politely knocking on the front door of the two story frame house. With patience she waited and knocked again until a good five minutes had passed. At this point she invoked her mother's prerogative, opened the door, and walked in. Phillip's house had a depressing and stiflingly uncared for feel. She tried to remember the last time she had been there. In her effort to give her son space in his time of mourning, it had been too long!

The house smelled of stale beer, whiskey, dust, damp refuse from the fireplaces, and something left to spoil in the pantry. It had never smelled like this when Caroline had been alive. Marie sighed. Not that she expected her son to take a sudden interest in housekeeping but he should never have let his cleaning lady go. Marie made a mental note to send Nora and whoever she chose to help her to do a thorough top to bottom cleaning of the entire house. Charity, Hope, and Grace were all old enough to lend a helpful hand and it was their home after all.

Marie doubted that the bed linens had been changed in months. Walking through, it was easy to see that when he did eat, Phillip never took the time to move the dirty dishes to the kitchen to be washed. Dried up food and scraps sat hard or moldy and disgusting on dishes pushed and shoved onto every surface.

Oh, Phillip, she cried inwardly, *you have been left to your own devices too long. Time to stand tall and be a man for the four daughters you have left who desperately need their father.*

Marie gathered her skirts and left but not before putting a note on the front door requesting her son's appearance at the family home as soon as possible. She had hoped to convince him to join them for Sunday dinner.

"It was difficult to see the state of the house," she told Richard later. "It is worse than an animal lair. I left a note. Something must change."

Richard nodded, reluctant to meddle. "We each grieve in our own way, *ma chère.*"

"When Rafe died you had Jacques and me to help you through, Louise had all of us. When Jacques died, I had you to help me through… Phillip has no one, he has cut himself off from everyone, even his own daughters. I wish John was home, perhaps he could convince his brother to return to work, something to bring some normalness to his life."

"When did John say he would be here?"

"It should be any day," she muttered.

"Come, *ma chère*, Helen and Thor have just arrived." He patted her hand and walked with her to the foyer.

It didn't take long for James and Cynthia to arrive as well but there was still no word from Phillip. Marie waited as long as she could. Everyone was growing hungry and the food was ready.

"Don't worry, Mother," Louise said quietly as they walked to the dining room. "It takes time… we both know that."

Marie nodded. Yes, she knew it took time but it was the drink and the children she was concerned about.

The dynamics at the dinner table were changing. With Caroline gone and Phillip absent, John and Ronnie not yet arrived, and Richie and Clarissa not home for the season, the qualifying grandchildren now equaled the adults at the table and conversation took off in a youthfully light-hearted manner. Talk of friends and hayrides, parties and the New Year dance filled the room, liberally laced with high pitched giggles and youthful snorts. Only Hope was very quiet. The girls had much to say about fashion while Thomas and Sebastian spoke of getting together a hunting party.

Marie looked up and down the table and smiled quietly to Richard. The adults were hard pressed to get a word in edgewise. But was this not better than to expect the children to be silent? At thirteen through seventeen these eldest grandchildren were now too old to be silent. And if the parents were smart, they could keep up with what was occupying their children's minds just by listening.

When dinner was over Richard pulled Thor aside.

"What is it that you need?" Thor asked quietly.

"I desire to establish a hunting party of my own."

Thor arched a blond brow.

"We go to hunt Phillip. His mother has not seen him in some time and I know she worries. We will start with his house in case he has been home and ignored Marie's summons but I suspect we are going to find him at Jozy's instead."

They indeed did find Phillip passed out in one of Jozy's small back bedrooms, too drunk to have any interest in a girl but charged a nominal fee "for the space." He had become a good customer. Thor picked Phillip up, tossed him over his shoulder and walked him out of the place and into the waiting carriage.

"He reeks of whiskey and cheap perfume," Thor commented as he laid Phillip's limp body out on the back seat.

"Marie will understand," Richard nodded as he settled in with the reins.

"I wasn't thinking of Mother Marie. I was thinking of my wife," Thor grinned.

When they got to the family home, Marie had them put Phillip into the "sick" room.

"Make certain he has a chamber pot and a pitcher of water but take away his clothes so he cannot disappear," she said as Thor carried him up the stairs.

The next morning arrived dark and rainy. Lyndyn assured Marie he had things at the store well in hand. No need for her to be concerned. She could stay home and see to Phillip. While the younger children were well occupied in the nursery, Louise decided to go with Nora and the girls and help set her brother's house in order. The other women found Louise could be quite ruthless and dispassionate about what she could remove from her brother's domicile in quick order and without any need for discussion. Half empty liquor bottles, stained clothing, torn linens, cracked or chipped crockery, and anything no one could recognize – it all went without a second glance.

Meanwhile back at the family home, Sebastian was assigned the task of checking on his Uncle Phillip periodically so he could alert his grandmother when the man awoke.

It was almost high noon but the house was still dark and gloomy. Between dramatic episodes of thunder and lightning, the rain continued to pour down in blinding sheets. Sebastian peeped in the darkened bedroom to see his uncle using the chamber pot. The boy immediately went running for his grandmother before Phillip could say a word.

Marie made her way up the stairs with a small tray filled with hot broth, hot coffee, hot tea, and fresh bread and butter. Sebastian lit the way with a candle and Rebecca carried a pail of hot water and fresh towels.

When they reached the sick room, Marie knocked lightly, opened the door a crack and said, "I hope you are decently covered, I have your niece with me." She heard a muttering of grumbles that passed for acknowledgment. Swinging the door fully open just as another clap of thunder shook the house, Marie signed for Rebecca to set down the hot water and towels and leave to get more hot water. Sebastian set about lighting the lamps in the room while Phillip sat under the covers.

"Please light the fire, Sebastian. There is a chill in the room," Marie instructed as she set up the tray on a small table. "Which do you prefer… coffee, tea, or broth?"

"What happened? And where are my clothes?" Phillip asked.

"Coffee or broth? Or would you rather tea?" Marie asked again.

"Coffee," Phillip responded truculently. "How did I get here?"

"You mean why are you not waking up in the brothel?" she asked easily as she handed him a cup of coffee. "Be careful, it is hot," she warned before pulling up a chair and sitting. "Richard and Thor found you and brought you home. Your clothes are being laundered, they reeked." With that she sat quietly watching as her son slowly cooled and drank his coffee.

"And when we are finished here you shall make a trip to the bathing room. Do you think you can tolerate some fresh bread? It is still warm."

Phillip barely shook his head.

"Then, some broth," she insisted and shoved the cup in his hand.

He set the cup down on the side table. "I don't want it, Mother!"

"Very well, then you will have a slice of this wonderful fresh bread." She set the small plate with the bread down on his lap.

"I don't want anything."

"I am going to sit here until you do," she replied with ample resolve.

He stared at her.

"I am still your mother and since the moment you were born my first order of business has been to see that you eat."

After a moment he picked up the bread and took a large bite, chewing through the hard, golden crust to the soft white interior.

"Phillip, I understand grief. When your father, my beloved Jacques died, God knows I was consumed by the ache, the pain, the loss, the desolation, the devastating loneliness. He was my knight-in-shining-armor, my closest friend, the love of my life for forty years… do you not think I know what grief is?"

Phillip sat silently and Marie saw tears spill down his cheeks. "I just don't know how to go on without her."

"But you must, you know you must. You have four daughters who need you. Patience is only nine years old. Your children have lost their mother, *mon fils*, they too know loss. They need their father, they need you, *n'est-ce pas?* Even in your own grief, you must not forsake them."

"They have you and Louise and their cousins…"

"But only one pa-pa. And this is not their home. They have their own home with you. This is only the place they come to… like school, to be looked after while their parents work. But if you are not going to work, then they can stay home with you. You are a family. Charity is seventeen, I would expect her to be marrying soon. Hope is fifteen. She needs you desperately, Phillip. Have you noticed how attached she is to her twin still? She grieves as much as you. All your girls need their father's love. Do not abandon them. Focus not on your loss but on your children… that is what Caroline would expect you to do. Anything else is incredibly selfish."

Phillip's quiet sobbing ceased and he nodded his head in the affirmative.

"I saw the state of your house. You cannot raise children like that. Get back your housekeeper and laundress and your cook. Nora, Louise, and the girls have gone over to restore order."

"They'll need a shovel, I'm afraid," he said in a lame attempt to joke. After a moment he added, "I'm not proud of it."

"Yes," Marie agreed. "Now, let me find some clean clothes for you. I expect you to wash yourself in the tub. Use plenty of soap to scour away the cheap perfume. Once you do you will start to feel human again, yes? Sebastian?" she called to the boy who was watching the storm from another room. "Go to Margo and see if your uncle's clothing has dried by her fire. If not, I can find something in the trunks. Quick, quick!"

Before Marie left the second floor, she stopped in at the nursery to invite the children to come to lunch with the adults. It was such a gloomy day and they could all use some cheer and laughter. And laughter there was when Nora led Louise and Phillip's oldest girls back into the house. They had ridden back in the carriage but just the trip to and from had left them rain spattered and a little chilled.

"Warm yourselves by the fire," Marie encouraged amidst the giggles.

"Go up and comb your hair out," Louise suggested. "I know that's what I need to do."

When they all reappeared in fresh aprons, they gathered by the fire to dry out the hems of their skirts. Patience came down from the nursery and finally Phillip appeared. When little Patience saw her father, Marie saw the child's eyes light up and she ran to him for an embrace. Marie smiled as she saw her son enfold his youngest daughter in his arms then move to kiss the other three.

The family had only just taken their seats when Lyndyn arrived looking drenched but drier than expected beneath his rain cape.

"I've closed the store," he told Marie as Nora took his cape. "No one is shopping today and now there's a fear of flooding."

"What?!" Marie spun around to stare at Lyndyn. "Where?"

"The rain is running down the hill so quickly, water is beginning to run up against some of the houses at the bottom."

"Jacques told them not to construct so close to the beach," Marie cried. "Tell Thor to close the lumber mill and have all the men go down to help fill sand bags to pile up against the water."

"Wait, Mother," Phillip spoke. "Before we rush into anything, I shall ride on horseback and see exactly what is happening."

"Yes, of course. Forgive me, Phillip, I have missed your presence," Marie apologized.

Phillip had risen from the table and was soon bundled in a long sealskin coat he had received as a gift from Rafe some years back. Before the others had finished eating he had returned.

"Several of the men have dug modest trenches to guide the water off without harm and if I dare to be so bold, there is nothing more to worry about."

Chapter 25

Spring 1729

The dark haired man sat at the corner table sipping his wine. The wine was decent but over-priced. As long as he paid he was allowed to just sit and watch the girls although Madame Molly preferred for her girls to engage each customer and have at least one of them get this one upstairs for a toss.

Pauline noticed him studying her but she didn't like the looks of him and tried to avoid eye-contact until she saw Molly staring her down and sending a clear command. Against her instincts Pauline rose up from the divan she had been sitting on and gracefully walked toward the stranger.

"You look very lonely," she said softly in a voice that betrayed her youth. One long ringlet of her soft blonde hair fell seductively into her cleavage. "Mind if I join you?"

"By all means," the stranger replied, gesturing vaguely to the chair across from him. "You look like you have a wealth of knowledge to dispense. Would you like some wine?"

Pauline nodded shyly and accepted the glass he offered her. After she had drunk a sip he reached over and ran his hand along her curl, from her throat to her breast. He saw her shiver and raise goose flesh while her nipple beneath the sheer cloth hardened.

"How old are you?" he asked.

"How old would you like me to be?" she retorted trying to sound seductive.

"Don't be cute," he said harshly. "I'm not interested in your games. I want to know how old you are under all that makeup."

She looked cowed and lowered her eyes. "I'm fifteen." Then looking up she saw him raise an arched brow in question. "Last month was my birthday."

"And how long have you been doing this?" he gestured to their surroundings.

"Madame Molly offered me a place last month."

"Fresh meat," he muttered unkindly. "Your Madame Molly is smart, believes in recruiting young."

She didn't understand half of what he said but she decided to move things along. "Would you like to go upstairs?"

"I thought you'd never ask. You must learn to ask to obtain your objective, don't expect things to just fall into your lap."

"Then I'll be asking for the money right here before we climb the stairs," Pauline said boldly.

"Very good, you're learning."

He paid her and together they climbed the staircase and went into the first empty bedroom they found. He closed the door behind them and stood looking at her.

"Take off all your clothes," he ordered and silently watched as she began to remove her garments. Finally, she stood near the bed completely naked and wondering what he wanted her to do next. He slowly walked around her.

"Your skin is completely unblemished; you haven't a mark on you. Did you never get a whipping? From your parents? A short-tempered master or mistress?"

"No," she shook her head. "My parents loved me. They would have never whipped me."

"So you didn't run away… they died and left you an orphan and you have no other family to which to go."

She nodded her head and looked on the verge of tears.

"Don't feel sorry for yourself," he said coldly. "It is a common tale, especially within the walls of a brothel." He turned his attention to the washstand and poured a goodly amount of water into the wash basin. "Come over here," he said with a gesture. She thought perhaps he wished to wash her cunny; she'd heard from the other girls that some men liked to do that. She walked over and was unprepared when he grabbed the hair on top of her head. "We really must do something about that makeup." And he pushed her face down into the water.

She held her breath and didn't struggle, then she raised her hands, intending to help the removal process, but when she tried to raise up above the water she felt the pressure on the back of her head. His hand was holding her down, holding her fast and she could not lift out of the water. She began to panic. Her heart was thumping as she sputtered beneath the waterline, struggling, grabbing at his hand. She would have knocked the washstand over but it was a sturdy, heavy piece of furniture and he was pinning it against the wall. Her lungs were beginning to scream for air and she suddenly thought to feign a loss of consciousness. She went limp and still and in response he finally released her.

Instead of falling to the floor, Pauline lifted her face from the water and screamed with all her might as she knocked aside the basin. She didn't stop screaming until ten seconds later when Big Dan, a huge mulatto, came bursting through the door which had no lock for just this reason.

"What go on here?" Big Dan demanded, filling the doorway. He had come into Madame Molly's employ in New York Towne from the islands. His father had been half white and half black, his mother, half white and half native and Dan had never been a slave. He was a brusingly big man, as his nick-name implied, with clearly defined muscles and a large barrel chest. He kept Molly's girls in line but he also watched out for them and kept the customers inclined to be respectful.

"He tried to drown me, Dan," Pauline cried hysterically and pointed to the basin on the floor and the stand and floor splashed with water. "He wouldn't let me up for air. He wouldn't let me breathe."

"And yet you can see she is perfectly all right," the dark haired man spoke confidently.

"What happened?" Madame Molly came running up the stairs and to the room. She saw the stranger with a smile she didn't like on his face. She saw Pauline standing naked as the day she was born, sobbing, her makeup running down her cheeks and chin, her hair a wet, disheveled mess. She saw the washstand and water.

"She say he push her face into bowl and not let up for air." Big Dan said succinctly.

"We don't go in for any rough stuff here. If that's your taste best you go to a bigger city but don't ever come back to my place again. You're not welcome. Dan, please escort the gentleman out."

Molly had a way of making the word *gentleman* sound like blasphemy.

Marie awoke and stretched. She was happy and spring was here.

John had been home all winter and was back to his old self. His headaches were gone and his eyesight and focus were back to normal. Ingrid Boot was a wonder with her magic massages. John now spent several days a week covering Doctor Ajax's office while Ajax rode out to his more distant patients. Between that, watching over the family concerns as patriarch, and spending time with his own wife and children, John was well occupied. Marie had heard no mention of going back to the military.

Together John and Ronnie had boosted the numbers in the emptying nursery to faithful Sarah's delight even if she did have to "share custody" with their very attentive mother. And Marie suspected Ronnie just might be pregnant again after the long cold winter.

Then Marie thought of her second son, Phillip. John had had a long talk with his brother and Phillip had finally returned to work at the mill. His children had all left the big house to live in their father's house again. But the two youngest still came to *Grand-mère's* after school and Marie often saw Charity and Hope in connection with the store. That, Marie smiled to herself, was working out extremely well. Both girls were trustworthy by nature and accepted responsibility well.

Marie rolled over and saw Richard, sleep tousled and grinning at her.

"Good morning, Richard. Do you always watch me as I sleep?"

"Of course, unless I am sleeping as well. I can think of nothing more pleasant to look upon. You have been awake for a while, first you stretched and then you were thinking, yes? And what were you thinking about, *mon petit four*?"

She reached out and stroked his whiskered cheek. "Just that I am happy. John and Phillip are both doing better and better. The store hums along requiring very little of my attention. James' new foals grow strong. The mill partnership goes smoothly. Richie and Clarissa seem very happy doing their treks. With so much contentment around me, I fear I will become fat and lazy in my old age."

"Never! I still see the girl who followed us to the New World. And… give me a chance to rinse out my mouth and use the chamber pot and I will work some fat off you."

She giggled and decided to do the same. She knew Richard enjoyed making love in the morning before the day brought out all the little aches and pains his body could feel. When she finished, she dove back under the covers to await his caresses.

Charity looked up at the sound of the door bell jingling. A dark haired man entered.

"Good day to you, sir. Is there anything I can help you find?" she called out hospitably. The man was well dressed and not unpleasant looking with very deep set, rather brooding eyes.

"I'm looking for a decent pipe tobacco," he replied and almost held his breath. She was young, virginally young yet old enough to be curious about the touch of a man. And a glance at her face made him doubt there were many young men seeking her attentions. It was obvious she had survived the pox. Her forehead under those bangs was a crater field and her nose had the oddest asymmetrical shape, no doubt also from pox scarring. Feeling unattractive and yet full of youthful urges, she would be easy prey and perhaps a willing student.

Charity showed him what the store had to offer in tobacco and he made his choice.

"Hold this while I take a look around," he said with what could only be called a flirtatious smile. Charity blushed. He retreated to the shelves of displayed merchandise, pretending interest as he watched instead. An even younger one came in from the rear. A more somber looking child he had not seen outside the slums of London, but she had flaming copper hair.

"How's it been today?" she asked quietly.

Must be family, he thought.

"Quiet."

"Should pick up now that school is out."

"Why would you think that?"

The younger one shrugged.

"Where's Uncle Lyndyn?"

"Upstairs doing some inventory."

So there is a man on the premises.

"Hope, you don't have to stay today. You can go home and do your lessons."

"I'm sick of lessons. They're no fun without Faith here to do them with."

"You have to learn to stand on your own."

"That's easy for you to say but you were never a twin, you don't know what it's like. I'm telling Papa I'm finished with lessons."

"Hush, we have a customer in the store."

With that the younger one left. The stranger went back to the counter to pay for his purchase and with a wink at Charity, he left the store. Once outdoors he took note of the direction the younger girl was walking. He followed at an easy pace and realized she was walking away from the town. He followed. She led him to a cemetery and he watched cautiously as she went into an impressive looking mausoleum.

He had gleaned enough from the sisters' conversation to know this one's name was "Hope" and she missed someone named "Faith" whom he was pretty sure was her twin. And was the twin buried here? He would learn later. For now, he was content to stay hidden and observe.

For several days he watched the movements and the habits of those who ran the store. A slim rather slightly built fellow in his thirties drove in with little pock face every morning. "Uncle Lyndyn," he presumed. The younger one came later in the day and if it was slow she left early and often went to the cemetery to visit her twin. The stranger went into the store again, ostensibly to purchase some handkerchiefs, then again to buy a new quill, then again for paper, then ink. He was becoming a familiar face.

He now knew Charity's name and had told her his was Ezekiel, but he added, with a soft touch to her hand, he asked his special friends to call him "Zeke." She had actually blushed. "Faith," "Hope," and "Charity," he thought to himself later, could parents be any more lacking in imagination?

He made certain he went in when business was slow but when Hope was there as well so he would become familiar to her. She was absolutely angelic to behold.

Once, when she was helping him to a selection of inks, he stifled a sob and asked her to forgive him but he used to write to his twin all the time. Now the letters went unsent and unread for he had lost his twin. She was instantly empathetic and they had a bond.

Then one day when they were alone in the store's front, he asked Charity if he could take her to dinner, she had stepped back even with the counter between them and told him in no uncertain terms that he would have to meet her papa first. He pretended to understand.

"And who is your papa?" he asked and saw her suddenly grow hesitant.

Charity thought of her father, his long hours at the mill and his current romance with the whiskey bottle.

"Well, he is a very busy man but let me see what I might arrange." She smiled so sweetly it could have broken his heart... if he had one. He left the store and did not return but watched from a distance.

His blood lust was growing stronger. He could wait no longer. When he saw Hope leave early two afternoons later he silently followed her to the cemetery. She was so free of care and caution, an innocent in this dark world. She went into the mausoleum and after a few moments he followed. She was startled at first but recognizing him, she relaxed and introduced him instead.

"This is my twin, Faith," she said quietly, pointing to the inscribed plate on the sepulcher. "I tell her everything that has happened in my day. And everything I am feeling."

"I understand. We twins have a very special bond, don't we? No one else can understand. And does she talk to you?"

She blushed. "Mostly she does but it's not like I hear her with my ears. I hear her with my heart."

"It would be nice to hear her with your ears again though, wouldn't it?"

"If only I could," she replied mournfully.

"Would you like to step into her world for a visit?" he asked with an air of mystery.

"Oh, yes, yes. Is that possible?"

"Of course. Only a few know the way... but I can help you."

"You can? But why didn't my family tell me? If there is a way to truly talk with Faith, why did they keep it from me?"

"Perhaps they do not know. I have studied many mystical things in this world that others have not." His voice was soothing, almost hypnotic in its ability to hold her fast. "There is a thin path between our world and hers and few can walk it. You must be innocent, pure of heart, and you must believe."

"It's not that I don't love my family but I miss her so much. You know how it is. So have you visited with your twin?" she asked solemnly.

"Of course but I don't tell just anyone."

"I won't say a word. Oh, please, tell me how."

"You must trust me," he smiled at her as he withdrew a razor sharp flint from his pocket. "This may sting a little but it's a small price to pay to see Faith again."

She gasped as with lightning speed he opened a vein in each of her arms. They sat together on the stone bench watching the blood flow from her body.

'It doesn't hurt now, does it?" he asked after a while.

"N-no, it just tingles a little."

"Blood is the avenue by which you can cross."

"When can I walk it?"

"Be patient," he soothed. "Your wish shall soon be granted."

They sat in the quiet as the sun shown its last afternoon rays into the high window. He saw her growing paler and weaker until she slumped back against the curved stone arm rest, unable to hold her head up.

"I feel so strange," she murmured.

"I know, my dear, it's all part of the process. The price of admission so to speak… to see Faith. Can you grasp my hand?"

She made an effort as the blood ran down to her elbow. "I feel so weak." Her hand fell back into her lap.

"There is another step to the process… so you can see your sister again.

"What is it?" she asked so faintly he could barely hear.

"A kiss upon your innocent breast," he replied steadily like a wizard and swiftly opened the front of her little bodice, exposing her budding breasts. He kissed each little naked nipple with the solemnity of a priest kissing his stole and she offered no protest. Then he retied her laces and snugged everything back. "And one more thing, it's very important…" he said softly. "You must offer yourself to your guide."

He knelt at the altar of her innocence and pushed her skirts back. Gently spreading her legs apart, he breathed in the smell of her down covered skin. She could offer no resistance, but moaned a little, much too weak to do more. He accepted it as a moan of pleasure. The first awakening of the guiltless. At long last he pulled back and smoothed down her skirts.

"That felt pleasant didn't it? My tongue is warm and comforting," he almost cooed. "You taste so sweet I could have gone on forever but now I give you leave to go to your sister." He saw her give a weak smile just as the light left her eyes.

He attended to his own throbbing arousal and caught his essence in his shirttail. He knew better than to leave any evidence he'd been there. Standing up, he stepped back and surveyed the scene in the fading light. She was stretched out rather primly, some blood had naturally dripped on the bench, the floor. Most had soaked into the top of her skirts. He dropped the flint in her lap. She had that faint smile on her face. Her eyes were open. It was perfection. He left and closed the door feeling extremely satisfied and gratified

The dark haired stranger sat on the small wooden bench outside the barber's shop. It was rather amazing what one could learn simply by being inconspicuous and listening.

The Power girl's funeral was today. The village was in conflict. There were many family, friends, and those associated with the Power businesses who would be there but there were also those who looked back to the old ways and didn't think a suicide should be buried in hallowed ground. But then again, *suicide* was only a rumor, one customer said. No one seemed to know for sure but they did know that the child hadn't been right since her twin died. Terrible case of small pox had taken her twin and her mother and left her older sister scarred.

And it wasn't even the real disease but illness caused by an inoculation.

It was a very busy morning for the barber and the stranger learned much of the history of the village from the chatty clientele. Jacques Power and wife Marie were the founders of Chartes Landing. Started out fur trading in a log cabin. All that trading had bloomed into any number of businesses including the emporium. The log cabin had been replaced by the largest frame home in town that put some in mind of a French chateau. It would seem that the couple and their family had lived under a golden rainbow for a long time.

He smiled to himself. The universe had a way of demanding balance. Sooner or later good luck had to be balanced with bad. One couldn't slide through life on nothing but sunshine and flowers. Rain had to fall. He liked to think he worked in service to the universe. He could see to it that rain fell.

When the last customer left, the stranger got up from his seating and walked amiably down the street until he reached the livery. There he found another bench where he had an excellent view of the town and the church. Half the businesses had closed out of respect. He watched.

The funeral didn't last long. After all, what could one say about a daft child who had taken her own life? The family filed out behind the casket. He made a game of identifying who was who from the stories he'd just overheard. The small, dignified woman with a full head of hair piled under a stylish black hat was undoubtedly the grandmother, the matriarch. And escorting her was a tall fellow with an equally full head of iron gray. Must be the second husband, the best friend who couldn't wait to jump into the widow's bed. He recognized Charity from the store, the man walking beside her was undoubtedly her father, the sympathetic drunk.

The stranger smiled. How many sleepless nights would that man have now, wondering if Hope would have taken her own life if he'd paid more attention to her? Yes, questions to live with, questions to gnaw away at your brain like a cut worm determined to have its fill. Once rot started, it perpetuated itself.

Then he saw the two younger girls and almost lost his breath. Copper red heads and such sweet milky innocence. This village was a cornucopia of pure delights. And to think he had until now been satisfied with only whores and street urchins.

The funeral dinner was at the big house and for several hours people came and went, bringing food, paying their respects, and giving their condolences. Doctor Ajax requested a brief meeting with John.

"What is it, Archie?" John asked as he led his fellow doctor into Jacques' old office and gestured for him to sit in one of the old wing backed chairs. "I don't think I've ever seen you quite so pensive."

Ajax accepted the glass of cognac John offered. "A few weeks back I was called upon to attend one of the young girls at Jozy's. She was hysterical, absolutely beside herself with fear. When I finally got her calmed down we had a little talk. Seems a stranger no one could remember seeing before had gone up to a room with her. He had her strip down naked as a jay bird then held her face down in a bowl of water until she almost drowned."

John's brows shot up in surprise.

"If it hadn't been for their resident muscleman, she was convinced he would have finished her off. You know we've never had that kind in our little settlement before."

"No, no, we haven't." John ran his hand through his hair, a gesture reminiscent of his father. "We've always had a very peaceful village. A few friendly fist fights after too much whiskey has been about the worst. So what happened to this fellow?"

Ajax shrugged. "He claimed it was a misunderstanding, a little rough game playing. Madame Molly threw him out, told him never to come back."

John nodded. "So why are you telling me now? He probably took a packet boat out of here."

"I don't think so. We have no hotel but I hear a stranger fitting the description the young whore gave to me is staying at Widow Angus' Boarding House."

John grunted. "I don't like the idea of someone like him staying in Chartes Landing but I don't think I have the right to run him off. As long as he obeys our laws and ordinances…"

"John, I took the liberty of talking to Charity at the store. Gave her his description and asked if she'd seen anyone like him."

"And?"

"She said 'yes.' A fellow matching his description has been hanging around quite a bit. He even asked her to go to dinner with him."

"What?! Have you told Phillip?"

"Phillip has enough on his mind right now. I can't imagine what torture the poor chap lives with. Losing Caroline and Faith and now Hope. Did I mention the young whore was *very* young? Only just turned fifteen. That seems to be his type."

"What did Charity tell him?" John was very agitated now.

"She told me that she told him he would have to talk to her father first… and he backed off. Hasn't been back since."

"Well, that's good," John said with relief. "I don't know how my father did it, staying civil while he raised three girls. Now I have a daughter of my own and nieces as well to worry about. I'll most likely not get a restful night's sleep again until they are all well married." He looked at Ajax and saw that his expression had not lightened with the attempt at humor. Obviously there was more. "What else?" he asked.

"Charity said she overheard him talking a good deal to Hope, but not when anyone else was in the front of the store. She could never catch what exactly they were talking about.”

John grew very still. “Archie, what exactly are you trying to say?”

Ajax took a deep breath and replied, “John, I don’t think Hope committed suicide.”

John was stunned.

“Murder? You think she was murdered? But why? You know she was very troubled and unhappy ever since Faith died. She went to that mausoleum to talk to her dead sister all the time!”

“I know but…”

“That’s a hell of a leap. There was no sign of violence or a struggle. What makes you think this?” John demanded.

Doctor Ajax looked thoroughly uncomfortable as he spoke. “There’s a romantic notion about slashing your wrists to commit suicide. The melancholic, the unhappy lover, the defeated hero, the jealous damsel… but most of the time nothing serious comes of it. They are discovered, bandaged up, and they get the attention they were really seeking… because they cut themselves like this.” He demonstrated with his finger on his wrist. “And they bleed rather slowly. I don’t know if you noticed how Hope was cut… straight up her veins which, as you know, is a very *efficient* way to bleed out very quickly. I do not believe a young girl like Hope had the knowledge to employ this technique or the skill to do it so neatly.”

“Why didn’t you say anything before this?” John snapped, angry with himself for not having noticed.

“I just thought it better to wait until the family had been through the funeral. To think that Hope was murdered is bad enough but if we cannot prove it, what then?”

The reasoning registered upon John’s face and he was instantly remorseful. Ajax was a good family friend.

“You’re right, you’re right. I’m sorry. Telling the family will just upset everyone and we have no proof. But I can tell Mother, Lyndyn, and Charity about this bastard’s history with the whorehouse.”

Ajax nodded and took a bolstering swig of cognac.

The stranger had been watching for what seemed to him like an eternity but finally he saw an opportunity. A ship had come into the harbor and the lumber mill had become a bee hive of activity. Half the family seemed occupied there and now “Uncle Lyndyn” had just taken off for the docks himself with a wagon. Charity was alone.

When the only customer he had seen all morning left the store, he walked in.

“Oh..hello,” Charity greeted in recognition.

“There seems to be a lot of activity with the ship in,” he said smoothly as he walked up close to her.

"Y-yes, it brings us supplies and takes on lumber. It is the first ship for the season. We're very fortunate to have them come," she chattered nervously.

"I was sorry to hear about your sister." His voice was like oil.

"Y-yes."

"Why are you shaking? You aren't afraid of me, are you?"

"No, of course not. We just haven't seen you for some time."

"I'm still waiting to take you to dinner." His hand brushed down the top of her arm. He could feel her trembling.

"Oh… well, that's impossible. We're a family in mourning now." She tried to move away but he blocked her path.

"Nothing is impossible if you want it badly enough," he said softly and bent over to kiss her full lips.

She was held there, frozen like a fawn before a wolf. His kiss was not unpleasant. She had never been kissed before like this and she liked it. She knew she shouldn't but she found herself responding. Her heart was racing and she could hardly breathe.

"No, please," she pushed halfheartedly against him. "You mustn't. It's not right."

"Love is never wrong."

"Love? How could you…?"

"Yes, love! I love every inch of you, every mark upon your face. They make no difference to me except to make me love you more."

Charity was speechless and then she began to weep.

"Don't cry my little darling. Has no other ever told you how beautiful you are, scars and all?"

She shook her head. "But I'm not, I'm not. It's my punishment. It's my fault for pushing my sister to take the inoculation, and because she died Hope killed herself. It's all my fault."

The man couldn't be more pleased. Scratch the surface of any young woman and one is bound to find a plethora of insecurities and guilt… and perhaps a need for punishment.

"But it's not your fault. Your family just doesn't understand. And I say you are beautiful. One man's ugliness is another man's masterpiece of beauty. All you need is a man's love to blossom into your best self. But is there any other man to love you? Like I do? I am here now and I want to take you away from your unhappiness. I want you to experience delights of which you have not yet dreamed." He held her close and kissed her more aggressively, pulling her into the shadows of the back and allowing his hands to move sensuously over her young body. He exposed her breasts and she gasped as he sucked on her nipples. She was putty in his hands.

He pressed her back onto a crate and began to lift her skirts.

"What…… what are you doing? No, no, you mustn't," she protested.

"Don't worry. There is no harm in kissing you there, you'll still be a virgin… you are a virgin aren't you?" he asked almost fiercely.

"Yes, of course."

He smiled. "Then let me give you pleasure without changing that."

"But what if someone…?"

"I flipped the sign to 'Closed' when I arrived. No one will come in," he assured her as he spread her knees and proceeded in his task.

In only a few minutes Charity was writhing, moaning, begging him not to stop which is precisely what he did. He wanted her in a state of frustration, need, and curiosity. As he pulled back and stood, she looked at him with complete bewilderment.

"Why..?"

"Your uncle may be returning soon," he said as he pulled her to her feet. She was flushed and panting. "Straighten your clothing and meet me tonight. Slip away after dark and meet me at the mausoleum."

"The mausoleum?" she repeated in startled surprise. "But why there?"

He smiled at her reassuringly. "It's the one place we can be alone and undisturbed with no one to see us. I'll be waiting for you, my sweet, and we can finish what we started here."

That night Charity slipped out of the house after everyone had retired. She knew she shouldn't. She knew what she was doing was wrong but she was eighteen years old and all beaus had melted away after she'd had the pox. She'd never been really kissed before and Zeke was there… and he said he loved her. Could it be true? Did he find her scars beautiful? And as long as she was still a virgin, what harm were they doing? Surely a man's tongue couldn't make her pregnant. True, she did not love him, well, she hardly knew him but he was exciting. And what he did to her was very exciting. What if Papa didn't approve of him? If Zeke was the only man to offer her a home and happiness, how could Papa say no?

As Charity approached she saw a very dim light through the high window of the mausoleum. She pushed the door open and found Zeke sitting on the stone bench waiting for her while one candle in its holder flickered to the side.

"Ah, my sweet," he purred. "My heart has been in such a state, wondering if you would come or if you had forgotten me."

"I could never forget you," she cried and he kissed her passionately. It was a soft spring night and he divested her of her wrap immediately.

"Too many clothes, my sweetness, I want to see your beautiful young body without all the encumbrances of clothing." Very quickly he had her down to her shift. "And now the final piece. It is yours to decide if you will grace me with a view of all your charms." He stood still, looking at her.

She shivered from nerves. "Perhaps, for now, I could just raise up my shift."

"Ahh," he leered seductively, "so now you know what you want of me."

"Oh, yes, it felt so good," she nodded quickly.

"And it will feel even better when you come to complete satisfaction but… if we are not going to destroy your virginity by copulating as men and women usually do, then you must learn to make me feel good as well."

"Of course."

"Have you ever seen a naked man before? I mean a grown man not a small boy."

Charity shook her head.

"I'll show you. There is nothing to fear." He sloughed off his coat, took off his shoes, and shucked his breeches. Then slowly he lifted aside his shirttails. Charity couldn't take her eyes off of him. "It looks something like what you saw in the nursery, doesn't it? A bit more buried in hair. But when a man gets excited and wants a woman, this grows, gets stiff and hard and is made to slide into the woman… only then she would no longer be a virgin and she could get with child."

He reached out and took her hand and brought it to him, showing her how to rub him. His skin was warm and velvety soft and she felt him respond to her touch. He begin to stiffen and grow. As she continued rubbing him, he exposed her breasts and sucked hard.

"Ohh…" she gasped.

"That is what you must do to me."

She looked at him in bewilderment, looking first at his chest but saw him pull back and look to his lower appendage. "You mean…?"

He positioned her along side him on the stone bench, her head down at his flanks. He noted how eagerly she opened her legs to him, straining to give him easy access as she worked clumsily to give him pleasure. After only a few minutes he felt her stiffen; she moaned loudly and pulled her mouth free with a gasp. She had just experienced her first orgasm, he thought. She was his now.

"I never dreamed…" she sighed languidly.

"Did I not tell you you would experience delights you had not yet dreamed of? And now you must allow me a finish. Get up from there and kneel in front of me," he commanded as he sat up.

He guided her until he reached his climax then they rested for a moment while he stroked her like a pet.

"What is it, my dear, you don't look happy?"

"No, I am… I mean…… what you did to me felt wonderful and I want you to do that again but… I didn't like the last part. I was choking."

"You will get used to it and I will warn you next time so you do not choke. Now," he ran his hands under her shift and over her naked body, "just think how much pleasure we've had and nothing has been harmed. You are still a pure virgin and no one is the wiser."

"Zeke?" she sighed, as she tugged on her clothing.

"Yes, my sweet Charity?"

"Do you truly love me?" she asked shyly.

"Of course I do. I could not do this with you if I did not love you deeply."

It was exactly what she wanted to hear.

"You are fortunate, of course, for not many would," he added and she was suddenly reminded of her ugliness.

Every fair weather evening, Charity crept from her father's house and made her way through the trees to the cemetery behind the church. She always found the stranger, with his odd mixture of honeyed words and harsh demands, waiting for her in the family mausoleum. By the third night she was comfortable removing her shift to be completely naked before his eyes. She didn't want to inhibit anything he wished to do to her. And she loved the way he made her feel.

Then one night, she did not appear. The stranger waited until midnight and finally left. The next morning he went to the emporium as soon as it opened. He strode in and found her alone in the front while "Uncle Lyndyn" was making noises in the rear.

"Where were you last night?" he demanded in a low whisper.

"Oh… I… my cycle began yesterday, I shalt be unable to meet you for another four days," she whispered back.

"Nonsense! I'll see you again tonight. Do not disappoint me," he said harshly and left before she could say another word.

That evening when she opened the mausoleum door she saw him sitting, waiting. There was a dark blanket spread out on the floor. He stood and walked up to her.

"Please don't be angry with me," she whimpered apologetically. "I didn't think you'd want to see me."

"Why? Your courses are no impediment," he said softly, caressing her. "I love everything about you, remember?"

"But it's embarrassing."

He stroked her cheek and began to undo her laces. "It shouldn't be. And I shall teach you another way we can have pleasure." He helped remove her clothing. "Now take off that clout and get down on all fours." He brought a bucket of water over and washed between her legs. Setting the bucket aside, he bid her stay still while he shucked his own clothing. He dug a small bottle of oil from one of his pockets and spread her small buttocks.

She felt his finger probe her and she tried to pull away.

"Don't be frightened, just relax," he soothed and with his other hand he fondled her breasts. "Couples often do this to avoid making a child, and you have such a beautiful arse," he cooed gently. He kissed her pale smooth skin and inserted a second finger at the same time, she was relaxing and opening. She was ready for him.

He seemed to find great satisfaction from his next actions. Charity only felt like she had to defecate and was simply glad when it was over.

As he lie spent, half rolled over upon the blanket, she began to put on her clout again.

"I really didn't like that. I don't think I'll come here again until my monthly is over," she said rather primly.

"Don't be ridiculous," he replied and sat up. "You're pouting. With sex sometimes you sacrifice for each other. Some things I like more than you do, and some you like more than I. That's normal. What we just did is most agreeable to me and it doesn't rob you of your virginity."

"But I don't want to be a virgin! I want to be a wife and a mother. You've said nothing about talking to my father, asking to marry me. I...... want to be able to make love the normal way so we can both enjoy it."

He looked at her with an expression of contempt mixed with horror and disgust, almost loathing. Then he grabbed hold of her and shoved his hand inside her clout. He could feel her sensitive nub, swollen and prominent with the night's stimulation and he fingered her until she was panting and moaning, begging him not to stop. As he brought her to climax he pinched her nipples painfully, and he felt her erupt again.

"You liked that, didn't you?" he demanded, his face an inch from hers. "You like the pain!"

She was breathing heavily and said nothing as he withdrew his bloodied hand, quickly washing it in the bucket.

"I know how to please you without the fear of getting you with child," he rumbled. "As for speaking with your father... I'm not ready yet and you are not to mention it again, understand?"

She nodded dumbly and after catching her breath she resumed putting on her clothing.

"I'll see you in three days," he said suddenly. "And be sure you wash yourself well before you return." With that he turned his back to her and began collecting his things.

Charity felt his displeasure and it shook her confidence. There was no good-bye kiss, there was no "good-bye." She left for home trembling inside, wondering what had so displeased him.

The next day Marie came to the store to look over the books and catch up on the recent receipts and invoices. It didn't take long for her to observe that her granddaughter was not her usual self.

Waiting for a moment when there were no customers, she pulled the girl to her side and looked her full in the face. "Charity? Tell me what is wrong."

Charity felt totally exposed before the scrutiny of those keen, changeable eyes.

"Nothing, *Grand-mère*, truly."

"Do not tell your *grand-mère* it is nothing. You are my oldest granddaughter which means I have known you the longest. Your ma-ma is gone, God rest her soul, and your pa-pa… well, I know he is still dealing with his own grief. And the sisters closest to your age are now gone but you do have your *grand-mère*. I am here and you can tell me anything, child, anything. Or ask me anything. There is nothing in this world that shocks me anymore. Think of any subject you want, no matter how bizarre or strange or seemingly forbidden and I have undoubtedly had some experience with it or close to it, eh?"

Charity gave a little nod and Marie gave her a little hug.

"Just ask your Aunt Louise," Marie continued. "She found out some things about me a few years ago, that shocked her. Things I choose not to make public but can share in confidence with someone I care about."

Charity almost broke down but was too humiliated and pulled a smile instead.

"It's nothing, *Grand-mère*, I'm on my cycle is all. I'm sorry to worry you. I guess I can feel really sad when I think of…" Suddenly she gave way to tears and her grandmother's arms. "It was my fault."

"What was your fault?" Marie asked as she held the girl.

"I believed so in Doctor Ajax and his inoculation. If I hadn't pushed so hard, they'd all still be here," Charity sobbed. "Hope would still be here if Faith hadn't died and Faith wouldn't have died if…"

"No-no-no, there is something you should know…"

Just then the door opened to the jingling of the bell and the stranger walked in. Marie felt her granddaughter tense and saw a look of recognition cross her face before she could hide it. Marie looked to the dark-haired man and saw that he was much better at hiding his thoughts.

"Charity, go to my office and put your feet up. We shall continue our conversation when I am finished." Then she turned to the stranger. "Good day, monsieur, with what may I help you?"

"I purchased some pipe tobacco here a while back. Your granddaughter helped me select it," he motioned toward the office. "I don't remember the name. Perhaps she…"

"She is not feeling well but I am sure we can find it again," Marie said easily and walked over to the tobacco. "I do not carry that many blends. If you have been smoking it, you will remember the smell, yes?" Marie smiled charmingly.

"Of course. I'm sorry to hear of your granddaughter's difficulty. I hope it is nothing serious."

"No-no, just woman's problems. She will be fine." She opened a tight container. "Was it this one?"

He leaned over, sniffed, and shook his head.

"Perhaps this?" Marie offered another and sealed up the first.

"Yes… yes, I believe this is it. I'll take eight ounces. And… I'd like some sealing wax and a way to melt it down of course. We seem to be heading into a rainy spell and all my footwear needs a treatment. If it's less expensive than going to the cobbler, I'll do it myself."

"Of course," Marie smiled and set about gathering the necessary supplies. She tallied the total and took his money. "Thank you, Monsieur…?"

He ignored her attempt to procure his name, tipped his hat, and left the store. The smile left Marie's face as she watched him walk down the short side street.

"Charity?" Marie called as she swept into her office to find her granddaughter sitting pensively in her chair. "Do you know that man?"

Charity knew in a face to face confrontation there was little she could hide from her *grand-mère*. "He has been in the store before."

"For what purpose?"

"Buying little things, paper, ink… but mostly he talked with Hope."

"Do you mean you think he came to the store mostly to talk to Hope?"

Charity thought for a moment. "I don't know, *Grand-mère,* perhaps. Oh, I'm sorry, I took your chair…"

"No-no, stay, sit for a moment." Marie pulled up a smaller chair and sat. "First, let us talk about this nonsense that somehow the deaths were your fault. Your ma-ma made a very carefully thought-out decision, just as Lyndyn did. They both worked here in the store, they both were constantly exposed to the public coming in off the packet boats, and they both decided of their own free-will to get the inoculation to prevent ever bringing the disease home to their families. Lyndyn lived, your ma-ma died. Who can understand the reasons why?"

"But Faith…"

"Faith and Hope were stubborn and competitive and eager to show the rest of us how grown up they were. Forget not how they always bemoaned the slightness of their stature. They forgot how their pa-pa's *grand-mère* was even smaller than I am. Of course, they never met Hélène but we all told them often enough. Do you think that your decision to go influenced them more than the decision of their own mother?

"Your parents agreed to allow them to do what they did… not you. They chose to draw straws. I'm sure they did not believe anything bad would happen but deep down they knew if something did, the survivor would be alone. It is not impossible to live when your twin dies. Many others had done it but Hope was in a very melancholy stage of growing up. And who knows but what she was assisted in morbid thoughts by that man who came in here. I do not like him. Every hair on my body tells me that we should all stay as far away from him as is possible. Charity, *ma chérie,* I do not want you going near him."

"But if he comes into the store?"

"Call your Uncle Lyndyn. Make whatever excuse you must but do not be alone with him. Promise me."

"As you wish, *Grand-mère*." The girl sat quietly for a moment, eyes downcast. "I'm feeling a little crampy. Do you think I could go home?"

"Of course, *ma petite,* but I have a better idea. I will have Lyndyn drive you to my house. Have the kitchen staff bring lots of hot water and take a long soak in the bathing tub with my perfumed soaps. It is very, very soothing. Then lie down for a nap. I will send word to your pa-pa that you all will be having dinner at my house tonight."

Charity felt it was best not to make any objection and simply accept her grandmother's directives but she wondered why Ezekiel had come into the store. He had told her to stay away for three days.

Charity took special care in her grooming as she readied herself to see her lover. She had seen her younger sisters to bed over an hour ago. Their father was not yet home. There was no predicting when he might stumble in but he never came to her room. She knew her scarred face was just another reminder of her mother's death. Charity couldn't help but believe her father would have rather it had been her who had died instead.

When she entered the mausoleum that night she saw the stranger in a mournful pose. Rushing to his side she gave him a kiss which seemed to do little to lift his spirits.

"So you finally came. I've been waiting every night for you," he lied.

"But… you told me not to come back for three days." She was bewildered.

"When I came to the store, I thought you would realize I had changed my mind," he said almost accusingly.

"Oh, Zeke, my dearest. I am so sorry. I didn't realize, I didn't know."

"Was that your grandmother?"

"Yes."

"She's very protective of you. Your family is never going to allow me to court you openly. I'll not be good enough for them."

"No-no, don't say that. Don't say that. You're everything to me. It doesn't matter what they say anyway." She kissed him repeatedly trying to lift him out of his hurt feelings, trying to apologize for not showing up the past three nights. "I love you. I'll do anything for you."

"Then take off your clothes," he whispered and she rushed to obey.

He was not gentle but his roughness excited her more.

When they had finished, he looked at her critically.

"What is it?" she asked.

"You're beginning to grow more hair. Angels aren't supposed to have hair all over their bodies." He thought of Hope's downy Mound of Venus and started to grow hard again. "You are my virgin angel, you don't want to look like an ape, do you?"

Charity cringed. Embarrassment, shame, and hurt all running through her now. An ape? A beast? Is that how he saw her? She couldn't help the hair that was beginning to grow all over her body.

He measured her reaction and came up to her, cupping her young breasts. "Don't worry," he whispered, "I'll take care of it, I'll take care of everything. You are my virgin angel and I worship every inch of you." He held her and stroked her and it made her feel special. "Now, if you want to please me, lean over the arm of the bench. I want you that way now."

And she did what he asked without protest.

The next night she found him bent over a utilitarian bowl being warmed by a small candle much like a chaffing dish.

"What are you doing?" she asked with a frown.

"Take off your clothes and lie down on the bench," he said softly. "I told you I would take care of you." He spread out the blanket and she noticed a small stack of cloth strips. She did as she was told. "Now put this in your mouth." He shoved a gag in her mouth and tied it about her head. "That is just in case you forget yourself. I don't want you waking up half the cemetery. Now raise your arm."

He used a tiny paddle to smooth melted wax over her arm pit and then patted a cloth strip over it. "Hold still," he admonished and proceeded to do the other one. "It must dry and grow hard," he added as he opened her legs and began to do the same to her nether region.

"It should feel warm and very comforting… does it not?" He looked her in the eye and she nodded her head.

He worked to cover her in strips then in silence they waited for the wax to grow cold and harden.

"Now control yourself, but you like pain, don't you? You should like this."

She nodded and he held her arm while he ripped the cloth away and the unwanted hair with it.

She gasped and then accepted the pain. She removed the gag.

"I don't need this."

An hour later he sat staring at his work with self-satisfaction. She was as smooth as a small child. His virgin angel.

He posed her immodestly. She could feel herself throbbing with desire as he stared at her.

"Stay like that," he commanded softly as he packed up his paraphernalia. "I want to admire my work." When he returned to her his fingers stroked her. She was so smooth, so pure, hairless and delicate. He began to grow hard.

She watched him as he unbuttoned his breeches and exposed himself, stiff and red. "My… little… angel," he moaned and she saw his essence spew forth onto her. Then suddenly he was at her newly exposed flesh, making noises like a gluttonous man sitting at a banquet table. She thrilled to his touch but was in an agony of desire because he would not enter her. Then she stiffened again… and again… while he bit her just hard enough to hurt but not hard enough to break the skin.

Chapter 26

Charity was constantly restless and frustrated. Every fair night she went to her lover who always had a new and inventive way to inflict pain upon her. He had her begging for satisfaction as it heightened her desires but even his roughest sodomizing now only served to inflame her more. And no matter how much she begged he would not breach the threshold of her womb.

His dialogue had shifted as well. He spoke much less of how he loved her, how beautiful and precious she was to him, and more about how fortunate she was to have him take an interest in her and teach her such delights.

"Very few could get over your face, you know. And I guarantee they couldn't excite you as I can. I'm the best thing that ever happened to you. Do you know that?"

"Of course, Zeke, I know that."

"Then say it! Say it!" he urged darkly.

"You're the best thing to happen to me," she gasped obligingly. "I don't know what I'd do without you. I truly don't. You can hurt me some more if you want, please… I deserve it. I want it."

"Tell me how fortunate you are!"

"I'm so fortunate, so very… Oh, please, don't stop… I'm almost there. Please, I want to feel you inside me. Oh……"

Her cycle had begun again and she had begged the day off from her grandmother. Marie could tell the child was not in a happy state but had no idea what the problem was and thought she might talk to Phillip about finding Charity a husband. Her cousin Rebecca was two years younger and had a string of beaus coming to the house. Rebecca had become a hauntingly beautiful girl with clear honey colored skin and hypnotic dark eyes like her father's had been. Marie wished just one boy could see beyond the ugly pox scars to the sweetness of Charity's heart. Marie, who had loved Jacques so very fiercely, did not like to think their granddaughter might only find a mate because of the richness of the dowry Phillip could provide. At the same time, she was aware that this was the basis of many sound marriages, with couples growing to love each other in time, if not with passion then with respect.

Charity had gone to *Grand-mère's* house for a soothing soak but as she wandered near the animal barn she heard a jauntily whistled tune. She saw Tommy, the tall young stable lad, cleaning out the stalls for the season. Unless the weather turned disastrous, the animals would be staying in their outdoor pens and pastures for the rest of the summer.

Tommy had tossed aside his shirt in the heat of the day and the heat of his labors. As he worked Charity watched the play of his muscles beneath his suntanned skin with fascination. She looked quickly around the barn; there appeared to be no one else around.

"Hello, Tommy," she said with a winsome smile.

"Oh, hello, Miss Charity," Tommy looked over in surprise.

"Where's Issac?"

"Gone into the village, said should anyone ask he's with th' blacksmith 'n' will be a while but I know when he says 'a while' that he'll be tippin' a few at the pub," Tommy replied with a wink.

"Is there no one else around?"

"Not right at th' moment. Why, Miss Charity? Is there something I can help ya with?"

"I want a fuck," Charity replied calmly while Tommy's mouth gaped open and he almost dropped his pitchfork.

"Miss Charity!!" he gasped in startled surprise.

"Is that the right word… *fuck*? When a man and woman…"

"Oh, I know what it means right enough though it's not a word I expect t'hear come out of a young lady's mouth."

"Is it very vulgar?"

"Yes. It might be better t'say *swive*." Tommy's face was beet red. "But even that ya don't want t'be sayin' in polite company."

"What would one say in polite company?" she asked earnestly.

"Nothing! I don't guess when folks is bein' polite they ever talk 'bout that."

"Well, I want a… swive…"

"*To* swive," he corrected her.

"Is that how you say it? Yes. I want to… swive… with you. Will you do it with me? I won't tell a soul even if I get with child. I'll just keep the baby for my own because no one is ever going to want me as a wife."

"Miss Charity, I don't hardly know what t' say," he gulped, "yer pa would skin me alive 'n' yer uncles would help him. That would be a'fore they chopped off me vitals 'n' roasted them over a fire like th' Mohawk do."

She came up close to him then and ran her hand slowly across his muscled chest, over his tight stomach, and inside his breeches. She heard him moan and felt him stir within her hand. "I want to swive," she said again softly. "I want to know what it's like," she sighed. "I don't want to be a virgin forever."

"Oh, Miss Charity…" he groaned, "you'll be th' end of me… but… if… if that's what ya really want…" He was getting hard as a rock.

"One thing though… I'm on my cycle. Does that put you off?"

"Good gracious no," he grinned and seemed to relax a little. "It be safer. Ya most likely won't get a child then. Come on, let's go up in th' loft." He led the way and Charity followed him up the ladder. He kicked off his boots and dropped his breeches as she removed her clout and hiked up her skirts. "Why Miss Charity," he exclaimed at the sight of her, "yer as smooth as a baby's bottom! I ain't never seen a grow-ed woman look like you before. Yer plum beautiful, like a statue I seen once!"

She smiled and opened her bodice to expose her pert, turned up breasts.

"Lord in Heaven, how did I get so lucky?" he moaned as he began to suckle them fiercely.

"Harder," she urged him and thought she was going to burst with desire. "swive me, Tommy," she moaned, "please, swive me… oh, yes, yes…"

It only took a minute or so for the dam to burst and all the weeks of pent up need to explode forth. Charity was beside herself with ecstasy and poor Tommy couldn't hold back but lost himself immediately after.

The two lie side by side on the hay.

"I'm sorry, Miss Charity. I jist couldn't help it. I'm so sorry but you surprised the tar out of me."

"Why?"

"Well, you bein' a virgin 'n' all. It generally takes a while, kind-a like primin' a pump, ya know. But you gusher-ed forth jist like that."

Charity smiled broadly. "And have you *fucked* many virgins, Tommy?" She giggled. "I think now that we've done it, I can say it, don't you?" He again went red in embarrassment. "Well, have you?"

"Not exactly but maybe one what weren't very… experienced."

"Well, it would seem not all of us virgins are the same, are we? Can we do it again? I know I can and I want to."

"Give me a few minutes," he replied, and turned to kiss and fondle her breasts again.

Tommy was not the most imaginative of lovers but to the lad's credit he managed to do the deed for a much longer duration two more times while Charity peaked again and again. Then they decided to stop with the growing fear someone might arrive and discover them.

"Where does Issac sleep at night?" she asked breathlessly before leaving.

"He's got a bed over th' stables with th' other men."

"And you?"

"Me too, but in th' summer I usually bed down right here on th' hay to get away from all their snoring 'n' farting."

"Good… then I'll find you after dark. I want to do *it* as much as possible while I'm on my cycle. It felt so incredibly good." She gave him an intimate caress down the front of his breeches which set his pulse throbbing again. "Do you agree?"

"Sure, Miss Charity, anything ya want," an unfocused Tommy grinned from ear to ear rather like he was the village idiot.

For three wonderful nights, Charity wallowed in sexual satisfaction until she was completely exhausted and forced herself to creep home. Then guilt again began to assault her and with it the need for punishment.

With her cycle over Charity went to Zeke in the mausoleum. He positioned her feet to spread her legs so he could gaze at her. But one look and he knew immediately.

"Who was it?!" he demanded with a menacing frown

She blushed. "Nobody important."

"Who?"

"Just a boy. I'm not telling you who. I told you I didn't want to be a virgin anymore."

"So now you're nothing but a whore."

"No, now you can make love to me the normal way."

"Make love?" he sneered. "What do you think I've been doing? Every touch has been filled with love…"

"You drive me wild with longing but then I want so badly to have you inside me, Zeke. But I can't get satisfaction from you shoving yourself in my behind."

"You're nothing but a whore now," he repeated coldly, "but at the moment you are *my* whore." He grabbed her hips as if to kiss her as he'd done so often before, instead he nipped and bit down hard.

"Oww," Charity cried out. "Stop it, stop, please, that's too rough."

"Customers don't care about driving whores wild, you take what we give you. Now bend." He bent her over the stone bench and sodomized her roughly. "Your tight little arse makes *me* feel good."

"Please," she sobbed, "you're hurting me too much. You said you loved me. Stop, please."

"You love being hurt!"

"It's too rough," she cried.

He drove himself with fury and twisted her around to discharge all over her face.

"Yes… well… feelings can change, you cheating whore. You think I'm going inside you now for his sloppy leavings? Put your clothes back on."

She wiped her face with her shift and put on her clothes as he ordered.

"Zeke, please," she begged and sobbed, "He was nothing, he meant nothing. I love you. I love you. Please don't leave me, please."

"Leave? No, I'm not leaving you. Now stop your sniveling and come with me," he said grabbing her by the arm and forcing her along through the dark at a brisk pace.

The night was moonless and Charity had no idea where they were going and knew she dare not ask. He was angry because she had been with someone else but he'd get over it. And when he calmed down they could return to their clandestine rendezvous filled with pain and pleasure and just take care not to get her pregnant until he got up the courage to ask for her hand. She knew how to submit and please him and he knew how to drive her wild with desires only half fulfilled. But now they could do it the normal way when she was on her cycle. Everything would work itself out.

They arrived at an old abandoned cabin down by the docks.

"What is this place?" she asked. He didn't answer but lit a candle. She saw an old bed. The stained, lumpy mattress smelled moldy. There was a rough table and one chair. She wondered if this was where Zeke lived. And in a sudden flash she realized he had never told her where he lived. Surely not, she told herself. There was nothing personal here. It was just some deserted hideaway.

"Stay here, I'll be back before you know it," he said calmly, "and you might want to take off your clothing if you want something to go home in." He left.

For a moment her heart raced as she wondered what new and exciting things he had in store for her. She went to the door and pushed and pulled. It wouldn't open. She removed her clothes as he had told her and stood waiting. She couldn't even guess where he might have gone. Then she heard several voices. She grabbed her shift to cover herself just as Ezekiel opened the door and came in with another man. Several more men stood outside gawking in at her.

"What's going on?" she asked in terrified bewilderment.

"Don't bother covering yourself, my dear. This is your first customer." Then he turned to the other man. "Have at the slut. I'll just sit here to keep her under control."

It was rather amazing how quickly the whispered words *free cunt* got around the all but empty dockside. Men kept coming, some of them were lumbermen but they didn't recognize her. How many of them had she waited on in the store, she wondered as they fondled her breasts and made her suck them because their wives would not. Many sodomized her because their wives wouldn't allow that either. Most of the lonely single men just wanted to swive her like Tommy had. There had been perhaps two dozen men in all. Or was it three? She wasn't certain; she'd lost count when they began to double up and penetrate her in every orifice at once.

As pre-dawn began turning the night sky into a pearly dark gray, Charity sat on the edge of the filthy bed, dry-eyed, numb to the sex act, bruised, painfully raw and swollen from abuse and over-use. It would take days for her body to return to normal, she thought. Ezekiel sat staring at her.

As she began to put on her clothes, he finally spoke.

"Fortunately your clothing will hide most of you… except your face. I suggest you tell your family that you got up in the middle of the night to use the chamber pot, stumbled and fell against your dresser or chair, whatever you have," he shrugged. "It's a plausible enough story for such a *good* daughter."

"How could you?" she asked with belated indignation. She was trembling and tears once again welled in her eyes. "I could see two or three as punishment for what I did but so many?"

"Just *two or three*? No-no, you would have enjoyed that too much just like you enjoyed your maidenhead thief."

"How could you just sit and watch them use me like that after everything we've been to each other?" She was crying now.

"And just what have we been to each other?"

"You know… you said you loved me; you said you loved everything about me. We've done so much with each other." He looked at her coldly. "I love you, Zeke, I need you. Was it all a lie?" she whimpered.

"Not a lie, a fantasy. You were my virgin angel that I could slake my desires with until you became a whore! So now I've given you a good taste of what it is really like being a whore. How did you like it?" he all but shouted.

"I didn't," she sobbed.

"You're the one who broke the magic. The fault lies with you. Now you better get home." He grabbed her hand and led her through the pathways until she recognized where she was. Despite the aches, bruises, and swelling to her body parts she broke into a run.

The next day when Grace and Patience walked to *Grand-mère's*, Charity sent a note along explaining she had fallen in the dark and bruised her face and didn't think she looked presentable enough to be working in the store. Marie made a point to stop at Phillip's home before going in to assist Lyndyn.

"Charity?" Marie called as she entered the back door. "Where are you?" Their housekeeper did not live with them and Marie knew she would not be there until after the noon hour.

Marie quickly looked around, then stood at the foot of the stairs calling upward. "Charity, are you upstairs?" She heard a faint voice respond.

She found her granddaughter in bed and was rather alarmed at her appearance.

"*Ma chérie*, what is this? You hurt yourself badly, *n'est-ce pas?* Had you no candle lit? We must have your Uncle John look at you."

"The candle had gone out and I was just so sleepy. I'm all right. I feel stupid. And I don't want to bother Uncle John."

"Bother? It is no bother to check on the health of his niece," Marie caressed the girl's hand. Her sleeve slipped down and Marie saw more bruising on Charity's arm. "And your arm? What else have you hurt?"

"I'm all right *Grand-mère!* You always make such a fuss," she said rather rudely.

"Ah, yes, well, you must forgive me for caring about my grandchildren, especially the ones who have no ma-ma."

"I'm sorry, *Grand-mère*, I'm sorry, please forgive me. I have a headache and it is putting me in a bad mood."

It was the wrong thing to say.

"You had a bad fall and now you have a headache?" Marie shook her head. "No! You will see a doctor. Do you prefer your uncle or Doctor Ajax?"

Charity heard the strength in Marie's voice and knew there would be no changing her mind now.

"Uncle John," she sighed in resignation.

"So what's this I hear about you having a fight with your dresser?" John looked over at the elegantly heavy piece of furniture with its three marble surfaces. "I don't think I would pick a fight with that," he joked as he put up his finger. "Look at my finger; now follow it." She did as he asked. "Well, that looks good. Do you have any dizziness?"

"No."

"Been out of bed today?"

"Not much."

"I'd like you to get up and walk across the room and back for me, can you do that?"

"Of course." Charity got up rather stiffly and walked as normally as she could despite the pain it caused her. She crossed the room and returned.

"When did you have your last menstrual cycle?" he asked very professionally.

"I just had one. It ended several days ago."

"Charity, did you know you are bleeding?"

"What?" she looked mortified and twisted around to see a spot of blood on her nightgown.

John turned away, got up and opened the bedroom door. He told the housekeeper to send someone with a message to his wife. "Tell her to please come over here as quickly as she can. I need her assistance." Then he went back into the bedroom.

"Now where was I? Oh, yes… any ringing in your ears?"

"No."

"Of course, I have to listen to your heart," he smiled and pressed his ear against her chest. "It's going a little fast, Charity. Are you anxious about something?"

"No, no, not at all. Just the headache and this is embarrassing."

"Why embarrassing? At the moment I am your doctor, not your uncle. Anything we say or do or talk about is confidential. No one else will know. It doesn't become family gossip and you don't have to explain it to anyone else. Do you understand?"

"Certainly, Unc… *Doctor* John," she giggled nervously. "Only everyone already knows I tripped over my own chamber pot and took a fall against my dresser. I must have scraped myself."

John returned her smile and fiddled in his bag waiting for Ronnie's arrival. He took out some powders and looked for a glass and water. He mixed up a headache powder with a mild sedative.

"Here," he offered, "drink this. It will help with your headache and relax you."

She took the glass dutifully and drained it.

Just then he heard Ronnie's voice in the entry hall. No doubt she had mounted a horse bareback to traverse the acre so quickly. "Excuse me," he said to Charity. "Up here, Ronnie," he called from the door. In seconds his wife was by his side. He led her into the bedroom and closed the door tightly.

"As my wife, your Aunt Ronnie often assists me. And when she does she becomes my official nurse and is bound by the same oath of confidentiality as I am. Do you understand, Charity? We're here to help you, not judge you. Now, you may hold Nurse Ronnie's hand while I examine the cause of that bleed."

"No! You can't do that," Charity withdrew in fear, pulling the covers high around her.

"I must. I wouldn't be a responsible doctor if I did not," he said gently and loosened the bedding from the foot of the bed.

She began to cry as she knew she was exposed. She closed her eyes and Ronnie held her in her arms.

A half hour later, John had finished a thorough examination and made notes of all the bruises and injuries he had found all over her body. He then applied some soothing salves to her raw and swollen flesh. Ronnie put Charity into a fresh summer flannel nightgown and back into bed between fresh sheets. The sedative was having its effect and Charity was ready to sleep.

"We both know you didn't get these injuries falling against your dresser," he said more calmly than he felt. "I want you to sleep now and when you wake, you will tell me exactly what happened to you."

She nodded, closed her eyes and was soon fast asleep. John took Ronnie aside.

"She's been raped, sodomized, bitten, and generally abused. And it looks like she's had all her hair removed."

Ronnie looked up at him questioningly.

"She's almost nineteen. Most white women have a very healthy patch of hair down there. I've no reason to think she's any different. Why would she do that to herself? Phillip needs to be told," he said softly.

"You cannot do, Jack. You told her you not her uncle now but her doctor. You must keep your word, be her doctor and keep her secrets."

"I've known her since she was a baby," he said sadly. "This reminds me of what happened to you when you were a child," he added, gritting his teeth.

"But she is not child. She woman full grown. She choose to leave her home and go out alone at night. She choose to try and keep what happened to her secret. If you want to know what happened so you might help her, you must keep her trust by keeping her secrets."

John looked at his wife. She was being calm and logical and he knew she was right.

Marie and Richard left for Phillip's house and she sent word to the mill that they would be joining him for dinner at his house. That would bring her second son home on time while they delivered Grace and Patience along with a large basket filled with tempting pastries and breads.

She left Richard to amuse the girls while she took the basket to the kitchen outback.

"And there are plenty of cream puffs for all," Marie told Cook Hannah who did live on the premises.

"Oh, them cream puffs from your kitchen are a piece of heaven, ma'am," Hannah smiled broadly, displaying very crooked teeth.

"If you like them, then you must keep some for yourself," Marie said as she placed many on a serving plate and covered them with a napkin. "These are ready to serve for dinner's dessert."

"Mistress Marie, you spoil me," the genial cook said as she greedily eyed the almost dozen cream puffs Marie had set back for the kitchen.

"Nonsense, you work hard. And I appreciate all that you do for this family. My son still grieves."

Hannah nodded sympathetically.

"I know you heard Miss Charity took a fall last night. Did you see or hear anything?"

"Not last night," Hannah replied licking whipped cream off her finger. Then she looked up quickly as though she'd said something she shouldn't.

"Not last night," Marie repeated, "but perhaps other nights?"

"Oh, ma'am, I don't like to be carrying no tales."

"Hannah," Marie prodded gently, "you carry no tales to the outside world. This is my son and my granddaughter. If you know something you should tell me."

"Well… last night was pitch black and I had my own candle burning but some nights, when the moon is bright, I don't burn a candle. I open my windows to let in the cool evening air and…" she faltered.

"Yes?" Marie encouraged.

"Well, sometimes I see Miss Charity leave the house and go off through the trees in the direction of the church."

"The church?!"

"Yes, ma'am."

"And how often does she do this?"

"I guess I couldn't say. I mean I don't sit up watchin' for her but I'd say she does it regular. Some nights when my lumbago is bothering me, I see her return, maybe two or so hours later."

"And have you ever seen anyone with her?"

"No, ma'am, never, and I figure if she feels the need to pray that much, who am I to question it?"

"Yes, Hannah, you are quite right and we shall keep this just between us."

When Phillip arrived home, he was surprised to learn his oldest daughter had been restricted to bed rest by his brother, her doctor. He went upstairs only to find her sleeping.

"So what happened, John?" he asked as they sat down to dinner.

"Please," Marie spoke out. "Let us say a blessing first. Phillip, do you mind?"

"No, of course not." He muttered a quick, short prayer. "Now can you tell me what has happened to my daughter?"

"She says she woke up in the dark to use the chamber pot," John said smoothly, "tripped over it instead and fell against that marble topped dresser of hers."

"Is she all right?" Phillip asked quickly.

"She'll live," John said lightly and then realized it was in poor taste. "I'm sorry, Phillip. Of course she'll be fine. She has some bruises… that is a beastly dresser, rife with sharp corners and pointy parts. She complained of a headache so I gave her a headache powder and something to help her sleep. I told her to stay in bed for the day."

Ronnie listened to her husband tread the path between not telling his brother a lie while not telling him the whole truth and keeping his patient's confidence.

Marie took note that Ronnie was unusually pensive at dinner. After dessert, Grace and Patience were excused to go outside and play while Ronnie and Marie kept watch and drank their tea.

"Ronnie, something more happened to Charity than stumbling over her chamber pot, did it not?"

Ronnie looked at Marie and lowered her eyes.

"Jack's Mother, I obey my husband in saying nothing more about his patient." Just then a ball the girls were playing with came rolling up to Ronnie's feet and she kicked it skillfully back in their direction. "It is good to watch children play. It brings to mind my own short childhood but when I think of my childhood I often remember what I suffered at the hands of a few bad men. I am reminded that bad people live everywhere."

Ronnie had just told Marie all she needed to know.

A short time later, Marie collected Richard and bid her sons good night. As they got into the carriage she asked.

"Richard, will you please take me to Jozy's?"

"Richard looked at his wife and knew it was not idle curiosity or a whim that motivated her but something specific. He didn't question. He never questioned Marie. In his eyes she could do no wrong. She wasn't perfect, no human being was but her heart was the purest he'd ever known and he loved her immeasurably.

When he'd come home that afternoon from his walk down to the waterfront, he relayed to her the story he'd heard about a young whore entertaining scores of comers for free. It had caused quite a stir especially among those who had missed out. Now he wondered if that might have something to do with Marie's request.

They arrived at the brothel and Richard shielded Marie from awkward stares as she asked to see Madame Molly. A young woman dressed in more than most of the others escorted them both to the madame's private parlor. In less than a minute, a stout, well dressed woman swept into the room. She wore heavy make-up which Marie realized was an attempt to cover her pox mottled face.

"Good evening, Mistress Power, oh, forgive me, I should say Mistress Bonchance..."

"Good evening and please, *Marie* will do fine."

"And Mister Richard," Molly nodded. "I must say I am surprised to see you both here."

"You know who I am?" Marie questioned in surprise.

Molly smiled. "There aren't many in this community I don't know. And there aren't many who don't know you, Mistress Marie. Have a seat, please. And tell me what I can do for you?"

Marie took a seat in one of the very elegant, velvet upholstered chairs.

"First, I must say, I have always wanted to thank you for the assistance you gave Doctor Ajax during the small pox scare."

"Oh, yes," Molly reflected, "you lost a couple family members, didn't you? I'm sorry."

Marie nodded. "My son Phillip's wife and their daughter Faith... I know you know him. Some wounds heal very slowly."

"Can I offer you something to drink?" Molly asked hospitably.

"Oh, no, thank you. I come on another matter, actually. I am certain you are aware of the story about the young whore who was being offered for free by her pimp two nights ago...?"

"Yes?" Molly replied cautiously.

"As a business woman myself, I know we must always be aware of any rising competition. Do you happen to know who this pimp is or who the girl is? My husband tells me one rumor is that she wanted to come under your wing and he was punishing her for it."

Molly slowly shook her head, a hard smile on her face.

"I can assure you there's no pimp trying to cut in on my territory. If there was, Big Dan would have to have a little chat with him. As for the girl… that was no whore."

"How do you know?" Marie asked.

"No working girl would ever open her legs like that for free, if you'll pardon my crudeness. They might get raped for it same as any other woman but they'd never just take a crowd on for free. That's their livelihood, they cannot afford to give it away."

Marie sat quietly, swallowing. Richard reached over and held her hand. Finally, in a very small voice she asked, "Molly, do you have any idea who the girl was?"

"No, Mistress Marie, I don't. But I did hear someone say she'd had the small pox."

§

I don't know, John, things just aren't the same as they used to be," Phillip said as he poured them each a snifter of brandy out on the garden porch. "We used to be a small little settlement of families and a few single lumbermen who came into town only in the winter and Father kept a tight check on them. Now we have a bona fide cathouse and a tavern that doesn't mind catering to a rougher crowd… people renting rooms to strangers who walk our streets. It's just not the same."

John looked at his brother. "What brought this on?"

Phillip shrugged. "It's stupid really. A story was going around the mill today about some young whore who was giving it away for free last night. Anything one wanted and all her pimp asked for payment was to watch. Rumor is fifty, sixty stiff pricks were lined up to take their turn," he grunted. "Well, that's the story anyway. Personally I think it must be a gross exaggeration. I don't care how seasoned the whore is, I can't see her taking on sixty customers in one night. Hell, if they could do that," he laughed, "they'd soon all be as rich as Croesus."

"Not if they don't charge anything."

"Yeah, funny that," Phillip took a long pull on his cigar. "My first reaction was that it was some kind of a punishment. Like maybe she wanted to go to Madame Molly and he didn't like that idea."

"And what do you know about Madame Molly?" John asked with a deceptive grin and playfully kicked his brother's foot.

"Caroline may have taken my heart to the grave with her," he replied sadly, "but I do still have a cock with a powerful appetite."

When John and Ronnie arrived home to Chartes Landing, Marie had consulted with them on their decorating preferences and then had Richard's old bedroom completely redone for them. Now in the privacy of that room, the couple talked quietly as they held each other in their large four poster bed draped for the summer in mosquito netting. They both liked to sleep naked with the windows open and the fresh breezes wafting through the room.

John told Ronnie the story Phillip had relayed.

"The pit of my stomach turned over," he said, "and I was doing everything I could to try to look normal."

"You do well, Jack. You have wise face."

"I don't know about that."

"I mean your face have wisdom. Very handsome face but it knows how not to show everything you think."

John took her hand and kissed it, just as he had so often seen his father do to his mother.

"I wish I didn't feel so sure that is Charity everyone is talking about," he pondered sadly. "It certainly would explain her condition. And I'm remembering the twisted bastard Ajax told me about, who held the young whore's head under water at Jozy's... for some kind of unnatural pleasure."

"You think maybe same man?"

John nodded. "I can see his kind getting sick pleasure out of watching a young girl being roughly used, abused, raped, and sodomized by dozens of men. But I don't understand why she didn't scream for help or run away or why she was even with that bastard to begin with... whoever he is. What kind of hold does he have on her?"

Ronnie tenderly stroked her husband's cheek. "Tomorrow you can ask but tonight you need rest."

John sighed and kissed his wife's forehead. "There's a lot to think about." Ronnie looked long into her husband's eyes. He saw the questions she had but she had been taught as a slave never to ask. "Something I haven't mentioned before... Ajax and I don't think Hope killed herself."

"Why?"

"It was the way she was cut. Too sophisticated... are you familiar with that word?"

"Means opposite of childish."

"Yes... that's a good definition. And we've said nothing to anyone else because it would just upset everyone when we can't say who and have no proof. This mystery man has just gone to the top of my list. God only knows why my niece would allow him to dominate her. But if she's sneaking out of the house to see him, Phillip really needs to know."

"Your mother suspects something. She very wise woman, she senses things. You should be honest with her. Tell her everything that does not break Charity's trust."

"Perhaps you are right."

"Is it not better to say everything to mother and Phillip before you speak with Charity… so you are not breaking trust on things she may tell you?"

"Of course. How did you get so smart?" he teased and planted a kiss on her nose. Then he pulled back and looked at her in the candlelight. "Not only are you a beauty and fruitful," he stroked her smooth, bulging belly as he gazed at her nude form, her swollen breasts and long legs. "But you have the wisdom of an earth goddess which makes you an enviable mate for any man, and this man appreciates you very much indeed." He gathered her to him and kissed her deeply, a kiss she returned with fervor. In minutes he was fully aroused as was she. He was ready to mount her but she chose to mount him instead, leaving his hands free to caress her enticing curves. In a beautiful duet set to the timeless music of the ages, they matched each other's rhythms with an accelerando to a blissfully satisfying crescendo.

In the morning John rose early, anxious to meet with Ajax, Marie, and Phillip before their work days began and before he checked in on his newest patient. Despite the pleasure of making love with Ronnie, it had taken him over an hour more to get to sleep as he mulled over exactly what he could say that didn't break his oath of trust to his niece.

As he left the bedroom, Ronnie was rising. She was heading to the nursery while he was heading down for a mug of strong, hot tea. Before parting she said, "I will be ready to go with you if you wish, to see your niece."

He nodded and descended the stairs.

"Good morning, John," Marie greeted her son. She and Richard were already having breakfast.

"Good morning," he kissed his mother's forehead and nodded to Richard. "Mother, I'm going to send Tommy out with a message for Phillip and Ajax to come here for a meeting. There are some troubling things that have been happening in our community and I think we need to share information and discuss them."

Marie's alert bright eyes were attentive but she said nothing.

"Call Tommy in here, would you please, Nora?" John said to their housekeeper as she set a plate of eggs, ham, and griddle cakes before him.

"*Jah, jah, mein heir*, right away," Nora replied and hustled out to the back.

"Before Phillip gets here I just want to remind you that as Charity's doctor I am bound to keep her confidences. I gave her a thorough examination but all I can say is she will recover and should not have any permanent damage. I wish

I could say more but until she is willing to speak, my hands are tied."

"It is all right, John," Marie said calmly. "My mother's instincts still function and I think I know what has happened. No details but enough and I have taken no oath to not *hypothesize*." She turned to Richard. "Such a word I would never have thought to know until I had a man of science for a son." She looked back to John. "I will tell Phillip what I know and think, that breaks no trust."

Just then Tommy walked in. His young heart was racing in double time, his pulse was pounding in his ears, and he was feeling light-headed. When he received the message to report to Master John immediately, he thought for certain his life was coming to an end. Somehow someone had seen him and Miss Charity together and he was going to be beaten within an inch of drawing his last breath. Shaking, barely able to breathe, with hat in hand and humbling bent, he barely got out the words.

"You asked for me, sir?"

"Tommy, I want you to ride a horse to Master Phillip's house and tell him I am requesting he come here immediately for a very important meeting. Then go on to Doctor Ajax. His clinic won't be open at this hour but pound on his upstairs door. Tell him the same and ask if he'd like to ride your horse to save time. Can you do that?"

"Oh, yes sir, Master John," Tommy almost passed out from sheer relief. He bowed and fairly ran from the room.

"That boy was as pale as a ghost," Richard observed. "He must have a terrible fear of you, John."

"Or he is guilty of something he feared he'd been found out for," Marie added with a smile. "Young Margo did say she thought a pie had gone missing. I cannot imagine what else it could be. He's a good lad."

By the time Phillip and Ajax arrived, Marie and John had finished their breakfasts, excused themselves, and retired to the privacy of Jacques' old office. Marie had more hot tea, sausages, fruit, cheese, and bread brought in. Who knew if Archie or Phillip had even had a breakfast?

John made certain everyone was comfortably seated and closed the heavy door tightly.

"At the risk of sounding melodramatic," he began, "I fear we have a predator roaming our community who needs to be stopped. To that end and for the protection of… well, I thought it was time we all shared information."

"What's happened?" Phillip looked to John with startled concern.

"A number of things, Phillip. Maybe by putting them all together, we can find some answers."

John called on Ajax first who relayed the story of the very young girl at Jozy's. He struggled a bit in front of Marie.

"Do not concern yourself, Archie. I know what a whore is and I know what

Jozy's is. Madame Molly does the community a fair service, *n'est-ce pas?*"

Ajax next shared the description he'd received from the girl. "Average build and height but surprisingly strong, with very dark hair and deep set eyes. And well dressed."

"*Well dressed* is not a description one would use for many of the men in our community," said Marie. "Our population is more rural, *n'est-ce pas?* But this entire description matches a man who came into the store just recently. I knew he wanted to talk with Charity but I sent her to my office. I did not like the man. I knew she knew him and asked her about him. She admitted he had often been in the store when Hope was alive and she said she often caught them whispering together."

"Whispering?" Phillip repeated.

"After the incident with the young whore at Jozy's and Hope's apparent suicide," Ajax spoke, "I also asked Charity about the stranger. She told me then that he had asked her to dinner but when she told him he must speak to you first, Phillip, he had backed off and they'd not seen him for sometime after that."

"Why didn't you tell me?" Phillip groaned. "I should… wait, you said *apparent* suicide?"

John spoke up. "Both Archie and I agree. Phillip," he said softly, "we don't think Hope killed herself."

"What?!" Phillip looked desperately around the room, feeling betrayed by his own family. "Did you all know and no one told me?"

"No, Phillip," Marie spoke quickly. "This I did not know until this moment. Explain to us, John, please."

"To be perfectly honest, Archie noticed it first and I kicked myself for not seeing it immediately as well. It was the way her wrists were cut… too sophisticated, too efficient, too precise to be the random slashings of a distraught child. But with no proof and no suspect, we felt it would only cause more unhappiness to say anything."

"I'll kill him," Phillip growled as he left his chair and began pacing.

"We all want to kill him but he needs to hang from a gibbet," Marie said tightly.

"If it is any comfort, Hope would have bled out very quickly and felt no real pain. Less than ten minutes, a short enough time for him to keep her mesmerized somehow. Who knows what pretty pictures he painted for her of joining her twin."

"But why? Why? What reason would he have to take our Hope?" Phillip cried out.

"Right now we must protect the daughters you have left," John said with compassion. "Grace and Patience should never be out of sight. The nannies should be told. And Charity… is vulnerable."

"I think she is already enthralled," Marie said quietly and the three men looked at her. "Your cook has observed her leaving the house many nights, perhaps every night, going toward the church."

"Why didn't she tell me?" Phillip asked sharply.

"Is it her duty to spy upon your children?" Marie asked just as sharply. "Have you been home to do bed checks, *mon fils?* The poor woman is either loyal enough or naive enough to think Charity has only been going to pray. Obviously someone has Charity bewitched." Marie stood then, she was shaking and she grabbed the decanter of cognac and set it before John. "Pour me a drink, please." He obeyed without question and they all watched as she emptied the glass.

"Phillip, this is not going to be easy to hear. Richard told me the story of the supposed whore who was making free with her body to so many men two nights ago. I assume you have heard it as well?" She saw him nod. "I had Richard take me to Jozy's last night. An experienced madame told me no whore would ever give her body away like that for free. And there is no rival pimp. She couldn't identify them for me but she did say she heard the girl had had small pox."

The room had gone completely silent as Phillip softly groaned.

Marie returned to her chair. "I am here with two doctors and my two oldest sons and it is now time for me to give up a secret. Not even Richard knows this but your dear pa-pa knew and he loved me as every woman should be loved all the same.

"When I was very, very young I was raped by a brute, hurt, and beaten into submission. Then he turned me into his tavern whore. One might well ask - but you were right there in a village, you saw other people all the time; why did you not tell someone, ask for help, run away? To them I would say - you know not what goes through the mind of a beaten down victim. The fears, the shame, the self-loathing, the feelings of worthlessness, the beliefs that somehow you are undeserving of anything better.

"Eventually… I did run away, but I was a terrified little girl running into a black abyss of fear and shame. Your father rescued me and gave me back my sense of worth, my dignity. But I know the signs. Phillip, I believe your daughter has in some way been beaten into submission, perhaps not physically, but perhaps verbally and emotionally. She has most certainly been devalued in her own eyes and in her mind and thinks she deserves to be punished. Did you know, Phillip, that she believes herself responsible for Faith's death and for Hope's? Believing she is undeserving of anything better, I think she has been turned into a sex slave. I think she was the girl in the story of two nights ago, accepting her master's punishment for some misdeed. John cannot say this because he has taken an oath as a doctor but I am *guessing* her injuries bare witness to this truth. And the worst of it is that somehow the poor child thinks she deserves it.”

"John, is that right? Was she… did she… was she the girl at the docks?" In anguish Phillip leapt over to confront his brother.

"Phillip, I have no proof of that."

"Was she used like that?"

"You know I can't say anything."

"But you're not saying *no*," Phillip challenged and brought his fist down hard on the solid oak desk.

"I'm going over to talk with her as soon as we finish here," John said calmly. "Right now everyone has been talking fears and guesses and opinions, you have no facts regarding anything. If I'm going to get her to confide anything to me, I can't break her trust in me now. I'll take Ronnie; I think they're developing a bond."

"What am I supposed to do?" Phillip almost howled in frustration. "I want to know who this twisted bastard is, God damn him to hell! And where is he?!"

"I might be able to help there. I heard someone fitting his description has a room at Widow Angus' Boarding House," said Ajax. "Perhaps…"

"I would resist going over for a confrontation," John spoke looking directly at Phillip, wishing Ajax had not shared that information. "Until we have some proof of his involvement, either Charity's word or a witness, we risk scaring him off. And we have absolutely nothing to link him to Hope. It's better he feel safe."

"How about we walk the docks and see if we can find any one who is a witness?" Ajax asked.

"Archie, you may be able to do that in a nonthreatening manner but who is going to speak up to the father of the girl they may have made use of?" Marie questioned.

"I doubt they knew who they were… *visiting*," Ajax replied, "but you are right. They might guess what we're thinking if they see Phillip. I'll go alone. I can put out the word that the girl had the clap and all who were with her need a dosing. That ought to bring them to me."

"So I am to just sit on my hands?" Phillip fairly snarled.

"Sometimes the hardest thing to do is *nothing*," John said sympathetically. "Go to the mill, brother, and try to have a normal day. We'll meet again before dinner to share what we have found out. Meanwhile, between Mother and Ronnie, be assured that your daughter will be well cared for. And for the love of God, when you see her do not betray that you suspect anything more than nocturnal clumsiness."

The meeting was over. John found Ronnie and they walked to Phillip's house while Phillip left for the mill. Ajax went on his mission to try and discover witnesses and Marie quietly went to her bedroom. She heard Richard still eating his breakfast and laughing with Nora. It sounded like Rebecca and Sebastian had joined him.

Quietly Marie went up the stairs to the master bedroom. She had a chest she rarely went into but now she pulled it out. Beneath an odd assortment of stored items she found what she was looking for: a handsome, well polished wood box. She lifted the lid and took out two pistols and proceeded to clean and oil them. When she finished she carefully loaded each one and primed it with fresh powder after which she put them back in their box and placed the box in the bottom of her wardrobe.

Chapter 27

"So, how is my patient doing this morning?" John asked warmly as he and Ronnie walked into Charity's bedroom. She was sitting up, a barely touched breakfast tray across her lap.

"I slept all day yesterday." It sounded like a complaint.

"Yes, of course. It is exactly what your body needed. You didn't get any sleep the night before, did you? I see the swelling has gone down some on your face. Now tell me who the man was who dragged you down to the docks and let all the men around have you?"

"Uncle John!!" she gasped in indignation. "I don't know what you're talking about."

"It is *Doctor* John. And it is what the whole town is talking about."

"What?!" All color left her face.

"Charity, I told you we want to help but you have to be honest with us. I am a doctor. I can see that you are no longer a virgin and you've been very roughly used and sodomized… you're covered in bruises and welts and have been rubbed until your flesh looks like raw meat while at the same time a story is flying around the village that a young whore was giving it away for free two nights ago while the man she was with just watched."

"That most certainly wasn't me!" she said defiantly. "I told you I tripped over my chamber pot and fell against the dresser. If I look abused it was those corners catching me in the wrong places…"

"Charity, you have human bite marks on your labia."

"How could you possibly see that?" she gasped. "It's not true."

"Would you like me to call Doctor Ajax in for a second opinion?"

"No!" she cried as she took on the look of a feral animal backed into a corner. Her eyes were wild as she tried to think. Then suddenly she broke down into tears.

Ronnie put a calming hand on John's arm. "Perhaps a quieter approach," she whispered. She reached over to sooth Charity. Ronnie undid the girl's sleep braids and began to brush her hair out.

"Doctor John is only concerned for your health," she spoke in her low, calming voice. "When I was very small girl, many men used me, forced me to be whore. I was only ten years and it ripped me apart. Doctor John sewed me back together and made me whole person again."

Charity pulled back and looked in Ronnie's face. "Why did you let them?"

"They threatened my small brother who was only four. They burnt his arm and threatened to do worse if I would not whore for them."

Charity looked down into her lap, obviously thinking.

"Your confidences are safe with us," John said in an equally calming tone, "but I don't like being lied to."

"I have a lover," Charity said at last. "I know we're not supposed to be doing these things but we do and I like them… and we try to be careful so I don't get pregnant. In fact, we did things for weeks and weeks and I was still a virgin."

"And then what happened?"

"I begged him and begged him…"

"And that made him angry?"

"A little… but I did fall against the dresser and bruised myself. And I have no idea who that was down by the docks."

"And it was for him that you removed your hair?"

"He did it and we both love it."

"I see."

"Why is this lover a secret?" asked Ronnie quietly. "Why has he not asked for marriage? You should introduce him to family."

"He's not ready for that." Charity looked away. "He thinks you won't approve of him."

"Why?" John asked.

Charity shrugged. "I don't know. Perhaps it's because he's an outsider, not someone who you have known all his life. The village can be very… very cliquish."

"Charity, you can't really think that. This entire settlement is made up of people from somewhere else. Or if not them, their parents. So what makes him so different? Does he have two horns and three eyes?"

She gave half a laugh. "No, of course not."

"Then you must invite him and if he is a man worthy of you, he will accept."

"I don't want to talk about it anymore. And as my doctor you must not tell anyone any of this."

He sighed deeply. "As you wish. Here is some more of the salve I put on you yesterday. Continue putting it on your raw flesh everyday. Remember to apply it with a clean hand, first to your front and second to your behind to guard against infection. And wash your hands after. I'll check on your progress. And you might as well know… I will keep your confidence as will Ronnie but I intend on telling your father you must remain at home for recuperative rest."

She looked up at him resentfully.

"Your paramour will just have to wait. I don't want him giving you an infection." John packed up his bag and prepared to leave. He was almost at the door when he stopped suddenly and returned to the bed.

"I've asked you to be honest with me so it's only right that I be honest with you. You are lying to me, Charity, and I know it. Yes, I believe you have a lover that you've been sneaking off to see for sometime now. But if he actually kept you a virgin for so long then something happened and it set him off. You don't realize the kind of sick individual you are dealing with. Whatever it was, he took you to the docks and invited dozens of men to be intimate with you. That is hardly the action of a man who truly cares about you." Charity began to protest but John stopped her with a gesture. "No single man is capable of inflicting the damage I've seen… neither is any dresser. The story is it was almost fifty men, give or take, sound about right? And you accepted it… why? Because you thought you deserved it? I don't know what's going on in your head but no woman deserves that and most certainly you do not.

"I can understand you being very curious about sex but they call it 'making love' because its supposed to be just that - an act of love, joyous and fulfilling, not an act filled with pain and punishment."

Her face had gone stiff and rigid and he could tell she was fighting tears.

"Your grandmother tells me you blame yourself for Faith's death, and for Hope… you shouldn't. It had nothing to do with you. She told me she explained that as well. Just as you cannot blame your parents because you got scarred. It's just something that happens but in time, Charity, your scars will mellow, be less pronounced, and no man worth his salt will see them as an impediment to loving you and building a happy home and family with you. You're just too fresh from your hurts to see that as yet. There is a difference between boys and men but not all men are good."

John wanted so badly to tell her what they believed of Hope's death but he couldn't risk her relaying it to the stranger. Instead he bent and kissed his niece's forehead then he and Ronnie left the room.

Before the door was even fully shut, tears were streaming down Charity's cheeks. What had she done? What was the matter with her? How had she let things get so out of hand, so… public? He said the whole village was talking about it. So how long before one of them walked into the store and some little thing she did, some little movement or gesture jogged their whiskey laced memory and they knew she was the one they'd bent over the table or the bed and she had allowed them to, accepted it, hadn't uttered a word of protest or complaint, just spread her legs and submitted. And then everyone in the village would know. Her uncle knew, he knew everything. The man was uncanny as though he could see into her brain and yet he had kissed her good-bye. She had shamed her family's good name. Shamed her father. And even if he forgave her, what about Tommy? He wasn't likely to forget. She could never go to her grandmother's again.

Then another thought struck her. During all these past months with Zeke, he'd been so concerned she keep her virginity and not get with child but then he allowed so many of those men to shoot their seed into her womb… what if she was now pregnant? And who could even say who was the father? Charity curled up under her sheet and cried until she had no more tears left.

She lie staring up at the ceiling and thinking. She hadn't bothered to really think in a very long time. Why had Zeke been so angry… really? Had he dragged her down to the docks and let dozens of men have her while he watched because she'd cheated on him with one young boy? That didn't make any sense. Or was he really so angry because she was no longer a virgin? He was always talking about her being his virgin angel, virgin, virgin, virgin… that was why. If she had asked Tommy to sodomize her, Zeke wouldn't have even known but more to the point, if she had told him he would have never dragged her to the docks. Not his virgin angel, even if she was a little tarnished. Didn't he tarnish her plenty himself?

So it was the loss of her virginity that maddened him. And since she was no longer a virgin perhaps he had no use for her at all. Charity felt a small pang of loss despite everything. Was he truly finished with her? Was he even now looking for her replacement? Some young virgin he could teach to enjoy his peculiar brand of love making? And now she felt a pang of jealousy. She tossed in her bed. She was sick of her room but she didn't want to face the faces in the rest of the house. She wanted to escape the house and flee to the mausoleum. It was not possible. There were too many people around all the time and she still couldn't even walk properly.

Two weeks passed. John had been brutally honest and vehemently opposed to Charity seeing her paramour for fear any continued relations might bring on a fatal infection.

"You seem to have no control around him so I am telling your father you haven't healed as yet and must remain home with clean sheets and a fresh nightshirt every day."

"But it's so boring. Surely it doesn't hurt for me to go help out at the store," Charity argued.

"Where you must use a communal privy instead of your own boiled out chamber pot? I think not. As soon as I can I am going to show you the world you cannot see with the aid of my microscope. You have no idea how many creatures live with us, invisible to the naked eye. Your skin is your body's barrier, the wall that keeps out the harmful creatures but when your skin is broken, cut or rubbed so raw it is nothing but an open wound, anything can get in."

One day he brought his microscope and what she saw had frightened her enough to accept her imprisonment and to use only her own chamber pot which each day Hannah saw washed out with lye soap and rinsed with boiling hot water per Doctor John's instructions.

They had fallen into a routine. Marie and sometimes Richard came over after breakfast to spend time with Charity. Sometimes there was sewing or mending to be done while Richard would amuse them with stories of past adventures. Sometimes Marie would bring her a new book which she had found as part of a shipment from New York Towne on the packet boat.

"Look what I have for you today," Marie said brightly. "It is called *Gulliver's Travels* by Monsieur Jonathan Swift. I wonder if Gulliver's travels are as amusing as your Grand Uncle Richard's have been. After you have read it, you must tell me what you think."

Around noon, John and Ronnie would always arrive, signaling the changing of the guard. Marie would leave for the store or home and after John assured himself that his patient had no fever, he too would leave to attend other patients. Later in the afternoon, John would return and take Ronnie home to rest. She was nearing the end of her term and they were expecting the new baby any time now.

Charity always came along for the short ride. They called it her ride for fresh air but it was really because John didn't trust her to stay put during their absence.

John stayed with her for the rest of the afternoon and they talked of many things. He shared stories with her of his travels and studies in Europe. Stories she'd never heard before of his visit to his father's parents' estates, the old chateau, and what his father had left behind when he had fled France.

Eventually John found himself sharing part of himself no one else in the family knew. His first love and how he had married her even knowing she was dying from a terrible blood disorder. And how she had fought with every fiber of her being to live but had died in his arms after only a few months of marriage.

"That was one of the things that drew me to Ronnie," he said quietly to his niece as she wiped a tear from her cheek. "She had a terrible childhood. Her father was murdered right in front of her, she and her mother were taken as slaves and turned into whores, then she was captured by another tribe, almost left for dead because of the infection she suffered in her nether region, from being misused," he added pointedly, "... but through it all, she never gave up. She fought to stay alive, she fought for every day and eventually she found love with an honorable warrior. I never really knew him. I only know what she's shared with me but I know they were deeply in love and finally married."

"What happened?" Charity asked, caught up in the romance of it.

"Ironically he was part of a faction of Indian allies that fought by our side in yet another set to between the French and English. It was the last battle of the season and he was bound for home and back to the arms of his pregnant wife who was carrying their first son. He was slain by one of the last arrows to be shot. I heard him cry out her name with his last breath and I knew I had to bring his body back to her."

"That was Gray's father?" Charity asked softly.

John nodded.

"Then you fell in love?"

"Oh no, it was another two, three years… but that's another story. I see your father coming so it's time for me to go back to my wife," he smiled at her and nodded to Phillip.

Phillip only nodded back. He was angry and upset with John. He'd been angry and upset for two weeks, ever since that first day when John promised they'd all meet back to share their findings and John had said almost nothing. Ajax, on the other hand, had reported that thirty-seven men had come to him for a dosing for clap and every description he'd been able to obtain of the girl, aside from being lewd and demeaning, had only vaguely resembled Charity.

Finally, a week ago, Phillip had reached the boiling point and marched over to Widow Angus' only to be told, the boarder she knew as *Mister Leslie*, had given up his room and left. She had no idea where he went off to but he wouldn't find any better prices for a room in all of Chartes landing, she grumbled.

And so Phillip still hadn't forgiven John. And worse, Phillip didn't know how to treat his own daughter. He wanted to have it all out, laid out on the table so to speak. Did she have a secret lover? Had he dragged her down to the docks? But how could a father accuse his own daughter of such horrendous and indecent behavior if she was innocent? To even think her capable of such behavior was unthinkable. Even now he told himself it was all a mistake. And he and his mother were creating monstrous imaginings out of rumors and suppositions.

Marie had spent the morning visiting with Charity and chatting about the store, the garden, the mischievous exploits of her youngest cousins, in short, anything but the reason she was confined to the house. All the swelling from rough handling had gone down in her face but John wanted one more pelvic examination before he would sanction her return to the store.

When John and Ronnie arrived, Marie excused herself.

"I must go on to the store and see if Lyndyn needs anything," she smiled and went out to her rig. As she drove she made a detour. She went to the cemetery.

Reining up the horse, she walked to the Power Family Mausoleum, the very place they had found Hope. She opened the door wide and let the noon day sunlight pour in. Marie saw the two little engraved plates, on the two little sepulchers:

Faith Georgina Power
1713 – 1728
Beloved daughter
of Phillip & Caroline

Hope Henrietta Power
1713- 1729
Beloved daughter
of Phillip & Caroline

Faith and Hope, side by side and next to their mother, Caroline.

Marie grabbed her breast and stifled a sob. Such a waste. Such a tragedy. But was it not for them to believe that they were now with the Lord in a much better place? She took a hankie from her handbag and blotted the tears from her eyes.

As she stood still she noticed the sunlight reflecting off an unusual spot on the stone floor and bent to scrape it with her nail. Candle wax. She followed an imaginary line upward and saw a very small wax drip on the back of the stone bench. In the bright light she also could see a few fibers caught in the carving on the bench. She pulled them out to examine them. They looked like blanket fibers. Next, she noticed a dried water ring stain on the floor. She stared. There was no explanation for any of these things unless…

Marie's heart began to thud in her chest. This, not the church, was where Charity was meeting her mystery man, in the very spot where her sister Hope had been allowed to bleed out in an act of murder! The blood stains were still visible, nothing could remove them from the stone. Marie had to leave. She was panting for breath and went to her rig to sit down. For several minutes she sat simply breathing. Then when she looked back at the mausoleum she realized she had left the door open. Climbing down she retraced her steps slowly, calm anger replacing her initial fury.

Lord God in Heaven, please help me and with your help I swear this demon shall not get another grandchild of mine.

Marie went on to the store but spent most of her time there just sitting at the desk in her office.

"Mother Marie," Lyndyn said softly, "you look a little peaked to me. Are you sure you're feeling well?"

"Quite well, I just have some unhappy thoughts to work through," and she gave him a brave smile.

Chapter 28

Ronnie had a tightly rolled up leather sheet she needed to put onto the bed to protect the mattress. The small, extraordinarily soft baby blanket of mink fur was next to it along with her birthing knife, a silken cord which had replaced the leather lacing she used to use, and the soft flannels they would use to bathe the infant. She remembered when she had birthed Mark in this house they had brought her a canvas treated with wax to protect the wood floor. She would ask for that again. The first supply of swaddling, the delicate goose grease, it was all there awaiting the coming of the child.

Ronnie pulled up her large cotton tunic exposing her huge belly and scratched at her itchy flesh. John did not like the smell of bear grease so she had gone to Marie who had given her a jar of French cream instead. It did not work as well but it did smell better. She stood quietly rubbing the cream onto the skin of her belly and wondering if this time she might give John a daughter although at the moment he might not appreciate another female to watch over. She knew Charity brought worry lines to his brow.

With the acceptance that is often the final state of mind for expectant mothers, Ronnie shrugged. They would soon know and if the child was a girl, they could hardly send her back. Sunshine would be six come winter. It would be nice to have another girl.

Ronnie stretched out on the bed. Her children were the youngest in the nursery, ages two, three, four, and five. Louise's Michael was the oldest left in the nursery, having turned eleven in January, and now he was the undisputed king. His siblings, Jeannette and Frances ages eight and six, were his devoted liegemen and when cousins came to visit in the form of Helen's Joseph, now also eleven, and Jean, who would soon be eight or Phillip's ten year old Patience, they would not think of challenging the status quo of the home kingdom or try to usurp the power of its ruler.

Ronnie smiled. Louise had loaned her a book which had belonged to her late husband. It had been one of Rafe's favorites she said and it was a romance all about honorable knights and ladies fair, powerful kings and kingdoms. Ronnie found the comparisons within the nurseries of the white man easy to see.

Then she thought wistfully of her absent son. What was he doing right this moment, she wondered? Gray Wolf's Son was a proud Mohawk warrior. Even at just seven and a half he would not simply accept the dictations of a child, even one four years older. Not without a physical challenge. Strength and skill are paramount to a warrior, not the mere passing of the seasons. She wondered what Wani and Yellow Rock were teaching her son. What precious pearls of greater wisdom might Gray Wolf have taught him as they shared warmth around the hearth on cold winter nights.

Ronnie fell asleep and as she slept she dreamed. Out of a soft mist Gray Wolf came to her with gentle words. He was her Gray Wolf, tall, strong, proud, and yet different, of another world. Without sadness or remorse, he wished her joy and happiness in her present life and left her with his promise to always watch over their son.

Ronnie woke with a little gasp. It had been so real she looked about the room half expecting to see him. Then she realized Gray Wolf had been so clear to her but she could not remember what he had been wearing... or what language he had spoken to her... or if he had spoken at all. It was as if all the thoughts had come to her without speech and his eyes had had a light she had never seen before.

Marie had asked Charity to remove the merchandise from the front display window. It was time to create a new display and wash the window. As Charity worked she looked past the glass and saw Zeke standing across the street, several shops down. He was watching her.

She felt her heart give a little flutter. How long had he been watching for her to come back to work at the emporium. She knew he dare not come into the store. He still cared. He still wanted her. He hadn't found another girl to replace her. He was still in love with her.

"Put this woven rag rug on the floor of the window," said Marie as she walked up behind Charity and Charity saw Zeke melt away. "Be sure to put a price card with each item. I think we shall display two place settings of our tableware. On one side arrange a place setting of our crockery along with our pewter tableware on a small checked tablecloth, folded neatly. On the other side fold a linen table cloth up into the same size. Place one setting of the good porcelain on it with a set of silverware. But we must remember to wipe the silver every night, yes?"

Charity was only half listening.

"Why bother *Grand-mère?* I'm sure anyone who can afford the porcelain already owns it. Setting the good silver out and having to polish it is just more work."

Marie looked at her granddaughter and saw the distraction in her face. Then she quickly looked out the window but saw nothing unusual.

"It is important for people to dream, *ma chère*. The housewife who can only afford to replace her chipped crockery one piece at a time still has the right to her dreams of owning fine porcelain. Dreams are what motivate us to push ourselves, they are what give us ambition as long as we know it takes hard work to make our dreams a reality."

"Yes, *Grand-mère*," Charity replied in a tone that made Marie feel she was talking to a potted plant.

"Are you listening to me?"

"Yes, *Grand-mère*."

"I would like you to look at me please, so I know I have your attention."

Charity turned and stared at Marie.

"So, behind them I think we should display one of the new iron braziers that just arrived. And behind that, let us put up a pair of sturdy coveralls and those thick, long, wool stockings. Then perhaps you can think of one or two more items to add, yes? Autumn is just around the corner and people will need the time to save for something that catches their eye now."

"Of course, *Grand-mère*."

Marie moved off but she continued to watch her granddaughter who seemed to be looking out the window more than she was looking at the display. She did add several more items, seeming to rush her time away from the window but slow down considerably once she was back in front of the glass.

"Are you finished?" Marie finally called over.

"Yes… I think so."

"Good, now stay there and I will go outside and see what it looks like from the street." Marie went out and saw that among a few other goods, Charity had added a small mirror which she had leaned against one leg of the brazier. Marie stood there for a time, apparently checking the display but she was really studying the reflections in the mirror. Then the hairs stood up on the back of her neck. She saw the dark haired man slip out from between the buildings and gesture boldly to Charity.

It was all Marie could do to remain calm and keep from turning around. She looked up at Charity and saw a huge smile on her face which she immediately turned on her grandmother when Marie looked at her.

"How does it look?" she asked through the glass. "Do you like it?"

Marie nodded and forced a smile as she returned indoors.

"Yes, very good. The mirror was a good choice on the porcelain side. Now, if you would be so kind as to stand behind the counter for the customers, I am going to ask Lyndyn to wash the outside of the window. I noticed many finger-prints."

Phillip was at the very end of his patience. John would not clarify because of his damnable ethics. Charity continued to take the stance that she had only fallen over the chamber pot and fell hard into the dresser. Now Marie had taken the girl back into the store with John's blessing.

"It will be good for her to stay busy" he had said.

So was that it? Was everything to now continue on as if nothing had happened? Over his dead body!

Phillip made a short end to the day as he belted on his scabbard and sword and took his musket off the wall. He'd loaded it with fresh powder just that morning. Walking briskly to the emporium, he was going to ask his mother to keep the girls for the night while he went out and turned over every rock in Chartes Landing to see what crawled out. The problem being their little village didn't have many rocks. There was no slum, no seedy section. Even the docks were generally quiet once the packet boat came and went. This stranger had already been banned from Jozy's so once Phillip hit the coarser taverns where was he to look next? And what proof did they have that the murdering whoreson had led one daughter to her death and the other to her degradation? Proof? Right now Phillip was of a mind to beat the proof out of him if only he could lay hands on him.

When he arrived at the store, Marie motioned him to her office and shut the door.

"Phillip, you and John both need to know this; I saw that man today."

"Where?"

"He was across the street, watching the store. Then while Charity helped me change out the window display he became bold enough to signal to her." Marie tried to remain calm.

"Signal how?"

"Signal, gesture. I know not what he meant but… I could not believe it and Charity took pleasure in seeing him and tried to hide it from me."

"He has her enchanted," Phillip growled.

"So it would seem. He ducked back into the shadows each time he saw me."

Phillip cursed softly under his breath. "I want you to keep the girls at your house tonight, Mother, will you do that?"

"Of course…"

"Between you and John and Ronnie, you can keep her safe. Lock her in her bedroom if you must."

"What are you going to do?"

"I'm combing every shelter in this village. Could be some decent family has rented a room to this monster, not knowing what he really is."

"Be careful, Phillip. You must tell John. Take him with you."

"Don't worry," he said and brushed a hurried kiss upon her forehead.

Late that afternoon, Marie closed and locked the store front.

"Come Lyndyn, we have put in a long day and dinner awaits us," she said.

"You go ahead Mother Marie, I just have two more crates to unpack and I'll be right behind you."

"Very well, don't be too late," she smiled but the smile did not reach her eyes.

Lyndyn and Louise only knew that Charity had taken some kind of a fall but with no bones broken, how serious could it be? Louise was of the opinion that her niece was milking it for all the sympathy she could get. Two weeks to lie around with no broken bones? Who ever heard of such a thing? Such was the information gleaned from nursery gossip exchanged by the children.

This day however, Lyndyn recognized a high level of agitation in Marie. Charity had returned to work in the store and yet Marie had not left all day and even watched out the back door when the girl went to the privy. Phillip appearing with a sword strapped on and a musket in hand was most definitely not normal. Lyndyn came within a hair's breadth of asking his mother-in-law if there was something going on and could he be of service but in an unguarded moment the look on her face said quite clearly there was definitely something amiss. At the same time, she could have asked for his help anytime that day if she had wanted it. Lyndyn kept silent, wishing not to pry. He didn't envy Phillip the solitary rearing of young girls. When Lyndyn married Louise he had taken on the responsibility of raising two himself and now he and Louise were expecting their first baby by winter. It might be another girl. Fortunately, his girls had brothers to help watch over them. The stunningly beautiful Rebecca was proving to be a magnet attracting every unmarried young man in the settlement but her tall, rather gallant brother Sebastian was almost always by her side. Instinctively, the lad saw a duty in protecting the innocence of his fair sister.

Marie invited all except the youngest grandchildren to eat dinner with them to liven up the table. The adults needed some distraction she decided. As she sat back with her wine and looked around the table she could tell Richard was having a bad day and expected he would beg an early end to the evening and head to their bed with a dose of his sleeping medicine.

Louise was still dealing with pregnancy nausea and Lyndyn was being most solicitous. Marie reminded herself that this was, after all, his first pregnancy. She was very glad that he and Louise had finally "found" each other and were so happy.

Phillip was absent and Marie had quietly told John why. To her surprise, he seemed to heartily approve.

Ronnie appeared to have no appetite at all.

"The baby come soon," she spoke softly to John, "does not want food in my stomach."

Charity had withdrawn into a world of her own. If it were not for her sisters and Louise's children, it would have been a solemn table indeed. Instead the young ones chattered and joked, poked fun at each other and cleaned their plates so that when dessert was served they could descend upon it like starving young wolves.

Marie had to laugh. Laughter was good. It was necessary balm to the troubled mind.

The children were sent to bed at their usual time. Louise and Lyndyn retired to their suite and Marie herself did a bed check before nine and settled in to read *The Penn Gazette* which the packet boat from the south had dropped off. Marie had never heard of the publication before and suspected that the free samples were an enticement to gain subscriptions this far away from...? She checked and saw "Philadelphia" printed on the front page. This Monsieur Benjamin Franklin was a smart businessman, she thought, an aggressive entrepreneur, and very witty if his gazette was a fair representation.

She had seated herself in the hall outside the master bedroom. Within their room, Richard's soft snoring assured her that for the moment he was pain-free and while she might use his snoring as an excuse, in truth she was keeping watch on Charity's door.

The clock in the foyer had just struck the hour of ten and she was aware of activity in John's room two doors down. It wasn't lovemaking, it was the beginning of labor. The door opened and Ronnie began a familiar walk, up and down the long hallway, with John at her side.

"Jack's Mother," she called softly when she saw Marie, "last time there was waxed canvas to spread on floor."

"Of course, of course, I will fetch it and wake the cook to boil water so it has a chance to cool down. Oh, this is exciting. I shall let Nanny Sarah know as well."

Just then a spasm gripped Ronnie's abdomen and she stopped and turned her concentration inward, breathing through the discomfort. It reminded Marie of the things Sheehoo, her Indian friend, had taught her in bringing forth a new life.

"She doesn't want a fuss, Mother," John said quietly. "We will keep the child with us for a while."

"Very well, no fuss, no fuss. We shall let Sarah sleep for now... but I have another grandchild on the way and she will be heartbroken if she is not able to help a little." Marie beamed happily at John and hurried down the back stairway.

Young Margo was alerted and Marie brought the wax treated canvas upstairs and handed it to John before she went to inform Sarah that there was a birth in progress. Sarah said she would go upstairs to the third floor and inform Nora. Marie nodded and turned to the empty hall. John had convinced Ronnie to allow him to stay with her at least until someone else came and they had gone back into their room where he was spreading out the canvas.

An empty hall. How long had it been empty? Marie looked into Charity's room and saw three forms sleeping soundly in the big bed behind the mosquito netting. She sighed in relief, closing the door quietly. Just then Nora came rushing down from the servant quarters.

"Oh my, oh my, big night tonight, *Jah!* She clapped her hands rather gleefully.

"Yes, yes. Do you have a catch bucket?" Marie asked.

"I go get, Mistress. Not to worry. Oh, whew, it so varm I sweat already," she exclaimed as she descended the backstairs.

Marie stopped. It was warm! And she rushed back into Charity's room. Grace and Patience each layed with the sheet half off as a warm breeze blew in the window. Marie reached through the netting to pull the sheet back on the third form only to find... pillows.

Charity ran to the mausoleum, threw open the door, and rushed into Ezekiel's arms.

"Oh, Zeke, Zeke, my love, it's been so long."

"Why has it been so long? You haven't been in the store for two weeks. What have you been doing?"

"Healing. And being kept a prisoner."

He pulled back and stared into her face.

"It's true, Zeke. My doctor wouldn't let me use a communal privy for fear of infection."

"Your uncle the doctor?"

She nodded her head.

"He noticed me bleeding and insisted on doing a thorough examination. I couldn't stop him."

"So, I suppose you whined to him about everything."

"No, I wouldn't tell him anything. He could see I wasn't a virgin anymore so I had to tell him I have a lover and we like to... do different things but I've never admitted to being the girl at the docks. I just keep insisting I fell against my dresser."

He grinned, a hard, dark grin and reached into her bodice to pinch her nipples. She gasped.

"You miss it, don't you?"

"I missed you. I love you, Zeke and I forgive you... do you forgive me?"

"You know you can never be my virgin angel again," he said as his hands ran over her body, loosening her laces.

"I know."

"You're a filthy whore now."

"I know."

"Say it!"

"I'm a filthy whore," she repeated.

"A dirty cunt."

"A dirty cunt," she echoed as tears filled her eyes.

"Now take off all your clothes and lie back. I have a new surprise."

Not certain what to expect, Charity obeyed.

He would not touch her with his mouth but he was soon bringing her to arousal with his fingers.

Then out of nowhere he brought forth a dildo and slid it into her. As she approached her climax he flicked a sharp flint across her upper thigh and poured a dash of alcohol on it.

Charity rose straight up, biting her lip not to scream out.

"What was that?"

"A thin flint," he replied, "it makes a very thin cut, nothing serious. It heals in a few hours but it burns and makes the feeling more intense, doesn't it?"

"I… I don't know, do it again."

"No!" shouted Marie as she stood in the open door. She had rushed up and heard the last bit of conversation.

"*Grand-mère!*" Charity gasped and tried to cover herself with the blanket.

"Would you like to join us, Grandma?" Ezekiel asked casually.

"Leave my granddaughter alone." Marie brought a pistol out of her skirts. "Charity get dressed."

"Don't move," Ezekiel commanded with a staying hand. "Your precious granddaughter is a dirty, filthy slut. Has she told you all the things she's done? How she went out and found someone else to fuck her when I would not? How she enjoyed being taken by over three dozen men? A very dirty whore indeed."

"So do you mean to do to Charity what you did to Hope when you are finished with her?" Marie asked darkly.

Suddenly his eyes took on a mad, glittering quality.

"You don't understand a thing! I helped Hope! She was too good, too pure, too innocent to stay in this world. She wanted to join her sister. She was an angel trapped on earth where eventually this filthy world would have sullied her. I helped her escape but you need have no fear of losing Charity." He laughed maniacally. "She belongs here. She's as filthy as this world. I knew that from the start."

Marie had seen Charity react to the man's confession as she withdrew and moved away from him.

"You killed my sister?" she gasped. "All this time I thought it was my fault that she killed herself because Faith was gone but you… you murdered her?"

"Come back over here," he snarled.

"No," Charity put the stone bench between them and was dressing herself hastily. "You murdered my sister! You deserve to hang!"

"Yes, he does," Marie agreed, "but I am not so foolish as to try and walk him through the forest in the dark so we shall wait here until you fetch help. *Ma chère* Charity, run to Pastor McCullen's house and get help."

"Yes, *Grand-mère*." She left.

Ezekiel began to laugh as he slipped on his coat.

"You don't really think you can keep me here, do you? I have at least eight inches and seventy pounds over you. Normally I tolerate little old ladies but stay out of my way."

Marie brought out her second pistol. "I have found these to be great equalizers, monsieur."

"I doubt you know how to shoot those things, Grandma, much less load and prime them. You can barely hold them up."

He took a threatening step toward her.

"I warn you, monsieur, I do not bluff! Stop!! Stop or I will shoot!"

He took another step and Marie pulled the trigger on both pistols. Ezekiel fell back, a most surprised look on his face as blood gushed from his chest. The sound of the musket fire was reverberating off the stone walls as Marie watched the light leave his eyes.

"Now you may try to tell the Lord why you took our Hope's life," Marie said softly as she stared down at the stranger.

In a few minutes, Charity came running up.

"*Grand-mère! Grand-mère!* Are you all right? We heard the shot."

Marie turned to block her granddaughter's view.

"I told him I was not bluffing but he would not stop. Who have you brought?"

"Pastor McCullen and his handyman but…" she stumbled vaguely, "I guess there's no need now."

"Someone must take the body away," Marie said calmly, abnormally calmly.

Just then John and Phillip both came riding up on horseback. They saw Marie's horse tied by the cemetery gate.

"Mother?"

"Mother?"

"Are you all right?"

"We heard a shot."

"Are you all right?"

"What happened?"

They were both calling and talking at once as they ran up to the mausoleum.

"He confessed, John… Phillip… no, he *bragged* how he had killed Hope. And how he had cruelly treated Charity. I would have liked to have seen him swing on the gibbet but he gave me no choice." She walked slowly toward her horse. "How is Ronnie?"

"She's fine, Mother." John took possession of the discharged pistols and took Marie's arm to steady her. "She's just given me another daughter… I think I'm going to name her Hope, if you and Phillip don't mind."

"Mind? Of course not, I think it an excellent idea." She turned. "Phillip, do you mind?"

"Of course not."

"Mother, I want you to ride up front with me," John said gently.

"Take care of your daughter," Marie said to Phillip.

"You've had a shock. You shouldn't be riding a horse alone." With that John lifted her, put her into his saddle, and climbed up behind. "I'm taking Mother home, Phillip, you take care of Charity. Bring her to the house so I can treat her."

"Whatever you say," Marie muttered. "Don't forget my horse." She looked back to see Charity in Phillip's arms. She was crying and he was surrounding her with fatherly embraces and kisses. *Good, this is what the girl needs, the loving attention of a caring pa-pa.* "What a wretched, evil man, so arrogant, so cruel," she mumbled.

"It's over now," John said as they rode slowly back to the house. "He will hurt no one ever again."

"He did not think I could shoot. He laughed for what he had done." She turned to look at her son. "I am not proud to have killed a man, *mon fils*. I am not proud and I ask God's forgiveness but this was a man who needed killing."

John sent to Trenton for a magistrate. While they waited, he asked the undertaker to stand the coffin up outside the jail, open for all to see. A sign above it read:

> *CONFESSED MURDERER OF HOPE POWER*
> *For the wages of sin is death; but the gift of God is eternal life*
> *through Jesus Christ our Lord. -Romans 6:23*

Parents brought their children to absorb the lesson. Here was a man who had done evil things and so now his body stood rotting away in the sun. The crows picked out his eyeballs.

A notice was posted that if anyone recognized the fellow and could identify him or had any of his personal effects that could lead to discovering his identity, they should come forward.

By the time the magistrate arrived along with his clerk, the coffin had been closed up as it was reeking so badly people across the street were complaining of the stench. An appropriately ignominious ending to an ignominious man, everyone agreed.

The magistrate took statements from Marie, Charity, John, Phillip, Widow Angus, Pastor McCullen, his handyman, Madame Molly, little Pauline, and Big Dan.

No one ever came forward to identify the corpse and John concluded that if the stranger had been renting another room elsewhere, his landlord was too embarrassed to admit it. And then there was the matter of money. The man they only knew as Ezekiel Leslie, which John felt strongly was a phony name, had been able to move around, pay for his needs, buy what he wanted. Presumably he had a stash of money. His landlord might have wanted to keep that for himself. John shrugged.

In an official judgment, the magistrate exonerated Marie from any wrong doing. He declared she was protecting her family and had acted in self-defense.

No one thought it worth digging a grave or posting a marker for such a man. His rotting corpse and reeking coffin were transported to the very outskirts of the town and burned. In a few years time very few would even remember that there had once been such a man but Charity Power would remember. She would never be able to forget him and the shame he had brought her.

Chapter 29

It was six weeks since the mysterious appearance of the young whore who had spent a night giving herself away. No one had seen her again nor the dark haired man who had sat smirking in the shadows like Mephistopheles auditioning entertainment for the Gates of Hell. In a year they would both become a ribald folktale that no one took seriously. Even the men who had had her would begin to disbelieve themselves and question just how drunk they actually had been.

Phillip had not had a drunken night since his daughter's "incident" and the shooting. And Marie had broached the subject of arranging a marriage for Charity.

"She needs a home of her own, *mon fils*, babies of her own, a husband to care for her... and for her to care for, yes? No rush, no rush, just think about it and think about the possible field of suitors. After all, she is almost nineteen and will be twenty before we know it."

Phillip had muttered something unintelligible but Marie knew the seed had been planted.

Charity had been working steadily in the emporium. It was a healthy diversion as she came to terms with her sisters' deaths. John approved. Marie spent less time in the store and more with Richard. She came in on occasion, reviewed the books, talked briefly with Lyndyn and left but not before she quietly asked Lyndyn how he thought his niece was doing. And he always nodded his head and said she was doing "just fine."

Then came the day when Marie drove the trap up to the back entrance and saw Charity outside with her head in the bushes.

"Charity? What is it?" Marie called as she hustled down from the vehicle and reined her horse to the hitching post.

Charity stood looking ghostly pale. "I didn't want the customers to hear me."

Marie took out a handkerchief to wipe her granddaughter's mouth. She brushed aside a stray lock of hair. "What is it *ma petite*, something you ate?"

"Oh, *Grand-mère*," she cried and threw her arms around Marie's neck. "I'm late."

"Late for what?"

Charity pulled back and looked full into her grandmother's face. "My cycle. I'm late."

"Ohhh. How late?"

"A week… perhaps two."

"That is still very soon to tell. How long have you been sick?"

"This is the first time."

"Come," Marie took her hand and proceeded through the back door. "Lyndyn, how are things going? Can you spare Charity for an hour?"

"Of course."

"I'm taking her to see the doctor. A stomach malady I think."

"Take care. Things will be fine here," he said agreeably and the thought struck him that his beloved Louise had started out her pregnancy just this way.

Once in the trap, Charity said, "I'm only seeing Doctor John. He already knows… my… how I look. I'll not have Doctor Ajax gawking at my… my body. If Doctor John is not there just take me home."

"Very well." Marie reined up the horse in front of the clinic and as fortune would have it, it was John who was keeping clinic hours that day.

"Mother," he greeted as they walked in. "Charity, it's been awhile. We've missed you at Sunday dinners."

"Yes, I know."

"It's almost like you've been avoiding us. Everyone misses you. Even young Tommy asked me how you were doing after the shooting." John noticed that she kept her eyes lowered. "Are you feeling unwell?"

"I'm late, Doctor John. I'm late and *Grand-mère* thought it best we come to see you."

"Oh, I see. How late?" he asked, gesturing for her to sit on his examination table.

"Maybe two weeks."

"I arrived at the store to find her vomiting into the bushes," Marie added.

"Have you been late like this before?" he asked.

"Not since I turned sixteen."

"Hmm. Are your breasts sensitive?"

"A little."

"Lie back, Charity. We'll drape you with this sheet. You are familiar with a pelvic examination. It may feel a little different now that you aren't all swollen and bruised."

John proceeded to do what he needed. When he finished he told his niece to sit up and he looked at his mother.

"She's a textbook case of early pregnancy." To Charity he said, "Unfortunately there is no way to determine who the father might be."

A silence descended on the office as they each took a breath.

Charity's mind was in turmoil. All she could think of was… *Be careful what you wish for.* She had told Tommy she didn't care if she got pregnant, she wanted a baby. Poor Tommy. She looked at her grandmother.

"The one man I know who could not be the father is… him. He never made love to me that way."

"Charity, he never made love to you at all," John said calmly. "Torture is not love."

"Oh," Marie sat down on the chair beside her.

"I can make it go away," John said. "It's not a decision to be taken lightly but I want you to know it is an option. The rest of your life need not be defined by what that man put you through."

"How?" Charity questioned.

"It's a very simple procedure, especially at this stage. A simple scraping of some cells from the wall of your womb."

"*Grand-mère*, please let me talk to Doctor John alone."

Marie nodded, her own head spinning. "I… I will wait out there," she spoke weakly and pointed to the waiting room. She could not play God again. She could not tell her grandchild what to do. It was not a matter of choosing a fabric for a new dress, this could have life long consequences no matter what Charity chose to do. Marie left the examination room.

As the door closed Charity spoke. "Doctor John, if… if a woman is in her menstrual cycle…"

"Yes?"

"Well, I mean… if she does make love with someone… repeatedly… during her cycle, is it true she can't get with child?"

"It's not usual but then most couples choose to forego relations during that time, but it's not impossible. We know the male…" he cleared his throat, "let's just say *seed* can be viable… ah, can live for several days within the womb." He looked clinically at his niece. "That was the something that happened, wasn't it? He told your Grandmother you had been with someone else."

She nodded. "He called him *The Maidenhead Thief* but it wasn't like that. I asked him to, I wanted him to and it all felt so good, so fantastic. It was wonderful. The way he held me, the way he worked for my satisfaction."

"And had you never had satisfaction like that before?"

"No, not really… only so much frustration."

"And over how many days did this occur?"

"The last three days of my cycle… but we did it so very many times," she added with a soft smile on her lips.

John cleared his throat again. "A very young man, no doubt."

Charity said nothing but dropped her gaze. "Is it possible I might have been pregnant already when Zeke dragged me to the docks?"

"Just one more question… did you experience any what you call *satisfaction* with anyone at the docks?"

"No," she groaned. "It was all horrible, mostly painful but I accepted it as my punishment."

"Then, there is a good possibility you were indeed already with child. The Greek Physician Galen wrote rather adamantly that women cannot conceive if they do not experience pleasure. It was, I think, as much an invective to husbands to insure they were attentive to giving their wives *satisfaction* if they wanted an heir. He lived in the Roman world where many a patrician husband left his wife from an arranged political marriage almost untouched while he spent his time and attentions on his mistress." He looked at his niece. "You see, human beings haven't changed much over thousands of years, have they?"

She nodded and dropped her gaze again.

"That was over fifteen hundred years ago but his writings and theories are still those adhered to by most physicians today… as well as the courts."

"What do the courts have to do with it?"

"If a woman charges a man with rape and she is found to be with child as a result, the courts will generally rule that it was not rape because she must have enjoyed it but is too embarrassed to admit it. Over the centuries, however, there have been intelligent doctors who have argued against this belief."

"Well, I wasn't raped, not really… I allowed it but I didn't enjoy it. It was what Zeke demanded of me. I can't believe how stupid I have been," she shuddered in disgust.

"Each generation makes its own mistakes. Now, can you tell me who this lover is?"

"I could… but I won't. I promised him I'd never tell so he wouldn't get into any trouble. He is certain you all will skin him alive before Papa chops off his vitals and roasts them like the Mohawks do… is that true? Do they really?"

"Very true and if you don't believe me, ask your Aunt Ronnie. Now… I think you need to take some time and think about all this. It's a big decision, but it was good to see a little smile," John said kindly, chucking her chin. "Your father should be told, Charity… not by me but by you. I doubt that he will be that surprised considering all that you have been through. And I doubt that he has read Galen. It's important to have his support, no matter what you decide."

She sat there for a moment staring at her hands.

"You know if you told me his name I am still bound by my oaths not to tell anyone else… but I could perhaps advise you, help you to think. Do I know him?"

She gave a non-committal shrug. "Maybe."

"Do we know his family?"

"No."

"Is he married?"

"Oh, no!" she said sharply.

"So he's an indenture perhaps?" And suddenly Tommy's name popped into his head along with the image of the boy scared out of his wits at being summoned.

"Stop! No more, no more. I must have time to think," she said as she jumped down from the table.

"I want to see you this Sunday for dinner at your grandmother's along with your father and sisters."

She nodded.

Marie drove Charity back to the store. On the way, the girl made her grandmother swear to keep her secret at least for three more days.

"Until I have time to think," she said very soberly. "But one thing I do know. I want to keep the baby."

Marie let out a sigh of relief and nodded her head.

"Richard, *mon cher*," Marie said softly as she sat on the settee beside her husband. They were in their bedroom, enjoying the fire. "If you were challenged to come up with a list of suitable young men for our Charity, who would be on it?"

He turned to look at her. "Who can say what makes one person more attracted to another than anyone else? And why are you asking?"

"Rebecca has suitors lined up so thick we must shoo them from every room... like flies. She is only sixteen whereas Charity will soon be nineteen and has no one."

"Rebecca is the very image of her *grand-mère*, Rafe's ma-ma," he said solemnly.

"Then she was very beautiful indeed," Marie said cautiously.

"She cannot be faulted for her beauty."

"No, of course not. Please, do not think that is what I meant. It is only that I look at Charity and think she is a girl who needs to marry."

Marie was treading lightly as she knew Richard's feelings were still a bit raw.

After the shooting they had had their first ever harsh words with each other. He had awoken to a new day only to discover his wife had gone out alone, in the dark, carrying two pistols, and shot and killed a predator in the family mausoleum.

"How do you expect me to feel?!" he had stormed. "While I sleep, my wife arms herself and goes off to do battle with a devil?! You unman me, Marie!"

"Unman...? No, Richard, no. I had no such thought. I only knew I must save my granddaughter. You had taken your medicine. You were sound asleep."

Marie, still reeling from her experience, sought no gentle words.

"I never take so much that I cannot roust myself to a state of alertness, that I cannot protect my family!"

"There was no time."

"If it had been Jacques, you would have found the time! You would have let him in on the family secrets to begin with. *Sacre bleu,* he would have been leading the charge because he would have been in on the meetings. Say this is not so," he demanded and she had stood there dumbly, her state of shock not helping her deal with an angry husband.

Later she had apologized profusely and discreetly shared everything she knew about Charity's situation. He was right, she had told him. If the boys chose to exclude him for one reason or another, that was their business but he was now her husband whom she loved very much, her helpmate, her partner for the rest of her life and he deserved her confidence and support within the family.

Her words and her sincerity had worked to mollify him somewhat for try as he might he could not stay angry with Marie.

Now as they sat upon the settee Richard looked at her again.

"Is there something I should know?" he asked.

"Charity has made me promise to say nothing to anyone for three days, time for her to think and tell her own pa-pa… she is *enceint.*"

"Ahhh, the poor child. Are you sure?"

Marie nodded.

"I took her to John when I found her today vomiting into the bushes. You must not tell a soul until she tells Phillip. And we must help Phillip make a list of possible suitors. I already told him a while ago… long before this situation came to light… I told him Charity needs a husband."

"Mmmm, you do not propose to keep her condition a secret from her bridegroom, do you?"

"No, no, of course not. I suppose we cannot set our sights too high. It must be a man willing to raise another's child. A man who can accept that his bride was raped, though I see no reason to tell him she was the girl on the docks. And someone who can see beyond the unfortunate scarring on her face. But on the positive side: he becomes part of a very good family, one well respected in the community, and Phillip can offer a sizable dowry and help in building a house."

"And who have you in mind to be on this list?"

"I honestly do not know. Every young man I know who used to court Charity is now at Rebecca's feet," she replied softly. "I am at a loss. Just another reason to wish Rafe were still with us. By now he may have seen the wisdom in allowing Richie to take over the treks so he could watch over his daughters. As nice as he was, I am certain he would have found a way to… how do they say it? Thin out the herd."

Richard pulled a wry smile as he often did when reflecting on a pleasant memory of Rafe.

"He might have sent his girls to a nunnery," he said with a small smile.

Sunday came and Phillip brought his daughters to his mother's for dinner with the family. It was a pleasant day and so they walked. As they approached the big house, Charity saw Tommy standing outside the stables waiting to tend to their carriage, but there was no carriage. Did he look disappointed, she wondered? When he saw that she was looking at him, he gave a broad smile and a respectful nod as she passed closer. She smiled back but then quickly looked around to see if anyone else had noticed.

When dinner was over, Charity told her father she had something to talk to him about and asked her grandmother to join them. They went to Jacques' old office where Charity calmly told Phillip she was with child but unfortunately, she didn't know who the father was. Phillip took it in stride.

"After an experience such as you endured, you cannot be expected to know who the father is." He opened his arms and she slid into them, clinging to him for comfort. "Oh, Charity, my daughter," he sighed without judgment as he held her.

"What shall I do, Papa?"

"It is times like these when I miss your mother most of all. She would know what to say... what to do."

Marie cleared her throat. "I think together we can figure out what to do, Phillip. There are several options."

Phillip and Charity both looked at Marie.

"Well," she said hesitantly, "you could go stay with your Aunt Izzy when you start to show. In Boston you could be a young widow. Perhaps you might even meet some nice man."

"And if I did not, how do we explain my return with a babe in my arms?"

"You might leave it in your Aunt Izzy's nursery," Marie suggested.

"Never!"

"No," Marie sighed as she looked to her granddaughter, "I could not do that either. Perhaps we could say you found it," she suggested weakly.

"Do you really think anyone is going to believe that?" Phillip verbally cringed. "She might as well stay here through her confinement and be honest about it all."

"I am certain Isabelle could help arrange a suitable match. She must know someone... perhaps a widower with children who is looking for another wife," Marie said hopefully. "Someone mature who can accept your circumstance."

"*Grand-mère*, I really don't think I am suited to the Bostonians and their society. If Aunt Izzy and her banker husband are an example of the crowd they socialize with, I'd never fit in."

Phillip gave a sigh of relief. He didn't want his daughter moving away to Boston.

"Is there someone here you would find suitable?" Marie asked before Phillip had a chance. "Your pa-pa can approach him and I am certain he would offer a handsome dowry..."

"Yes, of course," Phillip nodded.

"Perhaps better employment, and help in building a new house."

"Absolutely," Phillip agreed.

Marie noticed Charity did not immediately shake her head. "Charity?"

"Let me think, please. This is all happening so quickly."

"Of course, as you say," Marie nodded with a little note of resignation.

"I'm very tired Papa, I'd like to stay here tonight if I may."

Phillip nodded his head and the little meeting was over.

Phillip returned home with his two younger daughters while Charity was made comfortable in the same guest bedroom she and her sisters had shared before. It took a while for darkness to descend as she waited for the house to grow quiet. Finally, she crept down the backstairs, if anyone caught her she would claim a need for some food.

Outdoors, the moon was a quarter full but clouds kept slipping over it as she made her way to the barn.

"Tommy?" she whispered up to the loft. "Tommy, are you there?"

"Miss Charity?" she heard an eager voice reply.

"Yes. Come down and light a small lantern. We need to talk."

She waited as she heard him descend the ladder, make his way to the side wall and use a flint striker to light a small candle lamp.

"Miss Charity," he said again as he reached out and took her hand. "Oh, Miss Charity, it's been too long since I seen ya."

"I was ashamed, Tommy. My behavior was not the behavior of a lady. I don't know what got into me but I'm hoping you can forgive me."

"Forgive you? For what? For giving me the best nights of my entire life? I thought you were ashamed of me."

"Why ever would I be ashamed of you?" she asked softly.

"I know I ain't that smart 'n' my education is poorly. I don't talk as fine as you 'n' yer family but I do care 'bout ya Miss Charity 'n' I've missed ya some'in fierce."

"Speaking correctly is something you can learn, it only takes a small effort," she said as she smiled into his eyes, the kindest eyes she had ever seen outside of her family. "And I think you are smart enough to do anything you set your mind to."

"I love ya, Miss Charity. I've been so miserable these past weeks, wondering if I'd ever see ya again. Do ya suppose ya could learn me to talk better so yer family could accept me as a proper suitor? My indenture will be over in another two years 'n' I'll be free t' take care of ya. Won't be able to give ya nothin' fancy but I could hire on at th' mill 'n' make a family man's wage. Ya said no one would ever marry ya but yer wrong. I'm sure a lot of men would like to marry ya, but none could love you more than me or better than me. I'd consider myself blessed t'have a woman as fine as you for my wife."

Then he leaned in and kissed her and Charity felt the fire.

"Tommy, I promised I'd never tell and I haven't; I never will but you should know... we thought we were so safe because I was in my cycle, but we weren't. My uncle the doctor told me it's not necessarily safe if the woman really enjoys herself and I did *enjoy* myself so much. You were wonderful and we did it so many times and now... well, I find I am with child."

Tommy's mouth fell open as he tried to grasp all that he was hearing. "Yer havin' *my* baby?" he asked with a dumbfounded look on his face.

"I am."

"Oh, gosh, Miss Charity. How kin we wait two more years?"

"We can't but don't worry, I'm certain my grandmother will release you from the rest of your contract and my papa will help us. Tommy, are you very sure you want to marry me?"

He looked at her a little sadly. "As sure as I am th' sun will rise tomorrow... if you'll have me."

"Tommy, oh, Tommy, I will have you."

"I had no idea the lad felt so strongly about my daughter," Phillip said to John and Marie. "He faced me eye to eye and told me he cared for her very deeply and he knew about the child. Said he wanted to get married immediately and give the baby his name. Said he's loved her from afar for some time. I called Charity in and she agreed. Said she'd never said anything because she didn't think we'd approve, him being an indentured and all."

Marie was beaming. "I will tear up his contract immediately. Do you have a job for him at the mill?"

"Of course. Tommy is strong and well built, the kind of man we look for. I'll get a crew working on a house, possibly an acre down from mine, but perhaps they can honeymoon in the apartment over the store while it's being built. Like Caroline and I did," he added sadly.

"A very good idea," Marie agreed. "What do you think, John?"

John nodded. He was certain now that Tommy was the father, the secret lover who had set off the outrage of the stranger. He had to admire the way Tommy was assuming the role of knight-in-shining-armor, coming to the rescue of the pregnant damsel in distress when in all likelihood, he was the father.

"I think Master Shakespeare said it best," John agreed, "when he wrote 'All's Well That Ends Well.'"

Seven and a half months later, Charity gave birth to a little boy. She said nothing to anyone save her husband when she observed the child had the very same shaped earlobes as Tommy.

Author's Note

During the period between the early sixteenth century to 1787, hundreds of thousands of Huguenots left their homes in France because of repeated waves of persecution. They escaped to countries sympathetic to their situation and of protestant leanings. As Ester Forbes wrote in *Paul Revere and the World He Lived In* (Boston: Houghton Mifflin Company, 1942):

> *"France had opened her own veins and spilt her best blood when she drained herself of her Huguenots, and everywhere, in every country that would receive them, this amazing strain acted as a yeast."*

The revocation of the Edict of Nantes caused France to lose at least a half million of its best citizens. It was not until November 1787, after the United States of America had gained its independence from England, that the Marquis de Lafayette, impressed by the fact that so many of the American leaders were of Huguenot descent, persuaded Louis XVI and the French Council to adopt the Edict of Versailles, commonly known as the Edict of Tolerance, guaranteeing religious freedom to all in France.

Academic discussion continues around the issue of smallpox even some 500-600 years after the discovery of the Americas. In Europe rather consistent exposure to smallpox, cow pox, chicken pox, and measles had the population developing a degree of resistance if not immunity. People may have come down with the disease and been scarred by it (Queen Elizabeth I is an example) but if they were in relatively good health to begin with, they fought it and usually survived. Being undernourished, in poor health and with a sub par immune system like much of the peasantry, has always been a recipe for disaster.

In the Americas, however, the indigenous population had absolutely no exposure and therefore no resistance, no natural immunity, and the disease spread like wild fire with devastating results. Measles did the same. The survival rates differed and some speculate that sweat lodges and other "go to" methods of combating illness among the native tribes may have actually exacerbated the death toll within the native population.

One thing does appear clear. It only took one generation born and raised away from Europe for Caucasians to develop the same vulnerability. Within the native tribes one could expect at least a 30% death rate. Within the white population one or two generations away from Europe, a 30% mortality rate could also be expected.

The British knew this when during the American Revolution they purposely tried to infect the American rebels. George Washington, himself purported to be a survivor of smallpox, ordered his troops to be inoculated against this germ warfare. The 3% expected death rate was much better than 30%. John Adams was part of a group of leaders in Boston who volunteered for inoculation so they could stand strong against any British attempts to wipe out the leaders of the fledgling government via disease. He wrote to his wife Abigail of his experience after which she also volunteered for inoculation.

The vaccine developed in the 20th century was much safer than the rather crude methods of inoculation employed in the 18th century but still did its share of damage and even death. However, because vaccination was mandated amongst the citizenry of most countries, smallpox no longer exists and the vaccine no longer needs to be administered.

D.C. Force
Asheville, NC

<h1 align="center">Book Club Discussion Questions</h1>

1. Discuss the varying reactions with which John's siblings greet him. Are they justified?

2. Consider John's attitude when he introduces Ronnie to Izzy. Do you think he bears any responsibility for Izzy's negative reaction?

3. What is the old *Sigurd and Brynhild* legend? Who is John comparing Brynhild to when he says "you, too, should have chosen life"?

4. Consider Izzy's reaction to the loss of Jacques. Why do you think she reacted the way she did? Do you think she was more or less affected by his death than her siblings? Why?

5. Today, many vaccines are commonly administered. They normally undergo years of development, testing, and long term trials so their safety and effects are well understood. But in the 18th century, the process of inoculation against smallpox was very new and carried much risk.
Consider the various characters and their situations. Do you think they made the right decisions? With whose decision did you agree or disagree the most, and why? Which strategy might you have chosen for your family in their situations?

6. Who do you think Tonoaki hears in the woods?

7. Why would a girl from a good family and good home allow herself to be so mistreated as Charity did?

Editor's note

Dear Reader,

First and foremost, as the editor of this novel I have to express my sincere apologies for the delay in publication. Although the content was completed in early 2020, I have regrettably taken far too long to complete the final editing and publication.

2020 was... a year. That might be the best thing I can say about it. I saw an Internet meme that likened it to looking both ways before crossing a street, and then getting hit by an airplane.

Perhaps it was a year we would all prefer to forget. Or perhaps it was one we will most need to remember. We no sooner rang in that new year, when we were faced with the makings of a once in a century global pandemic. A new virus was making its way around the world, causing illness and death among the vulnerable. "Two weeks to slow the spread" dragged into two months, and has now become over two years of various lockdowns, mandates, self-quarantines, social distancing, masks, and vaccines. And there still doesn't appear to be a real end in sight.

Despite all that, my personal airplane was the loss of D.C. Force, my mother. Although it had nothing to do with the now infamous novel coronavirus - or perhaps even more so *because* it was unrelated to all that - it was a terrible surprise.

Fortunately, she had already completed her final two books, and it has been my privilege to do the editing and formatting on the books to bring them to publication in accordance with her wishes.

Writing the Huguenot series of books was a labor of love for her. She enjoyed all the hours she spent researching, writing, rewriting, and revising the stories as she fleshed out the characters and storylines. She had many more stories to tell and even had drafts of stories covering several more generations. While I know she was disappointed that she wasn't able to develop those additional stories any further, I also know that she was very happy to have been given the opportunity to share the stories she did. I(We) hope you have enjoyed reading these novels at least as much as she did writing them.

- T